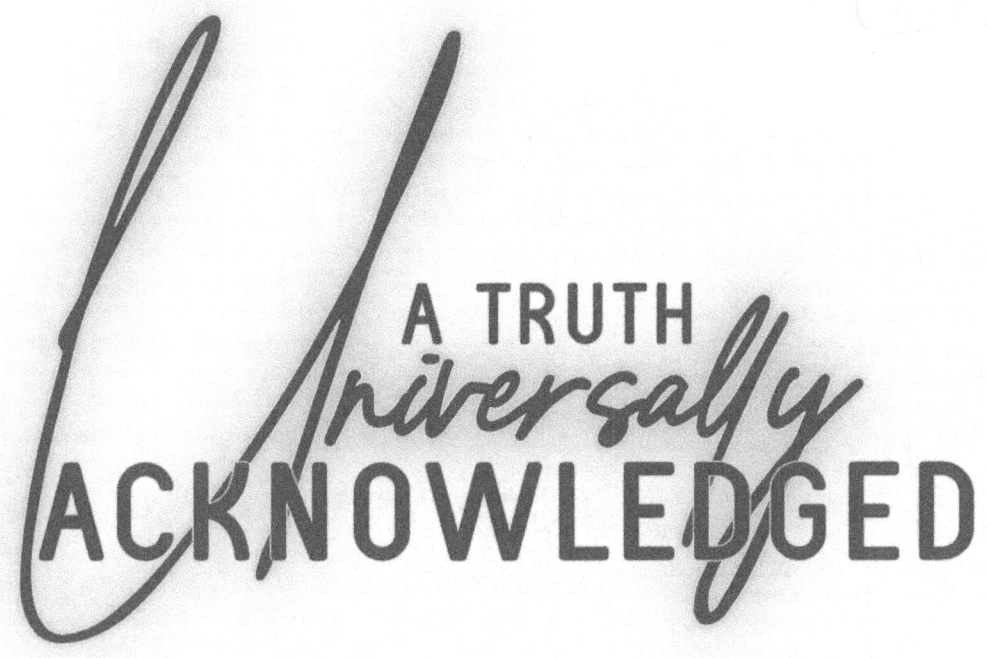

A TRUTH
Universally
ACKNOWLEDGED

QUEER FANWORKS INSPIRED BY
JANE AUSTEN'S PRIDE AND PREJUDICE

DUCK
PRINTS
PRESS

Duck Prints Press, LLC
Schenectady, NY

Stories:
"unwound thread and wilted roses" © 2025, Téa Belog
"Along the Way" © 2025, E. V. Dean
"Somewhere Other Than Here" © 2025, J. D. Harlock
"Trousers and Other Oddities" © 2025, Rascal Hartley
"A Charmed Life" © 2025, A. L. Heard
"The Parsonage Becomes Her" © 2025, ilgaksu
"To Her the Pride" © 2025, Lucy K. R.
"Much Ado (About Quite a Lot)" © 2025, Lyonel Loy
"The Magnificent Mr. Markham" © 2025, Mikki Madison
"Must Be in Want of a Wife" © 2025, Genevieve Maxwell
"It's Just You" © 2025, Sage Mooreland
"tell that to my tell-tale heart" © 2025, nottesilhouette
"Kiss and Tell" © 2025, Taliesin Owens
"Lyd, Not Lydia" © 2025, Linnea Peterson
"We Can All Begin Freely" © 2025, Em Rowntree
"The Iron Rose" © 2025, Vee Sloane
"A Constant, Fearful Longing" © 2025, Shea Sullivan
"Orbital Conjunction © 2025, Dei Walker
"The Triad Plot" © 2025, Terra P. Waters
"Silk Gloves and Second Chances" © 2025, A. D. Williams
"In Want of a Horse-Stealing, Troublemaking Swordsman" © 2025, Xianyu Zhou

Art:
"Rosa Canina" © 2025, Aceriee
"Nighttime" and "Token of affection" © 2025, Cris Alborja
"Gazebo in the Rain" © 2025, May Barros
"Pas De Deux" and "A Stolen Moment" © 2025, Zel Howland
"Follies and Nonsense" © 2025, mcdad arts
"Dueling Darcy" © 2025, Max Jason Peterson
"Girls' Night In" © 2025, Flore Picard
"Do me the honor" © 2025, Kendall Pletcher
untitled © 2025, radicalhoodie
"The Meeting At Pemberly" © 2025, J. Radin
"A Handsome Face" © 2025, Elizabeth Rose
"Distracted Glances" © 2025, Xanthe P. Russell
"'If only we had been blessed with a son!'" © 2025, Saro / Legendaerie
"A Moment Ripples Outwards" © 2025, Tomowowo
"Aroace Mary Living Her Best Life" © 2025, A. A. Weston
"If only they could see it" © 2025, Amalia Zeichnerin
"Moonlight" and "Glove" © 2025, Jagoda Zirebiec

Front cover art © 2025, Aceriee

Edited by Rhosyn Goodfellow, Catherine E. Green, A. L. Heard, Owl Outerbridge, Nina Waters, and Rachael L. Young. Art advisement by Aceriee and Pallas Perilous. Significant planning contributions made by the many members of the Duck Prints Press advisory team.

Print manuscript formatting by Hermit Prints and Pallas Perilous
E-book formatting by Nina Waters

Published by Duck Prints Press, LLC
Schenectady, New York
duckprintspress.com
ISBN: 978-1-962488-25-9 (reflowable ePub edition)
ISBN: 978-1-962488-24-2 (PDF edition)
ISBN: 978-1-962488-26-6 (trade paperback edition)

TABLE OF CONTENTS

ART

STORIES

Aeriee

COVER

The inspiration for the cover comes from a Gutenberg print of *Pride and Prejudice* from 1894. The book was illustrated by Hugh Thomson and the cover features a prancing peacock.

We decided to take the idea of the peacock and do a modern take on it. The original shows a single male peacock displaying his tail feathers, but we wanted to showcase the peahen instead. Though not as colorful and dramatic as their male counterparts, they are beautiful and fabulous none the less.

TAGS

bisexual, coming out, f/f, first kiss, friends to lovers, gender non-conforming, lesbian, love confession, masquerading as a person of a different gender, past tense, pining (mutual), post-canon, third person limited point of view

INSPIRATION

There is a scene in the 1995 BBC *Pride and Prejudice* miniseries when Mary is moralizing to her sisters, but she also specifically speaks much more favorably about women than men. It made me think that perhaps she preferred women, and that little nugget of "maybe" slowly got spun out into the story you see here. (And as for why Georgiana: because Georgiana deserved far better than the way she was treated by Wickham, dang it!)

Nikki Madison

THE MAGNIFICENT MR. MARKHAM

MARY STRODE UP the wide stone steps to the Ashworth's house, mingling with a group of people who had just disembarked from their carriages. At the top of the stairs, the doors were open wide, and with each step, she could see a little more of the ballroom: the three-tiered chandeliers, the massive tapestries, the ladies in their finest dresses, and the gentlemen in their smartest jackets. An airy string melody drifted out into the night air. Her heart fluttered with excitement.

She hadn't been certain she'd be able to attend tonight. Up until two days ago, Lizzy had been discussing taking Mary and Georgiana to the ball herself. Then Mr. Darcy had suggested the theater instead, and Mary had been so grateful to him she could have wept.

It was nothing to claim a headache yet again—she'd done it a dozen other times this Season—and as soon as Lizzy, Mr. Darcy, and Georgiana had left, Mary was out of bed to attend the ball with no chaperone and, more importantly, nobody around to learn her secret.

She stepped inside and spotted their hostess, Mrs. Ashworth, gliding toward the stairs. Mary angled to meet her, bowed deeply, and pitched her voice lower before she spoke. "Mrs. Ashworth, my deepest thanks for the invitation. Your home is absolutely lovely, as always."

Mrs. Ashworth tittered and covered her cheek as though she were blushing. "Truly, Mr. Markham, you're too much." She clasped Mary's hand. "It is so *good* that you could make it. I know Ariadne was very much hoping that you would come."

Mary smiled. "Then I will be certain to claim at least one dance on her card."

She bid Mrs. Ashworth farewell and made her way into the ballroom, greeting nearly everyone she passed along the way. She bowed low over the ladies' hands and claimed a few dances, and the gentlemen, she clapped on the back and extracted promises of a shared drink and a card game later. Everyone was happy to see her.

Or, well, they were happy to see Mr. Benjamin Markham, which amounted to the same thing.

"Markham! How've you been, old chap?"

A hand fell heavily on Mary's shoulder, and she turned to see Mr. Granville, a handsome man who had paid her not the slightest bit of attention last Season when she had come to these balls under her real name.

Mary grinned and shook his hand firmly. "Better now that I see I've another chance to win a few pounds off you in cards."

Granville guffawed. "We'll see about that. Come over and have a drink with us before the dancing starts. I'm sure your name's already on all the cards in this room."

Mary joined him and the other gentlemen readily, accepting the drink they passed to her, although she scarcely did more than taste it. Every one of these gentlemen had seen her during the two previous Seasons, and every one of them had ignored her when she'd been wearing a ballgown rather than breeches. It was delightfully subversive to be holding full conversations with them now.

She left them once the dancing commenced because, as much as she enjoyed those conversations with the gentlemen, they were nothing compared to her delight at dancing with the ladies. She spun her way through a dozen dances with flirtatious winks and charming words, and exhilaration brimmed within her every time a lady blushed and looked up at Mary—at Mr. Markham, rather.

On these nights, Mary disappeared into him and loved every minute of it.

At the first break in dancing, someone called her name. "Mr. Markham!"

Mary turned toward the older gentleman trying to get her attention. "What can I do for you, Mr. Edwards?"

Mr. Edwards—a bit portly and a lot gray, with a truly hideous mustache—pulled forward a young lady with a pile of blond curls on her head, her face mostly hidden by her fan. "I've a lady here who would love to make your acquaintance." He beamed. "May I present Miss Georgiana Darcy?"

Mary froze, her heart pounding like a chased rabbit.

"Miss Darcy," Mr. Edwards continued, blithely unaware that he had just done the social equivalent of shoving Mary off a cliff, "this is Mr. Benjamin Markham."

Only practice kept Mary's horror from showing on her face. She took Georgiana's proffered hand and bowed over it to give herself two seconds to compose herself. "Miss Darcy. How do you do?"

When Mary raised her head, she met Georgiana's blue eyes peeking over the edge of her fan. She could read nothing in their gleam.

She'd fooled everybody else. Maybe Georgiana wouldn't recognize her.

Even as she thought the words, she knew it for a dim hope. Georgiana had become one of her closest friends over the past few Seasons—truly, her only friend in London. Of course she'd recognize Mary, no matter what she was wearing.

Then again, she would not be expecting to see Mary here. Mary had learned she could get away with a lot by playing into what others expected to see.

"Mr. Markham." Georgiana fluttered the fan and curtsied. "A pleasure to make your acquaintance."

Mary allowed herself to feel the slightest bit of relief. No recognition whatsoever. Her disguise was holding. All she had to do now was make some vaguely polite conversation and then equally politely excuse herself to—

"Mr. Markham, I do believe Miss Darcy has a few dances available," Mr. Edwards said, his eyes sparkling.

Mary wanted to curse. This seemed like the proper time for it, and gentlemen cursed so often when they weren't aware there was a lady present. "I'm sure Miss Darcy has a dozen interested suitors. I should hate to deprive them of such a lovely lady's company."

She needed to get out of here before Georgiana suspected. It was entirely possible for her to get back to the house and into her nightclothes before anyone else returned. She could claim she'd been somewhere else—*anywhere* else.

"You're far too kind, Mr. Markham," Georgiana said. "Surely one dance wouldn't hurt? I've heard you do so enjoy dancing."

Mary *did* enjoy dancing, and it would be hard to argue that she didn't after having spent so much time on the floor. But dancing with Georgiana would be dangerous for far too many reasons to list, and her mind was too scrambled to think of a gracious way to get out of it.

Drat everything.

She swept into another bow. "Very well, if my lady insists. May I have the next dance?"

Georgiana's eyes lit like the sunrise. "I would be most honored, Mr. Markham."

Oh, Mary was going to regret this. She was going to regret this forever. Still, she held out her arm to Georgiana and led her to the dance floor as the next quadrille began. At least it was unlikely they would have time to talk.

For the first two passes, her hope held. Georgiana continued to meet Mary's eyes with a soft, bright smile, and Mary allowed herself to think maybe, just maybe, Georgiana hadn't recognized her. Perhaps they were really Mr. Benjamin Markham and Miss Georgana Darcy, and they would share a lovely dance, and they would flirt, and perhaps Mary could kiss her hand, and then—

She banished the thought. As much as she was enjoying weaving her way through the *ton* in disguise, she was well aware that she could not remain Mr. Benjamin Markham forever. She couldn't even be Miss Mary Bennet in breeches past the end of the evening. And she certainly couldn't ask for a lady's hand in marriage.

The most she could hope for, right now, was making it through the night with her secret intact.

"You know, your disguise is *excellent*," Georgiana said conspiratorially the next time she and Mary were arm in arm.

Mary choked on nothing and had to wait until they'd completed their turn before she could respond. "I'm sorry? Whatever could you mean?"

"Oh, *truly*," Georgiana scoffed after their next turn. "You've been at my brother's house for three Seasons in a row, Miss Mary Bennet. Don't think I wouldn't know you in a jacket and breeches."

Blast it. Mary's mind swirled like Georgiana's skirt on each turn. Georgiana *had* recognized her. Her weeks and weeks of careful planning were all for naught in the face of someone who knew her well. And the "don't think I wouldn't know you" made something warm tighten in her belly, at odds with the chilly fear of recognition running down her spine.

She couldn't find the words to respond.

She *had* to find the words to respond.

A second turn, and then a third, and then she finally said, "Are you claiming I'm a lady in men's clothes?" Mary gave a disbelieving snort for good measure. "You must be utterly daft, Miss Darcy, if that's what you think. This is hardly the place or time for such accusations."

Mary smiled charmingly at Miss Lexington in the couple opposite them in the quadrille and decided it would be best to ignore anything else Georgiana said. It was foolish to even *have* this conversation somewhere that they risked being overheard. The string quartet's jaunty song was certainly helping, and neither she nor Georgiana had spoken loudly, but the fact remained that any of the other couples could hear them if they put their minds to it.

"Very well," Georgiana demurred. "Have it your way. I'll make the rest of my accusations later, then."

The dance finally, mercifully, ended, and Georgiana curtsied deeply. "Mr. Markham, I thank you for the wonderful dance."

Mary bowed. Her hands were clammy. Thank the good, blessed Lord for gloves. "Miss Darcy. It was a true pleasure."

She waited until Georgiana disappeared into the crowd before she made her own escape.

Mary crept back into the house, the same as she'd done a dozen times before now, and slipped her way back up the stairs. Lizzy and Mr. Darcy were still out, and most of the servants were abed, so she wouldn't have any difficulty sneaking around.

She silently slipped back into her room and struck a match to light the candle on the table near the door.

"Why, Mr. Markham! How lovely to see you here!"

Mary swallowed a screech and spun to face her accuser. Georgiana lounged in the plush chair by the window in a most unladylike manner, her legs kicked over one of the arms while she leaned against the other.

"What are you doing in my room?" Mary demanded.

"You didn't want to talk at the party, so I thought I would wait until we were somewhere you might be more amenable." Georgiana gestured to the room. "Somewhere we won't be overheard, for example."

"I haven't the slightest idea what you're talking about."

Georgiana just raised an eyebrow. "Really, Mary. I was willing to go along with it at the party, but right now you *are* standing in your own bedroom dressed in breeches and a hat."

Blast and damn. "I…am aware of that, yes." Mary felt sick to her stomach, and she gripped the edge of the table. She could feel every seam of her trousers, the lines of her jacket and waistcoat, the disguise that had once felt like a second skin now laying her secret bare. "There is an explanation."

Georgiana tipped her head to one side. "Is there?"

Perhaps the worst part was that it was a genuine question. Her voice held a hint of skepticism, but it was overshadowed with concern and curiosity. She *would* listen to Mary, if she had another explanation.

But she didn't.

She took her candle and strode over to the dressing screen so she could change into her nightclothes. She'd rather have this conversation as Mary than as Benjamin.

Georgiana was still there when she emerged. "Why have you been going about the *ton* as a man?"

"Must we discuss this?" Mary lit another lamp and went to sit on her bed. "I'd really rather not talk about it."

"Understandable," Georgiana said, "but I would like to know. We are friends, aren't we?"

The confusion and hurt in her voice broke Mary's heart. In other ladies, it would have sounded false; with Georgiana, it was achingly sincere. They *were* friends, or at least, Mary would have claimed so—Georgiana had been nothing but kind to her since she'd come to London three years ago for her first Season. They'd spent hours upon hours together, going to parties and the theater, shopping for dresses, perusing bookstores, staying up for another hour or two every time they'd returned home near dawn to talk about everything and everyone they'd seen. More than once, they'd fallen asleep together in the same bed.

But it couldn't stay like this, Mary knew. Georgiana had an impressive dowry and had been of the object of no small amount of interest over the past couple of years. Even so, her brother, ever doting, had told her she had no need to pay any mind to anyone who didn't also capture her heart, and as grateful as Mary was for that, Georgiana would be getting married eventually. If not this year, then the next.

She would leave, and Mary would be alone.

Georgiana moved from the chair to join Mary on the bed. "You've been so distant these past few months. I simply wanted to know what had happened. It's been dreadfully lonely at the parties without you. And boring."

Mary forced a smile to her face. "You mean there haven't been dozens of gentlemen clamoring for your attention?"

Georgiana screwed up her nose and waved the words away. "You know very well that there have been, but who cares about them? They don't stop it from being lonely and boring without you." She took Mary's hand. "They're not my friend."

The warmth of Georgiana's hand made Mary's heart beat faster, and she immediately stood, not only to pull her hand away but to pace. "But one of them will be, eventually. You'll find someone who makes you smile, makes your heart dance, and he'll ask for your hand. Then you'll be married and mistress of your own house, and I'll be sitting at the spinsters' table."

Georgiana gasped, as if there were no more horrific fate. "That's not true!"

Bless her loyalty. Mary swallowed the lump in her throat. "It is. You know it is. I haven't had one single bit of interest from any marriageable gentlemen in three years. And as I get older, more girls will start coming out, and—"

"That doesn't mean you'll end up a spinster," Georgiana argued.

"You're far too optimistic. My chances are dim and getting dimmer." Mary's eyes burned, and she dashed her hand across her face before any tears could fall.

"Is that why…?" Georgiana glanced back to the dressing screen.

Mary nodded jerkily. "Nobody pays me any mind as a woman. I wondered if it would be the same if I were a man. And I thought…"

No, she couldn't say it. Not even to Georgiana.

"What did you think?" Georgiana prodded gently.

"I thought it would let me dance with ladies, at least."

No sooner were the words out of her mouth than Mary wished she could take them back. Over the past few years, she'd told Georgiana almost everything except for this, the one thing she hadn't admitted to anyone.

Georgiana's eyes widened. "You prefer ladies?"

Mary's face heated, and she looked away. "Not…prefer, exactly, but…" Oh, blast it; she might as well tell the truth. "Yes, prefer. Exactly."

She held herself still, unsure of what to expect next. Would Georgiana run away? Scream? Burst into tears? Tell her brother? Oh, God forbid that last one. Mary didn't want to think of what that man would say. He'd probably turn her right out in the street or send her straight home to Longbourn.

Instead, Georgiana clapped her hands to her mouth, her eyes shining with tears, and she whispered something Mary couldn't understand.

"Pardon?" she said, leaning closer.

Georgiana dropped her hands to her lap. "Me, too."

Mary's jaw dropped. "What? You…"

Georgiana leapt to her feet and grabbed Mary's hands. "Oh, I've wanted to tell you for ages. I like men, I do, but I've always found myself looking at ladies more."

Mary could scarcely believe her ears. She had known, logically, that she couldn't be the only one, but it had never occurred to her that Georgiana might share her partiality for the fairer sex.

"Were you hoping to marry a lady?" Georgiana asked.

"Oh, heavens, no." Mary shook her head. "I didn't think that far ahead. I just wanted to have at least one Season where I could spend time admiring the people I wanted to admire before I have to go up on the shelf."

Georgiana's pink lips tipped up in a slight smile. "Well, you certainly seem to have made a splash. I've heard nothing but good things about Mr. Benjamin Markham. What will you do with him at the end of the Season?"

Mary blinked. "I…"

"Didn't think that far ahead, either?" Georgiana asked gently.

"Well, I didn't expect it to actually work!" Mary raked her hand through her hair, only to remember it was still pinned to her scalp within an inch of its life so she could better fit it under a hat. Irritated, she sat back on the bed, closer to the bedside table, to pull the pins out. "I thought for certain they'd throw me out of the first party. Instead, I ended up dancing with every lady there. And it was just…"

That first night she'd been so nervous she could scarcely swallow her dinner. But by the end of the evening, she was bowing and dancing the man's part in every dance as if she'd been doing it her whole life. She'd become Mr. Benjamin Markham, if only for the duration of the party.

"It was wonderful," she finished.

Georgiana sat beside her and joined Mary in pulling out the hairpins. Her fingers were swift and precise, and each gentle tug that freed a pin sent a delicious shiver down Mary's spine.

"Have you been to call on any ladies?" Georgiana asked.

"A few. But less to court them and more to keep being invited to parties and balls." She half turned to Georgiana, the next question burning her tongue. "How did you realize what I was doing?"

"It took some time," Georgiana admitted. "At first I believed you really were sick when you begged off from attending parties with me or Fitzwilliam or Lizzy. And then I overheard one of the servants say they'd seen you come in late one night."

The servants. And she'd tried so hard to stay out of sight. Mary sighed. "Of course they had. And here I thought I was doing so well at keeping it a secret."

"You were!" Georgiana assured her. "As far as I know, Fitzwilliam and Lizzy haven't noticed a thing. Or if they have, they certainly haven't mentioned it to me. And the servants knew very little when I asked them about it. Only enough to suggest that you weren't spending your time cooped up in here nursing a headache."

She held out a handful of pins, and Mary accepted them and dropped them onto the bedside table with the others. "So that's what tipped you off."

Georgiana nodded. "And then tonight, when you begged off because you weren't feeling well, I came back so I could follow you and see where you were going." She smiled. "I confess, I did not expect Mr. Markham."

She wasn't the only one. "I didn't expect you, either." Mary forced one of Markham's flirtatious grins to her face. "I make a rather nice gentleman, don't I?"

"You do!" Georgiana clapped her hands and laughed. "Oh, you looked very fine in your breeches and jacket. I was so surprised. I almost didn't recognize you."

"But you did." Mary sighed and flopped back onto the bed to stare at the ceiling. "What gave it away?"

Georgiana was quiet for long enough that Mary wondered if she'd heard her. Then: "Your eyes."

Mary sat up on her elbows and frowned. "My eyes? But they're nothing special. They're half hidden by glasses, most times, and—"

"Your eyes," Georgiana cut in, "are lovely, and I've become very fond of them over the past few years. The only way you could've fooled me is if you'd found a way to change your eyes."

Mary's stomach fluttered, and she stared at her. Georgiana was staring determinedly into a corner, the edge of her face hidden by the length of her hair, so Mary couldn't see her expression.

The room felt so quiet that Mary was positive her pounding heart was audible. Her thoughts were scrambled, grasping for a perfectly innocent meaning to Georgiana's words, because she surely hadn't meant what Mary hoped she meant.

But she was having trouble coming up with any explanation other than the obvious one.

Which, well…maybe obvious explanations were the order of the evening.

Mary liked going to parties wearing breeches.

Mary liked women.

Georgiana liked women.

Mary liked Georgiana.

Georgiana liked Mary?

Mary sat all the way up, her racing heart making her unsteady, and she caught Georgiana's hand. "Your eyes are lovely, too," she said, her voice hoarse. "They're so blue—it makes my heart ache."

Ugh, really? She couldn't come up with anything more romantic than that? She had been flirting as Benjamin Markham for *weeks*, why couldn't—?

Georgiana whipped around and kissed her soundly.

Ah. Well, her clumsy confession seemed to have worked, then.

She closed her eyes and set a trembling hand on Georgiana's knee. She wasn't entirely sure what else to do with them.

Georgiana's nightgown was soft, as soft as her lips on Mary's, a sensation that made Mary's head spin. How strange and silly that something so gentle could have such a strong effect on her.

"I would ask you to forgive me," Georgiana whispered, her mouth a hairsbreadth from Mary's, "but would I be correct in assuming forgiveness is unnecessary?"

"Completely unnecessary," Mary croaked—her throat had gone quite dry at some point in the last few minutes. She still hadn't opened her eyes, afraid to do so and learn this was naught but a dream. "It was welcome. Very welcome."

She *felt* Georgana smile. How was it possible to be so close to someone that you felt them smile? "I'm very glad. I've been wanting to do that for some time now."

Mary opened her eyes. Georgiana's face was but a few inches from hers now, her blue eyes sparkling with a happiness Mary didn't think she'd ever seen in them.

She swallowed to wet her throat and confessed, "I pretended that so many of the ladies I danced with were you. I fancied that, maybe if my disguise were good enough, I could call on you here."

A foolish fancy, to be sure—if Georgiana had been able to recognize her, then Mary never could've fooled Lizzy—but Georgiana's expression lit as if Mary had said she'd hung the stars for her.

"Do you want to?" Georgiana asked.

"Pardon?" Mary asked.

"Do you want to call on me?" Georgiana took her hand. "Take me on walks? Ask my brother for my hand?"

"I—" *More than anything.* "Don't be foolish. I enjoy wearing breeches, but I'm not actually a man. I couldn't—"

"My brother knows my preferences," Georgiana cut in. "I mentioned to him, some time ago, that it might be nice to have a home in the country that I could share with a particular friend. I've always preferred the country. He agreed and said if it were amenable to me—and to my friend, of course—he had a couple of properties that would do nicely for two ladies who wished to retire to a quiet life outside the city." She batted her eyelashes. "Where, I imagine, one would only be considered eccentric if one wished to wear breeches about her own property."

Mary's heart went from thundering in her chest to thundering in her throat. She could hardly breathe at the thought. A house in the country? Just the two of them? And all she needed to do was ask?

"It sounds too good to be true," she said, though how she got the words out past her heart was a miracle beyond her ken. "Truly, tell me now if you're jesting."

Georgiana shook her head. "I am not. I wouldn't jest. Not about this, and not to you. If you…" She closed her eyes, cleared her throat, and wet her lips before she opened her eyes and spoke again. "If you would want that, we could go to Fitzwilliam tomorrow."

Tomorrow. They could have a future together settled as soon as tomorrow. It was both too soon and not soon enough.

"Yes," Mary said. "I would love that. But not tomorrow."

Georgiana frowned. "Not tomorrow? What do you mean?"

"Because"—Mary drew their hands up so she could kiss Georgiana's perfect knuckles—"I would like to give Mr. Markham one last night on the town. And I would like to spend it dancing with you."

Georgiana flushed and ducked her head. "Well. I imagine that could easily be arranged, Mr. Markham."

Mary tugged her gently, and Georgiana came readily to her arms. "You do me the greatest of honors, Miss Darcy."

A.A. Weston

AROACE MARY LIVING HER BEST LIFE

Mary Bennett is finally comfortable enough to drop her lifelong mask. Autistic and aroace, she surrounds herself with books and the trappings of her many hobbies. Mary and her husband married out of convenience but soon came to realise they shared a yearning for a platonic kinship, so they live their lives happily alongside each other.

Editor's note: aroace means aromantic and asexual.

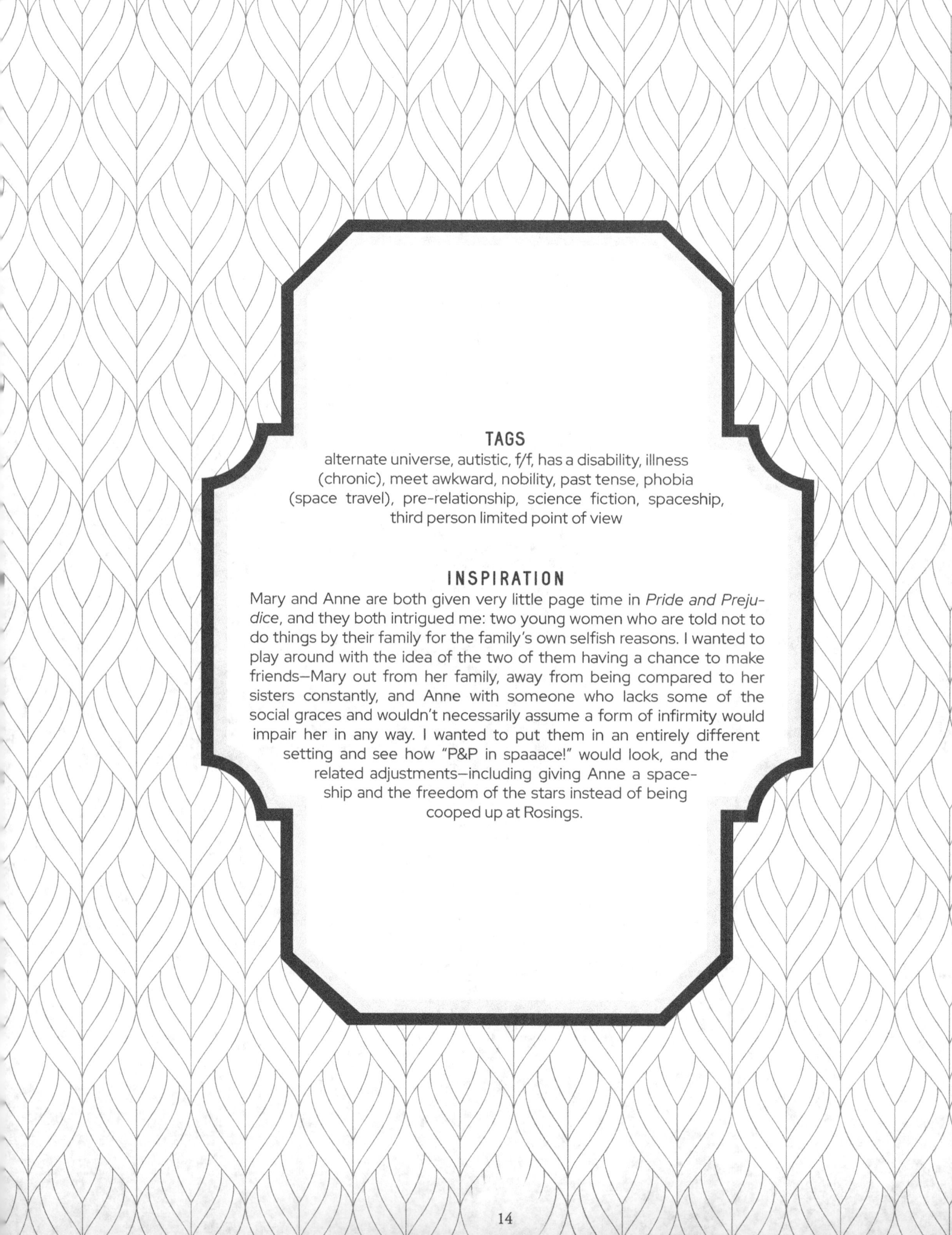

TAGS

alternate universe, autistic, f/f, has a disability, illness (chronic), meet awkward, nobility, past tense, phobia (space travel), pre-relationship, science fiction, spaceship, third person limited point of view

INSPIRATION

Mary and Anne are both given very little page time in *Pride and Prejudice*, and they both intrigued me: two young women who are told not to do things by their family for the family's own selfish reasons. I wanted to play around with the idea of the two of them having a chance to make friends—Mary out from her family, away from being compared to her sisters constantly, and Anne with someone who lacks some of the social graces and wouldn't necessarily assume a form of infirmity would impair her in any way. I wanted to put them in an entirely different setting and see how "P&P in spaaace!" would look, and the related adjustments—including giving Anne a spaceship and the freedom of the stars instead of being cooped up at Rosings.

ORBITAL CONJUNCTION

MARY BENNET'S STOMACH swooped, heart racing, pulse rushing in her ears. She'd never felt this way before—and if she were lucky, she never would again. Her fingers clutched at the armrest of the copilot's chair as centripetal force shoved her into the gel-filled seat while the tiny ship pivoted then shot off in another direction. At least she assumed it was changing trajectory; the sight out the viewport before her was an oppressive matte black dotted with white, every angle looking the same. It made the terrestrial animal in the back of her mind scream for the safety of ground and walls and all that was good and right in the universe.

In the pilot's chair, Anne de Bourgh's laugh of sheer delight filled the small ship. Taking control from the autopilot, she pulled back on sticks and her fingers danced over sliders, sling-shotting the craft around the Rosings Park habitat and off into the stretch of space toward the Pemberley habitat. Colloquially called The Gardens for the elegant views the area gave of the rest of the system, Anne said it was one of the prettiest places she'd ever seen. What was most important, evidently, was that it was clear of any obstructions; without the distortion caused by the habitat domes, every star and nebula visible from this part of space was painfully, petrifyingly clear.

All of it terrified Mary. She wanted to see this from the safety of a screen, not through a viewport, without the hum of a ship's engine vibrating through her boots and bones. When she wasn't wearing a ship-suit that clung to her and was ready to vacuum seal if something went horribly awry. She sucked in a breath of rose-tinted recycled air and tried to ease the pounding of her heart. Turning her eyes from the field of space before her, Mary focused instead on Anne's profile. Her skin's flush. Excitement stretched over high cheekbones. Hair pulled away from her face into a pilot's chignon at the back of her neck. She looked almost entirely unlike the woman Mary had met several weeks ago, with no sign of worry in the corner of her eyes, her motions confident and easy instead of abbreviated and stiff.

"Isn't it beautiful?" Anne sighed, smile dancing at the corner of her mouth. She flipped a switch and adjusted the joystick-like throttle with an absolute confidence Mary envied. "There's nothing like it anywhere."

Mary's choked sound, somewhere between laughter and despair, bounced against the walls of the little ship. "You're right about that," she agreed. "It isn't at all what I expected."

Anne rewarded Mary with a stunning smile, impish delight Mary had never anticipated from the de Bourgh heiress. There was a rightness to this moment that Mary had never anticipated. Two months prior, Mary would have been agog at the impossibility of it; even a fortnight past, she would have shaken her head in disbelief—and yet here they sat, spinning amongst the stars.

They had begun so wrong-footed, circling around each other like a pair of binary stars, neither sure why Catherine de Bourgh had called up the Collinses and invited the visiting Bennet girl to Rosings Park. And if there were one thing true in the world, it was that Mr. Collins would rather die than do anything to disappoint his benefactress. Mary hadn't been given a choice in the matter. She had been thrust toward Rosings like a peace offering—or a sacrificial lamb.

Standing at the shuttleport, Mr. Collins had smiled awkwardly at her. "Your parents have approved," he said as she slung her carisak of belongings over her shoulder, "and Anne is a lovely young woman."

"A lovely young woman" could mean many things; was it a polite, pat phrase to avoid offending Lady Catherine? Was Anne de Bourgh really a pleasant person to be around? What precisely *would* happen once Mary set foot in Rosings Park? There were too many possible interpretations and nothing firm to grasp onto. It reminded Mary of space flight: too many trajectories, too many possibilities.

Such thoughts consumed her during the shuttle hop from Hunsford to Rosings. Merely twenty minutes, but it was long enough for Mary to get tangled up with hypotheticals and not long enough to work anything through from start to finish. Lizzy's unexpected marriage to Mr. Darcy hadn't merely thrown the Bennets and Longbourn into disarray; it had heightened the tension between the Bennets and the Collinses—and the de Bourghs as well. Mary's visit had been intended to get her away from the sisters the world insisted on comparing her to.

Rosings had seemed like a whole new world when she stepped out of the shuttle, the gravity not quite the same as home's. Entering the de Bourgh family suites, the gravity had shifted again. Mary's firm steps had nearly launched her into the air, and only an indecorous scramble kept her from utter embarrassment. Rosings was an odd place, gilded carvings alongside sleek chrome, mirrors and the soft hum of wallscreens and bots moving through the hallways. Longbourn was shabby by comparison, with only a couple domestic bots and wallscreens which Kitty always wanted set to views of Bath and Mr. Bennet preferred to keep tuned to local and pastoral scenes. Those in Rosings displayed a variety of old art; on closer inspection, Mary discovered some of them weren't displays at all, but *real* art, with oil paint and brush strokes and everything.

Lydia would be beside herself. And probably trying to figure out how she could take advantage of the situation—uncharitable, Mary admitted in her heart, but not inaccurate.

Anne had been seated when Mary was presented to her; Anne had risen briefly to look warily at the visitor, shaking hands with the bare minimum of necessary politeness before sinking back into her damasked chaise. The way it conformed to her spoke of the latest self-molding furniture and piloting chairs. It should have been Mary's first sign there was something different about Anne, but she hadn't thought about it. It hadn't lined up with her knowledge gleaned off the 'net about the de Bourgh heiress, a young woman usually described as affable if quiet, seen little in public. Reality spoke of an ostentatious wealth Mary envied—and of a secret gone unspoken. Self-molding furniture was painfully expensive, indicative of either great casual wealth or the need for extra support, when pain or gravity or injury required extra assistance. None of the media outlets had ever dared to imply the de Bourgh heiress was anything but in the best of health. But if Mary put the pieces together…it was the edges of a puzzle, shaping up to mean something. She needed to fill the middle in, and time would allow for it.

Over a lavish spread of tea and sandwiches—"From Rosings' own hydroponics lab," Anne said proudly—in the elegantly appointed parlor, they began the delicate dance of first contact. The fish was pink and flaky, the herbs and vegetables fresh, the bread soft— Mary suspected it was made of real wheat.

"How far have you travelled?" Anne asked, raising a teacup to her lips. Her fingers trembled, which Mary attributed to nervousness: the same thing she was trying to hide.

"Aside from here? Bath with my family." Mary suppressed a shudder at the memory of the long flight, how she'd spent most of it in her berth, trying not to think of it as anything more complicated than a tram-car ride within a habitat. "London once," she added, hoping to establish some degree of credibility with the de Bourgh heiress. She drew her etiquette lessons up from the depths of her mind. *Reciprocate. Ask questions. Encourage your conversation partners to talk about themselves.* "And yourself?"

"I don't travel much," Anne said tightly, her fingers denting the soft sandwich bread. "Not to other habitats or planetside, at least."

Mary raised a brow, shoulders drawing back as she shifted in surprise. "Whyever not?"

The moment she asked the question, she wished desperately she could take it back, clapping a gloved hand over her mouth in horrified dismay. The salmon and dill sat leaden in her stomach, the tea churning with bitter acidity. *Tactless*, her mother's voice whispered in the back of her head.

Social interactions had never quite made sense to Mary. They were too difficult to qualify and understand, guided by unspoken rules she'd never quite grasped. There was nothing like perfecting a complicated piece of coding for the family business (or her own amusement) or mastering a complicated piece of music on the piano. Reading, memorizing interesting tidbits to tell at parties—all were technical skills, all of them quantifiable. Technical achievements made *sense*. The more difficult they were, the more satisfaction she took in attaining them, and the more delight in showing them off.

A look of irritation flashed across Anne's fine features, a line on her forehead and a delicate frown on her face ghosting away a heartbeat later. "Surely you're not *that* out of society in Meryton," she replied tartly. With her still-gloved hand, Anne gestured at the room around them, the couch she sat on, as though encompassing the entire system with the movement.

Mary blinked blankly. She set her teacup down harder than she had to, sloshing liquid onto the impeccable white tablecloth and her own gloves. Her skin heated, rising in a blush from her chest to her cheeks in a wave of embarrassment.

"I'm *ill*," Anne said, the frown appearing again. There was something to it Mary couldn't put a finger on—as though Anne were reminding herself more than Mary. "Kept out of society by my lady mother's request because I am…" She crinkled her nose. "Unwell. It's complicated… You must've heard the rumors, seen the newsflashes."

"You seem perfectly well to me," Mary replied honestly. Maybe the handshake hadn't been terribly strong, but then, her eldest sister Jane's wasn't either. There was no look of sallowness to Anne's skin, no bruising beneath the eyes to speak of exhaustion, no ports or unexpected bits of chrome on her skin to hint at medical enhancement.

Anne's frustrated look shifted into something verging on confusion. She managed to hide much of it behind raising her delicately painted cup to her lips again and sipping from it. After a moment's consideration, she set the cup down and levelled Mary with solemn brown eyes.

"They really do keep you sheltered," she said with an almost admiring snort of disbelief. "I am possessed of several illnesses, all genetic—nothing you need worry about catching," Anne added dryly. "They present most commonly as exhaustion and chronic pain. While there are possible medical treatments in testing, my mother has determined her only heir is not to use them until their effects have been more thoroughly studied. In the mean-time—*surely*," she added with that same hint of disbelief crinkling her nose, "you noticed the gravity here."

"Or lack thereof?" Mary nodded. She was certain if she tossed a ball in the air, it would—perhaps not hang, but certainly not drop with the same speed it would at home.

Anne picked up another of the delicate fish-and-herb sandwiches. "It is to accommo-date me. I exercise for muscle tone, but the rest…the lighter the gravity," she said with a hint of longing in her voice, "the less it all hurts."

It made sense; Mary bobbed her head in acquiescence. Why wouldn't Lady Catherine do everything she could on her daughter's behalf? If she could adjust grav-ratios in the rooms Anne was in, of course she'd do so.

"You exercise," Mary said, "and I'm sure you do other things. What do you enjoy doing? Do you draw or paint?"

"I think," Anne said, setting her empty cup down, "I am feeling tired. I should like to have a rest. Someone can show you to your rooms, and you can explore Rosings Park, I suppose." One shoulder rose and fell in a half-shrug, a gloved hand covering her mouth—ostensibly to hide a yawn. "You must be tired from your travels and wish to refresh yourself. Quinlan can show you what you need to know."

Wondering what she'd said that was so offensive, Mary opened her mouth again to refuse but thought better of it. She shouldn't risk making more of a hash of things. She'd already put her foot in her mouth; time to think about what she'd said, what else she might more appropriately say in the future, would be prudent.

"I hope you rest well," she said, trotting out familiar pleasantries and platitudes, "and I apologize for any offense I've unintentionally caused. I look forward to speaking with you again."

And then, as Anne didn't move from her couch, Mary took the other young woman's nod as a dismissal. The moment she stepped out of the parlor, heavier gravity sank onto her shoulders. A young woman in the sleek livery of one of the household attendants—Quinlan, Mary presumed—intercepted her, smiling politely.

"If you'll follow me, Miss Bennet, I'll show you to your rooms. Lady Catherine has left authorizations to hook you into the Rosings Park intranet, and we can prepare and outfit you for your stay with us." The smile flashed again, a hair too small to be genuine.

The worst part about Rosings was the gravity—not simply the actual gravity, but the seriousness with which Anne treated everything. She reminded Mary of Jane, or perhaps even Charlotte—now Mrs. Collins—with her tendency toward severity. She did not have the playfulness in her that most of Mary's sisters did, and it made negotiating the peculiar social norms of the de Bourghs, and Anne in particular, difficult.

They both read, at least—but neither seemed to have an agreement about a particular book. Where Mary preferred Starlitchka's literary slant on philosophy and social criticism, Anne unabashedly loved Gyuvany's travelogues and light humor. Mary had to admit she'd never read them—and then promptly found herself diving into them after dinner that night for the sole purpose of being able to argue her stance with Anne.

There was something to be said for the conforming furniture, Mary admitted privately as she curled up, her fingers running along the fabric-bound travelogue in her hands. They made curling up with a book far more comfortable than the lumpy stuffed chairs of home did. Over the fortnight she had been staying at Rosings, she'd grown to enjoy them more than felt reasonable, and she would certainly miss them when she had to leave for home. The de Bourgh library boasted real physical bound books, with the smell of paper and glue that accompanied them. Losing herself in a book was far easier this way. The habitat's lights faded around her, the stars gleaming and hazy in the sky outside the window, as she lost herself in Gyuvany's humorous stories of the different habitats.

"What do you think of them?"

Mary yelped and clapped the book closed, jerking upright. She'd been so caught up in the writing that she hadn't heard Anne's footsteps. She looked at the book in her hands and back to Anne standing in the doorway, clad in long, loose trousers and a sweater that looked soft as a cloud.

"They're…interesting," Mary allowed, pressing her lips together, turning away from Anne. "But I haven't made a decision yet. There's something about the words Gyuvany uses—so…subjective?"

Anne plucked a book from one of the shelves and settled herself on a sofa across from Mary. She opened the book, flipping to a ribbon marking a page. "That's part of the appeal, I should think. As if you're there, with him, among the people. In the fields and the factories, the markets, the spaceports." Her voice carried a hint of longing even Mary couldn't miss.

Tucking her feet beneath her, Mary returned to the book in her lap, paging through it to find the place where she'd stopped. "I suppose," she said halfheartedly, not sure why someone would want to imagine themselves in a country market full of noise and clatter, voices shouting and bickering, the hum of transport carts vying with the livestock some people insisted on keeping in more pastoral places. Still, he had a way with words, dialogue especially, that captured what it must be like to hear the conversations and fill one's lungs with spices and fish and sunshine.

Quiet settled around them, broken only by the turning of pages and the occasional contemplative sound from one or the other. Mary traced a nail across the page and paused her reading, glancing at Anne—

—to find Anne quickly averting her gaze, eyes focusing on the book before her.

Once, Mary could attribute to curiosity, but then it happened again. Catching Anne watching her twice was peculiar. She'd never paid so much attention to Mary before, and Mary couldn't fathom why she would begin to do so now. The third time it happened,

Mary pursed her lips to ask a question and then thought better of it. They were neither arguing nor coldly ignoring one another; it was a delicate bubble that might pop at any moment.

Mary was terrified. There was no social script for this. Should she say anything, it might be misinterpreted or be inadvertently offensive. It would be safest to keep her mouth shut. Say nothing, let Anne take the lead if she wished.

"Tell me," she found her mouth saying despite her best attempts, "which one of these, then, is your favorite?"

Anne's eyes lit up like dawn, and she was on her feet with a haste Mary hadn't believed possible. She stood beside Mary a moment later, smelling of recycled air and a hint of flowers—real ones, without the synthesized undertones. Her fingertips almost brushed Mary's as she plucked the book from Mary's hands and thumbed through it with familiarity to a particular passage, then thrust it back at her.

"This one," Anne said, eyes still bright. "Read it and tell me what you think." Her lips kicked up at the side in the hint of a smile. "Please."

Mary drew in a deep breath, roses and paper and Anne. With such a look of hope, how could she not?

Gravity was a fiddly thing at Rosings. Over the following days, she kept a mental map of where it shifted, which doors and hallways led from one place to another, the shifts in gravity enabling her to map out where in Rosings Anne most often went. Most areas had nearly normal gravity; Mary's familiar slippered steps bounced slightly and she covered a little more ground, her hair hanging for a fraction of a second longer before it settled against her shoulders.

But when Mary set foot in the parlor as she did now, the place she and Anne had wordlessly arranged as their meeting place, the pressure shifted. No matter how many times she went into the room to admire Lady Catherine's collection of figurines from across the habitats or to read one of the antique printed books there, the lighter gravity seemed at its peak, intended exclusively to maximally frustrate her.

Her steps, normally light, were too heavy for the parlor. They sent her bouncing into the air—not quickly nor particularly high, but enough that her feet left the ground like a girl who had never dealt with zero-g before. The weighted slippers which had unobtrusively entered her closet on the second day of her visit had confused her at first, but now had a subtle—though pointed—purpose. If only they didn't feel like walking around in lead-lined boots in the rest of the habitat.

Mary bit back a curse she had come across in one of the older books. It was not fair *bollocks* tripped so neatly off the tongue, the pop of the "B" and the angry sharpness of the "cks" at the end. She settled for muttering it under her breath as she grabbed for the edge of a table with one hand, hoping to hold herself down and collect herself before making any further attempts at movement.

The grab was too quick, her movement too wide, and by the time she collected herself, the sound of her pulse in her ears was loud as engines. She'd knocked down a handwoven market basket and a gilded figurine of a shepherdess. Tears of frustration hot in her eyes, she lunged, hands outstretched, to catch it before it hit the ground. It was like being a coltish teenager again, her body refusing to obey. When her embarrassment and mental haranguing of herself ended, another sound broke through—restrained and ladylike laughter.

Mary snapped her head up, mortified. Her body went all-over ice, goosebumps pricking along her skin, as she lifted her head to see Anne de Bourgh tittering in the doorway.

She might have hated Anne for a moment then, with her long legs shown off by trousers cut in this season's fashion, so perfectly at ease. She wore the short wrist-length gloves society demanded, though these had nearly risqué cutouts along the back of her hand. Mary's fierce flush of emotion vanished as quickly as it came.

"Still struggling with the gravity?" Anne asked, relaxing her expression into something approximating seriousness. Laughter yet lurked in the corners of her eyes.

There was no malice in her, but *oh*! How it rankled to be the source of someone's humor.

At least Anne was seeing *her* rather than comparing her to Jane and Elizabeth and Lydia and Kitty. At least it was *Mary* she was laughing at.

Anne rolled her eyes in a decidedly unladylike fashion. "If you'd like…I can help you. I'd prefer to discuss books and have tea in a civilized fashion, without you bumping all over the room." Her mouth twitched in what might have been a smile, the first one Mary had seen on Anne's face in the days Mary had spent at Rosings. She stepped fully into the room, each step calculated with the ease of long familiarity.

Mary's fingers curled around the carved wood back of the couch as she regained her footing. She eyed Anne with some trepidation. "I am used to being able to walk about without fumbling and feeling like a child. I…would appreciate the help."

Anne cocked her head, full lips tilting in the shadow of a smile. "It's all about using a light touch," she said, voice carrying a lingering hint of humor. She reached for the shepherdess figurine, her gloved fingers brushing against Mary's. They lingered there almost too long. Deftly, she lifted figurine and set it back on the end table where it belonged. "Gently. Easily. Smoothly. Every action has a reaction. Know what you—and your body—can do."

"I know," Mary muttered, pushing out her jaw. The heat of embarrassment was replaced by years of practiced, cool composure. "It takes—getting used to, with all the transitions in the house."

"I suppose," Anne allowed with a tilt of her head. She took several steps back toward the chaise, nudging a tufted ottoman out of the way and making an open space in the middle of the floor. "Come here."

Mary blinked several times. "I—"

"Come here," Anne said with a hint of her mother's demanding tone in her own. "It's the easiest way to do this. House"—Anne directed the localized system—"begin waltz music. Lanner and Strausses." She gave Mary a look that dared her to argue. "My mother is always after me about dance practice, even though I never go out to dances. And if you are to be my companion, you should be able to do this."

"Dancing?" Mary shuffled forward apprehensively. "I am *normally* capable of dancing. But given the circumstances—and the weighted slippers…"

Anne crossed her arms in front of her chest. "I looked into you, you know. I looked into all of you, after Fitzwilliam wed your sister. I wanted to know who had thrown a spanner into my mother's well-planned life for me. You have any number of certifications and achievements to your name. Is dancing one thing too many for you?"

Mary gave her a mulish look, admiring the appeal to her pride. "It's not so much that I can't, Miss—"

"Anne."

"—Anne," Mary said grudgingly. "But are you sure dancing is the best way to do this? Every time I turn around here, I nearly break something, or argue with you, or put my foot in my mouth. And now you ask me to dance?" She made a soft sound of disbelief.

"Light and easy steps. Let me lead," Anne added with another twitch of an almost-smile.

Mary lifted her hands into the customary position for a waltz, grateful for her gloves as she settled one on Anne's shoulder as light as she could. Anne's warmth was palpable through the fabric of her blouse, the muscle firm but mobile. It was a dance—just a dance, and she had danced many times before, with people she liked far more—and far less—than Anne de Bourgh.

"I won't break," Anne said tartly as the music piped around them, violins and cellos encouraging light steps.

The need to move filled Mary's body. But Anne had said to lead, so Mary waited. "You said light and easy," she said, toes curling in her slippers with the urge to follow the music.

Anne's dark-brown eyes flashed; this close, the challenge in them was unmistakable. She settled her own gloved hand on Mary's waist and pressed her other palm to Mary's.

Anne led, her movements slower and more deliberate than Mary's would have been; though the steps were familiar, there was a delicacy to them Mary would never have used herself. Each step was calculated to address momentum and trajectory, taking into account Mary's movements and adjusting on the fly. It was difficult, restraining most of her movements, the shifts of her feet and the way her body responded a struggle. She kept catching herself, leading to stumbles and jerky movements that made her seem like a badly programmed bot.

"You're being too analytical about it," Anne said. "Stop thinking about it and just let your body respond. You know the steps, you only need to adapt."

Allowing herself to sink into it and trust Anne was one of the harder things Mary had done. The first waltz finished; they let the music carry on into a second of the same composer's work, then a third.

"Better," Anne said with a smile as the music went quiet. A new song started, but Anne—and Mary—made no move to resume dancing.

Mary forced her hands from Anne, wondering if what she saw flicker in the other woman's eyes was the same reluctance she felt. "I'm not entirely hopeless," Mary replied. "I'd like to know what you're like when you are ready to let loose, though."

Anne rested her hands on her hips, clearly considering something. The music crescendoed around them. Suddenly she nodded, the first sharp and decisive movement Mary had ever seen from her.

"You want to see me let loose? There should be a ship-suit in your wardrobe. Put it on and I'll show you what it's like when I don't let gravity hold me down. May I take you for a drive, Miss Bennet?"

There was a gleam in Anne's eyes that hadn't been there before, and Mary found herself swallowing and inclining her head to accept.

"Excellent. I shall pick you up from your rooms shortly."

And now it was Anne shifting command from the pilot's seat to the copilot's as the Phaeton-class two-seater shot through space.

"You try," Anne said, her eyes bright with joy. Her lips curved in a smile Mary couldn't help but echo on her own face. "Come on."

Delight was not a common look for Anne, not nearly as common as Mary thought it ought to be.

"I can't—" Mary wet her lips nervously, pressing them together until they hurt, heart skittering in her chest. "I don't know how. I don't—do well in space."

Anne huffed, then made another sound of disbelief that carried a weight heavier than any g-force Mary had ever felt. "My mother brought you over to be my companion, and you can't pilot? You're *space-shy?*"

"I haven't ever needed to," Mary replied, chagrined. "We've had someone who can pilot for us when needed. And Jane can, a little bit," she added grudgingly. "I don't know where or how I would even begin. I'm—" She swallowed and met Anne's eyes. "It's too big. Hard vacuum, inches away? No thank you. I quite like letting someone else take control of this. You're enjoying this far more than I ever would."

"I suppose it's a good thing we have the Gardens, then." Anne shuffled the controls back to the pilot's seat. She turned a true smile on Mary, warm enough to make her heart beat erratically. "I'll take you for a drive. And then, I think—as long as you still trust me—we should be friends, shouldn't we?"

Friends. Mary tasted the word in her mouth, shaped it on her lips.

"Friends. Yes, I should like that, very much."

"Me too." And with a flick of her wrists, graceful and smooth, the little ship shot off into the spaces between the stars.

Cris Alborja

TOKEN OF AFFECTION

This artist has chosen not to share the inspiration behind her work.

TAGS

f/f, f/m, first kiss, historical with magic, love confession, past tense, pining (mutual), regency, second chances, story diverges from the original work's canon, third person limited point of view, time travel

INSPIRATION

Every time I read *Pride and Prejudice*, I like to focus on a different character. When it was Caroline's turn, I found myself delighted by her. She's everything you could want in a mean girl—witty and jealous and duplicitous. And I think she's also genuinely fond of Jane. At least, at first.

I started to think about her actions as if her jealousy was aimed not at Lizzy, but at Charles. Perhaps she tried to put space between her brother and Jane because of a hidden desire for the latter. Maybe she brought up Darcy's sister constantly as a way to get a feel for Jane's true emotions.

Then I thought… what if Jane held the same quiet affection for Caroline?

And this story was born.

SILK GLOVES AND SECOND CHANCES

Draped in feigned indifference and a gown the eye-catching colour of cerise, Caroline Bingley arrived with the rest of her brother's small party at the Meryton assembly.

The announcement of their presence caused conviviality to stutter into silence. The dancing halted. Not a clink of glass could be heard. Dozens of curious faces waited to see what amusement the newcomers might bring. Their attention would be fleeting. In another moment or two, the musicians would begin their aborted song anew and everyone would return to their jovial selves.

Caroline played with the tassel of her fan. She was in the unique position of knowing exactly how the evening would unfold. Each and every one of the people gathered beneath the warm yellow light of the chandelier, she'd met already. Only she was aware of this fact, being the only one to have lived this fateful night before.

The night she'd met Jane Bennet.

The night she'd fallen in love.

"Regrettably," Caroline said on the morning that Jane Bennet was to become Mrs. Charles Bingley, "I have been beset by a most terrible headache and cannot make the service. Do send my sincere regards."

Before her confused lady's maid could respond, Caroline shut the door between them. She kept her hands pressed to the wood and waited until soft footsteps hit her ears. Once satisfied she had been left alone, she elegantly pushed aside floral chintz curtains, flopped back onto her four-poster bed, and stuffed a pillow over her face.

She did not have a headache.

What she had, instead, was the sincere belief she would never be happy again.

She was not partaking in theatrics. There were many reasons for her to have such a conviction, and all of them distressed her greatly. She wished never to speak, nor think, of them for worry that if she allowed her mind to wander towards the *why* of it all, she risked getting lost in kind eyes, a gentle smile, and the lovely hands she would never be allowed to hold. Not in the way she wished to.

Oh, how *marvellous*!

As was the way of things, now she could think of nothing else. Muffled by the pillow, a most unladylike sound of frustration escaped her lips.

If she were forced to detail her woes in order of least to most unconscionable, the wedding of Jane's sister Elizabeth to one Fitzwilliam Darcy could not be ignored. It was to occur today, alongside the other couple's blissful union, despite how tumultuous and unseemly Miss Eliza's courtship with Mr. Darcy had been.

Not that Caroline was jealous, of course. She had long since moved on from her designs upon Mr. Darcy. If Elizabeth wished to marry a man whom she had once found detestable beyond measure, well, that was none of Caroline's business. While it would not be inaccurate to say that Caroline was frustrated in the wake of her most tolerable match having been yanked out from under her, like the hem of a dress stepped on by an unskilled dance partner, her jealousy had better aim.

Charles. Her dear, sweet brother.

The instant he had laid eyes on Miss Jane Bennet, he had been charmed. Despite her family's lack of wealth and lower social status, he had been set on making her his wife. A desire Caroline understood all too well. Who wouldn't wish for the hand of such a delightful young lady? To be able to take her by the wrist whenever he wished, and pull the thin glove from her fingers, and press soft lips to knuckles…

Caroline couldn't have that.

No, she couldn't let *Charles* have that.

Not with a member of the Bennet family. It was objectively unwise for a gentleman of his stature. As she was a good sister, Caroline had thus done her utmost to put space between him and the lady who had caught his eye. Yet her continued efforts had amounted to nothing. Less than nothing! What good was a sharp tongue and profound wit if one afternoon with Mr. Darcy—a man she'd thought was on her side, who had formerly gone out of his way to discourage Charles from such an unworthy match—had the ability to undo all of her hard work? She should have known better than to trust a person stricken with love for Elizabeth Bennet. There was truly no accounting for taste.

The worst part? Her resentment towards Charles's happiness was wholly undeserved. He was innocent. He had done nothing other than fall in love.

That brought her to the last of her vexations. A secret. The mere thought of it escaping from the hidden place beneath her ribs was enough to make her sweat.

But there was no point in dwelling on it.

All she could do was return to the brief oblivion that sleep would bring, and pray that the warm grey eyes of her beloved secret did not haunt her dreams.

Caroline released her fierce grip on the poor pillow and shifted onto her side, allowing it to rest against her cheek. She closed her eyes, and in the fuzzy moment before sleep took her, the linen that cushioned her face became Jane's hand.

And then the swaying movement of a carriage jostled her awake.

Odd, she did not recall having left her room.

Seated across from her was Louisa. Her sister's gaze had initially been caught on the scenery but had shifted to Caroline once it had become clear she was no longer a boring companion.

"I told Charles the country wouldn't agree with you," Louisa remarked. "It's no wonder you rest so terribly these days. No one will blame you should you choose to sit out tonight's ball."

Caroline's mind must have been clouded from sleep. The only event they had been set to attend was the wedding and its subsequent breakfast, not to mention she had grown used to their accommodations in the country many months ago.

"Besides," Louisa continued, "I doubt Meryton can offer much in the way of entertainment. Not for those of us with finer sensibilities. Though, I must admit to my curiosity regarding the Bennet girls. I hear the eldest is quite handsome. You have heard the same, have you not?"

More than heard! Caroline was intimately familiar with the beauty of Jane Bennet. Weren't they all?

She was about to say as much aloud when, smoothing her dress out of habit, she noticed the green muslin. It had not been worn since last season when the colour went out of fashion. She wouldn't dare wear anything other than the latest style. Perhaps she was still dreaming.

Caroline discreetly pinched the skin above her wrist. Hard.

Nothing happened.

She did it again. The only result was a tiny pink bloom where her skin protested the harsh treatment. If she truly wasn't dreaming, then—

"We have yet to meet the eldest Miss Bennet," Caroline said, not quite a question. "Are you certain?"

Louisa's dainty brows lifted nearly to her hairline. "Are you ill? Of course I'm certain. When would we have been introduced?"

Hope, terrible and bright, seared Caroline from the inside out. Her sister's sense of humour was on the sharper side, much like her own, but it was not ill-intentioned and she had no quarrel with Jane. Louisa would not pretend they weren't acquainted.

After some careful prodding, Caroline ascertained that her brother had not yet married. The only Bennet with whom Charles had met was the father, and the Meryton ball where they first made the acquaintance of Jane Bennet was set for that very evening.

It was impossible to think she might have been returned to a time before the dissolution of her happiness. And yet, there she was.

Caroline did not understand why a second chance had been granted to her, nor through what means, but she would not spurn a miracle. There was no harm in playing along. Even if she was still in her bedroom, conjuring up a fantasy in the wake of heartbreak, she was determined not to let Jane slip through her fingers again.

The first step: steal a dance from Miss Bennet at Meryton.

But how was she to do it? Perhaps she could disguise herself as a man? Her brother would not miss a single set of full dress attire… No. Her features were far too delicate and, while Charles was not the most observant man to ever grace her presence, even he would be hard-pressed to ignore the obvious familiarity of face and dress.

If she remembered correctly, this particular ball had fallen short of many ladies' expectations. There had been a lack of gentlemen. So much so that a good number of young women had been forced to sit during more than one dance for want of a partner.

The gender disparity, in accordance with the rules, could allow for partners of the same sex. She would have to receive permission from the Master of the Ceremonies, but that was a small matter. The larger issue would be dissuading her brother from lavishing all of his attention on the eldest Miss Bennet. In turn, Miss Bennet's affections would be swayed towards Charles the instant he walked in.

If only Caroline could take Jane away for a private dance. Forgo the stares and the gossip, and keep Miss Bennet solely to herself. It was a heady thought. Far too enticing. Ah, what great misfortune—now her heart would settle for nothing less!

She did not yet know how to achieve such a feat, but she had until the ball to figure it out.

Impatience buzzed beneath Caroline's breast as her brother led the way through the sea of men and women enjoying the ball. She could not resist the temptation to search for Jane, and her uncharacteristic interest did not go unnoticed by her companions.

"Were you not of the opinion that this gathering was beneath you?" Mr. Darcy did not turn towards her, keeping the proud jut of his chin straight, but he regarded her out of the corner of his eye. "I recall you saying so this morning."

It was never more apparent than in social settings that he and Charles were cut from vastly different fabrics. Mr. Darcy's dark countenance was in such contrast to his friend's enthusiastic sincerity, it begged one to laugh. And Charles, rosy-cheeked and carefree, could always be called upon to provide as much laughter as required, and then some.

"The gathering, perhaps." Wry amusement seeped into Caroline's tone. "The company, perhaps not."

Louisa attempted to share a look with her husband, but Mr. Hurst's attention was already engrossed by the nearest drink tray, and he could not be bothered with Caroline's strange behaviour.

"I wish I could share your optimism," Darcy said.

"Oh, my dear Mr. Darcy, I should not be so quick to set aside the ladies of the country if I were you. One never knows…" She trailed off, struck by a glimpse of light brown curls and sprigged muslin.

Time did not grind to a halt when Caroline caught sight of Jane. It leapt into motion, as if all the moments before had been trapped in molasses, sluggish and tedious. And Jane's unforgettable eyes, as kind as a candle was bright, were already trained on Caroline.

In the ensuing blur of introductions and curtsies and polite exchanges—why Charles was so adamant about cavorting with people like the Lucases, she would never understand—Jane slipped from view. Caroline's body moved by memory alone, smiling and conversing with ease, while her thoughts and heart were across the room. She could think of little else but the depth of Jane's gaze. It had been so profound, so utterly unlike the gentle cordiality she had expected.

It was not the look of a young lady meeting another for the first time. There was too much happening beneath it.

Unless that was merely what she wished to see.

"—my sister," Charles said, finishing another introduction.

Caroline straightened from her curtsy and was flung from the daze that held her captive by the very woman who had caused it.

"A pleasure to meet you, Miss Bingley." Jane's voice held a softness that had not been directed towards Caroline in many months.

Not since they had stopped exchanging letters.

"I cannot believe," Charles said, taking a seat on the sofa across from his sisters, "that Miss Bennet was in London. Did she not write to you?"

He directed that last part solely at Caroline. It was an innocent question, not meant to sting. How was he to know that his sister had, indeed, received a letter whilst Jane was in town and instead of alerting him to her presence, Caroline had taken great pains to break their correspondence?

Caroline shrugged an elegant shoulder. "Perhaps she did."

"Why did you not tell me?"

"Mr. Darcy was of the opinion that we should conceal it." Not a lie. But not the whole truth either. "Would it have made a difference had you known?"

Charles appeared utterly bewildered. "Of course! I've shared how deep my feelings are. If I could have married her the night we met, I would have."

"What's done is done." Louisa waved a hand as if to waft the conversation away. "She has agreed to marry you now, is that not enough?"

"Too true. It is more than enough." Charles smiled, thoughts already back on Jane. "I am to be the happiest man in England."

Caroline curled her fingers into a fist against her thigh, unable to stop her own mind from following a similar vein as her brother's.

Caroline's pulse jumped. Sweat gathered on her palms, hidden and uncomfortable beneath her gloves.

Jane had yet to step aside, still hauntingly close, but the sparks of her attention had drifted towards Charles. That hidden emotion in her eyes—had Caroline imagined it? Was she so pathetically besotted that she could not discern reality?

Caroline's fan dangled from a thin loop on her wrist. She wrapped her hand around it, eager for a brief distraction, and was met with slender gloved fingers.

"Pardon me," Jane said. Her fingertips lingered for a heart-stopping moment before she slipped free of Caroline's light grip. "It looked as if your fan was about to fall."

She glanced up, a swift flick that Caroline nearly missed, caught as she was by the pinkening of Jane's earlobes. Thank goodness she hadn't.

There it was again. That undeniable depth. Caroline had not imagined it.

Her heart began to race. The possibility that she was not the only person given a second chance did not take root so much as it burst from the soil, already flowering. She needed to find out for certain, but she could not do so in such lively society. The other Bennet sisters were thankfully preoccupied with dancing or, in Miss Eliza's case, sitting in wait for Mr. Darcy to put his handsome foot in his mouth. Charles excused himself to continue his cheerful sweep of the ball. He had promised Miss Lucas his first dance, giving Caroline the perfect opportunity.

"I beg your forgiveness, Miss Bennet," Caroline said, fluttering her fan. She tried not to think of how recently Jane's hand had been in its place. "I am in desperate need of some air. Would you care to join me?"

Jane nodded. "I feel a bit faint, myself." She held out her arm, elbow crooked slightly. An invitation Caroline did not take for granted.

They slipped away, arm in arm. Not pressed together, but close enough.

Caroline might have attempted conversation, but the places where they touched, fabric against fabric, were too distracting. They walked in silence, leaving the music and voices behind.

The empty room they happened upon had a large window. It was dim, lit by a single lamp and the moon shining through a crack in the curtains. The door creaked behind them, falling to a position near closed.

"Shall we rest here?" Jane asked. When she turned her cheek towards Caroline, the flush of her skin was undeniable.

Another time, another place, overlapped in her vision: Jane ill in bed, hair mussed.

"My dear Miss Bennet," Caroline said, touching the back of her gloved hand to Jane's forehead, "this brings back memories, does it not?"

Jane's eyes widened minutely. She did not pull away. "I'm certain I don't know what you mean."

Caroline searched Jane's face and found no ignorance or cruelty. Just fear. "I will state it clearly, then."

And the truth came to light in a thin, reedy stream. A match to the moonlight.

"I apologise for not calling on you before now," Caroline said, forcing her tone into one of indifference. Her goal in visiting Jane while she was still in London was not a happy one. "You have been well, I take it?"

The parlour of Jane's temporary residence was charming, though it lacked the affluence of Netherfield. Most places did. Caroline stood, hat in hand, aware that she was not to stay long.

Jane took in Caroline's cold countenance, much changed from their previous encounters. Her pretty brow furrowed. "Yes, very well. Have you—?"

"I do not think I shall be free to visit again before you return to Longbourn." Caroline watched hurt briefly unfurl on Jane's face before it was hidden as if it had never been there.

A pin pricked Caroline's chest.

Her feelings were too overwhelming. She had been the one to reach out all those months ago, had invited Miss Bennet while her brother was away dining with the officers. It was selfish. She should not have offered a friendship when she had always wanted more.

It needed to end. For the sake of her own heart as well as Jane's.

Caroline could not make herself stay after that. And Jane did not attempt to stop her from leaving.

Jane took Caroline's hand and said, "I thought it might have been a dream."

"If it was, then we have somehow shared it."

"Miss Bingley…" Jane hesitated. "Please tell me you aren't teasing me. I do not think my heart could take it."

Neither could mine. "I would not dare, Miss Bennet."

Laughter, high and loud, cut into the air. Faint music wandered in at its heels. A new dance had started.

Caroline tugged lightly at their joined hands. "May I request the honour of sharing the next two dances?"

"You may."

And with the barest hint of a tune, the women and the shadows around them danced. Hands pressed together, then apart. A slow circle of steps interrupted the brief, careful touch before they came together again.

"You cannot imagine my surprise," Jane nearly whispered, quieted by the intimacy of their surroundings. "When you did not arrive at my wedding, I was certain you had decided to hate me forever."

"Why would you come to that conclusion?"

"Your letter and general demeanour whilst I was in London gave the impression you wished never to see me again. And then—well, you did not act in a way that assuaged my doubts."

Caroline's lips parted, but all excuses shrivelled up before they could escape the confines of her mind. She had been cold to Jane. Cruel, even. It could not be denied. She could find no words to defend her behaviour, so she settled on: "I assure you, that was not my intention."

"May I ask you to share your true intention then, Miss Bingley?"

Caroline hesitated. It was not a simple matter to confess her feelings, to bare her heart.

Her most intimate desires were akin to a necklace dropped amidst still-growing roses. They had lain enshrouded and concealed for so long that it was now impossible to reach inside without getting caught by the sharp prickles that had wound around them.

She was not afraid of breaking past the protective stems. She was afraid of what came after. If she were to confess her feelings, and the woman who held her affections did not return them…

For such a genuine person, Jane was surprisingly difficult to read.

They stepped back in time with the music, slowly swirled past each other, then touched hands once more.

Jane must have sensed that Caroline was frozen, unable to share quite yet. "You sent me another letter."

"Did I?"

"You did," Jane confirmed. "Professing your sincere congratulations on my marrying your brother and your profound delight towards the notion that we should be sisters." She averted her gaze, long pale eyelashes casting shadows over her cheekbones. An exceedingly lovely image. "I must confess," she continued after a brief pause, "that I did not believe a word of it."

"I write a great many letters," Caroline said. "Is it to be expected that I recall the contents of each one?" It came out sharper than intended.

"No." Jane averted her gaze. "I suppose not."

"A letter for you, ma'am." The servant held it out for her. "From Miss Bennet."

Caroline's heart stuttered. She took it, immediately sliding the contents out. Jane's handwriting was as pretty and neat as the woman who wrote it. They had kept up a steady correspondence since the days she'd spent ill at Netherfield.

While she missed being able to knock on Jane's door and converse in person at the drop of a hat, she greatly enjoyed being able to keep the words written by her beloved. Each letter was safely tucked beneath her mattress, easily opened and read again and again. There was nothing untoward in their responses to each other—they spoke only of common matters and friendship—but each "Dearest Caroline" was as precious as the last.

Like the others, she would read the new letter so many times that she could recite it. She hoped that Jane, stuck at Longbourn, was doing the same.

Her foolish brother was just finishing the preparations for the ball he had promised the younger Bennet sisters he would hold. Perhaps when he went to Longbourn to deliver the invitation, she might tag along. To receive Jane's letters was a pleasure, but to see her in person was a joy second to none.

"I remember your letters better than my own." Caroline stepped past Jane, the two of them crossing the room, guided by the music. "You would ask after my brother." If she could determine whether Jane's feelings towards Charles were deep and true, then she would know how best to proceed. "You did so admire him."

"How could I not? Mr. Bingley is most agreeable. I daresay that no finer man can be found in all of Hertfordshire, though that is not to imply a lack of respectable gentlemen in the country, for I have made the acquaintance of many. I merely mean to note that his happy countenance and exceptional manners impressed upon me a certain good-natured-ness, a pleasant air, that inspired my admiration."

"The two of you are birds of a feather, to be certain."

The corners of Jane's lips turned down. "I cannot tell if you are teasing me."

"How duplicitous you must believe I am. Miss Bennet, you have wounded my heart."

"From those words alone? No, I fear that I hurt your heart long before now."

Caroline nearly protested it reflexively. What had Jane done to hurt her? The only answer was loving Charles. If she admitted her pain, was that not tantamount to admitting her feelings? Their shared past was built of unexplained glances and light touches, the cream space between words on a page, a breath between whispers. What if there was nothing more to it? If the hidden romance had been a fictitious invention by Caroline's sordid mind and Jane was about to spurn her affections—

But if she didn't admit it now, when would she? What was the point of getting a second chance at happiness if she allowed fear to get in the way again?

"You're right." Caroline stopped dancing in the middle of the floor. Jane followed her lead. "Your courtship with my brother hurt me. When you accepted his feelings, it hurt me. Your wedding—I think of it now and my blood boils."

"Miss Bingley, I—"

"Were we only friends? Is that truly all we were?" Desperation stretched between her words, thin and brittle and unable to be concealed. "Did you love my brother as a man loves a woman?"

"I did," Jane said. "I do love Mr. Bingley."

"I see."

"Allow me to finish. I know that he would have treated me well and taken care of my happiness. But I could never have felt for him...as I feel for you."

Caroline's breath caught.

"I did not mean to cause you pain." Jane's lips pursed, an obvious attempt at keeping a deep well of emotion from springing forth. "Marriage to a man like your brother would change not only my life, but the life of my family. I did not know that Lizzy and Mr. Darcy were going to wed. Poor Lydia had just eloped with Mr. Wickham. If I married Charles, then not only would it have been a Godsend for my family, but I also would have been able to spend countless hours with—" She took a deep breath, chest rising. "With you. The feelings I hold for you are unlike how I feel with anyone else. Marriage to a kind man did not seem like too terrible a trade in light of that opportunity."

"We would have been sisters." Caroline scoffed, a disdainful little sound. "I did not want to be your sister, I wanted to be your—" She cut herself off.

"My what?"

"Your wife."

Jane's ensuing smile was better than anything Caroline had seen before. Women did not marry each other, they both knew that it was an impossibility, but it was a heady and wonderful idea.

"I wish to be your wife, too." Jane laughed beautifully and pulled Caroline back into their dance. The beat of the music was lost on them. It didn't matter. They danced to music only they could hear. "You have no idea how happy you've just made me. I worried myself sick, thinking you did not feel the same. I commend your sincerity. It must have been difficult."

Caroline had never thought of herself as anything less than sincere. Had she danced around the truth at times? Of course. A lady was not to give away her true feelings unless it benefitted her. She had learned early on to smile and titter, elegant fingers lifted to her lips. To turn her head as she dabbed a handkerchief to the corners of her eyes, wisps of carefully curled hair doing their utmost to hide the lack of moisture. As long as one had developed the skill, it was not difficult to shift a gentleman's opinion.

She had thought, for a time, that all women were like her if they held sufficient wit. That they all played the same game together, keeping a careful eye on their cards and hiding the winning hand against their breast.

Until Miss Bennet.

"Difficult? Do you truly think I'm so insincere?" Caroline teased. "If your opinion is that low of your future wife, how can you expect us to possibly survive marriage?"

"I wish nothing more than to think the best of you," Jane confessed.

Caroline's heart swelled. "Then do so."

"You must show me how."

"I will," Caroline promised. Her actions had been lacking. It was not wrong of Jane to doubt. "My affection is no less true than yours. I will endeavour to prove so from now on."

Jane laughed again. "I believe you."

The music outside swelled, bringing their second dance to a close. Their silk-covered palms were pressed together. Moonlight reflected in Jane's eyes.

Caroline didn't know who moved first. It could have been her, or it could have been both of them at the same time. All she knew was that the gap between them closed. Her lips touched the warmth of Jane's.

She had never kissed anyone before. There was an undeniable hesitance to it. Slow and unsure.

Footsteps shattered the moment. They pulled back from each other, startled into reality. Laughter and hushed words gained volume then lowered, passing by the room where they hid.

Caroline was not unaware of her social responsibilities. She knew they had stayed away for longer than was wise.

Desiring the opposite, she suggested, "We should return."

There would be plenty of time to figure out how to move forward together, now that they were both clear about their feelings.

"I believe Charles desired a dance from you." Caroline reached for the door. The music began again. A new song, more upbeat than the last.

"I think he can wait." Jane caught her wrist, smiling. "May I have the next dance, Miss Bingley?"

Oh, well. Who could possibly miss them for another dance or two?

Caroline closed the door and took Jane's hand.

"How do you like Meryton, Miss Bingley?" Jane was slightly out of breath, having recently finished a dance with Caroline's brother. Her cheeks had a delightful rosiness to them, a warmth that seemed to spread from her to everyone she came into contact with.

"Quite tolerable." Not a moment ago it would have been a lie. With Jane's smile aimed at her, Caroline found that the tedium of the country was not as unbearable as it had seemed when she arrived. "More so after making your acquaintance, Miss Bennet."

Jane's smile shifted. She appeared genuinely surprised at the compliment. "Truly?"

Caroline nodded. "I find your companionship to be exceedingly pleasurable. You must visit me at Netherfield."

"I…yes! I would be honoured."

"Miss Bennet, I assure you, the honour will be all mine."

Aceriee

ROSA CANINA

The title of this piece is the Latin name of the dog rose. In the flower language, this flower symbolizes many things, among them beauty and immortal love, but also pleasure mixed with pain. I wanted my piece to show a love hindered by the rules of society. Stolen moments and fleeting touches while being pressured into unwanted but expected relationships.

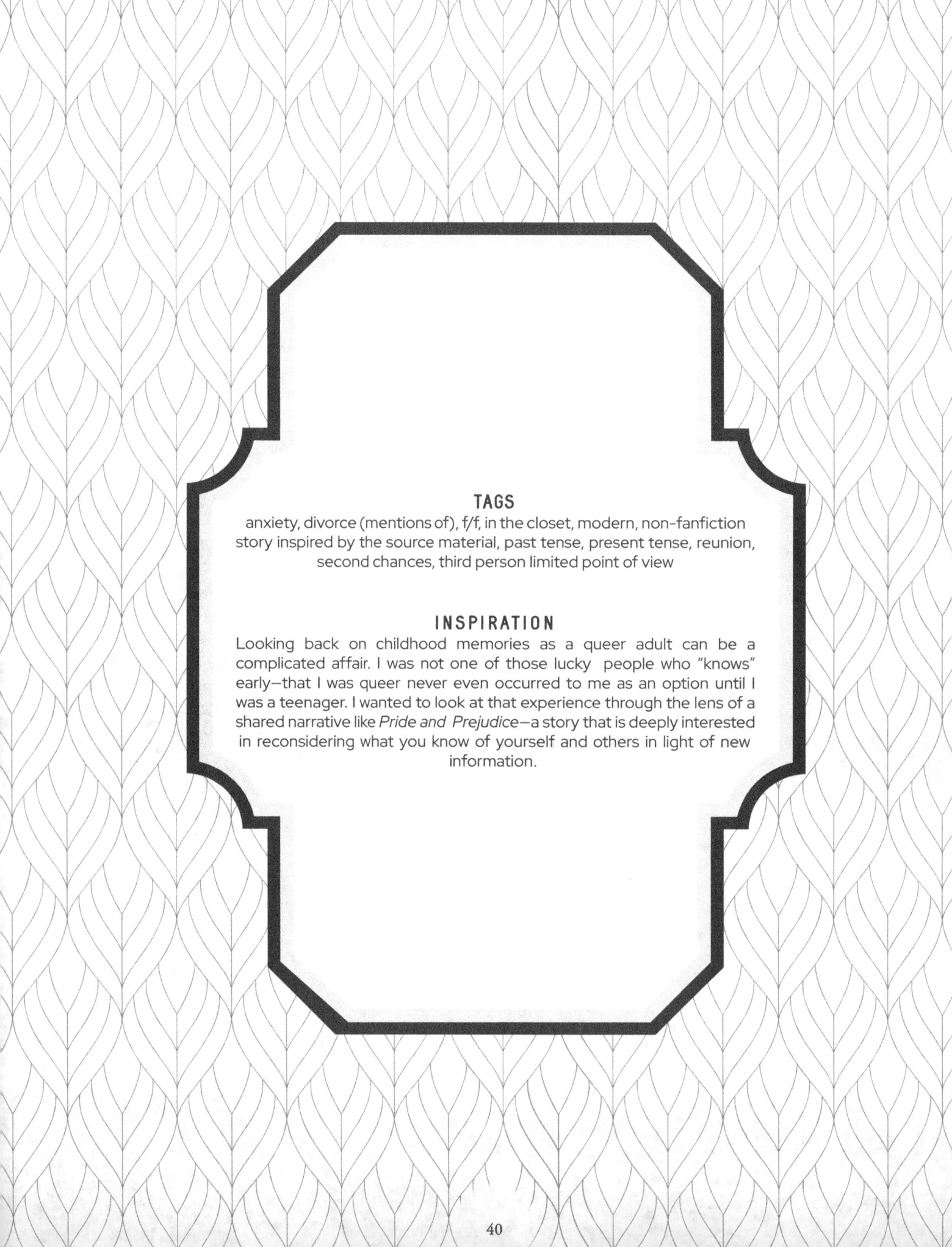

TAGS

anxiety, divorce (mentions of), f/f, in the closet, modern, non-fanfiction story inspired by the source material, past tense, present tense, reunion, second chances, third person limited point of view

INSPIRATION

Looking back on childhood memories as a queer adult can be a complicated affair. I was not one of those lucky people who "knows" early—that I was queer never even occurred to me as an option until I was a teenager. I wanted to look at that experience through the lens of a shared narrative like *Pride and Prejudice*—a story that is deeply interested in reconsidering what you know of yourself and others in light of new information.

TO HER THE PRIDE

WHEN THE AUTOMATIC doors of the library first open, a wash of smells assaults her—stale air, old books, aging carpet. Paige doesn't break stride, walking into the haphazard maze of folding tables with books piled onto them. It puts her in mind of display cakes with decadent icing layered on styrofoam.

It's an…*unusual* smell. Nothing like her library at home, where they'd done away with the carpet and sagging armchairs decades ago and switched to clean, neat tile and sterile seating areas. Glancing back through the glass doorways out of the foyer and into the library proper, Paige can see sagging armchairs and plush seats. They make her skin itch with discomfort.

Her calm, pleasant smile has not so much as twitched. She's had plenty of practice maintaining pleasant smiles in extenuating circumstances.

There are four patrons there, though it's still early at 8:30 a.m. Paige had planned her arrival to appear laid back for a sale that began at 8 without being too tardy to miss out on the best selection. She doesn't want to look like an over-eager bargain hunter, but neither does she want to wander in late as the volunteers with their card readers have begun to regret agreeing to spend their free time selling tattered old books.

It had been a near thing, whether to come here at all. True, her new bookshelf is empty, but she'd have been just as happy with the resplendent spines of newly printed books, ordered from the closest ethical source and delivered right to her door.

She's still practicing how to enter "Apartment Number" into order forms. She's never lived anywhere but a street address before.

But this sale benefits the library, and it's important to invest in a community. Even a new one. Even one with an *unusual* smell and unpleasantly aged seating.

Perhaps a piece of her is remembering the words of her coworkers when she'd left home to move here.

"Know anyone there?" they'd asked, pleasant and empty.

"I'm sure I'll make friends," she'd assured them in return, her smile perfectly even.

She's considered making her new neighbors cookies to introduce herself. It's possible, however, that they have gluten intolerances or are cutting out sugars. Perhaps there are allergy concerns of which she isn't aware. She's been considering her next move since—whether a small card inquiring after food sensitivities and allergies would be intrusive or welcoming.

It is loud in the apartment.

But books are the same everywhere. They are the familiar faces she can rely on in a new town, a new library, a new life, a new apartment. She doesn't touch their spines as she passes, but greets them in the privacy of her mind. A paper bag of books only costs ten dollars to take home, but she can't bring herself to pick up one of the bags. They're no doubt loud, crinkling with every movement, rustling more and more with every book placed inside, dampening and scrunching under the touch of moist, sweating hands…

This moment should be sweeter than it is. Better than it is. She's had beautiful times before, looking at books—reminiscing about the worlds within them and how she'd felt from one page to the next.

She remembers *Jane Eyre* calling her thoughts away from her strict study schedule for days, until she'd finally surrendered and read the rest in one fervent overnight.

She'd read *Frankenstein* on a gray day, and her soul had felt connected to the very spirit of Mary Shelly, hiding from the storm by building a new nightmare under her own control.

Today, those memories feel distant and artificial. The familiar faces of stories are separated from her by an invisible haze of the filth and unfamiliarity surrounding them. It's impossible for a person to dream when all they want to do is leave.

It would be rude—unforgivably rude—to leave without picking up anything. It's a benefit sale, after all, and she's one of only a handful of people there. Not exactly an anonymous situation that she can breeze in and out of like she would at a big box store. When she'd gone to purchase her new bookshelf, she could have left without a word and no one would have registered she'd been there. It might even have made their lives easier—the line shorter for the checkout, the day simpler for the man who'd had to help her carry the unwieldy box to her little hatchback.

But there's no doubt she needs to leave, and soon. She will not be filling a paper bag. She keeps one eye on the book spines, one eye on the door, and tries to pick one—*just pick one*—only to see—

There. An easy choice, finally. One simple thing. The spine is cracked—in worse shape than all the surrounding books—and yet, now that she's seen it, she has to have it. *Pride and Prejudice*, a favorite of hers from the moment her high school literature teacher had suggested it to her in freshman year.

It's in her hands before she can second guess, and she pulls out the ten-dollar bill she'd prepared for the day.

"Uh," the young attendant by the door says, "you can get a whole bag for ten dollars, ma'am."

"I just want this one," Paige assures him, smiling hard enough that she feels her dimples form before letting her expression settle into mild politeness again. She bids him a good day, then she *goes*, as fast as she can without drawing more attention than she already has.

Ah well. No one minded an eccentric person, so long as they had a little money to throw around.

At home, Oscar has overturned her potted zebra plant, cracking the ceramic. He's unapologetic to the extent of denying it ever occurred, despite the dirt on his paws. His croaking, frog-like meows only make her sigh instead of laughing this time.

After cleaning up, there's lunch to make. After lunch, intake paperwork for her new job. After intake paperwork, she needs to jog before she misses the window of bearable temperatures outside. It's colder here in the mountains, despite not being too far from her childhood home.

One thing adds to another, and it isn't until late that she actually opens the book. The chair by the window is the only place that feels real in her apartment. It's the one piece of furniture she'd put in the effort to bring. It sits beside her new, empty bookshelf, adorned with a now-cracked potted plant, its leaves pierced by a grouchy, snaggle-toothed cat.

The book feels light in her hands. The pages are slightly yellowed with age and a little brittle, like the manuscript of a monk rather than a mass-produced cash-grab edition from—

She opens the book to check the publication date to back up her internal diatribe, only for her thoughts to grind to a halt. There on the page, scrawled in blue ink with quick, spidery writing, is the name "Mia Turner," followed by an off-kilter heart, slightly smeared by a careless hand that hadn't waited for the ink to dry.

"Mia Turner," the precise voice of Mrs. Morrow called from the front of the room.

"Hello!" a chipper voice sang from behind Paige, bright and piercing.

Mrs. Morrow took a deep breath. Paige felt something within her curl in discomfort and second-hand embarrassment, like a leaf shriveling up in a fire.

"Please simply reply with 'present' in the future," Mrs. Morrow said with calm forbearance. "As for your volume and pitch—well, we'll be addressing such subjects today, so thank you for the apt entry point, Mia."

The class didn't exactly *laugh* in response—it was only day one of Miss Morrow's Etiquette School, and everyone wanted to make a good impression—but there was certainly something like a titter and the shuffling of a dozen skirts moving against chairs.

"Excuse me," the voice behind Paige called again, just as loud.

"…yes, Mia?" Mrs. Morrow's expression had emptied of genuine pleasure, leaving only politeness behind. Paige took note of it, and the burning leaf in her curled tighter.

"If we're going to call you Mrs. Morrow, shouldn't you call me Miss Turner?"

Nausea latched onto that burning leaf in Paige's gut. Cold crept down her spine—a physical manifestation of her desperate desire to turn around and attach a face to that voice.

"Respect must be earned, young lady," their teacher said, her smile curving upwards without actually warming.

"How'd you get yours?"

I'm going to throw up, Paige thought, closing her eyes. Her polyester top stuck to her stomach and sides with how damp her anxiety had made her.

"I try not to be harsh on the first day"—Mrs. Morrow's voice was clipped but calm— "so I won't ask you to relocate to the reflection corner, but please be aware that your statement was inappropriate and unappreciated, Mia. Now, if there are no more questions, may I finish taking attendance?"

"I've got a couple more," Mia said.

Paige couldn't stand it. Couldn't stand another moment of it. She turned around.

What an odd coincidence, Paige thinks as she slides her thumb over the name, half-expecting the ink to smear beneath her touch. Stubbornly, it stays rooted in place. The tenacity makes her lips twitch. How like Mia…

Back then, Paige hadn't known what to make of the girl sitting behind her. The wilting dandelion stuck behind her ear, the scrunched-up disapproval of her expression, the narrowed scorn of her dark-brown eyes, ringed beneath by a curve of freckles.

Paige hadn't had the words back then to encompass "mess" and "wonderful" at once. Now she thinks, maybe: bright sunset silhouetting industrial ruins overrun by soft moss, captured in tousled hair, drooping flower, chapped lip, angry eyes…

Paige runs the same thumb she'd traced Mia's name with over her lower lip, soft and sensitive. For a moment, she wonders if the blue might stain her, like a kiss. Then she realizes what she's doing and slams her hand back against the page.

It's terribly rude to be thinking such things. Who would want to be compared to a ruin? Much less some rusted iron machinery. Though, if anyone would, perhaps it would be Mia, with her set jaw, always raring for a fight.

A coincidence, Paige reminds herself again, trying to shake off the memory. Surely there were a hundred "Mia Turners" in the state. With a deep breath to center herself and prepare for enjoyment, she turns to Chapter One.

It is a truth universally acknowledged has been messily underlined in blue, with a line leading into the blank white space on the page.

"Maybe I'm really not smart enough for this," that spidery writing bemoans.

Paige blinks at the immovable words. Then, with a careful hand, she presses her thumb into the yielding page edges and begins to flip through.

Neat black text, weathered pages, and everywhere—*everywhere*—blue ink.

Paige lets the cover fall closed against her thumb, still pressed in place for "Chapter One," a mere three pages into the edition. Her head falls back against the cushion, and she stares at the ceiling. She *really* should have flipped through before buying. It was probably someone's assignment for college, full of homework notes.

…it's probably not *that* Mia.

The itch in the back of Paige's spine had turned into a fishing hook connected to her jaw. She wanted to turn her head. She wanted to look. She wanted to see. Whether Mia's curled hair was tame or wild today, and whether there was a flower behind her ear. Whether she was still glaring, or if she'd calmed down. When she was in the reflection corner, what did she do there? Paige had glanced once, and seen her with her fingers against the wall, walking upwards as if she'd made a spider of her hand.

Oscar swats his jingly ball toy with disdain, and Paige remembers to breathe. As if the book weighs ten times what it does, she lifts it and peels it back open to that first splash of blue: "Maybe I'm really not smart enough for this," she hears in a voice that *always* seemed loud back then, even though Mia mostly spoke in a dramatic whisper as malicious compliance with Mrs. Morrow's classroom rules.

"I bet you are," Paige whispers back to the book, then has to clear her throat.

She hasn't spoken to anyone but the library bookseller today.

Past experiences suggest she'll either learn to tune out the blue lines carving their way across the pages or lose patience with them.

"This dick doesn't like his own kids?" Mia's handwriting demands of Mr. Bennet.

"Why isn't there any narration? I don't know where we are!" she bemoans on one page, and then, "this is *funny*!" on the next.

"*This* is the hot guy?" she demands of Darcy.

"Give him time," Paige replies.

"None of these people have real jobs," Mia notes, then a short while later: "THEY DON'T?!"

Paige had meant to savor her re-read. A chapter a day at most, with a notebook to hand for keeping track of any stray aunts.

The blue writing compels her. She keeps turning pages.

"Two-faced bitches," Mia proclaims of Bingley's sisters, and "simp" of Bingley himself. Paige googles the accusation, and though the language is uncomfortable, she can't disagree with the sentiment. Not a new experience when it comes to Mia.

"You could be so pretty!" Annabell offered during one of their small-group tea party practices. "I can bring my hair straightener tomorrow."

"You're not touching my hair," Mia responded, pushing her untouched teacup away.

"Be polite," Paige warned past her discomfort, glancing toward the prowling Mrs. Morrow.

"Why?" Mia demanded in return, turning those sharp eyes on her. "I asked Mrs. Morrow what it was for the other day, and you know what she said? 'To make things simpler for people.' So I said: 'For who? It's not simpler for *me*. Why should I make things harder for myself so other people can take it easy?' and she didn't have an answer for that. She just made me go to the reflection corner."

"…did you reflect on it?" Paige asked, so mortified that she was in danger of getting sandwich crumbs on her dress from how her hand was shaking, but she was fascinated in equal measure.

"Yeah," Mia allowed with a shrug. "I decided I was right."

Paige had gone home that day with a spot on her lap from the cucumber slice that had dropped from her sandwich.

Mia likes Bingley, despises Darcy, and finds Wickham interesting more than anything, but she *loves* Lizzy. Every line of sass is underlined. Every snide remark, commented upon. The story through her eyes is new again, and Paige is alight with excitement for how it will continue—how she'll take the truth about Wickham, and where she'll land on the issue of Bingley, and—

She turns the page to a dense wall of blue ink.

"What?" writes Mia, beside where Charlotte accepts Mr. Collins's proposal. For a few more lines, there's nothing from her. Charlotte doesn't love him but will not die alone. She doesn't like him, but she can tolerate him. She's made a smart choice, and everyone knows it.

Everyone, that is, except Lizzy, and apparently Mia. Because here, that flood of words opens, pouring out not only into the margins, but at times overlapping the text itself. It's sloppy, quick, and fierce.

"Here it is in black and white! Here's that pretty future my parents wanted. *Security* at the price of *everything*. Predictability at any cost"—the next few words are smeared, impossible to read, but then—"and she *won't* be happy. If her daddy wants Longbourn that bad, she should've just married *Lizzy*, but no, of course, that wouldn't be Proper and Right. Women living happily together is the fantasy no Proper story can afford to indulge in. Never mind that Lizzy and Charlotte are *clearly* interested in each other, and—"

Her handwriting gets too cramped to read, perilously close to the bottom of the page but stubbornly persisting. Paige squints as if it will help, her hands shaking and her pulse racing. Part of her is saying: *no no, you don't know the whole story yet. Darcy's better than you think, Charlotte will be more content than you fear, and Lizzy will learn how blind she's been.*

Part of her is stuck on the words "Women living happily together," on the thought of Lizzy and Charlotte, on "she won't be happy."

"He wasn't happy," she'd heard her mother say over the phone the day after her dad stopped coming home. "But neither was I. Why does he get to go, while I'm…"

"What a shame," Annabell had whispered, eyes turned on Paige with the same sort of eager pity she usually only turned on Mia.

"Chin up," Mrs. Morrow had advised in a low voice, straightening Paige's collar. "It's a mark of strength to continue on with dignity in dire circumstances."

But Paige's hands wouldn't stop shaking long enough for her to be dignified. The heat of her classmate's stares curdled the already sour feeling in her stomach until she couldn't bear it. She asked to be excused. The chair rattled and scraped on the floor when she stood. The uncomfortable titter following her graceless rise chased her out the door.

It was the only thing that followed as she bypassed the restroom to go straight outside— out under the front porch awning, only barely sheltered from a pouring afternoon storm. The wind tossed fractured raindrops onto her face and spotted her hastily pressed uniform. It was a bleak, ugly Saturday in a world her father had just made her a stranger to.

The door opened behind her. Paige braced herself, ready to be scolded by Mrs. Morrow for a lie of omission—using the dismissal to escape the confines of the building. She couldn't tear her eyes off the rain; the vibrant, manicured flower beds being driven down and down and down into the brown, soaking earth where mud would stain the petals that survived the downpour.

But it wasn't Mrs. Morrow who stepped up silently beside Paige. It was Mia, her wild hair lashing in the wind, squinting her eyes against the sideways rain. It was Mia whose knuckles bumped into Paige's—a touch that she couldn't distinguish as accident or invitation. Her eyes were stuck on those flowers, and she couldn't peel them away. She spread her fingers closer, just in case—

Mia grabbed her hand in reply and held on tight, tight, tight. An anchor in the storm, silent and watchful. Until she huffed out a breath, stepped forward to be in Paige's line of sight, and said, "Come on."

The rain soaked Mia through in moments as she stepped out under the sky.

Paige clung to Mia's hand, her wrist drenched, her forearm splattered, but she couldn't bring herself to step forward. It wasn't proper, out there in the rain. It wasn't right. Even if someone else had gone first, even if she wanted it to drive down on her too, even if…

She pulled away, and Mia's bright smile shifted and fell.

Fingers trembling, Paige turns the page past that ink-drenched diatribe, hoping for more. Another word, another hint, another glimpse of "Women living happily together."

There's nothing at all on the next page. Nothing at all for pages more, until eventually, fed up with Mrs. Bennet's wailing, Mia has written: "She needs a banana and a nap," followed by: "Did they have bananas?"

Disappointment pings like a twisted tendon in Paige's chest and zips electric through her arms. She flips back, staring at that wall of blue. She thinks of the rain, of the hand in hers, of walking back into the classroom, still mostly dry, while Mia followed sopping wet. How she'd abandoned her to the others' scrutiny, only glad to have it off herself for a moment.

Her hand had been wet, her cheeks had been dry, and she'd still thought she was living in a story like *Pride and Prejudice*. A story with a man at the end, one she could be comfortable with. A story where she stayed at home until she moved into the house she would share with someone new.

That kind of story doesn't have room for Charlotte and Lizzy to stay together.

Oscar jumps onto her lap claws-first, and though she hisses through her teeth, she only lifts the book out of his way. It still occurs to her every time that there will be holes in the fabric, even if they are small. That everything she owns has become less perfect by the inclusion of her cat. He is rude, strange, and disruptive.

All those years ago, when Mia asked Mrs. Morrow what exactly the effort of politeness was for, Paige had thought it was shocking, bordering on ridiculous. Now…

Now she feels like she herself is the claw in society's fine clothes—the maker of holes that no one will notice but that those who *know* cannot fail to think of. A woman who will take no husband, no matter how tolerable he may be.

She looks down at the page where Charlotte accepts a proposal out of prudence and feels, for the first time, more than just mild discomfort and amusement at the twist. She feels sorrow, pouring down and drenching the page, smearing the ink. Disproportionate sorrow, not only for Charlotte but also for Lizzy, but not *really* for either of them. It's for herself. For Mia. For her mom. Maybe even for Mrs. Morrow. For women who are seen as unreasonable if they stop the constant effort of keeping others comfortable, no matter the cost.

Her vision blurs, and she only just snaps the book closed in time to save Mia's writing from salt water.

There was a girl in her etiquette class who shared a name with the person who used to own this book, and Paige should have followed her out into the rain. Should have walked back inside sopping wet with her. Should have held onto her until she understood why she wanted to hold her so badly.

With an apology to Oscar, she lifts him off her lap, wrapping him and the book both in her arms as she starts pacing. The apartment is still empty, so the room is very good for pacing. There are long swaths of space for her to move her discomfort through, painting it like a slime trail behind her.

Oscar bites the book in his annoyance, and she slows to a stop, still cradling him, grateful he's chosen to bite the book and not her. She should have followed Mia then, just as Darcy should have been kinder to Lizzy and her family from the start. She should have known why Mia's wild hair and drooping dandelion were mesmerizing before she'd dismissed them, just as a foolish man should never have proclaimed a woman he did not know "too plain" for him to dance with.

For decades, Paige has considered herself a kindred spirit to Lizzy. For the first time, standing in her new, empty living room, she thinks: *Oh no. I'm the Darcy.*

Paige had not packed her "Memory Book" from etiquette school when she moved, just as she hadn't packed the rest of her bookshelf. It wasn't a treasured piece of the past for her, then—merely a series of embarrassments and stresses. Only now, in the light of those blue words, can she consider it anything else.

Even if Mia had signed it, she can't check the handwriting or hope for an email address. They didn't have cell phones back then, and though she still exchanges letters with Annabell—married with her first son growing and her second on the way—it's more through Annabell's insistence than as a result of any routine Paige had formed of keeping touch with the other girls.

But the itch is there under the new light that has been cast on her memories. Looking back now that she's grown, she can't stand the thought of never seeing Mia again—of never telling her "I read what you wrote—that's me too!" or "Thank you for coming outside, I'm sorry I wasn't ready to follow you then."

Darcy was lucky. Mia won't be coming by with her aunt and uncle to tour Paige's apartment in a well-timed coincidence. If Paige wants to meet her again, she'll have to find a way for herself.

She only has one link to follow.

The website for Mrs. Morrow's Etiquette School hasn't been updated in three years. There's an announcement on the front page that classes have been suspended, with thanks to the school's many students through the years. It's clear, concise, and final. At the very bottom, in plain text rather than a link, is an email address to be used in case of any questions or concerns following the closure.

It's clearly intended for business purposes.

Paige takes a deep breath to quiet the acid in her heart at betraying that expectation. She paces again, shaking her hands as if she can dislodge the sticky feeling of failure at the fact that she's about to do something rude. Something *selfish*.

No one wants this but her. She picked up a book on a whim, and now she's gotten carried away. There's no evidence that it's the same *Mia*, except for distant, worn memories that might have only lined up so nicely because of the tone she'd read those blue words in.

And yet…

Her hands are shaking as she types.

Dear Mrs. Morrow,

I had the good fortune to attend your class for many years, and was hoping you might help me get in touch with an old friend. Her name is Mia Turner.

Alone in her armchair with her phone beside her, open to email, Paige opens the book again. Every few pages, she pulls one finger down across the screen, hoping for a reply.

Lady Catherine de Bourgh is met with a scornful blue comment of "Okay, boomer."

There is a sale from an online shoe store she forgot to unsubscribe from.

Darcy's proposal spawns a series of exclamation points, and Lizzy's refusal grants an enthusiastic "DESTROY HIM!"

The Nature Conservancy would like to thank Paige for her financial support last year.

Mia receives Darcy's letter with the same trepidation as Lizzy, and Paige's mouth goes dry. How will she receive a letter from a girl who left her out in the rain alone?

Re: An Inquiry From a Former Student, reads her inbox.

Paige drops everything.

Dear Paige,

Of course I remember you. You had a charming knack for napkin folding, and always spoke thoughtfully. I'm very glad to hear from you.

I would not feel comfortable sharing Miss Turner's information without her consent, but will tell her you have reached out and, with your permission, give her your information. How would you best like her to get in touch, should she like to?

I would also like to take this time to apologize to you. At the time you were my student, I was less understanding of the different lives my students were lead-ing. Since that time, I have had many conversations and experiences that have expanded my mind—many of them with our afore-mentioned shared acquain-tance. I sincerely apologize for my actions and lessons which I'm certain added to your stress. I wish I had been a better support to you during your time at my school, and hope that you have found happiness and stability in your life.

With thanks for reaching out and all best hopes that you are well,

Mx. Morrow

Paige carries *Pride and Prejudice* with her into the café. It's half an hour away from her empty apartment and forty-five minutes from where Mia reports she lives. Meeting in the middle. *Within thirty miles of each other*, Paige thinks to herself—a clear thought past the curling leaf of shame and uncertainty always present inside.

It should be raining, but it isn't. Her hand longs to feel the rain pound down on her palm joined to another, and for the rest of her to follow this time as she always should have. There is nothing she can do to repair that childhood mistake but this.

She opens the café door to a jingle of bells and the increased roar of milk foaming. A wash of smells assaults her from the book-filled coffee shop that Mia has chosen. Musty pages and espresso—lemony cleaning products and scalded milk. Something stranded between disaster and perfection. An industrial ruin, seen in silhouette before a sunset.

A woman in a jean vest, with a wild head of hair half-shaved and a drooping dandelion shoved behind her ear, looks up from her table. Paige clutches the book that brought them together again in sweaty hands and marches forward. She's practiced this so many times Oscar could probably do it.

"Mia," Paige chokes out, standing stiffly beside her table, "b-but one word from you will silence me on this subject forever. When last we spoke, I did not know my own affec-tions and wishes. But if yours are unchanged, I—"

Mia's lips lift into a baffled half-smile as she listens. Her head tilts, and Paige's train of thought jumps tracks, leaving her mouth stranded in the middle of her ridiculous speech that she had so ardently pieced together.

"You know, I only read that book once," Mia says, her voice deep and wild. "You might have to be a little clearer."

"I liked you," Paige cries. "I want to try again!"

There's a woman Paige knows who's like soft moss growing on steel ruins, and she kisses more fiercely than a downpour. The next time they meet, they pick a rainy day.

When Mia steps out into the downpour, Paige follows her.

DO ME THE HONOR

In this scene, I've chosen to reimagine Darcy as a woman. By removing the gender inequality between the two main figures, a queer retelling makes it clear that the central tensions of miscommunication in the story are due to prejudice rather than the imbalance of freedom related to romantic communication between genders in Regency England.

The scene I've chosen is the morning after Darcy's ill-fated proposal, when she finds Elizabeth and gives her the letter (which she doubtlessly labored through the night to write!) that will serve as the catalyst for Elizabeth's full understanding and eventual change in feelings. This scene appeals to me because of the tension between Darcy: understanding Elizabeth's feelings, assumptions stripped away; and Elizabeth: ignorant of the truth, full of misconceptions; and in Elizabeth's hand: the all-important letter.

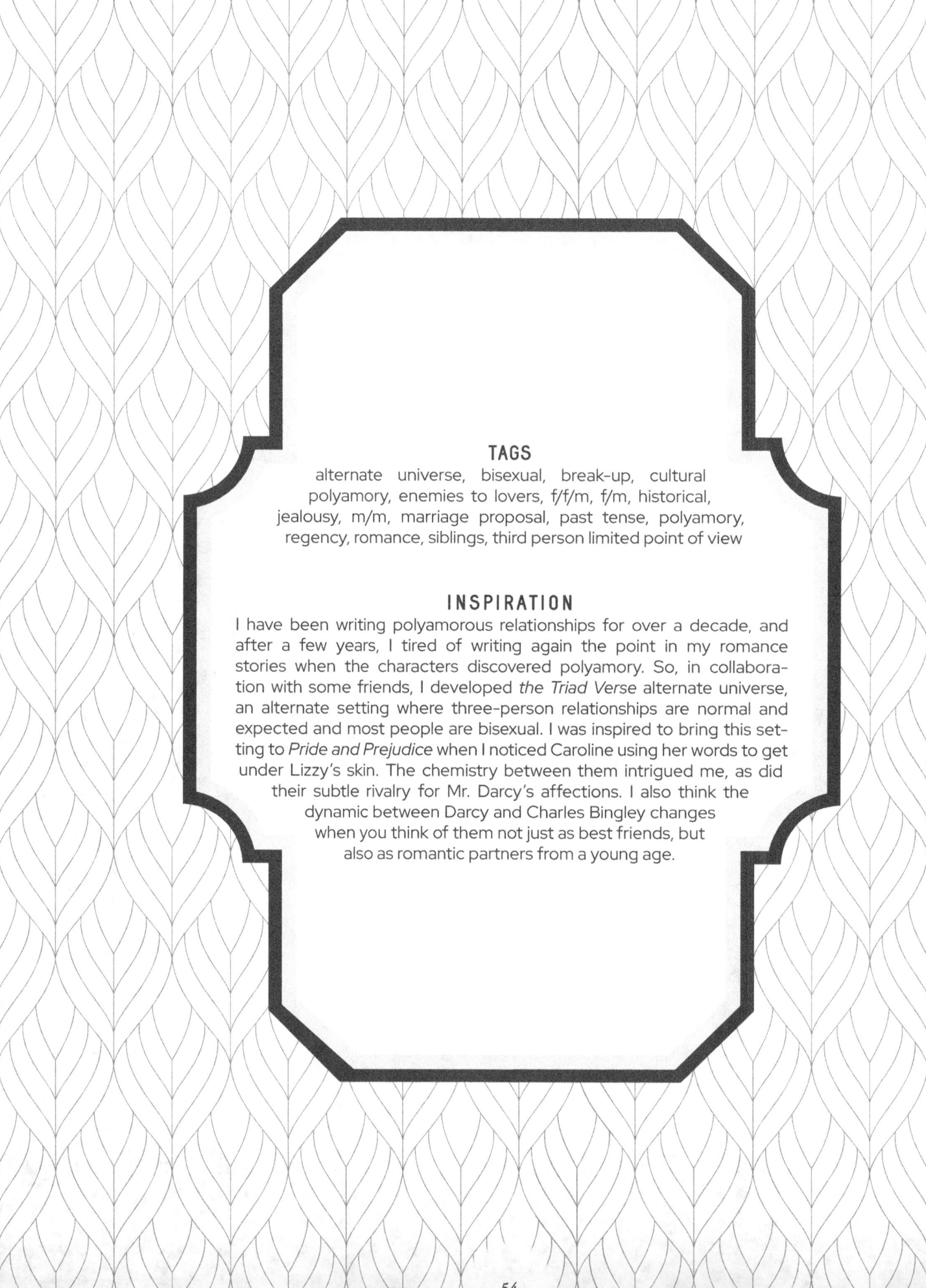

TAGS

alternate universe, bisexual, break-up, cultural polyamory, enemies to lovers, f/f/m, f/m, historical, jealousy, m/m, marriage proposal, past tense, polyamory, regency, romance, siblings, third person limited point of view

INSPIRATION

I have been writing polyamorous relationships for over a decade, and after a few years, I tired of writing again the point in my romance stories when the characters discovered polyamory. So, in collaboration with some friends, I developed *the Triad Verse* alternate universe, an alternate setting where three-person relationships are normal and expected and most people are bisexual. I was inspired to bring this setting to *Pride and Prejudice* when I noticed Caroline using her words to get under Lizzy's skin. The chemistry between them intrigued me, as did their subtle rivalry for Mr. Darcy's affections. I also think the dynamic between Darcy and Charles Bingley changes when you think of them not just as best friends, but also as romantic partners from a young age.

THE TRIAD PLOT

LIZZY BENNET STOOD beside the dance floor where her sister Jane was performing a traditional three-person waltz with Mr. Charles Bingley and Mr. Fitzwilliam Darcy. The stagnant air of the ballroom smelled of sweat and lamp oil. The musicians played loudly and brightly. Mr. Bingley smiled as brightly at Jane as they passed, but Mr. Darcy's expression was subdued.

Mrs. Bennet, Lizzy and Jane's mother, wriggled beside Lizzy with barely contained excitement. "Can you believe it, Lizzy?" She lifted her lacey peacock-print fan to hide her ecstatic smile. "Your sister may marry a couple of gentlemen worth 15,000 a year! Imagine that! With that much, Jane could care for us all when your fathers both expire."

A tight ache in her throat soured Lizzy's mood. "Be cautious, Mother. Mr. Bingley appears to admire Jane more than Mr. Darcy does."

"Excuse me." A young woman about Lizzy's age stood to her left. She wore a fashionable and expensive mauve dress, and her silk fan was intricately embroidered. "I see you and I watch the same triad." She gave Lizzy a polite smile. "I am Caroline Bingley, Mr. Bingley's sister."

Lizzy returned the introduction politely, then asked, "Do your brother and his partner often ask ladies to dance more than once?"

A pouting frown curled Caroline's lips as she shook her head. "I apologize for overhearing your conversation, but I agree that Mr. Darcy's feelings for the girl do not equal those of my brother. She is a member of your party, no?"

"She is my sister Jane."

As the dance ended, Mr. Darcy bowed and excused himself, leaving the dance floor, while Mr. Bingley engaged Jane in a brief conversation.

Mrs. Bennet asked, "Your brother and Mr. Darcy appear to be very close. Are they a primer couple?"

"Unfortunately, yes." Miss Bingley frowned unpleasantly. After a moment, she put on a polite, if grimacing, smile. "He and Mr. Darcy have been close since boyhood, and never have agreed on a woman they would like to court. In London, Mr. Darcy favored a woman introduced to him by his aunt, Lady Catherine de Bourgh. My brother detested her, so they never made her an offer. She married the son of an earl. And here…" Miss Bingley gestured to her brother, who backed away from the dance floor dreamily, his eyes still on Jane. "This is a most dreadful situation."

Mrs. Bennet gave a soft *tsk* of disapproval. "They must marry at some point. Two wealthy gentlemen will need heirs. They cannot run their lives without a woman's touch." Mrs. Bennet touched her fingers to her lower lip, then said, "Oh! There is Mrs. Garfield. I must say hello. Please excuse me, ladies."

Though Lizzy could excuse herself as well, this Miss Bingley undoubtedly knew about

London and life outside of Hertfordshire. "How are you enjoying your stay at Netherfield? It is a delightful—"

"Miss Bennet," Caroline rudely spoke over Lizzy, then stepped closer and lowered her voice. "I would like to ask for your assistance with an urgent matter."

"What is it?" Lizzy's curiosity was piqued. The richness of Miss Bingley's clothes and hairstyle suggested she would not normally condescend to speak to Lizzy. Perhaps at this country dance, she deemed Lizzy adequate for lack of better conversation partners? Lizzy burned with an embarrassment that almost overtook her curiosity.

Miss Bingley took Lizzy by the elbow and guided her into the darker, cooler corridor beside the ballroom. "I desperately need a co-conspirator in a plot."

Lizzy's heart pounded. Breathless, with voice low, she asked, "What plot?"

"Though this may sound cruel on its surface, I promise you I have only the best of intentions." Miss Bingley cast a glance around the empty corridor, then continued in a hushed tone. "I have been desperately in love with Mr. Darcy since I first met him, but he has always loved my brother. Though Charles returns Mr. Darcy's affections, I am convinced they cannot agree on a wife. If they remain attached, Charles will never marry your dear sister."

"What do you propose to do about this situation?"

"I think we should pose as a primer couple, and lure Darcy away from Charles." The edge of her mouth twitched up mischievously.

Lizzy followed Miss Bingley's suggestion to its logical conclusion. "It would leave Mr. Bingley and Jane to form their own primer couple. I doubt it would take them long to find a third."

"Exactly."

Still, Lizzy's conscience demanded she speak. "Miss Bingley, what you propose is quite immoral. We hold no affection for each other. We would lure Mr. Darcy away from his partner under false pretenses."

"No affection, Miss Bennet?" Caroline took a step closer and grasped Lizzy's hand. "One need not have an overabundance of affection to make a good match. I admire you, and I wish to know you better."

Lizzy's cheeks grew hot and her breath caught. Perhaps she could dismiss her concerns about Miss Bingley's plan. Mr. Bingley's separation from Mr. Darcy would undoubtedly help Jane find a happy marriage. Lizzy's future could depend on Jane making that match.

For the greater good, then.

Lizzy took a breath and squeezed Caroline's hand. "How do you propose we enact this plan?"

Caroline's lips parted to reveal sharp, white teeth as she smiled. "We accept Darcy's invitation to dance."

She gave Lizzy no chance to argue, and instead pulled her back into the ballroom.

Caroline and Lizzy approached Darcy at the edge of the ballroom. Her tone coquettish, Caroline said, "My dear Mr. Darcy, I have found a third for our scheduled dance. Have you met Miss Elizabeth Bennet?"

"No." Darcy frowned at Jane and Bingley, who were accepting a dance invitation from one of the Lucas cousins. Then, his eyes snapped back to Lizzy. He held out his hand. "Miss Bennet? Any relation to…?" He trailed off but gestured across the room at Jane.

"They are sisters." Caroline placed her hand in Mr. Darcy's. "Would you be so kind?"

Caroline had elegantly trapped Darcy in the prescribed script of politeness. He grimaced at the first few musicians' notes, but he reached for Lizzy's hand and led both women onto the dance floor. Despite attending several balls in her lifetime, Lizzy's dance partners had never been such new acquaintances. The warmth of their bodies and the press of their hands in hers stirred her heart. Miss Bingley was a great beauty, her hair and headdress impeccable, her smile charming. Mr. Darcy was just as handsome, though his expression of haughty distaste ruined the effect. His movements were stiff, and his grip on Lizzy's hand loose; she obviously disgusted him. Near the end of the dance, Caroline drew close to Lizzy and pressed a soft kiss to her cheek before glancing at Darcy. The warmth in Lizzy's cheek turned icy as she realized Caroline had kissed her more to appeal to Darcy than to express genuine affection.

Lizzy shook off her discomfort and asked, "Mr. Darcy, how are you enjoying your time at Netherfield?"

He cleared his throat as he performed the next few steps of the dance. "Netherfield has neither the excitement of London, nor the comforts of my estate at Pemberley. Thus, I am enjoying the company more than the setting."

Lizzy's hometown pride stung. "Surely there must be some aspect of the area that appeals to you."

Darcy's expression softened minutely. "There is more time to read."

Finally! Someone who might share her love of literature. She gave Caroline a thankful smile for putting her in contact with Darcy. Caroline's returning smile wobbled; her dark eyebrows rose high in surprise.

Before Lizzy could ask Darcy about the books he liked, the song ended. He gave them a polite bow, turned, and walked away.

Lizzy shared a confused look with Caroline, then followed her off the floor. "What went wrong?"

Caroline flicked her fan in a dismissive wave. "I promise, his mood is not due to you. He despises dancing."

"Did he like me, do you think?" Lizzy wrung her hands. "Perhaps I need to engage with him in a different setting."

Caroline leaned closer to hide both their faces behind her fan. "What do you have in mind, Miss Bennet? Though I love him, Mr. Darcy is slow to trust new acquaintances. This may be more difficult than I thought."

Lizzy agreed, now believing Mr. Darcy was a larger impediment to Jane's happiness than she'd previously realized. "If he didn't want to dance and meet new people, why did he come to this ball?"

"He's only here because Charles forced him to be."

"And Mr. Bingley slights him by showing Jane an abundance of attention."

Caroline nodded.

A young couple approached and asked her to dance, so she and Lizzy parted ways. Lizzy wandered away to think. There had to be a way to melt the ice around Mr. Darcy's heart.

An hour later, Lizzy moved through the crowd with one aim—a plan held confidently in her mind. All she had to do was put it into effect. She approached Mr. Darcy, who stood near the refreshment table, reunited with Mr. Bingley. The latter spoke. "You must dance again, Darcy. It would be impolite not to."

"Charles, you know me better than to ask."

"What about Miss Elizabeth Bennet?" Bingley asked him. "You and Caroline danced with her, did you not?"

"We did," Mr. Darcy said stiffly.

Had he not enjoyed their dance? Lizzy backed up a step.

"Well, Miss Jane Bennet is the most beautiful creature I ever beheld. Don't you agree?" Mr. Bingley took Darcy's hand and kissed it. "Please say you agree with me."

"She is merely tolerable," Darcy said, his chin raised haughtily. "Handsome, I suppose." He lowered his voice, but Lizzy still understood when he said, "She smiles too much, Charles. You know I dislike women who smile too much."

"I smile all the time and you like me." The tenderness in Bingley's voice squeezed Lizzy's heart. "I am enamored with her, Darcy. Can you at least *try* to like this one? For my sake?"

Mr. Darcy frowned, then said, "Miss Selby—"

Mr. Bingley cut him off with a frustrated huff. "You are impossible! I will go ask Miss Jane Bennet to dance again and actually have fun with her. You can stay here and rot!"

Bingley's fervor made Lizzy gasp, which drew Mr. Darcy's attention. His frown deepened, then with a haughty air: "Not to worry, Miss Bennet. Despite Miss Bingley's attempt at matchmaking, you are not handsome enough to tempt *me*." He walked away.

Lizzy stood frozen with shock, cheeks pink with fury and embarrassment.

When she regained her senses, she hid her face behind her fan and quit the ballroom. By sheer force of will, she held back her tears. It was only after she found a small, private alcove that she let some fall. Then she chastised herself for being so affected. Jane would be disappointed when Mr. Darcy took Mr. Bingley back to London and the girls they could never decide between.

At the sound of encroaching footsteps, Lizzy dried her face with her handkerchief, hastily shoving it back in her sleeve. Caroline Bingley appeared, lips parted and brows drawn together. "Miss Bennet? What happened?"

"Apparently"—Lizzy's voice wavered with emotion—"Mr. Darcy is not 'tempted' by my looks."

"He said that to you?"

Lizzy nodded, expecting to receive comfort from her new friend.

Instead, Miss Bingley snapped, "I knew I should have chosen someone prettier."

Lizzy spluttered. "Why would you ask me to be your partner in this scheme if you think I am—"

Miss Bingley had walked away, leaving Lizzy alone. She called out, "Miss Bingley, I should never like to speak to you again!"

As Lizzy returned to the ballroom to reunite with her mother and sisters, she took note of Jane still speaking with Mr. Bingley, her eyes sparkling. The indignity of Lizzy's hurt feelings would be worth it if Jane made a genuine love match tonight.

Several days later, a letter arrived at Longbourn inviting Jane, and *only* Jane, to visit the company at Netherfield. The narrow invitation didn't surprise Lizzy, though Mrs. Bennet found it rude until she saw both Caroline Bingley and Mrs. Louisa Hurst had sent it. A friendly visit with the women of Netherfield was much more proper than Mr. Bingley inviting Jane unchaperoned. Then, Mrs. Bennet had an idea: Jane should travel by foot, arriving as the threatening rain began. This would trap her at Netherfield until morning, giving her more time to spend with Bingley and Darcy, which would surely lead to the proposal Mrs. Bennet awaited.

Perhaps if Lizzy had protested her mother's plan, they wouldn't have received a letter from Mrs. Hurst the next morning, explaining that Jane had been caught in the rain and had taken ill. She would not be well enough to travel home until she recovered.

Without a care for her own comfort or safety, Lizzy decided she could not leave Jane alone and ill with *those people*!

An hour later, Lizzy arrived at Netherfield, her stockings and the hem of her dress wet and muddy from cutting through the fields between the estates.

Her visit started well enough when the butler showed her to the room where Jane was convalescing.

"Oh! Lizzy! You did not need to come!"

"Nonsense," Lizzy climbed onto the bed with her. "Now, let me take care of you. What do you need?"

Eventually, Jane fell into a deep slumber, and Lizzy sat with her for a few minutes before growing discontent from boredom. Her thoughts turned to the rest of the Netherfield party, whose voices periodically filtered up the staircase.

Mr. Bingley was the lord of this house while he held the lease, and Lizzy was sure he would be good company should she join the others downstairs, but her desire not to see Mr. Darcy or Miss Bingley caused hesitation. They had treated her so poorly. Plus, they had not invited her to visit, only Jane. Should she impose her presence on them, they might resent her for it.

No, she would not cower upstairs while there were interesting conversations to be had. She left Jane's room quietly and went down the stairs, pausing at the doorway to the drawing room.

All eyes fell on her.

Mr. Bingley stood, anxiety clear on his face. "Miss Bennet! How is Jane?"

"She's sleeping for now," Lizzy said with a polite nod. "I thank you for your concern."

Mr. Hurst asked, "Would you like to join us at cards?"

Though Lizzy occasionally enjoyed cards, she noted the only empty seat was across from Miss Bingley, between the two Mrs. Hursts and Mr. Bingley. "No, thank you," she said as she gave Mr. Hurst a polite smile and approached the bookshelf. "I shall occupy myself with a book."

"A book!" Mr. Hurst chuckled. "I have not met many ladies who would rather read than play cards."

Lizzy grasped a book. "Then you must not know many women." She realized the rudeness of her tone and looked up to apologize, only to find Caroline watching with a glint in her eye. Lizzy's heart thumped in her chest and her neck flushed hot. She straightened her shoulders and dedicated herself to reading.

Mr. Bingley said, "Most of the young women I know are quite accomplished." He gave Lizzy an encouraging smile, which she returned. Perhaps Lizzy should leave Caroline and Darcy to one another and marry Mr. Bingley along with Jane, in the French style of sharing a spouse with one's sibling. But as much as she loved and admired Jane, cutting herself off from a romantic relationship with a second spouse was a measure too drastic—even if it would save Jane from being coerced through her love of Mr. Bingley into marriage with the odious Mr. Darcy.

Caroline turned and met Lizzy's eye over her book. "I think to be *really* accomplished, a woman must study music, dancing, drawing, and all the modern languages."

"Is that all?" Lizzy's words made Caroline's lips widen in a smile that showed her eyeteeth. Heat crawled up Lizzy's neck; she could not tell if anger or attraction caused the sensation. How vexing that attraction was still a possibility despite how Caroline had treated her.

"I find," Mr. Bingley broke in, as if to dispel the tension, "that Miss Bennet's care for her sister makes her quite accomplished."

Vindication drew a smile on Lizzy's lips, and she gave Mr. Bingley a grateful nod. "Thank you. I also find care and compassion to be among a woman's most valuable qualities." Her gaze made Caroline scoff and look away. Curiously, Lizzy caught a hint of a smile on Mr. Darcy's lips. "Have you any comment on the matter, Mr. Darcy?"

His eyes held hers for a moment before they flicked to Mr. Bingley's. "Only that I find women more surprising than any other creature."

Lizzy set her book on her lap. "Surprising? How so?"

"I am surprised that a woman of your upbringing would walk so far for the sake of her sister. After all, Miss Bennet is safe here, in the house of a friend, despite her illness. Your father owns a coach, does he not? Horses?"

"My father and the coach are away," Lizzy explained.

Darcy continued, "Then did you think those here would not well care for her?"

Lizzy caught the implication that her appearance might have offended Mr. Bingley's pride as a host. She turned to him and said, "Though I am sure you would have done your best to care for Jane, when ill, one wants the comfort of the familiar."

"One can be too comfortable," Caroline said with another of her foxlike smiles. "Perhaps we need to be more uncomfortable, if only so we grow accustomed to new experiences."

"Then, if your sister," Lizzy said with a gesture to Mrs. Louise Hurst, "were ill among strangers, you would have left her there to promote the evolution of her character?"

"Strangers?" Caroline laughed. "We are not strangers, but friends! Jane and I became very close through our conversations before she took ill."

Mr. Darcy said, "I think it shows great character for Miss Bennet to attend to her sister at such great expense to her own comfort." He gestured at the still-dirty hem of her dress, which made Lizzy blush. "It was the charitable, Christian thing to do."

Caroline's cheeks flushed deep pink, but she did not refute Mr. Darcy's assertion. Though Lizzy still felt hurt over what Mr. Darcy had said about her at the ball, the ice around her heart began to melt. Still, the manner in which both Mr. Darcy and Miss Bingley had treated Lizzy was atrocious. Though Lizzy was Christian enough to forgive them, she would not soon forget the harsher aspects of their natures—spirited conversation notwithstanding.

Some days after Jane's convalescence and her return to health, a letter addressed to both Lizzy and Jane arrived at Longbourn.

"Oh! Open it!" Mrs. Bennet cried, flapping her hands as Jane read the envelope, then took out the letter, which she read aloud. It was an invitation from Miss Caroline Bingley to accompany their party to Pemberly for a duration of two weeks.

Lizzy scoffed as Jane gave her the letter. "I can't believe she thinks we would travel with them!"

Jane did not reply. Instead, she ran her finger across her name on the envelope as if she wanted to savor it. Her feelings for Mr. Bingley must be stronger than her anger at Miss Bingley on Lizzy's behalf. She wanted to go.

Lizzy pondered what the trip might be like, spending that much time with the Bingley party. Mr. Bingley was quite agreeable, and she was glad for Jane that her and Bingley's feelings appeared to be mutual. Could Lizzy spend two weeks with them and avoid arguing with Miss Bingley? Or Mr. Darcy? Could the three of them come to a truce for the sake of Jane and Mr. Bingley?

Lizzy watched Jane's face carefully as she said, "We should go. This will be your best chance to get to know Mr. Bingley and Mr. Darcy, and I am sure Mother and Father will not allow you to go on your own."

"I enjoy Mr. Bingley's company," Jane said, her cheeks blushing. "I am less sure of Mr. Darcy. He does not seem to like anyone other than Mr. Bingley."

Mr. Darcy had praised Lizzy for her care of Jane. Perhaps encouraging Jane toward him would be the best thing for all of them. "Mr. Darcy can be kind as well as proud. I am sure you will like him better if you give him a chance."

A broad smile grew on Jane's lips. "I would be ever so grateful to you if you would come. I cannot do this without you."

"Then it is decided." Lizzy took Jane's hand and clasped it. "We will accept the invitation. Let us craft our response."

The ride to Pemberly was surprisingly pleasant. Lizzy and Jane rode with Miss Bingley and Mrs. Louisa Hurst. The second Mrs. Hurst rode with Mr. Hurst, Mr. Bingley, and Mr. Darcy. Caroline behaved admirably, with none of her previous vitriol. Lizzy spent much of the ride surreptitiously watching Caroline and contemplating possible reasons for the change. Had Mr. Bingley instructed her to be more polite? Perhaps she'd come to accept that Mr. Darcy did not love her, and that their failure to entice him was not Lizzy's fault.

When they approached Pemberley, Mrs. Hurst pointed out the landmarks of the estate. Two members of the staff stood in the manor's entryway, along with a girl similar in age to Lizzy. She was handsome and well dressed, and Jane took great notice of her. Mr. Darcy introduced both his sister, Georgiana, and the housekeeper, Mrs. Reynolds, with uncharacteristic enthusiasm and pride.

Lizzy commented on her observation to Jane as they unpacked and settled in their room. "Darcy seems to hold genuine affection for Mrs. Reynolds."

"Mr. Bingley told me she raised him and Georgiana from a young age," Jane said, then her attention waned, as if she were lost in her own thoughts.

Curious, Lizzy asked, "What are you thinking about? Mr. Bingley proposing?"

"Oh!" Jane gave Lizzy a playful push. "No! I cannot think he would propose here. Not with things undecided between him and Mr. Darcy." She met Lizzy's eye and gave her a tepid smile. "Besides, I am not sure I would accept their proposal."

"No?" Lizzy stepped close and embraced her sister. "Why not?"

"Because my feelings for Mr. Darcy remain friendly. I may grow to love him in time, but I do not want to…" She sighed. "Perhaps I would accept. How else can I take care of you and Mother and our sisters?"

"Stop that," Lizzy admonished. "You should marry two people you love. Your future happiness matters as much as anyone else's. I could not stand you entering a marriage you did not want for my sake, no matter what Mother might say."

"But I want your future happiness as well," Jane cried. "I wish there were someone you loved the way I love Mr. Bingley."

Lizzy sighed. Mr. Darcy's warmth toward his sister and housekeeper showed a side of him he'd previously kept obscured. The pensive manner displayed by Miss Bingley during the carriage ride was new as well. What if Lizzy *could* find happiness with them? When conversation with Miss Bingley felt more like a chess match than a social event, Lizzy enjoyed her company. If marrying Darcy rounded her sharp edges, Caroline could be just the spouse Lizzy had been waiting for.

At dinner, Lizzy sat next to Caroline and across from Darcy, with Jane on her right. Miss Darcy sat across from Jane, and the two carried on a dizzying conversation about flowers and botany.

Then, Miss Bingley asked Mr. Darcy, "What is your favorite piece of literature in the library here at Pemberley?"

"Library?" Lizzy asked softly as Mr. Darcy listed several volumes, any of which Lizzy would be delighted to own.

Discussion turned to favorite pieces of literature, and Lizzy found she and Miss Darcy had a similar fondness for romances. If Jane were to marry Mr. Bingley and Mr. Darcy, she would never want for good books. Lizzy was almost jealous. Later, in their room, when Lizzy voiced this jealousy, Jane gave her an amused look but did not otherwise comment. What did Jane know that she did not?

To welcome the Bennet girls to Pemberly, Mr. Darcy's aunt Lady Catherine de Bourgh hosted a dinner. Also in attendance was Lady Catherine's neighbor, Mr. Collins, who was a cousin of Lizzy and Jane's. Though Lady Catherine condescended to everyone, save Mr. Darcy, throughout the meal, the food was excellent, and her daughter was sweet. It was after dinner, as the visitors were gathering their things, that Lizzy overheard Lady Catherine speaking.

"If a break with Mr. Bingley is inevitable, your cousin is a much more dignified choice than someone of a lower class. And Mr. Collins would make a fine—"

"Mr. Collins is an equal in class to Miss Bennet."

"Perhaps, but Miss Jane Bennet is bad enough," Lady Catherine continued. "I noticed the way you watched Miss Elizabeth during dinner. That girl is far too outspoken to marry into a family like ours."

Lizzy met Miss Bingley's eyes; Lady Catherine's words had tied her stomach in knots. Caroline scowled, balled up her fists, and stepped into the room. She said, "Lady Catherine, you are wrong about Elizabeth Bennet. She uses her outspoken nature to defend her sisters and friends, not to demean and condescend to people as you do!"

Lady Catherine gasped, and Lizzy joined Caroline, needing to see her scandalized face. "Miss Bingley! I expect such outbursts from people as common as the Bennet sisters, but not from someone as high born as you! I am shocked!" Lady Catherine met Lizzy's eyes. "What spell have you cast on these good, well-bred people that they can think of nothing but you?"

They think of me?

"I have cast no spell," Lizzy assured her, and when Caroline held out her hand, Lizzy took it. "Should you think them ensorcelled by my appearance, rather than my character, I can assure you that I would rather be loved for my mind than my looks."

Darcy took a step toward Lizzy and Caroline "You are *loved*—most ardently—for the liveliness of your mind and everything else, Miss Bennet."

Lizzy's heart swelled, and she squeezed Caroline's hand. Lizzy asked Darcy, "And how do you feel about Miss Bingley?"

Darcy took Caroline's hand and kissed it. "My deep affection for Miss Bingley has long been platonic, as my heart has belonged to her brother."

"Does it still?" Caroline asked in a breathy voice.

Mr. Darcy looked down and sighed. "You are correct, Aunt Catherine. Though I love Charles, he and I are not compatible in marriage." He looked over Lizzy's shoulder, and when she turned, Mr. Bingley stood there. "It is better for us to remain close friends and marry others, than to forever seek a third who does not exist. Could we learn to love each other as brothers?"

Though Mr. Bingley's eyes grew shiny and he swallowed audibly, he nodded. "It is for the best."

Caroline squeezed Lizzy's hand again. "And you, dearest Elizabeth? Can you forgive me the harsh, untrue words I said out of frustration? I promise, I appreciate your appearance. You are one of the most beautiful women I have ever met."

"Stop!" Lady Catherine barked. "Stop putting these thoughts in my nephew's head. He will marry his cousin, Anne, and another person of high breeding." She put her hand on Darcy's arm. "Such a match will be best for everyone."

"No, Aunt. That will not be best for me. In fact, it is your effort to keep us apart that has solidified my feelings. I do not love Anne, but I do love these women. If they will have me, I will marry Elizabeth and Caroline."

Lizzy heard a gasp and turned to find Jane standing next to Mr. Bingley, one hand wrapped around his arm and the other over her mouth.

"I will!" Caroline let go of Lizzy's hand and went to Darcy. She grasped his arm and held it tight, she and Darcy perfectly mirroring Jane and Mr. Bingley. Then Caroline reached out to Lizzy. "What do you think, Miss Bennet? Will you marry us?"

Though an assent perched on the tip of her tongue, Lizzy sent a questioning look at her sister. She valued Jane's counsel over all others, save perhaps their father's. When Jane gave her a slight smile and a nod, Lizzy knew that whatever she chose, her sister would support her. She could follow her heart. This was *her* decision to make.

Lady Catherine took a breath like she was about to start another screed.

Lizzy jumped in before she could ruin the moment. "I will!" As the words tripped off her tongue, Lizzy knew they were right. She stepped close to Caroline and Darcy, taking both their hands. "I accept your proposal."

Jane made a soft sound of delight, her smile growing bright as Miss de Bourgh and Miss Darcy joined them. Jane took Mr. Bingley's hand and asked, "Perhaps you may ask me again?"

"Ask what again?" Lizzy waited eagerly for her sister's words.

Mr. Bingley smiled, then spoke. "Miss Jane Bennet, will you do me the honor of being my intended bride as we search for our third?"

"Oh, not you as well, Bingley!" Lady Catherine cried, but no one paid her any mind.

Jane returned Mr. Bingley's smile and nodded. "Of course I will."

Cheers of delight filled the air as Lizzy and her party left Rosings, heading back to Pemberley to celebrate their declarations of love.

Elizabeth Rose

A HANDSOME FACE

My piece was inspired by a scene from the 2005 *Pride and Prejudice* film. I wanted to take a more painterly approach to the scene while keeping the emotional elements palpable through the color and lighting. I also wanted to impose more texture on the statue to make it feel older and more broken.

TAGS

the 1970s, alcohol use (casual), classism, family, fat, gay, historical, in the closet, lebanon, m/m, non-fanfiction story inspired by the source material, past tense, period-typical homophobia, reunion, rivals to lovers, second chances, third person limited point of view

INSPIRATION

Somewhere Other Than Here is a queer romance set in early 1970s Lebanon that was written at a time when I was critically analyzing Lebanese history for articles tackling the sociopolitical and economic concerns of Lebanese across generations. Even though these protagonists would be around my father's age and from a social class I could only join in my dreams, I wanted to portray their plight sympathetically due to their outsider status as LGBTQI+ minorities in spite of their elitist attitudes, which were unfortunately of the time and never went out of vogue. If anyone is familiar with Lebanese history, the Civil War is only a couple of years away. Needless to say, the bourgeoisie "circles" discussed throughout the short story had a major hand in leading us there.

As I was raised around similar people during a similarly turbulent time in Lebanese history, the reality of the political situation is basically background noise in the protagonists' lives as they reconcile with problems the less fortunate can't even afford to work out. This was intentional as it's unfortunately realistic. Still, it's important to note that the protagonists are young adults thrust into a situation where they'll have to take on the reins or run away, and in hindsight, the latter option is, ironically, the right one for everyone involved. For, as Lebanese history has shown us time and again, passing power down through hereditary lineages has been a disaster, and it would be best for the rest of us if the aesthetically pleasing scion of the Lebanese elite could take the money they stole and live their best lives elsewhere so that we can try and repair the country.

SOMEWHERE OTHER THAN HERE

IT WAS ALWAYS a curious sight when a young Lebanese man of good standing and good fortune hadn't yet taken a wife. No one seemed to draw more attention in this regard than Elias Bannout, who couldn't escape the fervor surrounding securing a respectable wife. Like many of his generation, he was reminded time and again of how important it was to start a family of his own to carry on his father's electronics import enterprise. Everyone had chalked his flagrant disinterest up to the changes of the 1970s, because there was no other reason someone so tall, dark, and handsome would have no interest in women. But no one was as concerned with this prospect as Monsieur and Madame Bannout, who were keen to remind him of the predicament whenever the matter seemed pertinent to them—and it always was.

Elias had returned to Rabieh for his father's annual party, hosted to indulge his business associates. He'd even agreed to wear a white tuxedo for the occasion, in the vein of his father's favorite spy, James Bond. Monsieur and Madame Bannout were naturally older than he remembered, but they looked much older than he'd expected them to appear after only a couple of years' absence. William, who, even as an artist, tried to fight his fixation with aesthetics, couldn't help but inspect the wrinkles that crinkled their faces and the silver hairs that once had been dyed over but were now left, as if his parents had reached a point in their lives where there was no reason to hide the ravages of time. Time and Lebanon, considering the precarious political situation that seemed to perpetually promise another civil war.

Really, it was no surprise that the elders had succumbed to stress as the youth had fled the country, promising never to return. Monsieur Bannout now required the assistance of a cane, and Madame Bannout, who'd always been heavier than the average Lebanese woman her age, had put on more weight. Elias and his sister Jana had been the spitting images of them when they were younger, making it all the more discomforting to sit before them now and be lectured on their futures. Jana was expected to have had children, and Elias was supposed to take the reins of the family business by endearing himself to his future network, now that his interlude as an artist in Beirut was ending.

"…did you hear that her son has married?" Madame Bannout raised the subject on a whim as she tended to the villa's veranda over Turkish coffee. Forgoing the assistance of the help, she had prepared it herself for this special happenstance but had forgotten how to pull it off properly. The quaint hills of Mount Lebanon surrounded them, opening up to the peaceful azure sky. Though Elias was relieved to be rid of Beirut's endless sprawl, he felt in Rabieh as if he were suspended in place with nowhere to run. He chose not to respond, only nodding pleasantly.

"Oh my, how time passes," she continued. "Tell us what's been happening with you, love." As Elias feared whenever he'd left Hamra, this family gathering had encouraged the rote routines of Lebanese traditional life that he'd spent his entire adulthood hoping to escape. "Are there any special women in your life?"

"Yes, Mama." Elias smiled curtly, trying to conceal his exasperation. "You."

Monsieur and Madame Bannout were visibly peeved, and Jana broke into hysterical laughter, adding to their chagrin.

"Oh, leave the poor boy alone." Jana turned to their parents with her commanding presence. She was a headstrong woman with far more personality and force of will than Elias could ever match. These traits were complimented by her sturdy frame and choice of dress, which covered her in shawls as if she were a grand dame from a faraway land. "We'll find out when he wants us to."

"Gentlemen aren't supposed to kiss and tell," Elias reminded them. "It's no one's business but my own."

"Depends on who that gentleman is kissing," Jana replied with a Cheshire grin. "Are you still seeing that girl from Hamra?"

"Which girl?" Madame Bannout lit up. "From what family? Did she relocate there for university, I hope?"

Elias shot Jana a glare before replying innocuously: "That girl has long gone."

"It seems they all have," Jana teased.

"You need to expand your social circle." Monsieur Bannout sighed. "You're spending too much time in West Beirut with these new friends. It's as if you don't know what you want anymore. Where is that driven young man who was ready to write the Great Lebanese Novel only a couple of years ago? All I see you do now is bounce from one article to the next while holding a position that is beneath your talent."

"I'll try harder, Papa." Elias rolled his eyes. "It would be much easier to expand my social circle if I could go abroad to continue my education."

"None of that nonsense, Elias." Monsieur Bannout sighed again. "Can't you be satisfied staying with us, now that you'll take over the family business? You've had your fun, but we can't let you run around the Hamras of the world forever."

"Oh," Madame Bannout intervened, trying to ease the situation. "William from the Darsi family is staying with us over the weekend so he can photograph the event. Perhaps he can introduce you to his friends and family in Achrafieh. You and Jana remember him, right?"

"The mischievous daredevil we used to be left alone with when his father visited?" Jana responded with unusual interest. "Is he still as handsome as he used to be? And single..."

Elias, on the other hand, was displeased. From competitive badge-collecting in the local branch of the Lebanese Scouting Federation, to their paint-offs in the art-and-craft school in Hamra, memories of a youth spent with William Darsi were unpleasant, and this time, of all times, was not one during which he wished to have him back in his life.

"Easy," Madame Bannout chuckled. "It's unfortunate, but after his mother passed away, he was sent to that aunt of his. I hear he's developed an attitude."

"Developed it from having to deal with her," Jana replied with uncharacteristic disdain. "I can't recall ever seeing her smile."

"We won't have to worry about that." Madame Bannout sighed. "Sitt El Bourji shan't stay long."

"So is *he* coming to stay?" Elias asked, worried. "You know he and I always had a…contentious relationship."

"Speaking of which," Monsieur Bannout interrupted, raising his voice. "William should be here any minute now, and we should be polite to our guest."

"You mean, we should be polite to our guest whose father's connections we rely on for our livelihood," Elias whispered to his mother and sister, who laughed.

"—ah, there! They are at the entrance!" Monsieur Bannout playfully brushed his hand on Elias's face to quiet him while trying to hold back laughter. "Tag along with me, Elias, and be nice. From now on, we greet guests together so you can get the hang of it."

"Righto…"

William Darsi was, as always, dressed to impress in a mix of Parisian high fashion and East Beirut's refined sensibilities. The feminine cut of his beige trench coat accentuated his svelte physique. Besides his designer shoes and red beret, it was the only article of clothing visible, as it was oversized and tied in an intricate knot. With his statuesque features, he came off more like a model on a billboard than a real person. Naturally, Jana was delighted, and William had to hide his interest, surrounded by family as he was. His aunt, Sitt El Bourji, looked as if she had crossed paths with him by accident and was trying to avoid being seen. Even though she was no older than Monsieur and Madame Bannout, she'd refused to update her attire and attitude for the times. Garbed in a tailored Bordeaux dress with a cinched waist and suffocating neckline, there was no opulence on display, but it was obvious she came from a lineage that predated the fall of Constantinople.

"Is this a permanent residence, or are you only renting for the summer?" Sitt El Bourji carefully studied the entrance hall with contempt for its modernist sensibilities.

Taken back, Monsieur Bannout wasn't sure how to respond.

"Stylistically, this is in vogue now," Elias chimed into the awkward silence. "This villa is a financial investment on our part; we aren't concerned with proper presentation."

"It seems you can't have both these days," Sitt El Bourji muttered, seemingly to herself.

Desperate to change the subject, Monsieur Bannout reached out with his hand: "Always a pleasure." He kissed each of her cheeks. "You remember my son, Elias."

William, who up to until now had been slowly running his fingers through the hanging macaramés with bewilderment, lit up with intrigue.

"Ah," he chuckled. "You seem so…different. I can't wait 'til we pick up where we left off."

"Can't wait." Elias shifted uncomfortably, trying to find an excuse to leave. "Sitt El Bourji, may I escort you back to your chauffeur?"

Wising up to what his son was up to, Monsieur Bannout intervened with a smirk. "On your way, you could show our latest pop-art installations. I'm sure that Sitt El Bourji would love that Roy Lichenstein piece we picked up in New York."

Sitt El Bourji was having none of it and stormed off, cursing in French.

Monsieur Bannout escorted William Darsi inside and introduced him as the son of a notable politician, impressing upon his family the importance of their work together. Jana rose to shake William's hand only for William to awkwardly receive it. There seemed to be a reticence toward what William had encountered here in the Bannout household, and it was easy to recognize his aversion to the nouveau riche. Elias had encountered the attitude many a time in East Beirut before relocating to the western side.

"Lovely villa you've purchased," Darsi said, inspecting the neighborhood from the railing. "You must be proud of how far you've come, Monsieur Bannout. Not many can make something of themselves in this country, especially these days, with all the riffraff causing trouble."

"Ah, thank you." Monsieur Bannout shifted uncomfortably in his chair. "We wanted to reintroduce you to our children, Elias and Jana. You'll find that you have much in common now. Elias fancies himself an artist, too—a writer, to be more specific—although it's more of a hobby."

"A hobby I went to university for." Elias rolled his eyes.

"Well," William smiled, "we all experiment in college."

It was another one of those picturesque mornings in Rabieh, uncanny in its perfection. As the warm sun rose gently over the horizon, it cast rays of soft light which, when filtered through the lush greenery, painted life in Lebanon with an ethereal sheen. From the terrace, Elias took in his surroundings, jotting down the first thoughts that came to him. Journal in hand, he then strolled down to the pool to find Jana on a beach chair in sunglasses, pretending not to ogle William as he swam laps in his Speedo. Even with the tensions between them, the roughness of their relations had smoothed over in the short period since he'd arrived, and it was as if he and William had fallen back into their childhood routine before their rivalries had taken precedence. Even when dealing with a problem as difficult as William Darsi, life removed from the dramas that suffocated Beirut was far simpler than he could ever be comfortable accepting. Perplexed by this realization, Elias sat in the chair next to Jana, refocusing on his writing, or trying to…

Though he preferred fiction, he found he could only write short poems in Rabieh. They were the only way to capture a mood accurately in a few pen strokes. Not that poetry would have gotten him far elsewhere, but there was no future for it here, and the program in France he'd been accepted to was the closest path out of Beirut and into the literary establishment he could find for someone from Lebanon.

"What are you writing?" William called from the pool when he noticed Elias.

"Oh, when Elias writes, he doesn't like to be disturbed," Jana replied. "Let's leave him be. *Artistes* don't like to be disturbed."

"Yes." Elias laughed. "Leave me be to write my miserable poetry."

"Misery loves company." William laughed and exited the pool. "Let us hear it then."

Usually, Elias wasn't keen on sharing his writing, but he felt he had to at this point. The feeling of malaise had been bringing down his mood since he'd left Beirut. The poem wasn't much, but he wanted someone to hear it. "If you insist, I'll serenade you with my pretentious fancy."

William lifted himself out of the pool, his physique glistening in the afternoon sun. Taking the beach chair by Jana, he dried off with a smile and sat back comfortably—too comfortably—with forced anticipation, so that Elias couldn't tell if he was being mocked. "I'm ready to be moved."

Elias hesitated, so Jana, much to his shock, snatched the journal out of his hand and started to read. "All right, it's called *A Life I Have Not Lived* by Elias Bannout:

> *I remember a life I have not lived*
> *for I am not who I am,*
> *nor who I want to be,*
> *and all I have left now are memories,*
> *and all I leave behind is a dream…"*

"Gosh," Jana murmured. She turned to her brother with a worried look, but he avoided her gaze.

William began a slow, thundering clap. "Loved it. I think you chose an utterly miserable narrator, but I can see how you got into a foreign program. You've got talent, Elias."

Elias was speechless. This was probably the only thing William had said since they were introduced that wasn't dripping with sarcasm. He didn't know how to feel about it, but it did make him feel better.

"Do you write, William?" Jana carried on the conversation.

"As a matter of fact"—William put on his sunglasses—"I've got a way with words, too."

"Then share with us."

"Nothing's coming to me at the moment." He stared out over the railing at the hills of Rabieh. "I'm not sure why."

It was the awaited night. Monsieur Bannout's gathering was an uneasy mix of arrivistes lacking in self-awareness and the scions of the feudal families who were all too aware of who they were dealing with. In line with the decade's ethos, Madame Bannout's attempts to appear modern to attendees were more tacky than regal. From the fondue fountain to the American cover band, an overwhelming sense of desperation had manifested as envy in the vieux riche, who wished they could still afford to throw this kind of money away.

Suffocating in an ivory dinner jacket with satin lapels and a black bow tie, Elias hung back uncomfortably in the room's periphery with Jana, who wore a jewel-toned gown of diaphanous silk and golden bangles that chimed softly on her wrist. Each watched the events unfold with indifference. In the past, Elias hadn't been able to wait to return to Hamra and continue the bohemian lifestyle he had grown accustomed to, but university was over, and he had lost interest in the pretentiousness of the scene long before that. Across the room, William, uncharacteristically dressed down in a high-collared shirt paired with tailored slacks and a slim belt, methodically took photographs of the guests, and Elias couldn't help but think he was mocking them.

"I think he's handsome, too." Jana winked. "Too bad about his personality."

"Ironically, it's not different from any of the others we know in our circles, even if he is from the other side," Elias responded, "but he seems particularly self-satisfied with his presumptions."

"Here he comes. Be nice," Jana reminded him. "Papa wants to be in his father's graces even though his father wouldn't even attend this event."

William walked over with a smirk and a snarky, "You seem to be enjoying this party just as much as I am."

"Well, we can make our own fun, William," Jana clapped back. "Care to dance?"

William seemed uneasy. "I'll pass on that tempting offer," he said, lifting his camera. "It's best if I focus on taking photographs."

Resilient as she was, Elias could tell Jana felt slighted by the rejection, but she chose not to express it.

"I'll leave you two at it, then." She held her head high and strutted off. "I'll dance on my own."

Their banter implied otherwise, but it was clear that his sister was disheartened, and Elias was not happy. Neither one believed William's excuse, which soured Elias again on the man, snark or not. Still, William seemed particularly interested in Elias, even though Elias couldn't hide his discomfort.

"What's it like being a writer in West Beirut?" he asked.

"Kind of like being turned down by you."

"Oh, temper." William latched onto his shoulder. "It was nothing personal. I just wasn't interested, if you catch my drift."

"I don't, and, well, I'm not interested in continuing this conversation." Elias turned toward the exit, letting William's hand fall off. "It's nothing personal, but I've had it with Lebanese people these days."

"Believe me, I know how it feels." He gulped his drink. "I sometimes want to get on the first plane out of here and start a life elsewhere."

"I was planning on that before my father stopped me. I can't stomach more of this place"—he turned back to William with disdain—"or its people."

Madame Bannout called out to Elias from across the hall. Elias rushed over, William close behind.

"It's your father; he's feeling ill. We should take him to the American University Hospital in Beirut for a checkup after the party."

"I can't drive." Elias panicked.

"It's all right," William said. "I'll drive."

Even though Monsieur Bannout was in the backseat of a vintage Aston Martin DB5, his dream car, he was too caught up in his discomfort for Elias's own. Having to share the front seat with William in an intoxicated state did not ameliorate the tension. Still, the fine leather and plush carpeting helped.

"Forgive the disagreeable driving." William tried to ease their concerns. "It's night, and there are no streetlights, and I'm a bit tipsy, but we should be all right."

"Thank you, William. I wish we didn't have to bother you with this, but Elias seems to have skipped the driving lessons we had purchased."

"Papa, where I'm going, I won't need to know how to drive."

"Your sister can drive."

"Then let her take over the company."

Monsieur Bannout was speechless.

Elias turned his face to the window, staring at the night sky.

Trying to ease the situation, William changed the subject. "My father would've loved the party."

"Would he, now?"

"Of course." William and Elias smirked. "I'll urge him to join us next time. You two will have a lot to discuss. I wanted to thank you for hiring me; it's tough to find work with the economy as it is, and I can always use the practice. My father greatly appreciates it."

"Nonsense. I sifted through your portfolio, and it was lovely. You're an artist. You know, Elias here is a writer, as I mentioned before."

"Copywriter," Elias corrected. "I was the one behind the jingle for the 'Ooh là là!' ad."

"'Indulge in the elegance and charm of French sophistication with every bite of Ooh là là!'" William whispered with glee. "'An authentic European experience.' You *are* an artiste."

The discussion with the doctor occurred as an out-of-body experience. In the back of his mind, Elias had always known something like this would happen, considering his father's age, but it couldn't have happened at a worse time. The last thing he needed was a reminder of the family's fragile position if the worst came to pass.

Elias walked back into reception and was surprised to see William still there.

"How is he?" William rushed over.

"The doctor tells me he'll be fine." Elias sighed in relief. "It was a stress reaction. He'll spend the night with them so they can monitor his condition, and we'll head back to Rabieh tomorrow. Do you know any hotels I can stay at tonight?"

"Nonsense. You'll spend the night at my place. I have an apartment in Achrafieh."

"Are you sure?"

"It'll be fun, but first…"

"First?"

"First, the evening is about to end, and the discos are about to open."

Once the velvet curtains of the underground nightclub were drawn back, neon lights painted the walls in hypnotic patterns, and the discotheque pulsed to the rhythm of the groove. The dance floor was a sprawling expanse of polished black tiles shimmering under the kaleidoscopic lights. Perched behind a fortress of turntables, the lone DJ intermixed the rhythm and bass, letting the music surge throughout the partygoers' bodies as they danced under the disco ball that scattered shards of light across the room.

Lebanese youth were dressed in the latest fashions imported from Europe and America. William, like the other men, was dressed in a sleek, high-collared suit that exhibited his rugged chest, while women in sequined dresses caught the light with every movement. The air was tinged with the mingling scents of expensive perfumes, cocktails, and cigarettes. It was intoxicating.

William danced in the center of the dance floor, taking on as many partners as he could. Girls nudged each other to try and share the spotlight. Elias watched from a distance, dancing by himself, trying to get into the beat. Once William caught sight of him alone, he moved in and shared the space.

"William, what are you doing? This is not the place for this kind of thing."

"Relax, it's the '70s. No one cares like they used to, and you could use someone to dance with."

Elias took him by the hand and walked out with him, panic spurring him into motion. "Let's head out. I don't want people to talk."

"Where do you want to go?"

"Let's head down the hill from here. I want to walk by the sea in Raouche. It's where I used to go to calm down."

"Après vous."

Raouche, at night, was as melancholy as ever. The stars in the sky lit the Corniche Beirut with faint flickers. In comparison, the lamps that lit the path by the railing cast a charged glow onto Elias and William as they strolled along. The Mediterranean Sea was to their left, and its uncharacteristic stillness left the Avenue de Paris uncomfortably quiet. Elias was distinctly aware that they were alone. And yet he felt exposed, as he always had, around William, who seemed to take on a different affect when speaking to Elias.

"You know, despite our history, I've taken a renewed liking to you in the time we've recently spent together," William blurted out of the blue. It had been a half hour since they'd walked down to one end, and they were half through their return by the time William dared to break the silence. "It's rare that I find others in our circles I can tolerate."

"That's an interesting development," Elias replied. "I'm surprised you would consider me a member of the circles you associate with."

"You could say that, since I don't usually take a liking to your kind," William teased. "But Lebanese money is like all other Lebanese money, no matter when that fortune was accumulated. I don't particularly favor my background over yours. Besides, the rough charm of the parvenus is lost with each successive generation of wealth. It's as endearing as those American films that have grown on me now that I'm bored with French cinema."

"High praise. I'm honored, sheikh."

"Honor's all mine." William chuckled. "Can I read more of your writing?"

"Why?" A feeling of discomfort came over Elias, as if he was being teased.

"Just curious." William winked. "Wondering if you were one of those artists like moi."

Elias hated sharing his art with other people, especially his fiction. In poetry, he could hide within the abstract, but in prose, his inner self, all his insecurities, was fleshed out in painful detail. If he struggled to share it with his sister, then he knew that sharing it with William would be impossible. And it was hard to tell what William's motives for asking for it were.

"I'm not an artist." Elias struggled to get the words out. "I'm not particularly interesting."

"Oh." William leaned in for a kiss. "You're fascinating."

Elias backed away. He'd wanted this since they'd first met again, but something wasn't right. "We should go back," he stuttered. "I'll stay by my dad's side for the night. Can you drop me off?"

"I was joking about the artiste thing. Don't let that bother you. I'm like that with everybody."

"I know, William," Elias managed to say with difficulty. "And I wish you weren't."

"But…"

"Let's head back."

It had been months since he'd heard from William.

Elias was sitting on the roof when he received the letter. Jana had snuck it in for him from Beirut. Elias had tried for the last couple of months not to think about him, but with the letter on the stand in front of him, he was tempted to look. After all, it was encased in textured stationery with a wax seal decorated with an intricate design. Holding it closer, he breathed in the delicate waft of bygone elegance.

William had gone through the effort of writing it, and it was only polite to take a peek.

Elias, mon amour, I sit in my studio and can't seem to draw a single brushstroke that doesn't reflect on our time together. I've wanted to reach out for weeks, but since your medium is the pen, I realized I should communicate with you in a way that shows my respect and admiration, something I regretfully made no attempt to do when we were getting to know each other. This persona I've maintained over the years was to drive people away because I can't stand Lebanon and all its phoniness. Still, I always held out hope I would meet a fellow artist with whom I could connect while stuck here. But, it seems I waited so long I forgot who I really was and committed to my act, driving away the only person I could have a connection with. All I'm trying to say is, if I were to remember a life I have not lived with you, then it would be a life I have not lived at all.

No doubt, the letter was penned with a careful hand.

William had been right about one thing: he also had a way with words.

Elias walked past the latest residential buildings in Beirut to an old estate in Achrafieh. Having friends throughout the area, he had passed such modernist structures multiple times, always wondering what kind of people lived within. Under his elbow was tucked a gift his mother had insisted he deliver for all the trouble his father had caused.

Expecting Elias, a servant answered the door and escorted him to the salon, where Sitt El Bourji sat staring out the window despondently. In her own residence, she seemed dressed to impress, even though no one was around.

"Are you one of Williams…friends?" She sighed.

"Yes," Elias replied uncomfortably, realizing she didn't remember him.

The woman turned from the window to look at Elias before returning her attention to the window. It was clear from her reaction to looking at him that she didn't think of much of him or his atypical attire, Greenwich Village by way of West Beirut. "Uncharacteristically charitable of William," she finally said. "I was always under the impression that he associated only with certain characters from East Beirut—ones cut from the same cloth as he is, or was, I guess."

"Seems like he's full of surprises," Elias retorted.

"And what is that you've got there?"

"It's a gift I've brought him as a thank you for helping my father." Elias presented the handcrafted journal he had sewn together with copies of his poems and short stories.

"It's…cute." Sitt El Bourji returned it to him. "Folksy."

"I think William will like it," Elias affirmed.

"Then you don't know William," she replied dispassionately.

"Who knows? He might startle you."

"I wouldn't count on that, dear. Really, no matter what happens in this country, nothing and no one ever changes." She turned toward her abode with despondence. "It seems that only our taste grows more garish."

Elias heard a door close behind him.

"Auntie, have you not left the house today? Wait…is someone here?" William walked into the salon. "Oh, Elias!"

Elias paced toward the door.

"Sorry, I have to go."

The night was serene, like it had been when they'd walked Raouche the first time. Cool air had Elias tugging at his coat as he walked by the seaside.

Just when Elias thought he could be alone, he heard the light footsteps of designer shoes. Of course William had tracked him down. More than anything, Elias had hoped he would.

"Why the change of heart?" William asked. "To be honest, Elias, I thought you would just chuck the letter away."

"I'm not sure," was all Elias had to say. "I wanted to give this a shot, but then I got… Oh, I don't know anymore."

"Well, I know, and I think you should still leave for the PhD," William paused, and there was an uncharacteristic genuineness to him.

"Oh," Elias sighed, disappointed. "I thought. Maybe—"

"And I want to come with you."

Without another word, William took him in his arms and embraced him in the moonlight.

Elias was, of course, speechless, and for the first time, there seemed to be a way out of Lebanon.

Zel Howland

PAS DE DEUX

This piece was inspired by the iconic dance between Mr. Darcy and Lizzy at the Netherfield ball, combined with my own love of ballet and wish to see more challenges to traditional gender roles in dance. In my mind, this comic is part of a longer alternate universe in which Darcy is a traditional Russian dancer and Liz is a transmasculine dancer pushing every boundary of the art (and causing plenty of controversy as a result).

TAGS

the 1800s, the 1810s, altered mental state (drunk-enness), alternate history, bath, bisexual, christian, death of a parent (mentions of), death of a sib-ling (mentions of), death of a spouse (mentions of), document-based storytelling, epistolary, f/f, f/m, great britain, historical, infidelity, london, non-fanfiction story inspired by the source material, open relationship, opposites attract, polyamory, regency, sex work, unreality

INSPIRATION

I was inspired for this story by the slow shift in depictions of queerness in museums over my own lifetime—it's been very real and marked, and I think it's easy not to realise how seismic the change has been com-pared to previously. Another major inspiration was real-life lesbian icon Anne Lister—specifically how her diaries were written in a code that was successfully decoded by a descendant in the mid-20th century, reveal-ing explicit discussion of her sexuality. He made the decision, apparently, to hide the diaries again and not tell anyone he'd managed to decode them, rather than destroy them, which was common to do with personal papers of queer figures after death (sometimes at their explicit request, like Wilfred Owen, the gay World War 1 poet, asked of his family). The deci-sion in the case of Lister's descendant to disguise, rather than destroy, them, really is perhaps the only reason we still have those diaries. And, finally—in a lot of ways I've always deeply felt for and related to Lydia Bennet, and the monologue given to her in a BBC adapta-tion of *Death Comes to Pemberley*, about what it is to be haunted by the decisions she made as a teen-age girl, has haunted me in turn ever since. Maybe this story is a sort of exorcism.

THE PARSONAGE BECOMES HER

12 Kings Inn Close,
Bath, England.
14th May 1811.

Darling Theodosia,

Well, today they buried the bastard. I cannot say I am shocked. He brought the final end to his long-seated dissipation fully and entirely on himself. Victor Whistham deserves the warm spot in Hell that has been waiting for him; and if women of my ilk are to join him, I will relish the quality seat to his suffering. No, what shocks me is how much the burying wounds me. For although I have longed—how I have longed, Theodosia!—to see the back of him, there's something about death that scrounges within you for the last scrap of tender feeling you possess towards a man. And isn't widowhood, for one such as me, just becoming a twice-abandoned wife? It reopens all the old wounds of it.

What am I to do, trapped amongst the horrible Ton, with you off in your blessed rolling hills? Won't you come to me? I can send a carriage for you as soon as you ask. You'd want for nothing, and think of how much we could laugh at them together. And when I awoke, there you'd already be—the luxuriant glimmer of your hair already pinned back in that severe style of yours, head bent as in prayer over your papers. I can picture the image of it, so clear and clean and sure that every fresh morning brings down your absence upon me anew.

Write to me soon, won't you?

Extract from the private letters of NANCY BALFOUR, written to Theodosia Radcliffe and dated 1811, copyright British Library Collection.

How does one remember a woman like Nancy Balfour? Part of the issue lies in the sheer expansiveness of her character and reputation cemented among feminists, fans of *Pride and Prejudice*, and the LGBT community. An oft-suspected Austen inspiration, unrepentant sex worker, and teenage bride who railed against the patriarchy—Nancy Balfour did it all, and in an era when women of her station were offered severely limited life paths. And yet, our attempts to categorise her into an ahistorical narrative of go-get-'em-girl defiance often strips her of the nuance that makes further study of her so compelling.

Extract from essay 'What Nancy Did Next' by historian Lucinda Jameson, from the collection MISBEHAVE AND MAKE HISTORY, published Penguin Random House, 2021.

INT.—GENTLEMAN'S CLUB, LONDON, ENGLAND—WINTER, 1808—LATE EVENING.

MID-SHOT, moving in a circular motion, panning to take in the scene:

A Christmas party is in full swing. Women in various states of luxurious undress are draped over suited male clients at card tables. There is loud chatter and piano music from an instrument being played in the corner. We see snow outside the large paned windows. Everyone is merry, drunk, and ready to spend money.

THEN:

The main doors burst open.

ENTER:

NANCY BALFOUR, our protagonist. Early thirties, extroverted, and striking, she has the manners of an experienced courtesan. She is wearing a crown of holly, an almost transparent muslin dress pulled down past her shoulders, and carries a small basket of candies, which she throws to various party-goers, laughing. Like them, she is clearly drunk.

NANCY: Felicitations from the ladies of the house!

An ATTENDANT approaches her.

ATTENDANT: (in a low voice) Nancy, he's here again.

NANCY: (Not paying attention) Who?

ATTENDANT: Uh, Lieutenant Whistham.

NANCY: (Annoyed) Again? I told you he wasn't to be let in.

ATTENDANT: Madam, he is your husband.

NANCY: He's nothing of the sort anymore. Throw him out.

ATTENDANT: Madam, it's snowing.

NANCY: He's used to a cold bed, believe me.

Extract from initial shooting script of BBC production *Remember Us* (2022), Episode One, Scene Seven.

Born Narcissa Bellshire in Suffolk, England, very little about Nancy Balfour's childhood differentiated her from the many upwardly mobile middle-class families of the era. Educated at home by her older sisters, one of whom had several stints as a governesses in wealthier households to supplement the strained family income, it wasn't yet clear that her fate would diverge from that of the Bennets immortalised by Austen. Naturally, to Mrs. Bennet, the social shame of a woman lowering herself to governess is a partial reason for the intensity through which she pursues the marriage market. However, this pressure was still on the young Narcissa. It's important to note, she was never educated in the topics she would later become well-respected for: architecture; languages; and, of course, through Theodosia Radcliffe, the politics of the day. Instead, she was likely taught what were viewed as the 'womanly arts': music; embroidery; and the minutiae of running a successful household.

From A SLATTERN THROUGH AND THROUGH: *The Life of Nancy Balfour*, **Cambridge University Press, 2012.**

J: And you know, what I find completely extraordinary about her is she was one of the few women of the era who really, uh, you know, really embraced the title of 'whore'. Like, if you look at her entry on the census of 1812, she literally positions herself as such. Like, 'occupation: whore'.

L: Oh, wow.

J: Yeah, I know right.

L: It's giving eighteenth century girlboss.

Conversation between hosts Jenna Harrison and Laura Blake, transcript from Whore-ible History Podcast, episode #45, "Naughty Nancy Balfour."

Had Nancy Balfour not made such an astoundingly bad match, we might never have heard of her. In another universe, she stays Narcissa. She does not accept Lieutenant Victor Whistham's advances, does not run away with him, is not caught in Brighton in a man's bedroom, and is therefore not married off under quick pressure to preserve family dignity. She is not condemned for the mistake of being, at her core, a teenage girl. The whispered scandal does not dog her on her honeymoon. She does not endure the first affair; nor the second, nor the drunken berating reported to be heard late into the night from her newly-wedded spouse. She does not risk venereal disease and death from Victor Whistham's constant exploits in the nearest brothels. She is not used as a cautionary tale by the ladies of the Ton to such an extent that, on her first married visit to Bath, a young single woman named Jane Austen witnesses her abandoned in the crush of a ball, mid-dance, by her lieutenant. A sight that was so spoken of in the gossip rags that Jane never forgot it, nor the story that swirled behind it.

Had Nancy Balfour, we are told in the prevailing narrative of literary criticism, simply made *better choices*, the character of Lydia Bennet might have been altogether different. But what better choices did she have?

Lecture by Andrea Fang (The Janeite Society, Steventon Chapter Representative) at the 2005 Jane Austen Commemorative Birthday Ball.

As we know, her marriage to 'her gallant lieutenant', enforced by her family after their elopement to Brighton, was a disaster from the very start. In many ways, they were well-suited: Whistham was vain, tempestuous, and deeply charismatic. In others, they were not: he was prone to long absences, infidelity, and gambling; and he chafed at the frugality with which the young Narcissa tried to desperately maintain their image with his ever-depleting income. Finances are something that breaks marriages in the modern day when women have careers, bank accounts, and credit cards in their own names. For a woman nearly sixty years away from the marriage act which would strike a deathblow to the social position that she was in as her husband's property, Narcissa rapidly found herself the recipient of what was seen as her just deserts. Her marriage was viewed with a great lack of sympathy and deemed a punishment for her own impropriety and expression of the inevitable results of extra-marital sexuality.

From A SLATTERN THROUGH AND THROUGH: *The Life of Nancy Balfour*, **Cambridge University Press, 2012.**

INT.—BOOKSHOP, SOHO, LONDON—EARLY MORNING.

MID-SHOT OF:

THEODOSIA, browsing the shelves. THEODOSIA is thirty-six, unmarried, and reeks of sensibility. She is dressed simply in a subdued cotton dress with the sleeves rolled up. Looking around the empty bookshop, she removes one of her gloves and reaches towards a pamphlet on display.

CLOSE UP SHOT ON:

The pamphlet in her hand, labelled *ON THE SUBJECT OF FEMALE EDUCATION*. THEODOSIA'S hand lingers over it, almost in a caress of affection. Her fingertips linger on the author name: FRANCIS DEWSBURY.

Then, at the sound of another customer entering, bell jingling, she withdraws her touch as though she's been caught red-handed in something.

Extract from initial shooting script of BBC production *Remember Us* **(2022), Episode One, Scene Seven.**

4 Priory Lane,
Kendal, England.
5th March 1812.

My Nancy,

Have you had a moment spare to read the latest pamphlet? I think it is very good, perhaps the best yet. It is, perhaps, Francis Dewsbury's finest work. I sent it along with this letter.

Your opinion is, as always, very much appreciated.

Your most endeared petit auteur,

Theodosia Radcliffe.

Extract from private letters of THEODOSIA RADCLIFFE, written to Nancy Balfour and dated 1812, copyright British Library Collection.

It is a SHAME and a DISGRACE upon us that this Empire, that is one claiming a reputation of GLOBAL INDUSTRY, disregards such a significant portion of its people as incapable of that great edifier of Man—LEARNING. How are we to INNOVATE THE FUTURE when we disregard the raw material of human minds? I tell you now: one day the world will look back upon us and denigrate our devaluing of the feminine intellect. I tell you now: that day is TOMORROW, and tomorrow always arrives faster than we think.

Extract from ON THE SUBJECT OF FEMALE EDUCATION, by Francis Dewsbury, private publication, Suffolk, England, 1813.

Theodosia Radcliffe was, socially speaking, a nobody. I cannot reiterate this enough. Radcliffe was the unmarried daughter of a deceased vicar, and in 1809, the suspected year Nancy Balfour and she met, was still deep in mourning for her beloved parent. Still, it appears Radcliffe was well-established in maintaining a secret life. In fact, since her late teens, she had been writing radically progressive pamphlets under her nom-de-plume, Francis Dewsbury. With no position, no money, and no great name, the sole reason Francis Dewsbury is so well-recorded as a socialist thinker today is the sheer quantity of his work. He more than flooded the market. Sometimes, he risked drowning it.

It is not clear when this practice of hers began, nor how she was radicalised. Her father did support the maintenance of her education, and in multiple areas not usually available to women of the era, but his motivations remain similarly unclear. Perhaps, as Theodosia's older brother had died of scarlet fever at age fifteen, she was distracting from this grief over a male heir. Perhaps the Reverend Charles Radcliffe was simply lonely, widowed himself. Perhaps he wanted a secretary who could keep up with what he viewed as the demands on his intellect, and he recognised the yearning for knowledge in his daughter.

Lecture on 'The Eighteenth Century and Development of British Socialist Thought', School of Philosophy, Durham University, 2010.

To this day, it is unclear how exactly the two met. Theodosia Radcliffe, aside from her fiery pamphlets as Francis Dewsbury, led a quiet and somewhat typical life for a parson's daughter in the rural England of the era. After her father's death when Theodosia was only twenty-five—a young woman by modern standards, but by the standards of her era's marriage market, anything but—she moved into a small cottage by herself, remaining in the same village she had been born and raised in. Less than an hour's walk from a coach house crossing in the Lake District, it still was hardly the cosmopolitan world in which Nancy, by comparison, moved. By thirty, Theodosia had taken lodgings in Kendal for part of the year, where she appeared to be entirely satisfied with her spinster lifestyle. In contrast, Nancy Balfour spent the years of Theodosia's burgeoning independence between Bath, London and the Parisian demimonde, a notable guest of many at the theatre, which she particularly relished, never without her opera glasses and a steady stream of witty repartee about her fellow attendees.

The mystery of their meeting, therefore, is one we are forced by the nature of history to accept. But meet, they very much did.

From A SLATTERN THROUGH AND THROUGH: *The Life of Nancy Balfour*, **Cambridge University Press, 2012.**

171 Headley Lane,
London, England.
14th May 1809.

My favourite Theodosia,

Today I found myself thinking of the first day we met, and how little I thought of it at the time. The irony is, on meeting the lieutenant, I can remember wanting to commit each minute detail to recall, as though I sensed something momentous was happening. Isn't it funny how those bad decisions can stay etched in our minds, like rot through a wooden cabinet? I remember that first introduction to him, like a man's long walk to the gallows might be remembered by his wife. Whereas, with you, it has felt like one long dream, for time does slow down when we are together, Theodosia, don't you think? It develops a grainy sort of quality, like golden light pouring into a dusty room.

Sometimes, I still remember seeing you across the room in that jet dress, the perfect mourning of a devoted daughter, and your head so studiously bent over your book. You looked like an ink engraving of a dear little mouse, and then I made some sort of noise and disturbed you, and you looked up and—

It was then I realised that I had come across no mouse, but a tiger. That perhaps I was, in fact, the mouse, a great cat's new plaything, lured in so soundly that I did not know the trap until it was sprung. I remembered the look, later, but dismissed it, told myself I'd misread. It is a rare one who can make me doubt myself like that these days.

It feels, sometimes, my darling, as if I have known you my whole life. I think of how it might have been to play together as children, you know, and it's a little silly to admit, but I think you would have been as superior a playmate then as you are a companion now.

Extract from private letters of NANCY BALFOUR, written to Theodosia Radcliffe and dated 1809, copyright British Library Collection.

EXT.—FIELD, OUTSIDE KENDAL, LAKE DISTRICT—LATE AFTERNOON.

GOLDEN HOUR.

CENTRAL CLOSE UP OF:
THEODOSIA and NANCY, hands interlocked, spinning in wild circles. They are laughing hysterically, whooping, free. THEODOSIA'S hair is loose and streams behind her. NANCY'S styled curls bob from beneath her bonnet, which threatens to escape her head. In light cotton dresses, their skirts billow in the bracing wind.

THEN: Someone trips.

CUT TO:

CENTRAL CLOSE UP:
Theodosia and Nancy, collapsing onto the ground. Where one has fallen, the other has followed. They are still holding onto each other, still laughing breathlessly. They look deeply into each other's eyes, mirth and joy across their faces, relaxed in a way we have not seen since the beginning of the episode.

THEODOSIA: (softly) You're lovely, you are.

And she kisses her to prove the point.

Extract from initial shooting script of BBC production *Remember Us* (2022), Episode Two, Scene Ten.

Through here, you can see the room where Theodosia Radcliffe stayed in on her many visits to Nancy. The radical pamphleteer was a bosom friend of Nancy Balfour, regularly travelling from her home in the Lake District to Bath, enticed by the promise of friendship and the healing waters. As you can see, the room is painted in a particularly beautiful duck's egg blue, which was Theodosia's favourite colour. We've found in household records that the paint itself was a custom request shipped to Bath from London, and if you visit Nancy's London townhouse, there is a guest bedroom painted in the exact same shade—likely, again, Theodosia's chosen room. To reflect this, the curators here have placed several objects of Theodosia's on the bed.

Here's an example of one of her day dresses, in all black, and therefore likely from the years after her father's death. In fact, it is only at thirty-two, a year after meeting Nancy, that she begins to wear colour again, something she references in letters as a testament to her friend's help in bringing her out of her long period of grief. Here is also one of her famous red notebooks, as she always carried in her reticule. And on loan from the British Library, you can see an early draft of one of Theodosia's pamphlets at the rolltop desk.

As I've previously mentioned, it is thought that the famous writer Jane Austen herself met the two during the Ton's various social events, and that the character of Lydia, especially, was inspired partially by Nancy Balfour's life. But there are literary critics who argue that the character of Charlotte Lucas was, in fact, derived from the quiet parsonage life Theodosia espoused at Bath's social dinners, often to the amusement of her less level-headed companions.

So, now we will proceed into Nancy's own bedroom, the master bedroom of the house. Don't turn around, because—as it turns out—we don't even need to go out into the main corridor again! No, if you look beside the armoire, there is a hidden door here. We will walk through it now and enter the dressing room of Nancy Balfour, which then links directly to her own bedroom. It is thought that the two rooms being linked in this way was done to prevent returning to their beds after long night-time conversations from disturbing any other household guests. Such a show of trust and esteem in Theodosia tells us that, to Nancy, she was no mere guest, but a dear and beloved friend.

Extract from recorded tour given by National Trust volunteer Janet Kirkgate of 12 *Kings Inn Close, Bath, England*, on July 1st, 1986.

Nancy, my Nancy,

It is too hot here tonight for England, and even if I could sleep, my heart is with you in Paris. I understand why you have gone, my darling, I really do. I have barely anything to barter for your love with. I am sure tonight, more than I ever have been, that my world, to you, must seem spare, little and mean. But I cannot help—my window open to the moonless heat—but long for you to be here, beside me, instead of winding your winsome way through politicians and officers. I am not envious, my Nancy, for you know as well as I that I have no tolerance for banal conversation, on account of having no art for it. I am merely lonely.

Were you here, I could offer you myself; press my face sweetly to your hair, your neck, your breasts, all of you that is made by God and ordained, so holy to him and I. You think it strange to see the Lord's hand wrought in our relations, I know, but I believe, like some leprosy-sick sinner, in the cure of your hand on me, much as scripture tells us. The word I am looking for, my darling, is 'miracle'. I would elevate your kiss to the benediction of a saint, if you'd be willing to let me.

Extract from private letters of THEODOSIA RADCLIFFE, written to Nancy Balfour and dated 1813, copyright British Library Collection.

Long before Oscar Wilde stood in court and was questioned on the 'love that dare not speak its name', there was Nancy and Theodosia, a match made up of opposites. Theodosia was bookish, religious, and yet still a political radical. Nancy was an unrepentant courtesan who continued to entertain male patrons for the long span of their relationship. And I do say 'relationship' with all of its weight, even at the risk of interpreting historical evidence through a modern lens of gender and sexuality.

In fact, it is my opinion that the nature of Nancy Balfour and Theodosia Radcliffe's love is only in such doubt due to the reservations of our society to accept the clear evidence of what appears to have been a deeply romantic, intimate, and yes—sexual—relationship.

Extract from 'The Vicar's Daughter and the Courtesan', 2008, Dr. Andrea Lockwood. Published by Picador Press.

While Dr. Lockwood's style of writing is personable, to be sure, her assertion that Nancy Balfour and Theodosia Radcliffe were in a homosexual relationship is one that feels politically motivated. While it's likely to sell her book on the pure scandal of it, these two women lived in an era when lesbianism was barely spoken of, and it arguably undermines the integrity and purity of female friendship under patriarchy to assume it was inherently sexual, romantic, or anything other than platonic. Given that the historian's goal is not to serve the homosexual agenda, perhaps flights of fancy, such as this, about long-dead women and their legacy, are best served in the realm of fiction.

Review by Harold Jetson of 'The Vicar's Daughter and the Courtesan' (2008, Dr. Andrea Lockwood), published in the London Review of Books, July 2008.

L: So do you think she'd have identified as bisexual? If she was alive right now?

J: Who, Nancy?

L: Yeah, yeah. Like, Theodosia, I reckon, she feels lesbian-coded to me.

J: Oh my god, yeah. No, yeah, exactly.

L: But Nancy—

J: I mean, the terminology didn't exist for—

[pause]

Did it exist then?

L: Uh, I don't know. We should look that up later.

Conversation between hosts Jenna Harrison and Laura Blake, transcript from Whore-ible History Podcast, episode #45, "Naughty Nancy Balfour."

My darling Nancy,

I was much concerned by the goings-on you reported in your last letter. I have known for some time, of course, that you have been supporting your husband—for he is, in name if nothing else—when he approaches you asking for coin. How could I not, when on our second-ever meeting, he interrupted our promenade to accost you? To this day, I do not regret striking him, for though I do hate to cause you unnecessary discomfort, it was, on this occasion, most necessary.

I know you do not wish to discuss the particulars of your business with me, for fear I will be disgusted. My silly girl, don't you see that I entered into our union with my eyes clear and my soul resolute? It makes no sense for sexual congress to be viewed always as sin. Although I may not agree with the circumstances that can force young women into such employ, I understand that the way of the world can give us little choice but to make the best of those professions the church considers bad callings. Had it not been for my father's care, who I might have become is all too clear to me, and without the dignity and protection you can now afford yourself in your manner of operating. I can only imagine how hard-won that must have been as, again, you do not speak to me of it.

And while I can respect that, and I can manage my jealousy of your patrons and your husband—the former are to be endured and the latter is a foolish man who threw aside a jewel and ought to suffer for it—I cannot stand the idea that the work you have poured body and soul both into is something he might skim the profits from as he pleases. It makes me near too angry to write…

Though it is sinful to say it, even think it, I shall not be sorry when the Lord comes to claim his due with that man. I give thanks that he is mortal.

Extract from private letters of THEODOSIA RADCLIFFE, written to Nancy Balfour and dated 1812, copyright British Library Collection.

And here now, we approach them! As you can see, Nancy Balfour is buried on the left, and Theodosia Radcliffe to her right, with matching headstones made of local granite. We were already getting some pilgrims to their gravesite, but after the release of the BBC's *Remember Us* last year, based on that book I mentioned, the one by Andrea Lockwood, who designed the route for this tour today… Well, oh, my God. People have been showing up in droves. We can barely keep the café in cake past midday now during peak tourist season. And there's something, you know, for me, as a local historian—

Because, you know, they spent their whole lives together, really, after they met. After Nancy Balfour's estranged husband died in 1811, she was entitled to his military pension, of course, and it's thought that's how she helped keep Theodosia's pamphleteering afloat even as it became increasingly risky to be known to spread seditious material. And, for all that Nancy lived in Bath during the Season and only came here to our little village outside of that, she insisted on being buried here, you know. It was her who bought both the plots in advance, although it's said that Theodosia Radcliffe was the one who picked them out. It's the kind of story that should be too good to be true. That you can meet someone, and that they be it for you. And really, we get all sorts showing up to see them. We get couples who have been married decades, and some who only just got married when the new laws came in, and a few parents bringing their teenagers, and you can see, the graves get heaped with all of these—the flowers and bears and things. The council have said we can let it happen, for now, so we're letting people leave what they like, as long as it isn't dangerous, you know?

And I think it gives people hope. There's something so reassuring about these two. They help you remember what's important. That even after death, love still matters. There's something so—you know what I mean—about that.

Anyway, that's all we have on our tour today. So, any questions?

Jagoda Zirebiec

MOONLIGHT (PAGE 94)

GLOVE (PAGE 95)

This artist has chosen not to share the inspiration behind their work.

TAGS

alcohol use, alternate universe, aphobia (internalized), aromantic, asexual, bar, blackmail, college, f/m, getting drunk, modern, one-night stand, predatory behavior toward a minor, present tense, rape (attempted), self-esteem issues, sex (non-graphic descriptions), sexual trauma, siblings, third person limited point of view, underage drinking

INSPIRATION

Lydia is a deeply misunderstood character—not as a person but in her circumstances. From Lizzy's perspective, Lydia's mother is ridiculed for her concern over her daughters' financial security yet is fundamentally correct about the necessity of wealthy marriage for her dowry-less children; Lydia's father is a gentle hero despite mismanaging their property's funds, leaving his children destitute past his death, and casting both mother and daughter under the same net of condescension as they utilize their few available options to secure their future.

Lizzy, for all of her critical powers, fails to recognize Lydia's vulnerability until Wickham's cruelty exposes it; I wanted to modernize and play on this complex sister relationship—delve into the pride that drives Lydia and Lizzy apart, the horror and guilt when the worst happens and finally comes to light, the shame of being "wrong" for the role she was cast in—and found myself grappling with the now-outdated Regency era institution of marriage.

How might someone struggle with the amatonormativity of marriage, romance, and sex in today's world? What might "other" someone from not just society but from their own family, and to some degree, their own self?

Hypersexuality is one potential presentation for an aspec person, and Lydia-in-denial relies on sex like a sword and shield to keep her safe, relevant, and normal. Her sisters' scorn and disgust over her slutty but "normal" behavior is preferable to their potential scorn and disgust when Lydia confesses how different and "broken" she is: unable to feel the things she's supposed to. While her relationship with Lizzy isn't mended over the course of this story, her relationship with herself is, and I think that goes a long way.

Ultimately, *tell that to my tell-tale heart* is a story about siblings and love. This is a companion piece to Téa's *unwound thread and wilted roses*, which touches on all the same topics in all different aspects, in all the best ways.

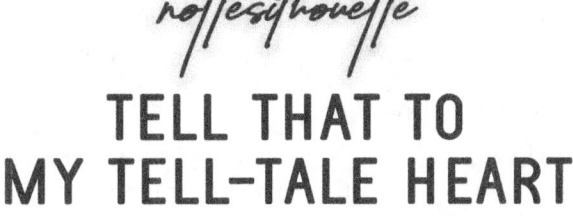

nottesilhouette

TELL THAT TO
MY TELL-TALE HEART

LYDIA COUNTS THREADS in the blanket Lizzie draped around her like she isn't unraveling.

There's a part of her heart still tangled up with George—a part of her life still tangled up with him that always will be once this stupid fucking video goes up—but right now Lydia counts threads in the blanket Lizzie draped around her, one-two-three, like she can see through the tears she pretends she isn't crying.

The blanket is heavy and warm, but it's no substitute for being in Lizzie's arms. Lydia misses her already. The question pushes at her teeth, bared and bloody and too vulnerable to bear. But asking shit like that has never led to the kind of results Lydia wants, so she bites her tongue and counts nine-ten-eleven until she can breathe around the desperation in her throat.

"I let him do it," Lydia warbles to Lizzie. Lizzie pretends, politely, that Lydia's voice is steady and stable, that it doesn't waver—even though *everyone* knows Lydia's never been good at being particularly steady. "I didn't mean to bother you with this."

In hindsight, she didn't mean to add that. In the moment, it feels inevitable.

"There's nowhere else I could be," Lizzie assures her, tucking tea into her hands—Jane's doing, no doubt. Lydia nods, looks up at Lizzie with big, wet eyes—hears what she isn't saying. *I have to be here, taking care of you*, Lydia knows. No one denies it. *You're a bother.*

She wouldn't believe them if they did. After all, hasn't George made it clear enough? Lydia's an easy lay, good for a laugh, not here for long. A leech, a loser, a little girl with something to prove. She's lithe, light, *loose.*

Lovable, though, she is not.

Going to college was a *great* idea. The thought feels slurred even in Lydia's own mind; she's three or maybe seven drinks in. That was a great idea too.

Another girl leans over Lydia's face with a brush and giggles. "You have *such* pretty eyes," she whispers. She's not very good at it, Lydia thinks, or maybe says out loud. She giggles again, though, so it doesn't seem like Lydia's done any damage this time.

The girl—Isabelle, or maybe Eleanor, or it could be Olivia, Lydia's not sure—pulls Lydia a little closer—her hands are so cold—and smudges gold onto Lydia's cheeks, then on her eyelids. Lydia's eyelashes flutter under this girl's careful touch, and for a moment she can imagine it's her sisters dolling her up.

It's been more than a few years since her sisters had the time or energy or, frankly, the interest to go clubbing with Lydia, but under the flickering fluorescent lights and with a creaky fold-up chair pressed against her back, Lydia's reminded of being nine years old and so excited to put on makeup, even if it was just for the school play; she's reminded of the way Jane fussed with her dress, the way Lizzie patted powder onto her cheeks.

Lydia stepped out onto that stage *shining*.

Now, she leans in closer to a girl whose name she doesn't remember. The bristles of whatever brush she's using are soft; Lydia nuzzles them. She hopes no one notices. She hasn't felt something this soft in so long.

As the girl's fingertips thaw on Lydia's skin, her touch starts feeling soft too. Her hands are wandering now, tracing over cheekbones and the bridge of Lydia's nose, dipping lower until her thumb rests gently on Lydia's lower lip. The other girl giggles again, leans closer; is someone watching?

Lydia chances a glance to her left. Yep—a couple boys have stumbled in, too impatient to wait for any of the girls in here to make their way out. This girl—Lily? Lisa? Liza?—is looking to put on a show.

That's fine. It's nothing Lydia hasn't done before. When the girl leans down to press their lips together, Lydia arches up, lets her lips fall apart just a bit—when they come up for air, their hair is mussed and lip gloss has smeared just a bit—just enough.

The boys look at them *hungry*. The other girl lights up, turns to them with a spin that makes her skirt flare up, and bounces away. Halfway there, she turns back and blows a kiss to Lydia; Lydia makes sure to catch it and press it to her chest, angle her shoulders just right, and wink.

Someone in the crowd hoots, and Lydia's little table-turned-vanity suddenly gets a lot more crowded. She doesn't feel too bad—the other girl has plenty of attention to stay occupied—but she keeps an eye on the situation anyway. She's not keen to be called any kind of whore tonight, attention or otherwise. Lydia peeks up to look at the person nearest her; he's cute, she guesses, in an awkward college-boy sort of way.

"Do you come here often?" Lydia blinks at his pick-up line; she thinks it needs work. The sharpest edge of the alcohol is wearing off, just enough for her to think meanly, *I live here*.

She reaches blindly for another bottle, purses her lips prettily, and throws her head back. Her hair flashes, red, and her cheeks flush, red, and the boy looks her up and down, she sees *red*.

But when he sinks into her that night, his dorm bed sheets are a cool blue, just like his eyes. Lydia closes hers and sinks into black.

George leans over Lydia; underneath her, silk sheets crumple in her palms. The thread count is over one thousand, but Lydia keeps losing track somewhere between thirty and forty, twice or maybe four times. Lydia's lost count: George is good at what he does, maybe. He's got her trembling, mind blank and heart racing, dizzy and flushed and too hot and too cold all at once. He's stolen away her breath; she can't *breathe*.

She's breathless in love.

His brown eyes are bright when he comes up for air, mouth even brighter—wet. He licks his lips, leans up for a kiss. Lydia holds herself still. His body is warm, so much bigger than hers when he flops over onto her playfully. Now she really *can't* breathe, but when she pushes at him weakly, still shaking from the aftershocks of his attention, he laughs and snuggles down for a moment too long. Just long enough for Lydia to wonder if maybe it's funny to him, the way her limbs hurt under his weight, if maybe—

Then he's rolling over, pulling her on top of him and peppering her face with more kisses. When he pulls away, Lydia is sticky but sated. He loves her. He *loves* her. He loves *her*.

George's eyes are bright with playfulness, with laughter, with the idea she knows is knocking around in his mind right now. He's only brought it up a few times, but she knows he hasn't forgotten—he's too bright for that. Lydia wonders what she'd look like on camera like this, hair mussed and skin spit-shiny. If she'd look too pale, a little off-color, or if her foundation would prove itself worth the space it takes up in her budget and hold up even after too-many-to-count rounds of sex.

It's not like Lydia was a virgin before George; she wouldn't be caught *dead* as something so uncool. That seems more like Lizzie's modus operandi, and Lydia is better than that. It's just that sex is a lot of work, and kind of boring, except for when it feels like her heart's in her mouth.

George is the only one who's ever made her feel that way. College boys don't care much for a woman's orgasms, not if Lydia doesn't make them work for it, and she never has. It takes too long.

Sex with George is fast too, the way they fall into it, all clumsy hands on each other and banging into walls with desperation, but once they're in bed, George always takes his time. Tonight, Lydia still has half her clothes on, with her underwear pushed to the side; he's stripped down all the way—Lydia remembers her insistent tugging on his shirt. It's easier when it doesn't get in the way. He hadn't minded, though, just flexed his muscles and grinned at her, then pawed at her skirt until he could get his mouth on her.

All the energy has bled out of him now; he's fast asleep.

Lydia rolls over and pads into the bathroom, grabbing his shirt on the way up, grateful for the way it falls down to her thighs. No point in getting a yeast infection. She hopes George doesn't wake up so he can't join her in the shower this time, though. She's not up for another round yet; if he does, maybe she'll just go down on him. It's quicker to clean up, and then he won't bother to touch her afterward.

The door clicks shut behind her. Lydia peeks over her shoulder, and when she's sure she's made herself inaccessible to the camera's blinking red light, she pulls off her underwear at last.

The bar is crowded, humming with the energy of too-many-bodies crammed into a too-tight-space. It's game night—basketball or something; Lydia hasn't bothered to keep track since she realized it doesn't matter to college boys.

Mostly they're looking for a pretty girl with hair to twirl while they talk her ear off about sports, promising intimate hand-over-hand demonstrations of how to throw the ball *later*. Lydia's not naïve enough to think *later* really matters when the bed is warm and ready and so is she. None of these guys will make it to *later*.

Behind her, Lizzie snorts. "Really, Lyddie? *This* is what you want to do for your birthday?"

Lydia immediately bristles, biting retort on her tongue—and what did *you* do, then, for *your* birthday that was so cool—then clocks the gaze of a cute boy in the corner and brushes herself down again. She turns, pleading, to Jane instead, who immediately delivers.

"C'mon, Lizzie, it's her day. Nights out can be fun, right?"

Lizzie immediately softens, like Lydia knew she would. A line like that would never work coming from bratty little Lyddie, but Jane can get away with so much more than she can. There's something special about a rebuke coming from your best friend—or so Lydia hears.

Not like she would know. Not like anyone sticks around long enough for her to find out.

"I just thought it would be fun to dance. With you two," she mutters before pushing her way past the crowd to the bar proper.

The threads on the friendship bracelets itch around her wrist. Lydia still remembers the ghost of Mary's warmth on her skin as she tied the knot. Jane has made her way forward and is already talking sweetly to the bartender. This is different, Lydia has learned, from sweet-talking, which is what *she* does. Meanwhile Lizzie's eyes have lit up at the flier for trivia night. Lydia has no doubt she'll be back, sans little sister, to smoke out everyone who dares show their face. They settle themselves for the night, vantage point perfect for keeping track of their trashy little sister no matter what trouble she stumbles into tonight.

Lydia calls out to them. Neither one follows her over. She tells herself it's the noise of the bar and pretends the threads on her wrist don't feel too tight.

Instead she makes a beeline for the cute boy she noticed earlier, now wearing a smirk he wields expertly in her direction. Almost immediately, Lydia finds herself in his lap, plucking his shot glass out of his fingers and tipping it back.

It stings as it goes down; Lydia's a little too used to it.

A few hours later, Lydia feels sloppy-drunk, on the wrong edge of tipsy. Lizzie's sending looks under her lashes to Jane, whose brows crease even as she tries valiantly to keep up her placating smile, each glance sharpened by the kitty-claw corner edge of her eyeliner.

The bass pounds loud across the dance floor, and Lydia lights up as the track switches to her current favorite song. Her skirt, short and light and the right kind of swishy around her thighs, wraps around her skin as she twists, euphoric. For a moment, in the dim lights, Lydia feels like she could be floating, punch-drunk on the peace between her mind and body and the music vibrating through her very bones.

This is *it* for Lydia, everything she loves about clubbing: the loud music, the dim lights, the crush of bodies that don't give a fuck about her, all bouncing and stepping and twirling neatly to the rhythm of whatever's playing. For a moment, it doesn't matter if she looks cute, doesn't matter if her makeup cracks when she smiles too wide, doesn't matter if she sings off-key because no one can hear her anyway.

She spins, loving the way her skirt flares out, and nearly tilts into a dip before she remembers. There's no one around to catch her if she falls.

The fun, floating feeling sinks like a rock, through her stomach and into the ground, then burrows its way into Hell when the guy she was eyeing earlier comes up behind her to wrap his arms around her waist. This song is too peppy to slow dance to, but he makes a valiant effort anyway, swaying gently to whatever beat exists in his head. He probably fucks like that too, all up in his head, with nothing to connect him to the person he's thrusting into except the tight, slick heat of her body.

His breath is too hot, too wet against her throat when he whispers, "Do you want to get out of here?"

Lydia casts a desperate glance over to her sisters, who've settled comfortably into their perches on the barstools where they've been keeping an eye on Lydia since arriving. They'd waved back when she waved them over onto the dance floor but hadn't gotten up—Lydia can still remember the snort in Lizzie's voice when she'd declined Lydia's invitation to join her.

"Looks like you're doing just fine on your own, Lyddie."

Well. That's fine, Lydia lets herself believe. She used her out-loud words like Mary had told her to, and other people made their choices. It burned up her throat to tell her sisters—her *own damn sisters*, who had never once had to ask each other for anything more than once—that she wanted them to join her, won't they come, *please?*

But Lydia's no stranger to that burn. She tosses down another shot, and nods yes to the stranger wrapped around her body.

Later, as he pulls the skirt off her body, letting it flutter to the ground, and tangles his fingers around the clasp of her bra, Lydia tucks her wrists underneath the pillow. This has the added effect of pushing her chest up, which seems to please the guy suckling messily on her, and that's important—but mostly she spaces out and plays with the loose thread of her friendship bracelet. Under the scratchy, maybe-unwashed pillowcase on a stranger's bed, Lydia considers it safe from the splash zone of sex.

Maybe she should care a little more about making this interaction satisfying for even a single person involved. She doesn't. Doesn't think about arching her back, batting her eyes, pulling the right moans from her throat as he does anything but satisfy her.

If she walks out of this house tomorrow with that knot still intact, she'll count it a win.

"So proline has restricted phi and psi angles given its 5-ring structure—you can see how it's an outlier on the Ramachandran plot here." Mary points to a tight ring, curled up on itself, tiny compared to the way the other amino acids sprawl out and take up space across the plane of the graph. "And that restricts its ability to bond with other amino acids."

Immediately, Lydia blinks back tears.

She feels ridiculous, sobbing over protein folding patterns, but *god*, proline's just like her for real. Bent all wrong, all sharp corners and stolen valence electrons. The way proline twists up into itself, the only amino acid to bond the protein backbone twice—it's like it's holding its own damn hand, no space for anybody else.

Lydia bends deeper over her work. Mary's always on her case to take better notes; now seems as good of a time as any to put that into practice. As she scribbles down a hasty axis, marking down oblong circles whose start and end don't quite make it back to meet, Lizzie's face flashes in her mind.

The thing is—Lizzie's not mean. Not to her little sister, not on *purpose* except when they fight, and in those cases, Lydia's a hell of a lot meaner. She'd just be confused, maybe, a little dismissive. *You're not a fucking amino acid*, Lyddie, *you're a human person.* Like it's obvious, like she's got all the right parts and can do all the same things as everyone else, can *feel* all the same things as everyone else. Like there's no way to be different while still being human.

So Lydia hasn't gotten around to using her out-loud words about that yet.

Jane would be sweeter about it. *Amino acids don't change, sweetheart. You can be anything you want to be!* Even in the privacy of Lydia's mind, Jane doesn't sound sarcastic or wry or cartoonishly positive like the voices Lydia imagines for the inspirational posters she remembers scattered around her elementary school classrooms. She just sounds encouraging.

The paper nearly tears under Lydia's pencil; she doesn't want to be *encouraged*. But really, Lydia admits to herself, being encouraged would be better than the reality of not being noticed at all.

A piece of fabric shoves its way underneath Lydia's tucked chin, obscuring her view of her notes. Lydia startles, bites off an instinctive growl and looks up to see Mary looking exactly as no-nonsense as she always does.

"Proline is critical in beta pleated sheets—next to a glycine." Here, she pauses until Lydia dutifully fills in the blank.

"The smallest, most flexible amino acid."

Mary nods and continues. "Yes. Next to a glycine, proline creates the bend that holds each sheet of the beta-pleated sheet together. Proline also starts the first turn of an alpha helix." Mary lets that sentence hang for almost too long, until Lydia peeks up out of sheer curiosity. The fabric is pleated over in Mary's hands in a mimicry of the protein structure they're discussing, but that's not what she's waiting for Lydia to look at.

When Mary can look her dead in the eye, she finishes her thought. "Life wouldn't exist without proline. It's a leader and a binder—it holds us together."

It's not like Mary to be so anthropomorphic about protein folding, though she often plays along when Lydia does 'cause "it helps you learn, after all."

After a long heartbeat, it occurs to Lydia that maybe, all these months that she's been using her out-loud words with Mary—maybe Mary's actually been *listening*.

The thought that she might have noticed Lydia's upset and done something about it— not shamed her or tried to make her change or understand someone else's perspective but just talked her through it, reminded her that she's good enough exactly as she is—

Her throat closes up, choked on her words; her eyes sting with tears. It feels *amazing*.

Later that week, with the folds of the fabric ruffling pleasantly under her fingertips, Lydia aces a college test for the first time.

The camera clicks on. Lydia, with nothing to hold onto except herself, digs her nails into her palms and reminds herself that the red of the camera light means she finally, *finally* loves George enough.

Loves him the right way. The way he loves her.

When the news hits that the website got taken down, Lydia smears on a smile like she used to smudge gold over her eyes and cheeks before hitting the club; her heart sinks. The door, heavy mahogany, creaks closed with a *thunk*, but the walls still shiver in winter storms, and Lydia can hear Darcy's quiet rumble as he murmurs his everlasting devotion for Lizzie in the next room over.

None of this would've happened if she hadn't been whoring around, *again*, fucking things up like she always did. Fucking, like she always did.

She can't even do *that* right. Lydia can picture her sister's face, tilted up at Darcy like he's the sun; their voices are so *warm*. She shivers; everything's in the wash and the sweater she's left with is too thin. It should make her feel good that the damn video got taken down. Instead, all she feels is blank.

At least the video was proof that she cared. That she'd *tried*, even if everything she did was irrevocably broken, not unlike Lydia herself. Maybe even George cared, in some kind of evil, schadenfreude kind of way. All *this* proved was that Lizzie, for all her brashness and bold commentary and incessant bitching, was loved. Loved despite it all, and Lydia *wasn't*.

A sob hiccups through the room. Lydia tries to swallow it before it echoes through the house, passes through thin walls and interrupts the *moment* building to a crescendo one thin wall away.

The door bursts open. Lizzie's there in a heartbeat, and it's so unexpected that Lydia's heart damn near stops.

The bouncer looks Lydia up and down like he knows she's too young to be here—seventeen and a little too experienced sneaking into bars. She plays with the necklace strung across her neck. It shimmers, gold like her makeup; long and layered and easy to roll between her fingers.

Lydia drops her gaze, smiles, and the bouncer ushers her in with a sigh.

Almost immediately, there's a guy on her; he looks almost thirty, and Lydia immediately scrunches her nose at him. He's leering at her, gaze lingering too low on her body. "Want a drink, doll? I can give you a good time," he promises.

Lydia is ready immediately with a retort, blood on her teeth and tongue. "I don't like you like that."

"Ha! You think you'll find anyone better than me 'round here?" He sneers, leans over her. Lydia doesn't back down.

"I don't like *anybody* like that," Lydia tells him, because she hasn't learned not to yet.

Later, Lydia calms herself down with deep breaths. That stranger hadn't *done* anything to her—she's fine. It could've been a lot worse. She walked away with scraped-up shoulders on exposed brick and a ring of bruises that contrast her bracelets nicely. It could've been worse.

Still, his words linger on her skin so long they sink, branded, into her soul. "What the hell kind of woman are you? Freak. Get your shit figured out, girl, or no one'll *ever* give a shit about *you*."

Lydia bandages herself up before her sisters notice and makes sure it doesn't happen again.

Lydia is a fun girl, a party girl: the girl you take home at the end of the night, the girl you help sneak out in the morning, the girl who's down for anything, with anyone, at any time, at least just once.

Lydia is a fun, cool girl who let the guy she said she loved film them having sex because she couldn't love him right, then broke down about it in front of the entire internet when he blackmailed her with it, and now she's sobbing into her sister's arms, which are holding onto her so tightly it might push away all the lonely nights, so maybe for once things really will be okay?

Lydia is a fun, cool, totally normal girl who's slept around and fallen in love exactly like she's supposed to. Every step of it was awful, not that she'd ever mention that—it wouldn't be very fun-cool-normal of her—but what does it say about her that, right now, wrapped up in her sister's steady love, is the first time in a long time Lydia's felt even halfway close to okay?

And what does it say about her that the man she loved (loves) is a monster, and her sister (sisters) won't talk to her until she's broken down by revenge porn and blackmail?

And what does it say about her that she sleeps around like she won't have a bed unless she's in someone else's, when really she's ten miles away from the nearest allosexual spectrum?

And what does it say about her that, for all she runs her mouth, she's never once spoken out the honest goddamn truth she's known her whole life: that her sisters will *never* be there for her like they've always been for each other?

And what does it say about her that she might be *wrong*?

"I thought that, for *once*, I might be good enough for—somebody," she tells Lizzie in a broken whisper, like if it's not loud it isn't real.

Lizzie's arms around her are warm, and solid, and *there*. She's not pulling away. *For once*, Lydia thinks, *for once*.

Lydia presses a little closer to Mary. The crush of the crowd shouldn't be so unfamiliar, but she feels underdressed in her slinky black dress and heels when half the crowd is in cosplay. On stage, a little off-key but rough and raw and so enthusiastic that Lydia can't help but bounce to their beat, a band warbles lyrics about Beatrice and Hero. No one looks twice at Lydia—no one catches her eye, looks her up and down.

The door swings shut behind them, Lizzie trailing just close enough to slip through without opening it for herself.

Mary curls her fingers around Lydia's wrist, pulling her forward under the flickering bar lights. They hadn't pre-gamed, and Lydia doesn't plan to drink, but she feels Champagne-bubbly already. There's a group of people already chatting, leaning against barstools and sitting up on the counter, casual and in each other's space with the quiet intensity of years-long friendship, hyping themselves up into a frenzy over ridiculous theories.

A few of them are talking about the newest science fiction book that's just hit social media full force. Lydia hasn't shut up about it—she's had a lot of free time to read, after everything.

Her thoughts fizz with hope and nerves and something entirely *else*, something that skirts the edge of belonging, maybe, or home. Before she can stop herself, Lydia's already blurting her thoughts out. "Isn't it possible she doesn't like anyone at all—?"

Ten minutes later, Lydia's been swallowed up by her new friends, who are buzzing over the idea of a main character with no love interest—"the themes are *impeccable*, Lyd!" Mary's deep in conversation with someone else, but catches Lydia's eye whenever she looks in that direction. Lizzie isn't saying much. Her smile is small, but so, *so* warm.

They stay late, downing soda like it's a shot and stumbling over each other on the dance floor. Nobody makes a pass at her; no one looks at her funny when she doesn't fall into someone's lap. Lydia gets passed from person to person and doesn't feel like she's holding onto anything at all. She thinks about the ways she could rearrange her wardrobe to pull costumes together, imagines running her fingers through the strands of hair on a wig. They'll come back the week after, and again after that. Lydia has plenty of time to try on different characters.

Tonight she just enjoys being herself.

TAGS

aromantic, asexual (gray), break-up (past), canon compliant, character study, coming out, f/m (past), past tense, present tense, siblings, third person limited point of view

INSPIRATION

When her first name is given to the reader, Georgiana Darcy is introduced in the context of marriage. According to Caroline, she's unmatched in her accomplishments and elegance, and Caroline hopes to have her as a sister. For much of the novel, we hear nothing about Georgiana except for how she excels. Both Caroline and Catherine de Bourgh praise her constantly, and her name is a weapon against the Bennet sisters, who are found lacking in comparison. The narrative is insistent: Georgiana Darcy is not just the ideal woman, but the ideal wife.

Then, the reader learns that Georgiana nearly eloped with George Wickham in a scandal that could ruin her and her brother's reputations.

Unlike nearly all the other characters in this book so centered on marriage that it frames that narrative from its iconic first line, Georgiana has no romantic intentions in the original story. Caroline is the only person to imply she may marry, and only to deliberately taunt Jane. In fact, her closest and only relationship seems to be with her equally isolated brother.

Though Darcy is highly sought after, he shows no interest in marriage before meeting Elizabeth. While it would have been unusual to remain unattached, rich men have the privilege of being "eccentric." Despite her wealth, Georgiana would have no such protection from societal scrutiny, especially after her brother does marry.

What if a girl as accomplished and desirable as Georgiana Darcy—with all her skills and wealth, held up as the ideal wife—decides she doesn't want to marry at all?

unwound thread and wilted roses is an exploration of the loneliness of amatonormativity, but more, it is a story about recognizing yourself in others and the complexity of sibling bonds. This is a companion piece to nottesilhouette's *tell that to my tell-tale heart*, which touches on all the same topics in all different aspects, in all the best ways.

UNWOUND THREAD
AND WILTED ROSES

Georgiana chews on her thumbnail as she paces up and down the room.

It's a terrible habit, very unladylike, and one she thought she had been well on her way to breaking, but she can't help herself. It feels as though she's coming undone at the seams—just like the handkerchief she partially unraveled earlier.

In her defense, there had been a loose thread. She had just pulled. And pulled and kept on pulling until—

Georgiana presses her palms to her cheeks and takes a deep breath. "It'll be all right, Gigi," she says to herself. "You are perfectly capable of having a conversation with William."

"What kind of conversation?"

She whirls toward the door, heart rabbiting in her throat, to see her brother standing on the threshold. "William!" she squeaks. "You're back!"

"Weren't you waiting for me?" he asks, giving her a confused look.

Georgiana stares at him, her "Yes" trapped between her tongue and her teeth, echoing in her ears and screaming to be released.

All she can manage is a smile.

Georgiana stared at the beautiful spread of pastries and felt a gnawing emptiness open inside her. Her tea sat unsipped, but Caroline hadn't seemed to notice. Not yet, at least.

"You're a beautiful girl," she said. "You'll have half the eligible men in England clamoring for your hand." The corner of Caroline's mouth quirked up. "The dowry doesn't hurt either."

The empty hole inside of Georgiana took a turn toward nausea. "I...I suppose you're right..." She stared into her tea as if it held the answers. Maybe it did—but she didn't know anyone who could read the leaves.

"It should be easy enough to find someone you tolerate." Georgiana's eyes flicked up to see Caroline staring out the window as she talked. It was a gloomy day—thick, roiling gray clouds threatening to open and weep at any moment. "Plenty of acceptable men are tolerable."

Georgiana's mouth tasted like ash. "Someone tolerable," she echoed. She wondered if she would melt away into nothing but a repeating voice.

"Your brother won't leave you out in the cold," Caroline continued, shredding a finger sandwich with deft fingers. "He loves you too much for that. He'll make sure there's someone to take care of you—someone *more* than tolerable."

"Sit down!" Georgiana insists, sinking onto the nearest sofa. Her hands are shaking. Her gloves are thrown over the back of a random chair on the other side of the room. She hopes her pacing didn't leave tracks in the carpet. "You must be tired!" She wonders if he can hear the slight strain and tremble in her voice. It's deafening to her.

William gives her an odd look as he enters the room. It makes Georgiana feel like she is trying to breathe underwater. She doesn't know what that look means. Does it mean she no longer knows her brother, or does it mean something else?

She looks down to smooth out her skirt and steady herself. She's panicking and she *cannot panic*. She needs to be calm and in control. Assuming the worst won't help.

William takes her hands in his, stopping her from smoothing out her already smoothed skirts. "Georgiana, is everything all right?"

She can't meet his eyes. She just stares at their hands.

"Gigi," he says softly.

His hands have always been so much larger than hers. Able to cover more space on the pianoforte than hers could. Able to hit each key with more grace and ease.

He has calluses in different places, but they have a near-identical bump on their middle finger from the way they hold their quill when they write. Hers is probably unladylike—though maybe some think it shows how accomplished she is, all the letters she has to write. Should a lady have calluses on her hands? Is it only acceptable if they're from embroidery? Or even then does one need to always remember to use a thimble, something Georgiana often finds herself forgetting?

She blinks back tears as their clasped hands start to blur. He has to know how badly she's shaking.

William squeezes her hand tight.

George Wickham had been a constant in Georgiana's life since her birth.

He wasn't family, but he was close enough. He was always nearby, sometimes by William's side and sometimes on his own, growing up as she did.

Wickam grew up dashing. Charismatic. *Enticing*.

And Georgiana knew him so well. She understood his personality, his sense of humor, his goals and dreams—and he understood hers. Wickham wasn't some stranger who she danced with at a ball or who was introduced to her with the intention of possibly making an advantageous match.

He grew up in the same halls as her. On the same pathways.

He was right there, smiling and charming, already having made a spot for himself in the home that she loved.

The butterflies Georgiana felt seemed destined. The rush of emotions and the heat in her cheeks when Wickham gave her his full attention. When he smiled for *her* and was drawn to *her* it wasn't just chance. It was what they had always been growing toward, as they grew together.

So when George told her he loved her, she believed him.

When Georgiana opens her mouth, it's with the intention to confront William about what is going to happen. To talk to him like she knows she's needed to for weeks—like she's *wanted* to for weeks—and finally know where she stands in this world.

But instead of broaching the subject with any delicacy, she says, "Your wedding is soon."

William studies her face. She tries to imagine herself as he sees her, splotchy and teary-eyed and asking about a wedding.

"Yes," he says, clearly hoping she'll guide him to understanding.

Georgiana swallows. She licks her lips. She pulls her hands—they're sweating, they're clammy—away from William's and stands. She moves over to a side table and pours herself a tumbler of water. She raises it to her lips with trembling hands and manages to take a sip without spilling it down her dress.

All the while, William watches her from the sofa, waiting for her to make the first move. To lead the way in this conversation.

"I'm getting married," he repeats as she stares down into her water. Her throat still feels dry. "I thought you liked Elizabeth."

"I do," Georgiana says in a small voice. "It has nothing to do with Elizabeth; it has to do with…with me."

When William first told Georgiana that Elizabeth had accepted his proposal, she had thrown her arms around him with a squeal and tears in her eyes. She went to bed smiling but awoke with sore cheeks and a cold, quiet burning in her chest.

She tried to recall her easy joy from the day before, but it had fled in the night to be replaced by a sinking dread that was slowly spreading throughout her entire body.

As much as she wanted to return to the simplicity of the day before, she couldn't just bask in the joy of having gained Elizabeth Bennet as a sister. The warmth and delight of the announcement was gone, and the knowledge that crept up on her as she slept and swallowed her dreams whole lingered in the cobwebbed corners of her mind. She wandered Pemberley like a ghost, tracing the edges of furniture and windowsills, trying to find that piece of herself again.

William hadn't noticed her poor acting; as much as she fancied herself a talented performer, she knew better.

He had happier things on his mind.

"I don't understand," William says.

"I know." Georgiana puts down her tumbler. "It's…"

Sometimes, she thinks her worries are silly and unfounded. But she can't be *certain*, not until she asks, and that's why it's terrifying. There's the possibility that she's making something out of nothing or that her worst fears could come true.

It wasn't something she ever expected, not before Bingley and his party went to stay at Netherfield. Despite all the barely disguised offers, batted eyelashes, and pointed looks, Georgiana never expected her brother would actually fall in love.

William never cared for courtship or marriage; he never had any inclination toward romance. His friends, while few and far between, were loyal and platonic and nothing more. In Georgiana's eyes, he was never *looking* for romance in the same way others were. And maybe most importantly of all, he never seemed unfulfilled or restless in the way that some people did when they were searching for love. Or even just *marriage*. Despite the grand fortune bestowed upon him, William never mentioned looking for a wife.

And that…that had been a relief.

Georgiana had never broached the subject of him marrying before. And he had never addressed hers.

But then: Netherfield.

Then: Elizabeth.

As Georgiana's friends talked of marriage, she found herself drifting from the conversations. It was one thing to smile and listen and talk about the men *they* found interesting, but the second they turned their attention to her, she would divert their conversation to safer waters.

There was a realization she would have to come to—one she would discover as she embraced her aloneness in a way that made her feel whole—but she wasn't sure how to broach the question in company. If she even should.

From what she knew, it wasn't typically done. She was a young woman of station and wealth, and young women of her stature married.

Men showed interest, they smiled and flirted and wedged their way into an introduction, and Georgiana would give them her best smile and most polite manners and hold them at arm's length.

And in those moments, she felt like she understood her brother more than ever before.

There was an unspoken understanding between them, a *knowing* about the other, that meant Georgiana didn't need to say it out loud. She simply *knew*.

At least, she thought she did. And she thought William had known too.

There's a dish of calling cards next to the pitcher of water.

Georgiana doesn't know when they arrived or how so many had accumulated. She flicks through them, feeling William's eyes on her as she tries to figure out how to start.

Before he entered the room, she had been so certain she knew exactly the words to say. How to approach her fears head-on and force them out into the daylight, where she and William would both stand and—hopefully—laugh at them until they turned to dust.

Somehow, seeing her brother's face makes it harder. The happy sparkle in his eyes that was so much rarer before Elizabeth.

It isn't that William was unhappy *before* Elizabeth, Georgiana knows better than that. It's that the simple thought of Elizabeth makes William light up from the inside in a way few other things do.

She knew this was coming. In fact, this is what she had wished for, wasn't it? When her brother was moping about, haunting the halls of Pemberley after Elizabeth refused his proposal.

Georgiana had had to claw that story out of William one painful sentence at a time, and she was still fairly certain he was holding back. And maybe, in that moment, with his heartbreak spread across the table like tea, she hadn't expected him to actually *marry* Elizabeth—not after such a rejection—but she had hoped he would be happy.

She grips one of the calling cards in her hand, takes a deep breath, and turns to her brother. He straightens, his brow furrowed in concern, and she feels a slight pang in her heart.

"I'm sorry," she says, and he shakes his head.

"What for?"

Georgiana opens her mouth, trying to voice the frustrations swirling inside her. "I don't want to get married."

Maybe it had been because Georgiana was fifteen. Maybe it had been because she was in London and caught up in the season. Maybe it was as simple as her really, truly loving George Wickham.

Despite all the attention she knew he received, he chose *her*, he wanted to marry *her*!

He wanted to elope with her.

George said her brother would disapprove. For petty, childish reasons. And Georgiana believed him because she had seen how their relationship soured. How kind and caring George was in the face of William's cold rejections. How unfair William was being to George.

(If only she had believed William. But she had been fifteen.)

Mrs. Younge had known George. She had been more than happy to help them meet and plan. For a few painfully short weeks—a few blissfully long weeks—Georgiana was overwhelmed with emotions in a way that she never had been before.

Love! It was love! It was love and secrets and rebellion and spontaneity.

And then it was over.

And Wickham was gone.

Wickham was gone, Mrs. Younge was dismissed, and William was there, standing over the pieces.

"You don't want to get married," William repeats. Confused. More confused than he was before she spoke. "Is there something you haven't been telling me?"

Shame burns in Georgiana's chest for a moment before she snuffs it out. "No," she says quickly. "There's no one. There—there hasn't been."

Which is the problem. She lets her words sit in the air, hoping he'll catch them and their meaning.

"You wanted to talk to me about…not getting married?" he clarifies.

Georgiana nods. "I imagined that you may have been thinking about it."

"Because *I'm* getting married?"

"Yes." She twists the calling card in her hands. "And Charles and Jane the other week," she adds quickly. "And Elizabeth's younger sister married a few months ago—"

A pained look crosses William's face. "*Gigi—*"

"It has nothing to do with him!" she interrupts. "I promise. It's…it's more complicated than that." The card turns to snow in her hands, dusting the floor in misshapen pieces. "It has to do with me."

She takes a deep breath and stares her brother in the eyes. "I don't know if I'll *ever* want to marry."

Georgiana had been prepared for love, but nothing could've prepared her for heartbreak.

She hated William for longer than she dared to admit. Then she stood in his shoes and felt the crushing pain all over again, this time not merely tinged in betrayal but steeped in it.

In that moment, she felt more a child than ever before—a little girl whose entire future was held in the hands of the men around her. Those carefree moments at balls and picnics were nothing in the face of the power that her marriage would hold: thirty thousand pounds.

Thirty thousand pounds and revenge on her brother.

Georgiana had thought her relationship had been solely hers—something tied not to her surname but her given one. That because this was something born in childhood, grown on her family's land, it was real.

She had been promised a union and a lie, and in the end, she received neither. The truth bit like a snake, and the venom burned as it raced through her system.

And just as George Wickham had wielded a marriage, William brandished his own weapons. And Georgiana—she was adrift.

No one knew what had happened, no one but William, but he was with her when she railed against him, when she sobbed, when she stared out the window at nothing at all, and when she finally stepped out into the gardens and was able to take a deep, full breath of chilled autumn air.

The silence in the room stretches long and thick.

William studies her from where he sits on the couch—that intense, inquisitive look that he brings to most social situations and usually scares people off with.

Georgiana stares back, probably looking like a hare confronted by a hunter's gun: small, terrified, and about to bolt.

"Ever?" William asks.

She straightens, ice shooting down her spine. "That's what I said, isn't it?" She's attempting for firm and confident, but her voice wavers and her lip trembles.

"Yes, but"—he rises from his seat—"forever is a long time to be certain of something."

Georgiana lifts her chin as he approaches her. "I'm well aware."

"As am I." He takes her hand and gently pries half a crumpled calling card from her fingers. "You're not old enough to be this worried about marriage."

"I'm plenty old enough."

William frowns at her. "Much older women than you aren't married, Georgiana. And my own wedding brought this on?"

She searches his face. It has, and she doesn't want to admit that fact. She feels guilty about it—mostly because she doesn't want *William* to feel guilty about her state of mind.

His gaze is steadying, comforting. The same reassuring eyes she's known all her life. She's kept her secrets from those eyes, and in the past, it's never ended well.

Georgiana has to turn around to even open her mouth. It's too hard when William is looking at her like that. "Yes," she says to the wall. She tries to inject some humor into her voice, hoping it will buoy this conversation. "Your impending nuptials may have inspired some…deeper thought."

"Will you share any of those thoughts with me?"

Georgiana looks down at the floor. She's standing on scattered pieces of torn calling card. She doesn't even know who it belonged to. Now, she'll never call.

"I was supposed to," she says. Not exactly to her brother. Perhaps, she says it more to herself than anyone else.

With time, Georgiana had thought the feelings would return. That she'd meet another dashing young gentleman and be swept off her feet, that she'd feel that flutter of butterfly wings and *know*, in the same way that she had before, that this was a man that she was falling in love with. That she could marry and be the wife of someone and be happy for the rest of her life.

Except…the feeling didn't come.

She knew she was young, but with each passing month, it felt less like another romance was potentially right around the corner and more like finding one at all was a rare treasure.

A rare treasure that turned out to be nothing but a cheap forgery on Wickham's behalf, but a gem to her nonetheless.

There were other girls her age who swooned over soldiers, who blushed over the men they danced with at balls, who snuck away with each other when no one was looking, who felt the possibility of romance in the air.

With the illusions of first love no longer clouding her vision, Georgiana found that romance had no real draw for her. More than anything, she longed for things to stay exactly as they were.

People would talk. They always did. They talked of her cousin. They talked of her brother. But why would she care? It wasn't as if she wanted for anything at Pemberley.

Georgiana would be delighted for her friends as they found relationships they could thrive in—or at least tolerate. But she wouldn't suffer on her own, she decided. And she truly believed her brother to be of the same ilk.

The Darcy siblings would face the future together: unmarried, but secure and happy.

"I was supposed to," Georgiana repeats, determined to hold back her tears. "It's difficult. I don't…I'm not sure you'll understand."

"I promise to at least try," William answers automatically, which makes her feel like crying even more.

The last time Georgiana truly broke down in front of her brother, she had been planning to elope. Now—

"When I say 'ever,' William, I mean *ever*," she says. She traces a pattern on the wallpaper with her eyes, trying to focus on the gentle swirls instead of the way her stomach is lurching. "I don't think that I…" She searches for the words she had so carefully planned and practiced, "…feel that way toward men. Toward anyone."

Georgiana whirls around, breath frozen in her lungs and tears shimmering in her eyes, *daring* William to be contrarian.

The expression on his face has softened, but that inquisitiveness is still there. Georgiana knows exactly what he's going to ask, and even though she thinks she's prepared for the question, it still hits her like a tidal wave.

"And George Wickham?"

Her knees feel weak. "I don't know," she murmurs.

When she first received William's letters from Netherfield, she had read them over and over, her fingers creasing the papers as she bent close in flickering candlelight. She reread them under the cover of night—hoping for clarity or understanding or some hidden message, she wasn't sure. She was looking for *something*.

In all those pages of elegant writing, there was much more than just a summer in the country with friends. There was something more developing between the words.

It didn't take many letters for Georgiana to put together the pieces. She knew how to read people, but more importantly, she knew how to read her brother.

Her brother had met someone.

It was an odd thing to accept into her worldview. At the same time, reading about this Elizabeth Bennet as the weeks went on, it felt natural.

Georgiana had done her best to resist asking about Elizabeth when they met up in London. She managed her way through the polite pleasantries before giving in to her curiosities, taking mental notes as William attempted to dance his way out of the conversation and implications.

He wouldn't say it aloud, but Georgiana knew. She wasn't even sure if William had admitted it to himself yet, but *she* knew.

Fitzwilliam Darcy was in love.

William leads Georgiana back to the couch and barely has to tug her down before she's practically collapsing among the pillows.

It's terribly unladylike, and every single one of her governesses would be horrified, but Georgiana can't bring herself to care. Instead, she looks to the ceiling to avoid William and says, "I truly think I loved him, you know. I just don't know if I'll ever love anyone else in that same way."

"I've been told love is different every time."

Georgiana tilts her head to look at her brother. "Have you?"

He shrugs. "I wouldn't know."

She looks back to the ceiling. That feels like an admission of sorts. "I don't mean to say," she starts slowly, "that he…ruined me for other men, or anything like that."

"I should hope not."

Georgiana smacks his arm with the back of her hand. "Elizabeth is rubbing off on you, I swear." She sighs and sits up a little straighter, drawing herself out of the depths of the cushions. "I've looked for romance again, and it's never there. Everyone knows what to expect, but it's like missing one of my senses. One that I used to have."

She pauses, hoping William will say something. He doesn't, so she swallows her fear, takes a deep breath, and prepares herself for the leap.

"I thought you might understand that."

Every time Georgiana told herself that *she* wouldn't have to marry just because William did, she was forced to confront the reality that this was not how things were done. Young women of her station married men of similar or better prospects. They married men and ran their households. They married men to secure their fortunes and their futures.

When it was just only her and William, it was a thought that lived in the back of her mind: present, but ignorable.

With him engaged, it was always at the forefront.

Perhaps William never thought of her marriage before. But with his own pending, why wouldn't he? Why wouldn't he wonder why his sister never showed particular interest in any of the men she was introduced to? Why wouldn't he wonder why no one had asked for his sister's hand?

Caroline said to marry someone tolerable, but Georgiana didn't know if she was *capable* of tolerance. How did she explain that the thought of marriage for marriage's sake, for stability's sake, for security, made her feel ill?

If anyone understood, it should be William. Even if he didn't understand the *feeling*, he understood *her*.

Didn't he? Wouldn't he, if he tried?

Would he try?

William's eyes widen imperceptibly.

Georgiana resists the urge to bite her nails. She can practically see the mental calculations that he's doing to prepare the proper response. But she wishes he wouldn't. She wishes he would just blurt out what he thinks in a fit of impulsivity.

"Was I wrong?" she asks, voice meek.

"No." William furrows his eyebrows. "No, you weren't. It's difficult to put into words. I suspect that I felt something of the opposite."

"The opposite?" Georgiana repeats, not daring to breathe lest she flame the sparks of hope in her chest.

"With Elizabeth," he says softly. With that gentle smile that seems to be reserved for only *Elizabeth.*

The rush of relief is so overwhelming that Georgiana feels faint. She holds back a bubbling burst of laughter, not sure if it'll startle William's words back into hiding.

William shakes his head. "Bingley was convinced I would be a lifelong bachelor."

Georgiana tries not to grin too wildly. "I noticed he stopped introducing you to nearly so many women."

"Yes, well…" William looks uncomfortable. "I believe he felt bad for their…hurt feelings."

"You're an acquired taste," Georgiana teases. "Elizabeth got used to you."

He shoots her a half-hearted glare, which she returns with a smile before his expression turns serious again. "Why would our marriage make you feel you need to tell me all this?"

Georgiana hesitates. "I…don't know if it reflects well on either of you."

"And if I still wish to know?"

She bites her bottom lip. "When you marry, Elizabeth will be the lady of Pemberley." William nods. "And I…" Georgiana shakes her head. "No, it's silly! Never mind. It was foolish." She starts to stand, but William touches her elbow and her legs go weak. "It's silly," she insists.

"It's not if it's distressing you," he promises. "At least let me assure you that you're being silly."

He's trying to make her smile, but she can't.

"When Elizabeth becomes the lady of Pemberley, I will live here on her generosity," Georgiana says seriously. "As long as she wishes."

William's eyebrows furrow. "Do I not have a say?"

Georgiana hesitates, just long enough for the rest of her implications to sink in, and he sputters. "Elizabeth would *never*—"

"I know," Georgiana interrupts, even though no, she hadn't. Not for certain. She's only met her future sister a handful of times and had to base her hopes on the words of those who knew Elizabeth more intimately. And her most knowledgeable source is also her most biased.

"I know," she repeats, "which is why— It was a foolish fear. Truly." She has to look away again, his eyes too hot against her face. "Once it caught, I couldn't be free of it. I had to ask. I had to…know if…" Pursing her lips, she forces herself to stare straight ahead. William had *said* Elizabeth wouldn't remove her from Pemberley. It should be easier now.

"What would you have done?" William steps carefully, as if performing a practiced dance. "If we…?" He doesn't seem to be able to face it either, which almost makes Georgiana laugh.

"I don't entirely know," she admits. "I knew I would tell you that"—she straightens her shoulders and spine—"'I won't marry for a roof over my head.' I was too afraid to plan for after. But…" Quickly, she cycles through their acquaintances. "Perhaps I would beg a room off Anne. Or Caroline—she might've allowed me to be a guest for several months. I would've…figured something out…"

When Georgiana braves a glance at William, his expression is stoic, but there is a deep misery in his eyes. A sadness that *she* has put there again.

"I'm sorry!" she blurts out. "I really don't think that poorly of you *or* Elizabeth, I *swear*. It was just nerves. Anxiety! I was overthinking and—"

"I'm not sure you were," he says, stopping her waterfall of words. Her heart flutters in her throat for a moment before he continues, "I think…there are many households where you would have been right for being worried. I can't fault you for putting your own well-being first—even if it means thinking the worst of me." He raises an eyebrow at her.

"Not the worst," Georgiana murmurs. "Probably."

"How long did you say you've worried about this?"

A heat creeps up her neck. "I'm not sure I did." And when he lets the moment hang, she adds, "I'm not going to tell you, William."

"However long was too long," he decides. "I don't like seeing you worry, Gigi."

She gives him a tired smile. "I'm rather sick of worrying myself."

William takes her hands in his, warm and solid and grounding. *Safe.*

"Pemberley is your home," he says. There is a weight to his words that makes them ring through the room, as if they're reaching the farthest corners of the estate. "It will always be your home. You don't have to ask permission or generosity; it belongs to you just as much as it belongs to me or Elizabeth. You never need marry to keep it—and I do not wish you to marry unless you find yourself truly and deeply in love. In fact, I forbid it."

Georgiana bites back a smile.

William meets it with his own serious eyes, with the smallest spark of humor. "You will never be asked to leave Pemberley and you will never be driven away."

"You promise?" Georgiana asks, feeling a little silly doing so with how solemn William is, but she needs this final assurance to fight the remnants of her fears.

His words are a flame that alight the darkest corners of her mind, burning the slinking shadows to ash.

"I promise."

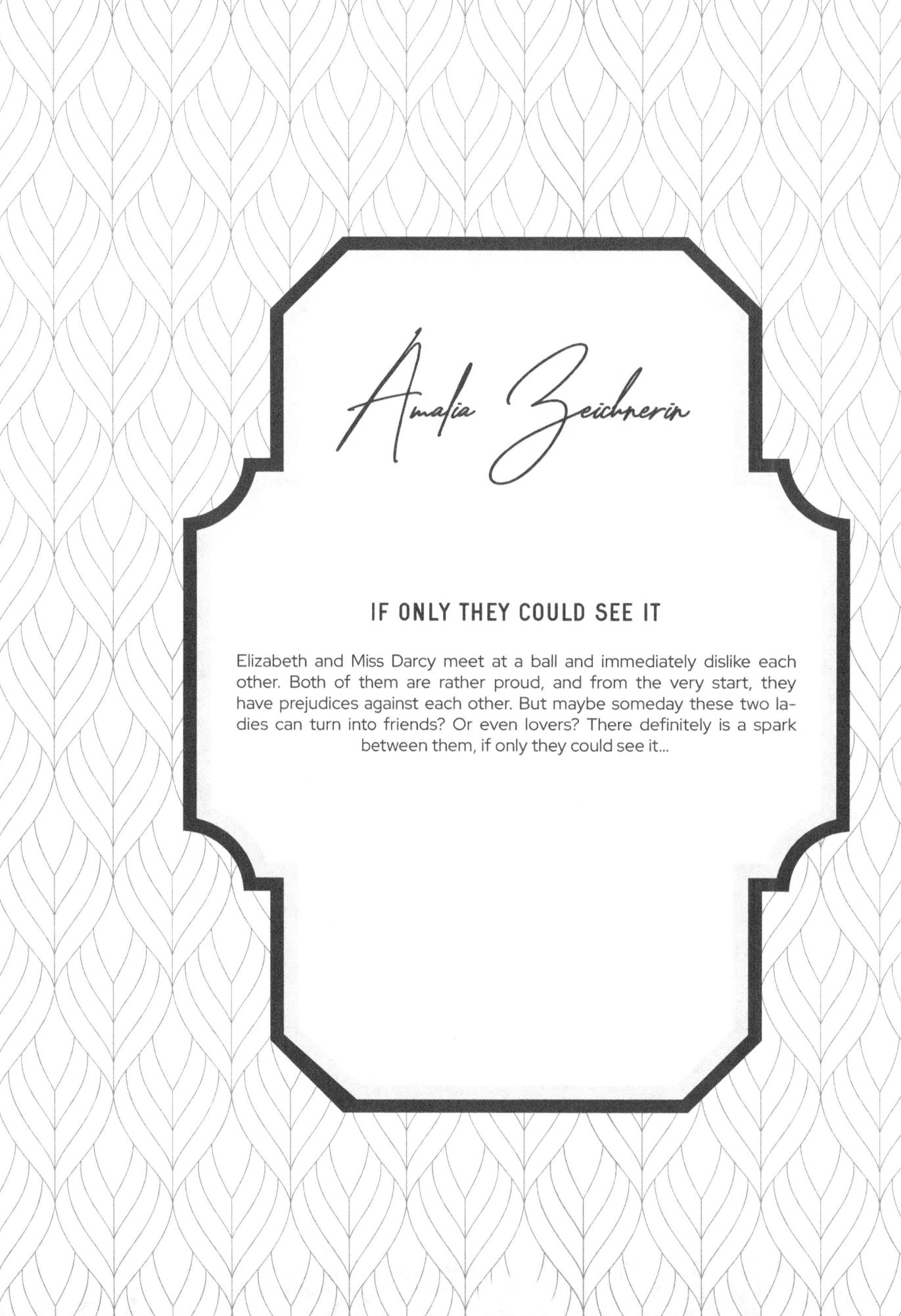

Amalia Zeichnerin

IF ONLY THEY COULD SEE IT

Elizabeth and Miss Darcy meet at a ball and immediately dislike each other. Both of them are rather proud, and from the very start, they have prejudices against each other. But maybe someday these two ladies can turn into friends? Or even lovers? There definitely is a spark between them, if only they could see it...

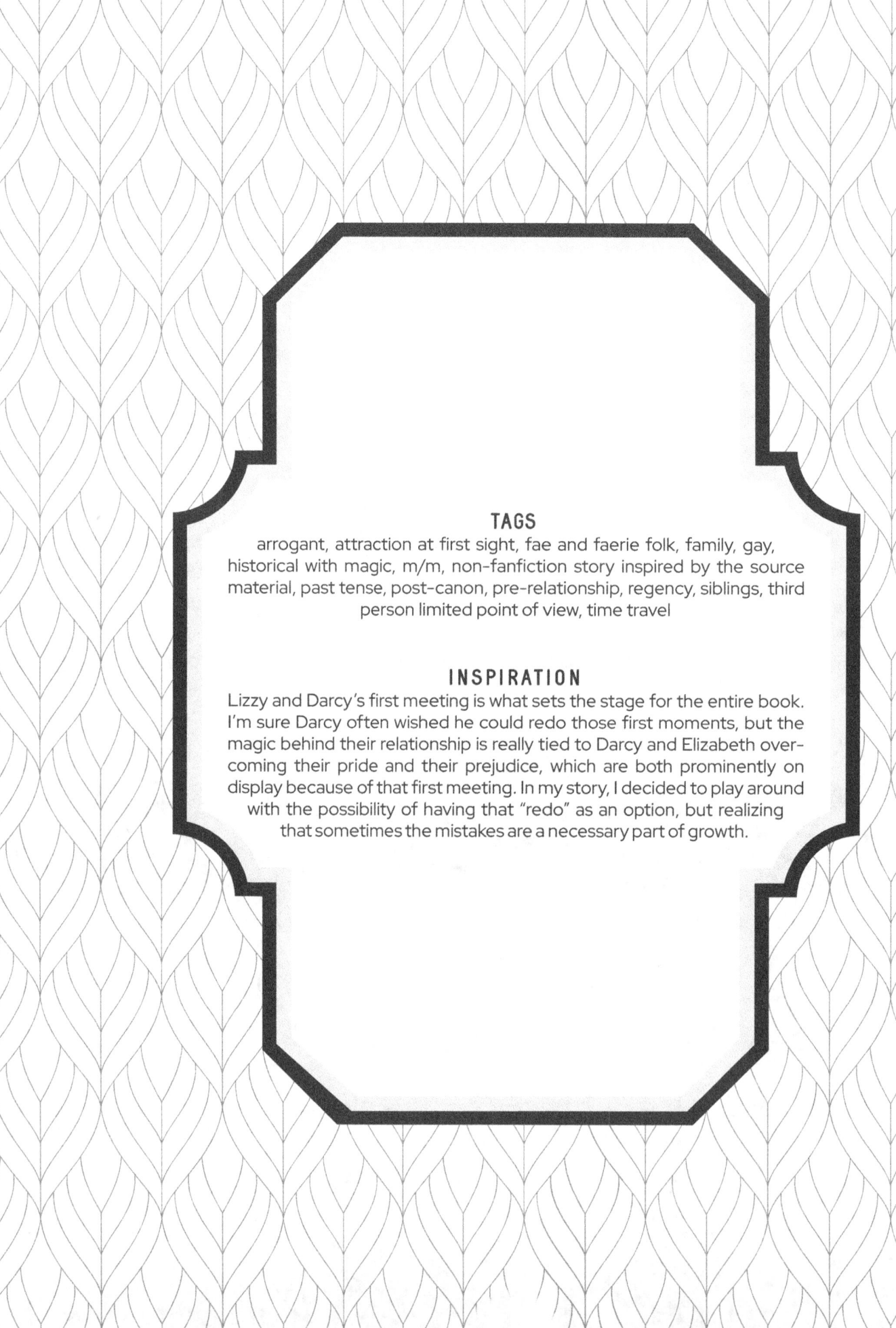

TAGS

arrogant, attraction at first sight, fae and faerie folk, family, gay, historical with magic, m/m, non-fanfiction story inspired by the source material, past tense, post-canon, pre-relationship, regency, siblings, third person limited point of view, time travel

INSPIRATION

Lizzy and Darcy's first meeting is what sets the stage for the entire book. I'm sure Darcy often wished he could redo those first moments, but the magic behind their relationship is really tied to Darcy and Elizabeth over-coming their pride and their prejudice, which are both prominently on display because of that first meeting. In my story, I decided to play around with the possibility of having that "redo" as an option, but realizing that sometimes the mistakes are a necessary part of growth.

A CHARMED LIFE

HENRY LUCAS OF Castlebury Abbey led a charmed life. And while he did indeed enjoy the many benefits of wealth and rank, of a good temperament and pleasing looks, his life was charmed in a much more literal sense.

His family had been bestowed stewardship of Castlebury not by any English king, but by a fairy one who lived in the forest surrounding the estate. The specifics of the tale had been lost over time, but some generations ago, Henry's great-great-great-someone-or-other had rendered the fairy a considerable service, and in turn he had gifted them the Abbey and the land. More importantly, the fairy king visited each child of Castlebury on their fifth birthday to bless them with "that which they most need."

Henry's elder sister, Louise, had been given a magical book that would show her any text she wished. A voracious reader, she'd made short work of every book in England, and last he'd checked, she was reading the lost memoir of the empress Agrippina.

On his younger brother's fifth birthday, Henry had watched as the fairy king had whispered secrets into Emmett's ear and then handed him a bronze bell. No matter how hard Henry shook it, it never rang, but ever since, Emmett had been composing the most beautiful songs.

Henry, though—he still shuddered when he recalled the king's otherworldly eyes piercing him, looking through him in a way that had made him feel undone, like he was simultaneously everything and nothing—for Henry, he had placed his hands on his shoulders and breathed into him a weighty power.

Without speaking aloud, the king's voice rang inside Henry's head: *"You can undo all that ails you and those you love. Choose wisely how you wield this blade."*

And then instead of the sword Henry had imagined, the king had given him a tarnished pocket watch that felt a little too heavy for its size. The watch ticked loudly and perfectly without ever needing to be wound, though Henry's family swore it didn't run at all, that the clock face was fixed at the hour of his birth. As useless as it appeared to the rest of the world (and as disappointing as it had been to a five-year-old hoping for an actual blade), the trinket had been a talisman for him for many years, proof of the spritely favor his family enjoyed. He'd kept it in his breast pocket, ignoring its faint heat and thinking it mostly decorative.

It wasn't until he was ten that Henry realized its true power.

The watch would sometimes hitch in its rhythm and grow warm. Usually he ignored these oddities, as he did on one summer afternoon.

Later that evening Emmett was found by a servant, his leg broken after falling from a tree.

Henry was devastated for his brother, and that night, through tears, he took out the watch and glared at it. Hadn't he been promised it would undo what ailed his loved ones?

What good was the damned thing if it couldn't help his brother? In angry frustration, he'd turned the time back to the afternoon when it might've done him good. The watch thrummed in his hands, protesting the change but obliging it all the same.

Henry looked up to find the world around him had shifted. Instead of his warm bed and the dim candlelight of his room, Henry found himself standing in the garden at the back of the house. Blinded by the sudden sun, he wondered whether he was dreaming. Or perhaps he *had* been dreaming, and now he was awake?

The watch ticked ominously in his hand, the metal suddenly so hot it nearly burned.

Henry ran to the woods where they had discovered his brother and caught him before he hit the ground. The whole family praised him for the timely rescue, only his father eyeing the pocket watch; Henry had tried not to fidget under his father's knowing gaze, but he couldn't help putting a hand to it protectively. His father had nodded then, understanding perhaps better in that moment than Henry did. He was determined to figure it out, though.

After much trial and error, he learned how to use the watch to its best advantage. The irregular ticks and heat were warning that he learned to heed, and he was able to prevent other disasters. He stopped his sister from accidentally setting fire to the library, rescued his mother from a runaway horse, and prevented a thief from pickpocketing his father. It made him—already heir of the family and now its protector—a golden child who could do no wrong.

It wasn't until he reached his more independent, teenage years that he began to abuse this power for purposes less lofty than intended. At a ball at Pemberley, he spilled wine on Mrs. Darcy's fine new dress. Although she laughed off the mishap, he undid the blunder to avoid her husband's ire. If he wished to avoid his tutors, any time he was caught by them he would simply rewind his steps and choose another hiding place. Any faux pas he made was easily erased, any game lost given a second go, and occasionally he used it at the races to earn some extra pocket money (though he found, much to his consternation, that it did little to improve his luck at gambling).

Spoiled as Henry was, it suited him to make himself the type of man all admired, all thought entertaining, and with whom all wished to be friends.

It wasn't until he met Charles Morland that such frivolous use of his pocket watch was rendered completely useless.

Their first encounter was just after Henry's twentieth birthday, on a gloomy Tuesday afternoon.

Louise had accosted him on his way out of the breakfast room with the hope of wheedling him into accompanying her to a tea party, and without any more amusing prospects for the day, he'd gone willingly. The party was hosted by some friend of his sister's whom he couldn't recall at all, though he suspected he should. Henry rarely bothered to pay attention during introductions, knowing that he could simply ask anyone their name and title, enjoy the brief moment of their embarrassed annoyance at his candid rudeness, and then repeat the last few seconds with the appropriate details (no doubt immediately forgotten once again).

Among the crowd of mostly ladies, he'd regretted the decision to attend. He liked women well enough. Their dresses were pretty and their attention pleased him, but he found their accomplishments dull. He hated having to feign interest in a poorly played work or splatter of paint that he could barely decipher as a landscape, yet such was his social obligation. Worse, attention he granted them might be perceived as courting, which was the very last thing on his mind.

(Sometimes, when he felt particularly wicked, he would let his true thoughts loose. He would tell the mercenary ladies trying to obtain his affection exactly how little he thought of their art and their singing and their poetry recitations. It was satisfying to let it out, and flipping back the minutes relieved him of any guilt he might have otherwise felt, their appalled devastation his own secret delight.)

He braced for an afternoon of such superficial social niceties, and was pleasantly surprised to see a handsome youth standing as a solitary sentinel in the far corner of the room. His jacket was well-pressed, pristine lines of charcoal with a beautiful purple cravat that drew the eye to the elegant line of the young man's neck. Only a year or two older than Henry himself, he was tall with blond hair slightly too long to be fashionable, the more wild strands at his ears and the nape of his neck curling. His features were set into grim lines that did nothing to detract from his soft cheeks and rosy lips.

Henry was certain the two of them would be fast friends. It was a simple matter of course: anyone Henry decided to be friends with would indeed become his friend. It was with this confidence that he strode across the room, too self-absorbed to notice the warning burst of heat from his watch, and stood next to him.

"Terribly dull business, isn't it?" Henry mused aloud. He rolled back on his heels and gave a conspiratorial look. "Can't stand these lady's tea parties."

The young man raised an eyebrow. "Then I wonder that you came," he said with an air of such indifference he might not even have expected a response.

"My sister"—Henry gestured vaguely in Louise's direction—"has solicited my attendance, which is hardly enough reason to tempt me, honestly, but I'm sometimes too indulgent." He spoke in jest, hoping to see the handsome if solemn face light up in a smile.

It didn't.

"I, too, come at the behest of my sister," he said, his tone softening as he looked across the room, then sharpening once again when his gaze returned to Henry. "Though I don't consider it a chore to indulge her."

"And yet you stand here alone in the corner," Henry pointed out. He offered a hand. "Henry Lucas."

The man lifted his chin and stared down his nose at Henry's outstretched hand. The pause was long enough that Henry was certain, if their luck were reversed and this stranger was in possession of the pocket watch, he would have told Henry off simply because he could and then completely undone the meeting, avoiding Henry so thoroughly the introduction would never happen. The thought made his heart skip a beat and heat rise in his cheeks.

Mercifully, the man accepted the gesture. "Charles Morland." He let go of Henry's hand as quickly as was socially acceptable, though not so fast that the fleeting touch didn't feel like a brand.

"You said your sister is in attendance," Henry said, trying a different tack. "Would I know her?"

Charles glared at him. "As hostess of this event and the intimate of your sister, Miss Louise Lucas, I would've thought so."

Henry cursed himself. The name and details were only faintly familiar, a friend he'd no doubt been introduced to before, information Louise had surely told him on the carriage ride over. If he'd hoped to rise in Charles's estimation, he'd failed miserably.

"Ah yes, of course—"

"If you'll excuse me." And then Charles was gone, halfway across the room before Henry could stop him.

"Unacceptable," Henry growled, not sure whether he was more angry at himself for such a failure or at Charles for giving him so little a chance.

He practically tore his pocket watch out of his jacket and wound it back five, no, ten, no, *twenty* minutes. To the very first moment Louise had parted from his side and left him to his own devices. The world shifted around him, a blur of fine dresses and waistcoats until he was at the entrance to the room, Louise's hand tucked into the crook of his elbow.

"Who's the hostess of this event?" he whispered urgently to her.

"Maria Morland," she said slowly, looking at him in disbelief. She didn't scold him for not knowing—unlike their mother, she never bothered to correct his ill manners. Instead she leveled a piercing look at him and narrowed her eyes in suspicion. "Whatever for?"

"No reason." He patted her hand gently. "Go enjoy your tea and gossip."

His sister spared him a raised eyebrow before shaking her head and wandering off. He was glad his odd behavior wasn't enough to detain her, and that she held no lingering suspicion about his motives. He wasn't even certain what his motives *were*.

It took Henry a moment to spot Charles, once again alone, and he walked over.

"You're Miss Morland's brother," he said with amiable assuredness. "Maria's such a lovely girl." He held out his hand, and though Charles accepted it automatically, there was little warmth behind his eyes as he watched Henry skeptically. "I'm Henry Lucas, Louise's brother."

"Charles Morland," he answered back, their touch fleeting but no less potent than the first time.

"What a charming tea party your sister has put together." Henry had never put so much effort into appearing cheerful at a tea party before, and he hoped Charles appreciated the effort. "Delightful!"

"She is a gifted hostess," he admitted. Though he obviously meant the words and the sentiment behind them, it was equally clear he wished to have no part in whatever it was Henry was doing. Indeed, it cost him so much to voice it that he said no more, leaving the burden of conversation once again upon Henry's shoulders.

Not that he much minded; Henry loved few things more than the sound of his own voice. "You must be a doting brother to attend when you otherwise find no enjoyment in such parties," he babbled on. "It's honestly rather noble of you—"

"What makes you think I find no enjoyment?" Charles interrupted, the perpetual scowl on his face deepening. It somehow rendered him more handsome, though Henry longed to see what a smile might do.

"You've completely distanced yourself from the whole affair," Henry said, gesturing to their solitary position, so far removed from the nearest circle of ladies that they could hear no more than the gentle cadence of their voices. "What type of enjoyment is that, hiding away by yourself?"

Charles looked around the room, arms clasped behind his back and feet firmly planted. Despite his growing annoyance, he seemed otherwise perfectly at ease; Henry didn't know what to make of the contrast.

"Some," Charles began, "find enjoyment in the enjoyment of others. My sister is here among her friends, having a delightful afternoon on an otherwise gloomy day. I see her friends, your sister among them, also enjoying each other's company and making the most out of their time here in London, freed momentarily from the expectations of their parents, the requirements of society, and the pursuit of suitors. I'm not sure why I should not find some amount of contentment in such a gathering, even if I would prefer to observe it from afar than interfere with it, nor do I understand why you took my isolation as an invitation to come over and make conversation, since you yourself have observed that I chose it."

Henry's jaw dropped. It was the most he'd heard from Charles yet, and it showed one thing above all: he found Henry utterly lacking.

"Has anyone ever told you that you're infuriatingly hard to get along with?" Henry grumped.

Instead of looking shocked at Henry's words, Charles seemed rather pleased by them. "Only to those with nothing of substance to offer."

Henry's cheeks heated. He reached once again for his pocket watch and very pointedly started to unwind it while Charles watched with a bemused expression. "We'll see about that," Henry said and held up the watch before slipping back to the entrance to try again.

This time, he stayed with his sister, much to her chagrin. He was a dutiful brother, in a way that would surely impress even Charles Morland. Louise, eyeing him like a lioness unsure whether she should pounce or not, obligingly introduced him to her friends one by one. They fawned over him in a way that gratified his ego, and soon Miss Maria Morland was hanging on his every word with delight. Henry preened at the attention, waiting, waiting—

"Oh, Charles!" Miss Morland called to her brother. "Do come over! Meet Mr. Lucas, my dear Miss Lucas's brother. He's quite charming, isn't he?"

Henry smiled triumphantly as he turned to Charles Morland, sure he'd finally found the right path to his good graces. "Pleasure to meet you," he said, offering a hand.

Charles accepted, polite to a fault…and that was it. He showed less interest in Henry now than when they'd met before, his attention mostly on his sister and her friends. The only time he smiled, the only time amusement crystalized in his eyes, was on account of them. He seemed to barely remember Henry was there. Which was worse, honestly—the indifferent tolerance that was afforded him.

In all his life, no one had ever thought so little of Henry as Charles Morland clearly did. Given the right inducement, everyone could eventually be prevailed upon to admit Henry a delightful young man. True, in many erased moments during the last decade, Henry had offended and misspoken. But aside from Henry, no one remembered those lost moments, and he was certain they shouldn't be counted against him.

He went about the rest of the party in a daze, not bothering to reset that more tepid first meeting. Instead he let lady after lady pour him tea and tried to push the problem of Charles Morland from his mind. He couldn't, though; the more he tried, the more it festered. By the time he'd returned home with Louise, his heart was heavier than he could ever remember it being.

He had never before found himself so unable to manage someone's estimation of him. If he were smart, he'd let it go. It was hardly a requirement that everyone he met should like him. There were plenty who no doubt didn't and were simply better at pretending. What did it matter that Charles Morland couldn't be bothered to pretend?

After days of being unable to turn his mind to anything else (any*one* else), he had no better answer, just the certainty that it *did* matter.

"You're in an awfully foul mood," his brother said, looking down his nose at Henry with confusion. "People tell me all the time you're the nice one in the family. Why don't *we* ever get to see it?"

"Piss off," Henry mumbled. "I'm not in a foul mood." And he wasn't. He was simply reflecting on how frustratingly useless his watch was, and had maybe told Emmett to stop playing his damned pianoforte so loud.

Emmett raised an eyebrow. "Of course you're not," he deadpanned. "How could I have been so mistaken? You're clearly the epitome of good humor."

"What? Just because I don't want your bloody concertos, day and night—"

"You have been rather surly this past week, darling," his mother chided from the window seat. Her eyes were on her embroidery, but he was sure the slight downward turn of her brow was all for him.

Henry bristled but bit back the impulse to argue. They were right, of course; he simply hadn't noticed his brooding had gotten so bad. "Sorry," he said with a sigh of resignation, and left the drawing room so as not to further dampen their moods.

If only he could wipe his mind clean of Charles Morland, perhaps then he wouldn't feel so haunted by him. Haunted by the possibilities that seemed to thrum around Charles like an aura, and the pull he exerted on Henry without his even knowing it. He couldn't bear to let him go. He couldn't.

"I'm *reading*," Louise said, and Henry startled slightly. He hadn't meant to come into the library, but here he was.

"You're always reading," he said automatically, and went to sit at the other end of the settee. His sister's feet were in the way, but she moved them just in time, then kicked him once in annoyance. He swatted back at her, then secured her feet in his lap so she couldn't easily retaliate. "What can you tell me about Charles Morland?" He'd been completely unsure what he would say until the words were out; suddenly, he understood what had drawn him to the library.

To his surprise, Louise immediately set her book down. "Pardon me?"

"Charles Morland. He's your friend Maria's older brother—"

"I know who he is," she said, her tone making it abundantly clear she thought him an absolute idiot. "I just didn't know *you* did." Her eyes narrowed. "You're doing it again, aren't you?"

"Doing what?"

"Rewriting things."

He blinked at his sister. It should be impossible for her to remember the moments she'd lost through his machinations, he was sure of it (at the very least because she would've been angry at him if the changes were to her detriment, and Louise had never been one to hide her anger). "How do you know about that?"

There was a devious glint in her eyes. "You keep a journal, do you not?"

The implication sank in.

"You read my journal?" he nearly shouted.

"Of course I do," she said dismissively. "I read everything."

"Since when?" he asked, mortification making him calculate how much time he was willing to rewrite to stop her, before he realized he couldn't. So long as she had her book and the inclination, there was nothing he could do, save keep no journal at all.

"Does it matter? What do you want with Morland, anyway?" She wrinkled her nose. "Oh Lord, you mean to seduce him, don't you?"

"I—I didn't—" His cheeks burned in embarrassment. He hadn't realized anyone knew about his proclivities, nor did he ever expect his own sister to mention them so casually.

"What? You think it's a secret? I knew even without reading your journal, though it was most informative in other matters."

"*Louise*," he begged, panic rising.

She ignored his plea. "I'm not judging you. Charles Morland is a handsome man, so I'm hardly surprised. He might even be good for you. If there's anyone who would be able to see you for who you are, it'd be him."

That stopped Henry short. "What do you mean?"

"Well," she said slowly, studying him, "perhaps you're drawn to him because he's not so easily fooled by the way you perform for society. Maybe you even like that you can't fool him, so that he could know the you that's hidden beneath the unflappable, ever-charming portrait of yourself you put forth to the world. He needs to see that you're a man who makes mistakes…and occasionally needs help from his sister."

Henry hated that she was right.

"Yes," he said, seizing that last point in an attempt to get things back on track. "I need help from my lovely sister who will help me convince Charles Morland that I'm not a complete ass."

"So you can seduce him?"

"My aim in doing so is irrelevant," he said. She gave him a sharp look, and he wilted under it. "That was my original intention, yes," he admitted, and fidgeted under her unwavering gaze.

"But?" Louise prompted.

Henry couldn't quite pin down the strange emptiness that had been growing in his chest from the moment he'd laid eyes on Charles Morland. "I know I shall probably never convince him I'm worthy of his time, but I cannot bear to think that he's alive in the world and thinking ill of me. If I could only show him I'm not a cad, that might be enough to soothe this…this *feeling*." He gestured at his chest. "I can't escape it."

Louise looked at him with such pity and understanding that it made him squirm in discomfort.

"Henry," she said, not unkindly, though her voice was tinged with chastisement. "What you seek is a real connection, and that's not something that can be written the way one writes a letter. You cannot simply cast the attempt in the fire and start anew, not when you are the only one aware of what you've chosen to discard. A real friendship—or whatever more you might one day seek with Charles, or anyone for that matter—must be shaped together by both parties."

It was discomforting to be so seen by her, though he was glad she did see him as he truly was and cared for him just the same. In all the world, he was closest to his family, and in all the world, they were the ones he most allowed to see his blunders. If he teased Louise more than she liked, or she him, he didn't unravel the moment; he let it linger. The same with Emmett: when he and his brother argued, he let the disagreement stand. So long as the consequences weren't dire, he changed very little of his day-to-day life at home.

If his family could overlook his faults, perhaps there was hope that others could as well.

"If you wish Charles to like you," Louise continued, "and I mean the *actual* Henry Lucas who sits before me, and not the well-constructed facsimile of him I often see about the ton, then he must *know* you. If he angers you or if you anger him, you must commit to that moment, because it shapes you. Whatever mistakes you make, Charles must know of them, especially since you have the power to always know of his. It's wildly unbalanced to be the one in complete control of the relationship, erasing moments here and there as it suits you. You must take the bad with the good, and learn how to salvage those times when you misstep."

The weight of such a notion nearly crushed Henry. While that was much how he lived with his family, it was safe to do so with them. They *had* to love him, even when he was an ass, just as he continued to love them despite their faults. Charles was under no such obligation, and the idea of opening himself up like that terrified Henry.

…and yet it offered a sort of authenticity he couldn't deny he yearned for. What a notion, to not need to perform for someone. Even if Charles wasn't that person, that was what he should be aspiring to, was it not?

"I understand," he said slowly. He didn't fully, not yet, but the idea had taken root. He would nurture it and let it grow into whatever he needed it to be. His eyes focused on Louise once again, and he flashed her an abashed smile. "Thank you."

"That's what sisters are for," she said smugly, then her expression darkened. "You won't be erasing this whole conversation, will you? I should like to get satisfaction for this advice beyond this very moment."

He startled slightly. "Erase it? Why would I do that?"

Louise arched an eyebrow. "You really don't undo much at home, do you?"

"Not unless you accidentally set fire to the library, no."

She rolled her eyes. No doubt she'd read that bit before. She might even be glad he'd interceded and saved her precious gift.

"Good," she said emphatically, then settled back against the settee and opened her book. "Mama's having a luncheon next week. I'll invite Maria and ask her to bring Charles. Hopefully she won't think *I'm* the one interested. Lord knows that's the last thing I need—her playing matchmaker."

"Thank you," he said. "You're amazing."

"I know," she said, nose in her book once more. "Don't interrupt me again."

A week was hardly any time at all—especially to someone like Henry, who'd sometimes lived three weeks' worth of time in the span of one—yet time seemed to crawl. He was too nervous to imagine different scenarios, to act out conversations with an imagined Charles. He didn't want to sound rehearsed, and he found he was completely unequipped to picture how the real Charles might respond to anything he said or did. No, best to save it all for the real thing.

Finally, the luncheon was upon them, and he stood sullenly in a corner observing the guests as they arrived. It wasn't lost on him that he was very much like Charles had been when they first met, and he thought he better understood his severity at that moment.

When the Morlands arrived, Henry's stomach twisted into knots. Maria clung to her brother's arm, but Henry hardly noticed her. Charles was so...so handsome. He wore a sleek dark-gray jacket that contrasted wonderfully with his blond hair and a sprig of lavender pinned by the lapel. He was quiet but confident as he moved about the room. He was, as always, the epitome of genteel male beauty.

"You're not subtle," Louise said as she appeared next to him. "You haven't stopped staring since they arrived."

"I can't help it," Henry said. He really couldn't.

"Are you perhaps going to speak to him, or...?"

Henry scowled at his sister, realized it made him turn away from Charles, and immediately looked back. "I shall," he said with far less confidence than he felt. "Wish me luck."

Charles was next to the windows at the far side of the room, but instead of rushing over, Henry stopped to get a cup of tea. Once he could hold it without the cup rattling against the saucer, he knew he was ready.

"You're Miss Morland's brother, aren't you?" he said, his nerves leaking into his voice. His palms were clammy, and his stomach roiled uncomfortably. He hadn't felt this anxious...ever, actually.

"I am," Charles said guardedly, then he seemed to soften in recognition. "We met at my sister's tea party a fortnight ago, did we not?"

"We did," Henry said. His smile was shaky, he could feel it, but he was so relieved to know he'd made some sort of impression on Charles, no matter how fleeting. "Could I ask you a very peculiar favor?"

Charles looked equal parts suspicious and curious. "Perhaps?"

Henry reached into his pocket and held out the watch. "Would you mind holding onto this for me?"

"Your watch?" Charles asked in bewilderment. "Whatever for?"

"Ask me again in a few weeks," Henry said as breezily as he could manage, then offered his hand. "I'm Louise's brother, Henry Lucas. I've been looking forward to seeing you again."

"I remember." Charles accepted his hand and, for the first time, it lingered. "I'm Charles," he said, and it sounded like the most wonderful beginning in the world.

Tomowowo

A MOMENT RIPPLES OUTWARDS

I took inspiration from my dates with my wife. We love going to museums and also sharing books together. So I thought looking at a painting with somebody special might awaken feelings. Said painting is the confession scene that made me feel very moved, and I wanted to capture that in a detailed painting.

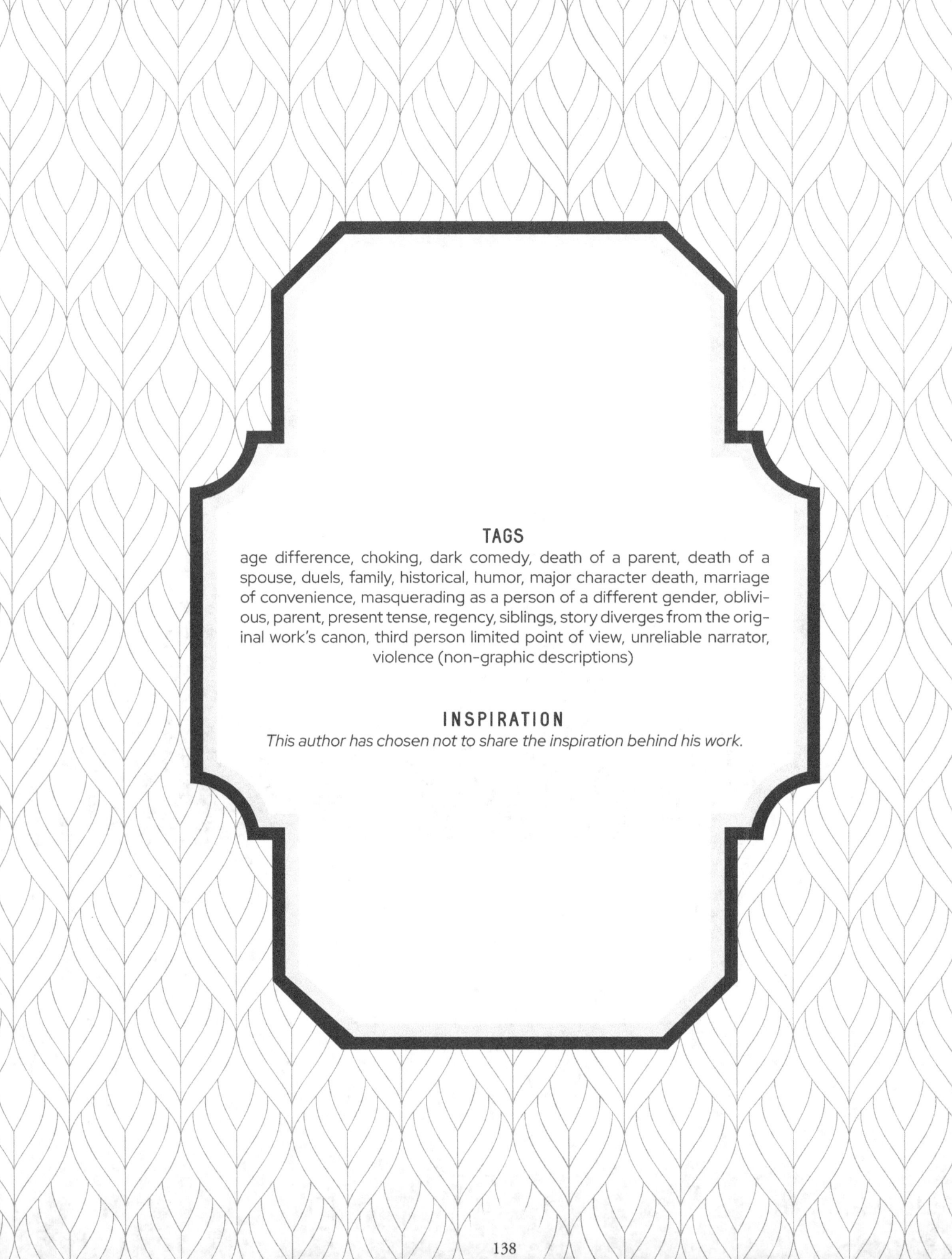

TAGS

age difference, choking, dark comedy, death of a parent, death of a spouse, duels, family, historical, humor, major character death, marriage of convenience, masquerading as a person of a different gender, oblivious, parent, present tense, regency, siblings, story diverges from the original work's canon, third person limited point of view, unreliable narrator, violence (non-graphic descriptions)

INSPIRATION
This author has chosen not to share the inspiration behind his work.

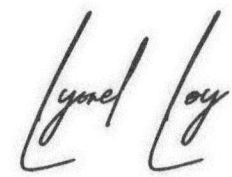

MUCH ADO (ABOUT QUITE A LOT)

"Lackaday!" Mrs Bennet cries. "I do believe he is indeed quite dead."

There is a clamour, and a hullabaloo, and much to-ing and fro-ing and rending of clothes and gnashing of teeth. Lizzy pounds Mr Bennet's corpse, quite belatedly, on the back.

It flops all over the good dishes.

"Dearie me," Mrs Hill exclaims, peering in from the kitchen door, "and on the day I made my special figgy pudding too. He always was fond of it."

'Twas fondness for figgy pudding that did Mr Bennet in, in truth. Mrs Bennet is also very fond of figgy pudding in general, and Mrs Hill's in particular, although unlike her now-late husband, *she* has enough good sense to be wary in its chewing.

It is very typical of Mr Bennet to expire of the one enjoyment they still shared.

She does hope that he does not expect her to lose her taste for the stuff in her widow's grief, because she shan't.

"Ought we send for the doctor, Mamma?" Kitty asks, peeping timidly at the body from behind Lydia. "The poor man was just here, and it's about to snow heavily, too. Quite the shock he'll have that it was Papa who went, when this morning it was *you* half-dead of your poor nerves."

"My poor nerves indeed!" Already, Mrs Bennet feels a great resurgence of her morning nerves coming upon her. Now they shall all die of cold, and misery, and the most hideous deprivations! "Of all the inconsiderate times to depart! Now there shall be doctors indeed, and lawyers aplenty, and then we shall all be turned out into the snow by some coldhearted lout barely related to your father!"

There is yet another tremendous clamour and tremendous-er hullabaloo: Mary begins pontificating on the legal processes of entails, but Kitty and Lydia are shrieking more loudly over her. Even Lizzy has gotten in on the weeping and wailing, no doubt over their collective impending demise.

"I'm sure it will all be well," Jane tries to say. Her voice does not overcome even Mary's.

The very nerve of her husband! To succumb in his own warm house with a mouthful of desserts! It would have done Mr Bennet a great deal of good to be vexed for once in her place. If only it were *her* dead of pudding! Mrs Bennet will surely be vexed unto death long before the cold and misery can take her.

How right Kitty is: the good doctor will have such a shock, that all of Mr Bennet's vexations have not yet driven her into the grave—

"But why, Kitty, you clever girl!" Mrs Bennet cries. "Hold, hold! No one is to send for the doctor yet, for I have a most splendid idea! Longbourn is Mr Bennet's as long as he lives, so live he shall! We will convince the doctor that 'twas *I* who departed of some great apoplectic attack—no doubt of your father's doing—and henceforth I shall play his part!"

How taxing a task could that be? Mrs Bennet can sit around in a warm study with her teeth in her mouth just as well as her late husband.

"What! Mamma!" Lizzy cries.

"She's Papa now," dear Lydia says. "Weren't you listening?"

"That just might work," Mrs Hill swiftly agrees. "What with Mr Bennet no doubt retired to his study in grief, that's the good Misses Bennet and myself left alone to manage this dreadfulness. No one could fault us mere women for forgetting, perhaps, not to keep a corpse too long by a warm fireplace."

"Indeed no one could," Mrs Bennet declares. "Well, girls, gather round. We must have your father—well, your mother—laid out nicely someplace."

"The front parlour, I dare say," says Mrs Hill.

"The front parlour," Mrs Bennet agrees. "Kitty, run and have a table in place. The rest of us shall heave-ho!"

So they heave and they ho, and they ho and they heave, until Mr Bennet lies in good state on the spare table before the parlour fireplace. Mrs Bennet darts off to fetch the largest and most staid of her dresses, feeling as nimble and sprightly as a young miss—or perhaps as a bachelor. Certainly she feels much more a bachelor than a widower; her poor nerves have wholly receded.

"Well, then," Mrs Hill declares, when the late Mr Bennet's corpse is properly dressed up as Mrs Bennet and all his whiskers have been carefully shaved away. "That ought to do the trick!"

Outside, blessed snow is already falling. The doctor cannot possibly be sent for for some days; this is a splendid idea.

"O, pew! Mercy me," cries the doctor. Even from behind the locked study door, Mrs Bennet hears the trampling of his feet as he skedaddles. "Well! I dare say she is indeed quite dead."

"He's bought it," gasps her sister Phillips, clutching at Mrs Bennet. "O thank the heavens, he's bought it."

"Hush!" hisses her brother Gardiner, clutching at them both. "O merciful Lord above, here he comes!"

They hush, all three clinging to each other, hardly daring to breathe.

"Have you got a coffin coming?" the good doctor asks, and from so close! Mrs Bennet had her ear pressed to the study door to listen; she snatches her face away in haste.

"One's finally on the way now the dratted snow's let up," they hear her darling Jane reply.

"Well, have the body safely in and sealed away before the vicar gets here, is my advice," the doctor says, his voice retreating down the hall. "His poor old heart mightn't take the shock to that enormous snoot he has, and then we'd have a mother and a Father both to bury. And speaking of fathers, I suppose Mr Bennet's shut away in his study?"

"Yes, with our uncle and aunt tending to him," says Jane, and sniffles. "Poor Papa! His dear heart is so entirely broken, he could scarcely bear to have anyone see him at all."

The doctor mutters something that might be, *of course he couldn't*. If there are more words to his muttering, they do not hear; the big door squeaks open and squeals shut, and the greatest danger is past.

"O gracious," Mr Gardiner gasps, and stumbles away from the door clutching at his chest. "O gosh. O my poor nerves—and look here, now you've got me sounding just like *you*, Fanny."

"You always have, you goose," Mrs Phillips exclaims, steering him firmly into Mr Bennet's big armchair. And he always has indeed, ever since he was a little sprout of a boy escaping his lessons on fencing and dancing to trot around behind them—Mrs Bennet had to learn both parts of the dances to teach him all the bits he missed.

A difficult boy to teach, when Mr Gardiner was still their little Eddie—always wanted to dance the lady's parts.

But none of them ever held with sword-fighting. Such a useless, fussy business! Any fighting man would be far better served with a cunningly wielded broom or stout walking stick, as they had until her brother Gardiner was grown and had to go about pretending to be a Proper Gent.

For the Gardiners never were Gentlemen and thus had to be more Gentlemanly than Real Gentleman, or so Mrs Bennet always heard their Papa say.

It does no one any good to be Proper so often, in Mrs Bennet's view.

"You *must* get away from Hertfordshire, Fanny, and soonish. My poor heart can't take this."

"Darling boy!" cries Mrs Bennet. "Your poor heart's far younger than ours! But I shall spare it nonetheless: Mr Phillip's already found us a place in ——shire."

"Merciful Father be praised," Mr Gardiner groans. "Very well! I'll make arrangements for Longbourn to be put up for let. Fortunate timing, too! I hear Netherfield Park's to be likewise put up, and soonish; best we beat them to it."

"And right quick we shall be out! My darling Jane has been running about with packing lists all through the week; when the body goes, we too shall be gone."

"Splendid of her!" Mrs Phillips says, exchanging a look with Mr Gardiner. "I must say, my dear, that we have been thinking: now that Jane's mistress of the house, as it were, it might do her a great deal of good to have the management of the household purse."

"Important thing for a girl to learn," Mr Gardiner agrees. "Certainly the late Mr Bennet never would've given her the chance, I reckon."

"Important indeed, and *this* Mr Bennet will!" exclaims Mrs Bennet. She means to be nothing like her late husband—her darling Jane shall have the household purse in full, without any sort of petty quibbling on the part of the master of the house.

"Then I'll have the papers sent directly to her, when Longbourn's been let," Mr Gardiner says, and sighs so deeply he almost throws his back out, and puts his head into his hands. "O gracious, I can't *believe* we're doing this."

And so softly that Mrs Bennet can barely hear him, he says, "I'm so glad you're not really dead, Fanny."

They sit quietly together, all the three of them, and hold each other's hands for a very long time.

"There is to be a ball at ———, the evening after tomorrow," Mrs Bennet announces. It is her first such announcement at their new home in ———shire. How she has missed such announcements, and how she has missed balls! "We shall be attending."

Kitty and Lydia must miss balls greatly, too; they shriek and tumble about at once in sprightly joy. But her sweet Jane asks, quite worriedly, "Surely we should still be in mourning, Mamma—I mean, Papa?"

"Nonsense, my darling! It has been half a year since your dear Mamma passed." It is so tremendously *darling* of Jane to worry of mourning still, but truly it has been long enough—Mrs Bennet will go quite mad if she sees another square of blacks. "That is quite a respectable enough period for daughters to be in mourning."

"Half a year!" cries Lizzy. "It has just gone by four months!" She sounds quite vexed—over what, Mrs Bennet cannot possibly fathom. *Does* the girl wish to spend more months doing nothing but sewing quietly, or staring sorrowfully out at the flowers in the little yard, or crafting yet *more* parasols?

"Dear girl! Four months is very nearly half a year." Truly, Lizzy has been inside too long if she's forgotten this. Mrs Bennet must have her darlings back out in Society, and soonish, before they all go completely out of their minds. "And it is only a smallish ball to ease your way into the thick of things. We certainly must attend, and you shall all show off your new parasols! Mrs Phillips sent word: that splendid young Mr Bingley who's taken Longbourn for let is visiting hereabouts; *he* might be in attendance. Such a coup your uncle Gardiner managed to snare him for Longbourn, as clever as any ploy of the great Nelson's; do you know that Mr Morris almost had him for Netherfield Park instead? How dreadful that would have been for that fine young fellow! So far from anywhere of consequence, and him an unwed gentleman!"

"Netherfield's only two miles from Meryton, Papa," Lizzy says.

"An entire two miles! *Our* wonderful Longbourn is only separated a mile from parties and balls." Everyone ought to be as close as possible to parties and balls, in Mrs Bennet's view, and the unwed in particular. "Nonetheless, *we* shall attend this one. Your uncle's success must not be wasted; I must introduce you girls before every fortune-hunting mamma in Hertfordshire descends upon *our* tenant."

"Yes," says Jane, in a certain sort of voice, "I suppose you must."

"O!" says Charlotte Lucas.

Mrs Bennet had never before considered the girl to be of the dimmer persuasion—although, of course, no Lucas could be half as bright and lively as Mrs Bennet's own darlings—but she might have to reconsider her previous high assessment. Charlotte has said nothing but *O!* since they stumbled upon each other by the table of refreshments at the ——shire ball.

"As you see, my darling *Papa* is quite well," Lizzy hisses, clutching Charlotte's arm as tightly as a barnacle to a boat. "He has, well, done away with his whiskers, which I suppose you might find strange, but I hear it common in widowers to change up their looks."

"O!" says Charlotte again, and at last, "Mrs—I mean, Mr—Bennet! Why, I mean. How do you do? I'm so terribly sorry for the loss of your— Ah, um. O!"

"A delight to see you again at last, dear Charlotte," Mrs Bennet declares, even though it is most certainly not. "Are you here visiting? 'Tis a long way from home for a young lady!"

What devilry could a Lucas girl be up to in these parts? Has the news of Mrs Bennet's splendid and splendidly eligible new tenant already reached the ears of Hertfordshire's fortune-hunting mammas? Is Charlotte here for an early chance at *Mrs Bennet's* tenant, for a sly leg up over the rest of the Hertfordshire set?

Admirable, in most circumstances—Mrs Bennet has great appreciation for this sort of cunning in a young lady—but in *this* case it will not do at all. The good Mr Bingley has taken Longbourn for let, and in Mrs Bennet's estimation that makes it only natural that a Bennet girl has first (and second, and possibly third) crack. Not that a Bennet girl ought to need more than a single crack—the agreeable Mr Bingley is already dancing with her darling Jane, and how smitten the man looks!

It is their second dance, and there cannot be a third; Mrs Bennet must contrive to be at his elbow as soon as they part, to steer him towards another of her girls. And then perhaps Mrs Bennet herself ought to ask Charlotte for a dance, to keep the devious creature safely diverted from her husband-hunting for a pass or two. It will be no sacrifice: Mrs Bennet is very fond of dancing.

But she gets no chance for such machinations: the wonderful Mr Bingley is captured by a Disagreeable Young Buck of his own party as soon as he parts from Jane.

Mrs Bennet has already heard much of Mr Bingley's Young Buck. All the assembly buzzes with the news of his discourtesy—he is above his company, they say, and above being pleased, and has condescended to dance only once, and then only with a young lady of his own party.

A terrible waste of a ball, in Mrs Bennet's view.

She—a gentleman twice this Young Buck's age!—has danced already thrice, and she means to dance again the precise moment she has gotten the agreeable Mr Bingley safely back in the arms of one or another of her girls—perhaps Lizzy, who has not yet had a chance to dance.

But— Oh, blessed day! For Mr Bingley and his loutish hanger-on are swinging of their own volition—or of Mr Bingley's, at least—towards Mrs Bennet.

"My most wonderful fellow," cries Mr Bingley. He thumps Mrs Bennet in a hearty and manful way on the back; it is a new and rather pleasing experience, to be thumped on the back like a gentleman. "Allow me to present Mr Darcy, a dear friend of mine; Darcy, Mr Bennet!"

Mr Darcy only sniffs and looks down his nose.

Mrs Bennet is none too pleased herself to be made an acquaintance to this uncouth young man, and doubly displeased to have the gentleman presented to *her*. Surely she is not so old that rank must defer to age?

But it is *Mr* Bennet's age that the agreeable Mr Bingley must be deferring to, and of course he could not know her own; she is soothed once again.

And thank goodness! There is the cunning Charlotte being swept away to dance by some second-rate gent—but then all gentlemen are surely second-rate next to the amiable Mr Bingley, saving perhaps Mrs Bennet herself. Lizzy has been left to sit alone, and there is Jane walking to join her.

But Mr Bingley has machinations of his own. "You must help me have Darcy here dance," says he. "I hate to see him standing about in this stupid manner, when all around are uncommonly pretty young ladies—like that one over there!"

He swings Mr Darcy around towards Lizzy, and raises himself twentyfold in Mrs Bennet's esteem. Now this handsome Mr Darcy must dance with her Lizzy, surely—she could forgive him all his past discourtesies if he dances well with Lizzy.

But Darcy only looks upon her Lizzy with a horribly cold eye.

"She is tolerable," says he, "but not handsome enough to tempt *me*; and I am in no humour at present to give consequence to young ladies who are slighted by other men—"

"What, my good sir," cries Mrs Bennet in a fine fury. "That is my own daughter whom you so malign!"

"Erm," Darcy says.

"O! Good gracious," the agreeable Mr Bingley gasps. "I'm sure Mr Darcy only misspoke. Isn't that so, my dear chap?"

"Well," Darcy says, which sounds nothing at all like misspeaking to Mrs Bennet.

What a setting-down she must give this young lout! No finer setting-down will the good people of ——shire have seen or heard in all their days, and blessed day! Mrs Bennet can freely do so because now she is a he, and a gentlemanly *he* at that. And so—

"La, sir," cries he, "I shall call you out!"

"O gracious me, Mamma," yelps Lizzy, leaping to her feet, and, "*Ouch*, Jane, don't pinch me—I mean, O darling Mamma in heaven, lend our Papa your wisdom! Papa, cease!"

But Darcy has rallied: he straightens as though he thinks himself as tall as a stag—the effect, if there is meant to be any, is unfortunately lost, for Mrs Bennet has no particular interest in stags. "I have not duelling pistols in my current accoutrements," says he, "nor have I my sword; but if it is satisfaction you wish, I will have them sent for."

"La, sir! For shame!" Pistols and swords, how ridiculous! Mrs Bennet is as unfamiliar with such unladylike objects as he is with any sort of deer. "We shall most certainly not be duelling with pistols or swords! You forget yourself, to speak thus amongst young ladies."

"Whatever is your meaning?" Darcy demands. "We shall set a time—"

"Good sir!" Charlotte Lucas interjects. Wherever did she spring from, and has she already cast aside her second-rate gent? "You are in polite company! The good Mr Bennet—being *most* considerate of the delicate constitutions of us young ladies in attendance—will certainly not be so *uncouth* as to duel in this fine company with *pistols or swords!*"

"And I am saying that that is not how duels go," Darcy tries to say, but Charlotte—the most wonderfully devious girl!—cuts him off once again with a shriek.

"O! Heavens forfend," the splendid girl exclaims in tones of scandalised horror, and the gathering crowd gasps with her. "Surely the gentleman does not mean to imply that an *elder* like the esteemed Mr Bennet is incorrect in the proper protocol of a duel? How faint I feel! Mary, dearest, I beg you take my arm—I simply *must* sit down."

"But—" Darcy says.

"See!" Mrs Bennet cries. "How dreadfully you have shocked this young lady with your words, my good sir!" The moment has seized him—how shocking this man is, indeed! He must teach this young lout a fine lesson. "Infamous! Most infamous! We shall have no more talk of pistols or swords in this polite assembly, or some *other* Papa might have to call you out also for besmirching the tender ears of his daughters—but twin weapons we must have!"

Mrs Bennet's knowledge of duels begin and end at twin weapons; he is very fond of things that match.

"But my good Mr Bennet," exclaims the agreeable Mr Bingley, wringing his hands, "I of course do not wish that you duel with pistols or swords—I do not wish that you duel at all—and especially not in the presence of young ladies!—but surely, there are no options aside of the two?"

"Nonsense, nonsense," Mrs Bennet cries. "My darling girls are most accomplished creatures, and have brought today fine parasols they crafted with their own hands—and of course all match most splendidly! Lizzy, I shall wield yours for your honour. Jane! Arm the rude gentleman also, that we might match."

"O! Goodness," says Lizzy, but she hands over her parasol; Jane has to plant her own very firmly into Darcy's limp hand and close his fingers around it.

"But I do say," Darcy begins, "surely this is the most infamous—"

"Infamous indeed!" Mrs Bennet exclaims, and shakes Lizzy's parasol at him. "Never in all my years have I heard a gentleman speak so infamously of a gentleman's daughter! So en passant, my infamous sir! I will have satisfaction!"

Darcy, to his credit, squares his shoulders. "En *garde*," he replies, in a tone that reminds Mrs Bennet greatly of the late and former Mr Bennet when he thought he was making some sort of grand point, and a great fierce fire rises in his bosom.

How grandly and properly this Young Buck Darcy stands, too, with Jane's parasol held swordlike before him! But a good stout walloping wins over lunges and parrying and all of that other Proper Stuff, Mrs Bennet has always found, and a parasol is far more like a stick than a sword.

Darcy advances, feints once, and lunges—and Mrs Bennet opens his parasol.

"What!" Darcy cries, into a wide expanse of laced canopy.

"What indeed!" Mrs Bennet agrees. He shuts his brolly as swiftly as it opened, and *thwaps!* Darcy soundly about his squared shoulders.

"Egads!" Darcy cries, and raises Jane's parasol; Mrs Bennet seizes it with his free hand—try *that* with a sword!—and thwaps him again, much harder. "O! Alas!"

"Alas indeed—for you!" Mrs Bennet shoves Darcy's sword-parasol aside, that he might have enough room to dart in close and seize him around his grand staglike neck, just as Mrs Bennet used to seize his brother and sister when they were being particularly odious little geese.

Young Darcy is stronger by far than Mr Gardiner is even now. But all the little Gardiners had been squirmier and cannier and a great deal more prone to biting—it is no work at all to have him locked firmly by the neck under Mrs Bennet's free arm, well-placed for a sound walloping.

And wallop him Mrs Bennet does! The unfortunate Darcy must not have had siblings close enough in age to serve as playmates—if he had, they failed him dreadfully. Mrs Phillips would by now be chewing Mrs Bennet's arms bloody, and Mr Gardiner kicking his shins to sorry bits; Darcy only squeals most piteously and tries to swat at the back of his legs with Jane's brolly. Doesn't he know that his angle is terrible for it? He would be much better served with his fists, but he does not try for his fists.

Mrs Bennet almost has pity—but then he remembers how his darling Lizzy's face had fallen at Darcy's cruel words, and how the poor girl straightened and tried at once to play it off, and all pity vanishes.

His angle is superb. He thumps the young lout as though he were Mrs Hill beating the dust out of the hallway carpet with a slipper, and perhaps he ought to have demanded to duel with slippers—a slipper would be stouter by far than this unfortunate parasol, which is splintering already in his hand.

"Fiddlesticks!" Mrs Bennet cries, and indeed his parasol is now quite fiddly to hold, and little more than a handful of sticks. "How vexing! See! Now we no longer match. But fear not, good sir, I shall have use of this one since you do not, and break it again upon your bottom until we are once more Twinly Armed."

He casts his broken brolly aside and snatches Jane's from Darcy's feebly waving hand.

"O mercy," Darcy cries. "Enough, I beg you!"

"O mercy," the agreeable Mr Bingley echoes, "I beg you cease, sir, for I'm sure he is most terribly sorry!"

"Well," says Mrs Bennet, with immense magnanimity, "I suppose if he is." He should not like to thump *too* soundly a bosom friend of the man who must surely be Jane's future husband—and it would be rather a shame to ruin a second parasol.

Darcy looks nothing at all like a stag when Mrs Bennet releases him. He totters and trembles, as spindly-legged and sorry-looking as a fawn abandoned in the rain. "Pardon! Begging pardon," cries he, as he trips his way to Lizzy to bow low before her; he even kisses her hand. "The beautifulest young lady in this room you surely are—I have seen none lovelier. Will you honour me with a dance?"

"What! Dance? Are you daft?" Lizzy demands as she grabs him by the collar and hauls him upright. "'Tis a hot cup of tea with lemon and a lie-down you need, not a dance!"

She shakes her head, looking tremendously put-upon even as she drags him away. "Come—I suppose we must find you a soft settee, for these chairs will be unkind to your derrière."

"An angel from the heavens!" Darcy cries, and follows like a lamb. Jane and the agreeable Mr Bingley trail along after, leaving Mrs Bennet to the crowd of ——shire gentlemen who thump him on the back and say wonderful things like *Good sport, old chap!* and *Splendid! Quite splendid!*

Mrs Bennet feels quite splendid indeed—he feels like a grand prancing stag himself, ready to strut about. He shall dance. He *must* dance; he will be *he* for just a while longer.

And there is the wonderfully devious Charlotte Lucas standing alone; the second-rate gent is nowhere to be seen. For the better: surely this is too clever and cunning a girl to be wasted on second-rate gents, or left to the decrepitude of spinsterhood.

"Dear girl," Mrs Bennet cries, "come, come! Let us dance!"

He has a most splendid idea.

"This is terribly irregular," her brother Gardiner says cheerfully—the horrible, wonderful little goose. "But I suppose that's quite ordinary for *you*, Fanny. I have the marriage offer drawn up exactly as you asked."

"I thank you," Charlotte says politely to him. "And, er—you don't find this *too* odd, I hope?"

"I've known my sister all my life," Mr Gardiner replies. "Therefore—no, and of course I approve of anything that helps keep her secret. Meanwhile: if you'd like a look for yourself, Miss Lucas, this settles enough on you that you'll be quite comfortably independent when my dear sister passes. As much as I hate to think of it! But some things must be prepared for. I hope your Mamma and Papa will find this sufficient?"

"They should be quite relieved for any offer at all, I fear," replies she, "but I will speak well of this to them on our return—and I thank you again for your kind offer of an escort to Hertfordshire. *Mr* Bennet, forgive my trespass, but I overheard your saying that Jane will travel also with us?"

"Indeed she shall!" Mrs Bennet cries, in tremendous, renewed excitement. "Mrs Phillips sent word that the agreeable Mr Bingley has secured his uncouth friend within Longbourn for the convalescence of his sore derrière; I have most cunningly arranged for Jane to assist in the nursing as mark of our forgiveness. How excited the agreeable Mr Bingley was to see her again, even in his letter! You are stepmother-to-be; I beg you deliver her safe to Longbourn in my stead."

"It will be my great honour, husband mine," says the indissoluble Charlotte, and all of Mrs Bennet thrills, unfathomably, at that. "But if I may—Lizzy ought to go to Longbourn, too. It is, ah, a hunch."

"If you feel so, so she shall," Mrs Bennet declares. She will be nothing like *her* late husband; she will pay heed to the cunning of her new wife.

Husband! She is to be a husband!

This is surely a splendid idea.

May Barros

GAZEBO IN THE RAIN

This art piece was inspired by the _Pride and Prejudice_ (2005) movie, Darcy's first confession is a moment that has stuck to me through the years, and I wanted to reimagine that scene as a queer moment of vulnerability.

TAGS

age difference, alcohol use (casual), alternate universe, break-up, college, coming out, dead-naming, family, first person point of view, fraternity/sorority, fraught family dynamic, gender dysphoria, infidelity, m/nb, misgendering, modern, naive, non-binary, predatory behavior toward a minor, present tense, secret relationship, siblings, student (college), student (high school), teenager, transphobia, underage drinking

INSPIRATION

I've had ideas about a modern *Pride and Prejudice* adaptation floating around in my head for a while, and one aspect that has really fascinated me has been how to adapt Lydia's "scandal." I think Austen judged Lydia too harshly—Lydia is quite young in *Pride and Prejudice*, and George Wickham takes advantage of her. *The Lizzie Bennet Diaries* were brilliant in their adaptation of this part of the narrative into a story of relationship abuse and revenge porn. But I wanted to put my own spin on it. What if the youngest Bennet is trans, and George (who was always a creep) turns out to be a transphobe?

Another super interesting (and often overlooked) part of *Pride and Prejudice* is the relationships within the Bennet family, especially among the sisters. It's not just a romance! While I didn't have room in a short story to explore a lot of interpersonal relationships, and definitely couldn't have fit in all five siblings, I wanted to pay attention to the dynamic between Lyd and Lizzy. While Elizabeth is not terribly supportive of Lydia in Austen's original, I think there's a lot of potential for solidarity and healing in that relationship.

LYD, NOT LYDIA

I DON'T WANT to be here. But 'cause my only other option is to talk to my mom, I'm sitting in the driver's seat stewing about how I wound up in this position, on the way to visit my nerdy, obnoxiously straightlaced sister Lizzy at college.

Usually, I'm thrilled to get out of my tiny hometown. My parents call it "quaint," "charming," and "sleepy," but to me it's backward, bigoted, and boring—not the kind of place any teenager wants to live, let alone a teenager like me. I'm definitely queer, and I've started to get the sense that the term "girl" doesn't fit me, though I'm still trying to figure out which labels and pronouns *do* fit. For the past couple of years especially, I've jumped at the rare chances I've gotten to skip town.

But this is different. I recently got my learner's permit, so Mom is making me practice driving the family car the full two-hour trip to the nearest state university, where Lizzy is in her first semester. I'm not comfortable behind the wheel yet, so it's stressful even though I'm driving in a straight line through cornfields.

And the destination holds basically no appeal. Lizzy and I have clashed for as long as I can remember, so it's not like I want to visit her. But I'm currently failing math, and my parents decided that getting a taste of college life might motivate me to get my GPA up. I doubt it, and I'm not looking forward to a weekend of sleeping on my sister's floor, but my parents had one of their rare moments of agreement when Mom suggested I stay with Lizzy for the weekend, so here I am.

Finally, we reach the freeway exit for the school, and I manage to navigate us to Lizzy's dorm building, Longbourn, so I can at least turn the car off and get out and stretch. I don't think I adjusted the seat far enough forward; my right leg is tired and sore from stretching for the pedals all the way here. Mom calls Lizzy to come let us in, and a couple minutes later, my sister is ushering us inside.

Lizzy shows us to the dorm she's sharing with her childhood BFF Charlotte, and Mom coos over how cute the room is. (It looks pretty normal to me, but apparently the musical posters and twinkle lights make it *perfect* in Mom's eyes.) Then she frets over whether Lizzy is eating enough and sleeping well and getting good grades in her classes (which she is, of course).

After about half an hour, Mom finally looks my way, paying attention to me for the first time since we reached the dorm, and tells me to make sure to catch up on homework this weekend.

Then she leaves, and it's just Lizzy and me in the dorm.

"I can't believe Mom is sticking me with you for a whole weekend," Lizzy grumbles as soon as the door closes.

"That makes two of us," I say, kicking at my duffel bag. "Are there any good parties this weekend?"

"Oh my *God*, Lydia," Lizzy groans, putting her face in her hands.

"I've *told* you, I'm going by Lyd now," I snap, running my fingers through my lavender-dyed pixie cut to remind myself of the ways I've recently changed my appearance to feel more at home in my body. "And I suppose you wouldn't know about good parties, seeing as you're such a boring goody two-shoes."

"I'm not boring. I'm in college to get an education, and I care about my future. There's a difference."

"I'm pretty sure that's the literal definition of being boring."

Lizzy rolls her eyes and then says, "Well, anyway, going to college parties as a woman significantly increases your odds of getting sexually assaulted. I'd just rather not."

"That sounds super victim-blame-y," I point out.

"It is not blaming the victim to make choices to *keep myself safe*," Lizzy argues.

I'm trying to think up a good counterargument when my stomach growls loudly, reminding me of how long it's been since I ate lunch. "Look, can we just get dinner?"

Lizzy sighs and grabs her purse. "Yeah, let's eat."

We don't talk much on the walk to the dining hall or during dinner. On the way back to Longbourn, though, we pass a house with thumping, bass-heavy music spilling into the street as people stream in and out and congregate on the porch.

"Lizzy! Is that a party? Can we go?" I ask.

"No," says Lizzy. "We're not going to a party, and even if we were, we would not be going to the Mu Rho Tau frat. They suck."

The song changes to one I recognize, and I want to run inside and join the dancing, but I'd prefer to be wearing better clothes and makeup if I were to crash a party, especially a college party. "But it looks so much *fun*!" I whine anyway.

"No," Lizzy repeats. "That's where George Wickham lives. We are not going."

"Come on," I say. "You're going to let your ridiculous rivalry keep us from an awesome party?"

Lizzy huffs. "It's not a rivalry, and it's not ridiculous. George is a bad person."

"Because he copied *one paper* from you," I grumble.

"Plagiarism is a serious problem! And if you don't understand that, maybe Mom and Dad are right about your chances of getting into college."

Now I'm upset for real. Screw my clothes and makeup. I turn back to the frat house and speed-walk in its direction, slipping inside with a gaggle of girls wearing strappy dresses and heels. I'm worried I'll stand out with my T-shirt, jeans, and sneakers, but I get in fine. I can hear Lizzy following me, but I don't turn around.

Inside the house, the air is hot and humid, smelling of sweat and alcohol. I beeline for the nearest keg and grab a solo cup. The beer (or whatever it is) tastes gross—I've only tried alcohol a few times before, all after sneaking out last summer, and I definitely haven't gotten used to the taste yet. I drink it anyway, keeping my cup in my hand as I move to the music.

Lizzy is arguing with someone at the door.

It's not long before a guy with curly brown hair and a tight T-shirt approaches me and starts dancing with me, inching closer until we're moving in tandem.

"Hey," he says after a minute or so. "I haven't seen you around before. Are you a freshman?"

"I'm just visiting," I say, his question surprising the truth out of me even though I realize immediately that I should have lied and said I was older.

"Even better," he murmurs. He reaches out and puts his hands on my hips, pulling me closer to him. "Do you have any idea how hot you are?"

I don't know how to answer that, but I want him to keep dancing with me, looking at me with that hunger in his eyes, so I reply, "Do you have any idea how hot *you* are?"

The guy smirks and opens his mouth to say something, but then Lizzy storms over and grabs my arm. "Lyd, we're *leaving*."

The guy and I both stop dancing, but rather than cutting his losses and getting away from Lizzy, the guy puts an arm around my shoulders, anchoring me in place while my sister tries to drag me bodily to the door. "Don't be like that, Lizzy," he says.

"This is none of your business, George," Lizzy snaps. "Get away from my sister."

I suppress the urge to wince at the word "sister." I'm not sure I'm trans, but I'm pretty uncomfortable with most feminine descriptors these days.

"You should let people make their own decisions," George says to Lizzy. Looking at me, he adds, "Do you want to go with Lizzy, or do you want to stay?"

"I want to stay," I say.

"Lyd, oh my God," Lizzy groans.

"What a compelling argument," I reply, proud of myself for sounding more put-together and adult than Lizzy does.

"You know what? Fine," says Lizzy. "Stay at this gross frat party with these terrible people and let something awful happen to you. I don't care." She turns and stomps out.

George and I watch Lizzie leave, but as soon as she's out of sight, we turn back to each other and get back to dancing.

"So you're Lizzy's sister, huh?" George asks.

"Unfortunately," I say, once again forcing myself not to react to the word "sister."

"Yeah, I wouldn't want to be related to her either," George agrees. "Especially because if I were it'd be pretty gross of me to do this." He slides a hand into my hair, leans down, and kisses me.

Oh, hell yes. I've been wanting a first kiss for a couple of years now, but I live in a tiny town where I've known my entire grade since kindergarten. I haven't been enthusiastic about kissing anyone at my high school. But this? A first kiss at a college party, with a guy who just stood up for me to Lizzy? Bring it on.

George's lips open and close against mine, and then he licks into my mouth, lighting up nerve endings I hadn't realized I had. I kiss back eagerly, my excitement stronger than my fear of messing up. Our tongues tangle, and I never want this to end.

Someone stumbles into me, pushing me into George, and our teeth knock together. George steadies me with a hand splayed on my back as he separates his face from mine and asks, "Do you wanna take this upstairs?"

"Uh…what does that involve?" I ask. My brain is still coming back online from all the kissing, but I'm vaguely aware that I only had my first kiss a couple minutes ago; I'm not ready for sex.

"Whatever you want," George says, rubbing his hand up and down my back. "I won't rush you."

I smile at him. "All right."

George leads me through the crowd in the living room, up the stairs, and through the second door on the left, which he unlocks with a key from his pocket. He doesn't turn the light on, so the room is dark other than the glow from the streetlight outside. The heavy bass of the music from downstairs penetrates the floor and thuds through the room. George locks the door behind us, drops down onto the bed, and asks, "Sit with me?"

I join him. I'm surprised by how hard the mattress is.

He turns toward me, putting his near arm around my waist and his other hand in my hair. "Cool to keep kissing?"

"Yep."

We kiss for a while, eventually lying down on the bed on top of the covers. It feels so good to be here, to be kissed, to be wanted. I want it to last forever—and not just because this is infinitely better than trying to sleep on Lizzy's floor. At some point, though, we're interrupted by pounding on the door.

"Not the bathroom!" George calls.

"What are you doing to my sister, you pervert?" comes Lizzy's shrill voice from the other side of the door.

"Shit," George hisses. Then he grabs his phone, unlocks it, and hands it to me, open to the contacts screen. "Do you wanna give me your number?" he whispers. Without waiting for an answer, he stands, adjusts his pants, and goes to open the door.

I've just finished adding myself to George's contacts—as Lyd, not Lydia—when Lizzy shoves past George and rushes to the bed. "Are you all right?"

"I'm fine," I say.

"Are you sure?" Lizzy asks, sounding frantic.

"Relax, Lizzy," says George. "We were just making out. We never even took our clothes off. You can ask Lyd if you don't believe me."

"Is that true?" Lizzy's been looking at me this whole time, ignoring George.

"Yeah," I reply, sitting up. "I'm totally fine."

Lizzy lets out a breath and then turns to George. "You know she's fifteen, right? And that sixteen is the age of consent here?"

I roll my eyes. "I'll be sixteen in a few months. It's no big deal."

Lizzy huffs, shakes her head, stands, and pulls me to my feet. "We're leaving."

As Lizzy drags me from the room, I look back at George, but it's too dark to see his face well.

"I've been texting and calling you for the past hour!" Lizzy seethes as she tows me outside.

"I was *fine*," I reiterate.

"How was I supposed to know that?"

"Stop being such a nervous mother hen and let me live a little!"

"I'm trying to protect you!"

"Why?" I demand. "You clearly can't stand me, and you're dragging me away from someone who actually likes me!"

Lizzy's head whips toward me. "What does George like about you? Have you even had a conversation?"

"Well, no, but still. Unlike you, at least he doesn't hate me."

"I don't hate you!"

"Right." I cross my arms.

We don't talk again on the way back to Longbourn. When we get there, I pull out my phone. In addition to a bunch of missed calls and texts from Lizzy, I have one text from a number that's not in my contacts.

Lizzy makes me study most of Saturday; it's not worth the drama it would cause if I were to sneak off to another party, so I let Lizzy and Charlotte drag me to an open mic in the evening. It's totally boring and nerdy, but whatever. George and I exchange texts throughout the day, which is surprising but nice. I would have thought he wouldn't want anything more to do with me after being confronted with an angry Lizzy, but he seems much more interested in me than I expected.

Mom picks me up after lunch on Sunday, and after we get home, I keep texting George, and he keeps replying. We talk about my hometown and his frat and both of our schools, and we complain about Lizzy. We don't talk about gender, but I keep googling terms like "nonbinary," "genderqueer," "genderfluid," and "agender," and I have a whole bunch of tabs open on my phone from different queer advocacy sites and blogs.

After a couple weeks, on a night when I'm feeling brave (I may have stolen a bit of my parents' vodka), in the middle of a text conversation with George, I ask,

I wince. I want to date him. I want to kiss him again. I want someone to want me the way he clearly does. I like the way he listens to me, and I miss the way kissed me and stood up for me to Lizzy. But I don't think I want to be anyone's girlfriend.

I'll worry about the gender stuff later.

Later comes sooner than I want it to. The next week, I fail a chemistry test, and my parents give me a lecture about what they expect from any daughter of theirs. The whole thing is gendered, peppered with phrases like "We know you're a smart girl" and "Society will try to sell you a lot of messages about how girls can't be good at math and science, but…" and such, and by the end of it I'm sobbing uncontrollably. Luckily, this means I can't talk, so I don't out myself to my parents before I'm ready, and they assume I'm crying because they're mad at me or because of my grades, not because I wish they'd stop talking about me with feminine language. I let them make their assumptions, and as soon as they're done talking, I run to my room and start looking up binders and pride flags on my phone. I don't buy anything, but I keep the tabs open.

My parents send me to visit Lizzy again the following weekend. It's another boring, stressful drive with Mom, but I don't fight it this time because it means I get to see George. Lizzy tried to persuade my parents not to send me 'cause she has a big group project due on Monday, but my parents wanted me to go, and with me on their side for once, it was three against one, so here I am.

For how glad he's seemed to be texting me for the past few weeks, George honestly hasn't seemed thrilled that I'm coming to visit. He tells me he has "other plans" on Friday night but suggests we meet up on Saturday afternoon at a coffee shop called Greta's Green Mug within walking distance of campus. I'd rather see him right away, but I can't force that to happen, so I agree to his café plan. Lizzy makes me study with her on Friday night, which is super annoying—who studies on a Friday night?—but I do actually get some schoolwork done. It's not like I have anything better to do 'cause George isn't even texting me back.

On Saturday, I'm trying to think of how to get away from Lizzy to meet up with George when Lizzy announces she'll be in the library all afternoon researching with her group. When Lizzy goes to the library, I leave Longbourn, too, following the walking directions my maps app provides to get me to Greta's.

I don't arrive early, but I've been there for ten minutes and have already received my fancy coffee when George shows up.

"Lyd!" he says when he spots me sitting near the door. His grin melts my insides, and my annoyance at his lateness evaporates. "Good to see you! Sorry I'm late. Oh, did you get your coffee already? I was gonna buy it."

I smile and shake my head. "It's fine."

"Aw, come on, what kind of gentleman would I be if I didn't even buy my girlfriend coffee on a date?"

I hadn't planned on coming out to him—I hadn't planned on coming out to anyone yet. The idea of telling George feels both more comfortable and more fraught than telling anyone else; we're so at ease with each other, but also gender is so relevant in relationships—and I can't keep from flinching this time when he calls me his girlfriend.

"What's up?" George asks, taking the seat opposite me instead of continuing to hover near the line to order.

"Can I tell you something?" I can barely get my voice above a whisper.

"Of course," he says.

"I'm not a girl," I whisper.

George reels back. "What do you mean, you're not a girl?" he demands, voice loud. "Of course you're a girl! Unless—are you saying you've been a dude this whole time? Like, do you have a dick?"

"I don't—shh, can you please not yell that? I don't have a dick. I just—have you heard the term 'nonbinary'?"

George rolls his eyes. "What a load of bull. No matter what those snowflakes want to think, guys are guys and chicks are chicks. I'm a dude. You're a girl. Simple."

"But that's what I'm saying—I'm not a girl," I repeat.

"That's ridiculous. Is this why your hair is short? Because it's not going to fool anyone," George says. "You've got the tits. You've got the hips. It's pretty obvious what you are."

I realize two things at once: first, I'm not going to get through to George no matter how hard I try, and second, I'm about to cry and I should really get out of here before that happens. I stand, leaving my drink on the table, and flee the coffee shop. George shouts, "Fuck you, you said you wanted to be my girlfriend!" just as the door slams shut behind me.

I'm sobbing before I reach the first intersection, and I keep crying all the way back to campus. At times my tears are so heavy that it's hard to see my phone screen displaying the route. I'm most of the way back before it occurs to me that I don't have anywhere to go. I'd need a keycard to get into Longbourn, and I'm pretty sure most of the other buildings on campus are locked as well. I don't remember Lizzy needing her keycard to access the library when we studied there last night, but I'm pretty sure she did need it to get into the dining hall. I don't want to go to the library, especially 'cause Lizzy is there right now, but it's too cold to stay outside, and I can't think of anywhere else I'm sure will be unlocked, so I don't have much choice.

I head to the library and beeline for the bathroom as soon as I get inside. I hate having to pick men's or women's, but I can't do anything about that right now, and I know I'll get fewer weird looks if I'm in the women's room, so that's where I go. I'm cleaning myself up at the sink—still crying, but less—when Lizzy exits a stall and does a double-take as soon as she sees me.

"*Lyd?*"

"Hey," I reply dully.

"What's going on?"

I shrug. "Don't you have a group project to do?"

Lizzy unfreezes, walks to the sink, and starts washing her hands. "Yeah, but that can wait. What happened?"

I sigh and run a hand through my pixie cut. I don't want to talk to Lizzy about this. I want to talk to George. Except—right. George. He's the reason I'm crying in the first place. "It's kind of a long story."

"Are you okay?"

"I will be," I say with more confidence than I feel. "I'm not injured."

"Okay, those are good things," Lizzy says, grabbing a couple paper towels and drying her hands. "But seriously, please, can you tell me more than that?"

I try to think of where to start and how to boil down the story to its most important parts. After a few seconds, I come up with: "I've been dating George Wickham, and I just came out to him as nonbinary, and it went—uh. Badly."

Lizzy's face does several things, one right after the other, a mess of wide eyes and frowns before settling on a soft expression that I've never seen from her before. "Oh, Lyd."

Someone enters the bathroom and gives us a curious look on their way to a stall. Lizzy and I make eye contact and then both head for the door. Once we're out of the bathroom, Lizzy continues, "I'll tell my groupmates that I need to take a break. Will you wait for me?"

"Sure," I say. It's not like I have better options.

Lizzy speed-walks toward a table where a few other students are sitting, plants her hands on it, and says something that I'm too far away to hear. The other students nod, and then Lizzy's speed-walking back to me, now carrying a backpack. "Let's go back to Longbourn," she says when she reaches me.

"All right."

We're mostly silent for the few minutes it takes to get from the library to Lizzy's dorm. She doesn't ask me anything, and when we get to the room, she takes the desk chair and leaves the chair that's actually comfortable for me. Only when we're settled does she finally speak.

"Do you want to start with the 'nonbinary' part or the 'dating George' part?" Both her tone and the question itself are far kinder than I'm used to from her.

"Um," I say, and my voice breaks. "I guess…maybe the nonbinary part?" I know Lizzy hates George, so I'm pretty sure she's going to judge me for dating him even though she's being nice right now. But she might be okay on the gender front.

"All right," says Lizzy. "I want to say up-front that I support you. Nonbinary identities are real and valid, and you *are* valid."

"Says the person who's literally never nice to me," I scoff.

Lizzy opens her mouth to reply and then shuts it again. After a second, she says, "You know, that's fair. I'm sorry."

I stare at her. "Who are you and what have you done with my sister?"

Lizzy's quiet for a few seconds, and then she says, "I think the last time I saw you cry, you were eleven. The past few years, you've just been all tough, all the time, always about to pick a fight. I'm not blaming you—I'm older, and I could've done better—but there hasn't been a lot of, like, real emotion to grab onto from you, either."

I think about it. "Yeah, I guess," I allow.

"So, you're nonbinary. Who are you out to? Do you want me to use different pronouns for you?"

"I'm only out to you and George," I say. "Well, and whoever George tells, I guess."

Lizzy leans forward, bracing her elbows on her knees. "Oh, this was *early*-early. For you."

"Yeah. So I'm not ready to switch pronouns yet."

"Right. That makes sense." She takes a deep breath. "So, uh. You and George?"

"We swapped numbers the night of the party," I explain. "And we've been texting a lot since then. It was really nice, until today. I felt like he understood me. And he definitely seemed to like me better than anyone else I know."

"I'm sorry," says Lizzy, leaning forward farther and taking both of my hands in both of hers. "It sucks that you felt so disliked and misunderstood. I'm sorry that so many people in your life haven't been good to you, and I'm sorry for my part in that specifically."

"Thanks," I say, feeling myself tear up again. "I thought things were going well. But today we went to get coffee and he called me his girlfriend and I just couldn't handle it, so I came out to him, and he said some transphobic stuff, and then I left."

"That bastard."

I nod. "Yeah."

"Well, the transphobia, yes. But also…did you know he's been dating this girl Alicia for the past few weeks?"

"What? No."

"I'm sorry, but yes. They've been *really* obvious about it."

"Fuck," I say.

"Yeah."

"That bastard," I agree.

"I'm really sorry, Lyd."

"Thanks."

"You know you can do better, right?"

I roll my eyes. "Yeah, right."

"You really don't think you can do better than a transphobe who cheats on you?"

I shrug. "It was flattering that a college guy would be into me. No one's ever shown interest before."

"Okay, two things," says Lizzy. "First of all, a college guy who's into high school sopho-mores is probably a creep. And secondly, you're really young. You have so much life ahead of you."

"Lizzy, you're literally three years older than I am."

"Which is twenty percent of your life. But yeah, we're both young. And that means what we've experienced in our love lives so far is not everything we'll ever experience. Sure, you don't know that anyone other than George has had a crush on you, but that doesn't mean that no one else *has* liked you, and even if no one else has liked you, that can change—maybe next month, maybe next year, maybe next decade. But like, what you've experienced in fifteen years in a tiny town is not all that's out there for you."

"I guess."

"That's probably a hard thing to feel right now," Lizzy says. "I'm really sorry about today. How can I support you better going forward?"

"Um…" I try to think, but my brain feels waterlogged from all the crying. "Can I get back to you on that? I'd ask you to argue with me less, but I think the bickering was on both of us."

"Of course you can get back to me on that. And yeah, I think we were both picking fights. I'll try to do less of that now."

"Thanks. For, like, caring."

"Literally the least I could do," Lizzy says. "Do you want me to text my group and tell them to finish without me, or would you be okay if I went back to the library?"

"You can go back. I need some Netflix time. Or maybe a nap."

"All right," says Lizzy, "but text me if you need anything. I'll put my phone on vibrate and keep it where I can feel it. I love you, Lyd, okay?"

I smile, even though I can also feel tears in my eyes again. "I love you too."

Lizzy's hardly out the door before I start crying again, but I feel a lot less empty than I did earlier. I'll be okay, even though I'm not right now.

mcdad arts

FOLLIES AND NONSENSE

I've always been inspired to show Caroline and Jane in such an intimate setting after reading that Jane was stuck at the Bingley estate after being soaked in the rain. Having Caroline visit Jane to confess that her ill behavior toward Jane was because she's actually in love with her and that her desire for Jane not to wed her brother was due to her feelings really sat with me; it felt more interesting and compelling than Caroline's poor attitude toward Jane per the original novel.

TAGS

alternate universe, engineer, f/f, first kiss, fluff, historical with technology, mecha, meet cute, past tense, steampunk, third person limited point of view

INSPIRATION

Mary Bennett intrigued me from my first reading of *Pride and Prejudice*. Of the three younger Bennet sisters, she seemed the most unfairly maligned. Her great sin was having interests and talking about them, something that Lizzie is rewarded for as the book unwinds. But Mary is not as naturally magnetic or witty as Lizzie and is thus consigned to the role of The Bore. I wanted to give her a chance to shine.

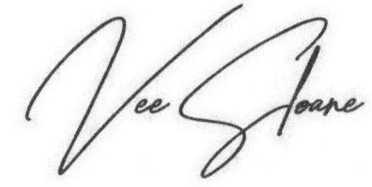

THE IRON ROSE

THE MYTH OF Pemberley had a shape in Mary's mind like a clenched fist. She had imagined it a fortress of technological wonders, but instead it seemed as mundane as home, if five times as large. Two complete searches of her room had failed to turn up a single button, lever, or toggle.

"You're the only person in the world disappointed by the most gorgeous estate in England," Kitty huffed.

"You have your own room," Mary reminded her, not looking up from the blueprints she'd carried in her lap all the way from home so they wouldn't get wrinkled. There was an elegance to them that only the Iron Rose could manage. How enchanting it was that someone could make the internal workings so concise and neat!

"You've been in here all morning!" Kitty threw herself on the bed. "Just because Mamma lets you tinker endlessly doesn't mean that you can get away with it here, you know. People will talk if you're absent."

Mary made a note in the margins. "Let them talk if that's the most interesting thing they have to speak about."

"You know that's not fair," Kitty groaned. "I want to get married! If I have a sister who is always disappearing, or worse, is known to have such an…undesirable hobby, then I'll be a spinster forever!"

It was best to ignore Kitty when she was like this. Eventually, her lecturing became as inconsequential as the twittering of the birds outside the window. Mary wasn't sure when Kitty left, only that when a maid fetched Mary for tea, she was gone.

Lizzy presided over the sisters-only tea, entirely the lady of the house with nothing left of the young girl Mary remembered. The teasing sarcasm, once her hallmark, was replaced with a knowing twinkle in her eye.

"It's so good to have you both here," Lizzy said as she poured the tea. "I'm sorry Miss Georgiana can't join us today. I know you'd both adore her, but she's been poorly as of late."

Mary murmured, on script, "I'm sorry to hear that." Her eyes were on the tracks cleverly carved into the floor and nearly hidden by the carpet. Here was the promised technological supremacy of Pemberley! The tracks led out into the hall and, in theory, might extend all the way to the kitchens. She heard the distant rumble of a mech, and sat up straighter to catch a glimpse.

"I'm sure she'll be well soon," Lizzy continued, "and you'll be fast friends. In the meantime, I'm having every young person in a twenty-mile radius at dinner tomorrow night."

"Fantastic!" Kitty clapped her hands once in excitement.

At last, an automaton wheeled in to serve biscuits. It wobbled on its tracks, and when it came to their table, it let out a terrible wheeze, stumbling and spilling the biscuits from its porcelain tray.

"Oh, you poor thing!" Mary cried before she could stop herself. She heard Kitty's protest as, heedless of her gown, she got down on her knees to look at the mech. "One of the casters is entirely loose. Who let it get into such a state?"

Mary touched the axle and reached for her tools, only to recall they were in her room.

"Our mechanic hasn't been in recently," Lizzy said with a hint of amusement that made Mary's neck burn. "It's one of a kind and a bit of a favorite with us. If you wish to fix it, I'll have to ask Mr. Darcy."

"I do wish that. Such a fine piece shouldn't be left to rumble itself to bits. It's easily worth as much as all of the books in the library, and you wouldn't let those molder." She looked up from the mech to meet Lizzy's eyes with a frown. "Just because a thing isn't alive doesn't mean it isn't doing its best to serve."

"There's no need to lecture, dear sister," Lizzy chided. "It wasn't malicious negligence."

Mary sat back down as gracefully as she could manage, feeling a bit lectured herself. Her fingers were smeared with grease, and she didn't dare touch Lizzy's pretty china with them. Kitty wouldn't even look at her.

This visit was off to a perfect start.

The next morning, she was conscripted into helping Kitty prepare for the afternoon walk that would precipitate the promised youthful dinner.

"It's to put us both on the market," Mary said darkly as she mended a tiny tear in Kitty's dress. She always had the neatest hand with mending, even if she couldn't dress a bonnet for all the ribbon in town. "Mamma wants us out of the house, I'm certain."

"Very much in line with my hopes." Kitty eyed her, pausing in pulling on her gloves. "Or do you enjoy growing moss while everyone else grows up?"

"I'll have a quiet afternoon by myself, then be ready for dinner," Mary said flatly, her eyes drifting to the Iron Rose's schematics.

Despite that declaration and a trip down to the library after Kitty's departure, she barely managed to be alone with the books for a handful of minutes. Just as she was getting to an interesting part of a text the Iron Rose had frequently cited, Mr. Darcy appeared like a wraith.

"Miss Bennet?"

She had been doing nothing wrong, but felt caught out nonetheless.

He continued, "My dear wife suggested you might be interested in seeing the workshop."

"I'd like that," Mary managed, flustered.

Mr. Darcy turned on his heel, expecting her to follow. She did.

"You're interested in mechanicals," Mr. Darcy said abruptly.

"Yes," Mary replied. "I think they're foundational to modern society, and we don't give them nearly enough attention. And—" She stopped herself.

"Go on," he said in that bland tone. "Tell me about the mechanicals and society."

Mary knotted her hands behind her back, heart thumping in her chest. "It seems to me that these machines make our lives a great deal easier. They free up time for servants to do more delicate tasks, relieve our horses, and work tirelessly. Most people see them as no more complex than furniture, instead of as something that takes labor and consideration to create. Each helpful tool represents hundreds of hours, and people often treat them as disposable—or worse, as annoyances—instead of as what they really are."

"And what are they really?"

The question plucked at the heart of her, at the thing that made her pour over schematics and create things by candlelight until her eyes ached.

"Art!" she cried. "I…apologize for my fervor."

They reached a staircase that Mary hadn't seen before. The rich smells of oil and hot metal rose to greet her as they descended into a wide space with neatly organized shelves and three long worktables, each with still more shelves beneath. On one of the worktables lay the mech with the loose caster. Someone had laid a length of fabric over its midsection, as if it were a human patient.

"You are welcome to come and go as you please, as long as everything goes back where it belongs," Mr. Darcy said.

What an array of materials! She never would have had access to these at home. Mary ghosted her hand over a series of bins: smoked glass, wire as fine as hair, and tiny bottles of enamel paint. "Theoretical amateur that I am, I'm sure I shouldn't."

"No one is working here just now. Enjoy being theoretical as much as you like." Mr. Darcy was already starting back up the stairs.

Mary's summer was not so dire or lost after all!

True, in the days that followed there was too much time spent socializing with people she barely knew. The dullness seeped into everything, robbing the world of its color. One sweet summer morning was particularly difficult, when she spotted some large automatons working in the far fields. No one else wanted to walk that far out to observe them, leaving her bereft as talk drifted aimlessly about her.

Between tea and dinner, though, there was a glorious bliss of hours in the neat workshop. Mary took over a table, and once she had fixed the poor broken mech, she merrily built the little dog automaton that the Iron Rose had so meticulously detailed.

Sometimes when she came down, there were bits out of place: a tool hung back on its hook when she'd left it out, or a stack of bolts on the other worktable where none had been before. She chalked it up to some curious servant.

One night while Mary was in bed, half planning her next project, half dozing, Kitty crept into her room. Startled, Mary lobbed a pillow at her; Kitty tossed it back, smacking Mary in the face, and got into the bed.

"Do you remember how Jane and Lizzy used to whisper to each other all night?" Kitty asked.

"They were loud about it," Mary groaned. "It was difficult to miss."

"Lydia and I used to whisper, too."

"I know."

Kitty fussed with the edge of her nightgown, curling and uncurling a piece of lace trim. "It's just—"

It took Mary a painfully long minute to figure out what was wanted…then a few more heartbeats to decide if she wanted to give it. Kitty was so small beside her, always so doll-like. But she wasn't a child any more than Mary was, and they had both witnessed the cruelty the world could turn on a woman who made mistakes—a woman who didn't confide in someone.

"Tell me about him, then."

Kitty wore herself out talking in circles about the two gentlemen she was trying to choose between and whether she should wait a few more weeks or give in as soon as she was asked lest the chance be snatched from her. Mary had little more to offer her than the etiquette books she'd memorized feverishly as a younger, more hopeful version of herself. Eventually, Kitty fell asleep, her breath a percussive wheeze against Mary's arm.

After listening to an hour of nonsense about men who were as interchangeable as cogs, Mary needed to ground herself in the firm reality of metal. Slipping from bed without waking Kitty, Mary made her way to the safety of the workshop.

She was brought up short at the top of the stairs—there were gaslights flickering, throwing shadows around the room!

Perhaps she should go alert someone, but her curiosity overpowered any sense of danger. With care, she eased the door at the top of the stairs closed behind her, then took each step on light feet.

There, at the workbench, was the mysterious other: a young woman, her brow furrowed beneath a lacy cap, bottom lip held between her teeth as she carefully glued down a wire with a tiny brush.

Mary had never met another woman who built mechs.

"Not yet, Fitz!" said this vision without looking up. "I'll go to bed soon. I just want to finish this."

"I—" Mary exhaled shakily. "Hello?"

The woman dropped her brush, looking up in wide-eyed alarm. Her eyes were the kind of deep brown that Mary had always admired—the inviting warmth of suede and leather waiting to be pulled over metal joints to soften them.

Recovering herself, the woman offered a small smile. "You must be Miss Bennet."

"And you must be—" Mary floundered, trying to think which young lady was unaccounted for, until the very obvious answer slapped her square in the face. "You can't be Miss Darcy."

"Can't I be?" Miss Darcy's smile went from polite to almost indecently large. "I've been wanting to introduce myself since you arrived, but I had a bout of some illness and my brother insisted I rest. Even Lizzy won't let me escape my rooms. I have to sneak away at night."

"That's terrible! Diligent work for a limited amount of time can be healing."

"Do you think so?" Miss Darcy blinked those lovely brown eyes at her. "Most people would say I shouldn't be down here at all. In any condition."

"Most people are fools. I think a lady's mech work should be as valued as her embroidery," Mary said firmly. "I hope you don't mind that I worked on your lovely fetch-and-carry mech. You must be the one who usually tends to him."

"I made him." Quiet pride lifted Miss Darcy's chin.

Mary stepped in a little closer. "Once I had his gears in his hand, I could tell he was finely made."

"That's very kind of you to say," Miss Darcy said. "That was one of my first functional efforts. I named him Mr. Butler. Not a particularly inventive name, I know."

"How old were you?" Mary asked, taking yet another step nearer. Now she could properly see the details of the work before her, and of her new acquaintance: there was a burn mark on the back of her hand and grease on her cuffs.

"Fifteen." Those keen eyes dimmed a little. "I was convalescing then, as well, from a different ailment."

"Fifteen! I only just finished a full mech this past summer, and it can't bend at all, let alone offer up a serving tray and bow! Did you have a tutor?" Mary asked. "I only had books, I'm afraid."

"Oh, it's the same for me!" Miss Darcy exclaimed. "Isn't it something? The things we can conjure from just words on a page."

"Imagine what we could do with a teacher," Mary said wistfully.

Miss Darcy laughed, and it was musical and not at all mocking. "A teacher, Miss Bennet? Look at what we can do without one!"

Mary clasped her hands together, delighted by Miss Darcy's show of fire. "It would be nice to at least speak with someone sometimes, though."

Miss Darcy ducked her head, voice softening. "Why can't we just speak with each other?"

"Why can't we, indeed!" Mary smiled the kind of smile that Kitty would scold her for. Too many teeth. "Would you like to see the project I recently finished? I subscribe to the Iron Rose's schematics, do you?"

"Oh, well—" Miss Darcy started, but Mary eagerly pressed on.

"They're truly extraordinary, but I enjoy tinkering a little with them. I like to think she'd approve!" Then she winced. How terribly rude of her to carry on and talk over someone!

Miss Darcy didn't seem to mind; she met Mary's enthusiasm with her own. "I'm sure they're excellent improvements!"

They spent a very happy hour in the still of the night. Mary showed off the little dog and the plans she had built it from.

"You haven't used the same circuitry," Miss Darcy said without glancing at the schematics. How much she must know to not need to refer to them!

Mary started explaining, and though she spoke far too quickly, it seemed that Miss Darcy understood every word. As Mary talked, Miss Darcy reached behind her and picked up a pair of goggles, fastening them around her head. Once settled into place, they comically magnified her eyes and pushed up the lace edging of her work bonnet. The sight made Mary feel as fond of her as she might one of her dearest, oldest friends.

"How lovely!" Miss Darcy remarked, leaning in closer to study the circuitry. "You've streamlined it all wonderfully. It's much more elegant now."

"I was just seeing what worked." Mary fiddled with the edge of the paper. "I'm sure the Iron Rose has thought of it before."

Miss Darcy nudged her gently with her shoulder. "I bet you could give the Iron Rose something to think about."

"Are you teasing?"

"Not even a little."

"But—"

A sound upstairs made them both freeze. "Georgie?" a voice called, and Miss Darcy winced, frantically shoving off her goggles.

"He can see the light under the door," she bemoaned. "I'm going to get in such trouble!"

Mary couldn't bear the idea of ending this night on a sour note. "Then you duck around that cabinet, and when he comes down here, I'll apologize for being out of place."

"Won't you get in trouble, too?"

"Go on," Mary insisted, though her stomach tightened at the thought of being scolded like a child. "I have it."

The door opened just as Miss Darcy tucked herself away, revealing Mr. Darcy silhouetted by candlelight.

"Miss Bennet!" he exclaimed. "What on earth are you doing?"

"I heard a noise!" she said, which sounded utterly stupid as soon as it left her mouth. "Kitty woke me. Then there was a *bang* and I just needed— I'm sorry."

"I see." Mr. Darcy's gaze flickered around the room. "Allow me to walk you back to your room if you have completed your investigations."

The air felt thick with her embarrassment as they walked in silence. It was only when they reached her door that he spoke again. "If you wish to work down there on a certain night, please alert my lady wife, so no one is alarmed by the noises."

Mary's brow furrowed. "Shouldn't I be getting a lecture on keeping good hours?"

"Time spent on the things we love are always good hours, Miss Bennet." He gave her a stately bow.

Then he was sweeping back down the hall. Bemused, she went inside and climbed back into bed.

Kitty stirred, yawned, and turned over to face her, blinking.

"I think Lizzy might have chosen the right husband," Mary whispered.

"Mmm." She yawned again and fell back asleep.

This time Mary followed her.

The next day flowed along; if Mr. Darcy had told anyone of her late-night escapade, they kept it to themselves.

That evening, Mary was allowed to descend to the workspace unimpeded, and to her great delight, the room was occupied once more.

"My brother relented!" Miss Darcy said, gesturing Mary into the stool beside her. "He realized I could do with some companionship and that he'd be wrong to deprive me all summer. I suppose that means I'll have to attend social events, though. Maybe it will be easier with a friend?"

"Surely it will!"

"I was thinking of a way to use your clever circuits in one of our newer serving mechs. Would you work with me on it?"

"Absolutely!" Mary took her seat, their knees pressing together as they bent their heads over the plans.

In the days that followed, Miss Darcy made appearances at the myriad picnics and dinners that Lizzy had planned in an endless parade. With them came tiresome young men who were tempted by the pretty Miss Darcy. Mary quickly despaired of ever having her friend's full attention on an outing.

The young men would ask such dull questions as: "Isn't the weather fine?"

Miss Darcy's face would go as blank as a doll's. "Most fine, sir."

"I made a perfect shot on this morning's hunt," another would say.

"Is that so?" Miss Darcy would murmur.

"What do you think of this latest fashion in sleeves?" another would drawl, and not listen to Miss Darcy's answer as the men prattled on.

Mary's only consolation was carrying a parasol to offer Miss Darcy a bit of shade, giving them an excuse to stay close together.

It was the pointlessness of it all that got to Mary. Today they were on the world's slowest stroll to some pond or another, which they'd admire for far too long, then return home with the same plodding slowness.

After a bare five minutes of peace, one gentleman fell into pace with them. "Miss Darcy, is that oil on your cuff? You shouldn't get so close to automatons, or you could get one of your pretty fingers caught up."

"Quite," Miss Darcy said coolly.

The man that Kitty had been walking with fell back to offer his opinion. "I always say that women and automatons don't mix."

"Nonsense!" Mary exclaimed. She heard Kitty's scandalized gasp but plowed on. "One might as well say that women and sewing don't mix!" She felt her face heating even as her surety hardened. "Circuitry is no more difficult than embroidery. Furthermore—"

"No woman could ever create a circuit worth using," he interrupted, looking to the other men for support. Several of them laughed nervously. "Why would they even want to?"

"Because it would be a far more productive use of one's time than speaking with an ignorant man!"

Mary closed the parasol with a huff, turned on her heel, and set back toward the house with a headful of steam. Likely she was about to say goodbye to her entire summer of freedom and be consigned to spinsterhood.

There were worse fates, she supposed. The righteous ire bubbling inside her was subsiding.

The sound of hurried footsteps turned her head. Behind her was Miss Darcy, her cheeks as flushed as Mary's felt.

"You're unbelievable!" Miss Darcy said, reaching her side.

It occurred to Mary that she might have made some trouble for her friend. "I'm sor—"

"Don't you dare apologize!" Miss Darcy scolded. "It's nothing I haven't wished to say, and more beside. If I had half your bravery!"

"I wasn't brave, just very angry," Mary admitted.

"You really made him sputter. What a buffoon!"

Mary gasped as if she were Kitty. "Miss Darcy!"

"Georgie," Miss Darcy corrected her in a whisper, as if the wind might steal away the nickname. "When it's only the two of us, can we be Mary and Georgie?"

Mary's poor heart fluttered wildly. "Yes. Yes, I'd like that," she managed to say. "Who was that fellow, anyway? I do hope Kitty doesn't actually marry him."

"Kitty will be doing no such thing," said Kitty from directly behind Mary, startling her. "What a show. What a drama!"

"I hate being the drama," Mary mumbled as her sister took up her other side, swirling her parasol in lazy circles over one shoulder. "Mamma will say I ruined everything."

"Ruin everything! It was the most exciting thing to happen all week!" Kitty linked her arm through Mary's. "Mr. Richards is terribly boring. I was only walking with him so that Sir Devinshire would pay me more mind than he did yesterday. He approached me after you flounced off and asked if he might pay me a call tomorrow. He said your defense of your ideals made him think better of our family! He thinks women should be allowed to speak their minds, can you imagine?!"

"How strange," Georgie said, so quietly and slyly that Mary almost laughed.

Her humor died before it reached her lips. All this fine camaraderie was about to end.

Kitty's droll commentary accompanied the rest of their stroll, and somehow she was able to get Mary laughing again even with the heaviness in her chest. The three of them were a merry party upon returning to the house, despite whatever consequences awaited them.

Kitty dashed off for dinner. Mary and Georgie shared a look and, in silent agreement, went down the stairs to the workshop.

Mary declared, "I shall be sent home tonight, so I must set every corner of this room to memory." She turned in a slow circle. "It's the loveliest place I've ever been."

"It's been so much lovelier with you in it," Georgie said wistfully. She kept reaching for a bit of wire or a tool, then letting her hand fall away, unsettled. "If this is to be our last evening together, may I show you something? It's a dear secret."

Mary took a step toward her. "Tell me."

Georgie clasped Mary's hand. Silently, she led her to the back of the workshop and, with a touch to a shelf, there was a faint hiss as a drawer opened.

"Clever!" Mary leaned in. "How does it work?"

"Focus, dear Mary." Georgie gave her hand a tiny squeeze. "Look inside."

Peering into the drawer, Mary spotted blueprints. Georgie's handwriting was all over them, but as she drew out the first one, she found it wholly familiar for other reasons.

It was the blueprint for the dog automaton: the Iron Rose's dog.

"You!" Mary turned to her. "You must've thought me very silly not to know!"

"How could you have! My brother helps me hide my identity, publishing things for me through a friend. If people knew it was me…I don't have the stomach for scandal." Georgie shook her head, one curl coming undone and falling out of her bonnet. "I wanted to tell you, very badly," Georgie went on, "because I wanted you to know that I meant it—that you could teach the Iron Rose a thing or two. You already have! That magic bit of circuitry alone will change how I make everything! Wouldn't it be grand to keep learning from each other? Think of all the marvelous things we could build!"

In the flickering light of the gas lamps, with that single dark curl touching her flushed cheek and the knowingness in those eyes, Georgie was utterly perfect. Mary, who had never so much as entertained the thought of kissing a man, could now do nothing except lean in and brush her lips against Georgie's. For a terrible moment, nothing happened, and death would have been kinder than the pain of waiting.

Then Georgie made a low, happy sound and kissed her back. Mary relaxed against her, undone by the tenderness of the moment.

Only footsteps overhead tore them apart—two servants talking about dinner. Mary and Georgie exchanged another peck before separating, and reluctantly departed to ready themselves.

Dinner itself was stilted, but no one commented on Mary's outburst. In fact, as the ladies adjourned to the drawing room to play whist, it seemed the evening would pass without incident.

Occasionally, Georgie would find Mary's eyes, and the electricity of their shared secret fizzed between them.

It was only as Mary stood to go to bed that Lizzy addressed her: "Darcy and I would like a word in the study."

Mary went quietly, planning her defenses, but the short, doomed walk was over before she could come up with something suitable. Mr. Darcy was standing behind a great desk, and Georgie sat in one chair on the other side, looking very small. Mary took the chair beside her. For once she felt she perfectly understood her mamma's nerves, and rather wished she too could throw a fit about them.

"Fitz and I were talking," Lizzy began, crossing to her husband and standing beside him, "after we heard about this afternoon's disruptions."

"You talked, I listened," said Mr. Darcy.

"Oh, hush," Lizzy huffed. "You'll make me seem rather less serious. This is meant to be a scolding."

"It is?" Mary asked, bewildered. A scolding seemed on a much lesser scale than banishment.

"Yes. That was very rude," Lizzy said with mock sternness. "You've been scolded. Do you feel scolded?"

"Yes?" Mary ventured, hope kindling in her.

"Good," Mr. Darcy said gravely. "We expect that you'll look very contrite should you ever encounter that donkey again."

"Yes, sir." Mary looked between them. "What's going on?"

"It seems to me, Miss Bennet," said Mr. Darcy, "that the best cure for my sister's ongoing health struggles has been having a lively companion. Since your arrival, the color has returned to her cheeks, her passion for her work has rekindled, and she speaks your name in every other sentence."

Mary glanced over at Georgie, who was blushing fiercely. She did look very healthy. Then again, Mary had never thought she looked poorly to begin with.

"I'm glad of it," Mary said with some caution.

Lizzy picked up where her husband had left off. "We were thinking of writing to Mamma about having you stay past the end of summer, as a companion for Miss Georgiana. For her health, of course. And maybe a little for the greater good."

Stay! Mary stared at her sister, wordless and overcome. To stay here with Georgiana! To make wonderful things together!

"Miss Bennet?" Georgie put her hand on Mary's arm.

"Yes!" Mary erupted. "Oh, yes please!"

This time she didn't care if Lizzy laughed at her. When Lizzy sat down right then and there to pen the letter, Mary felt as though some electric impulse was coursing through her, a frisson of potential. Beneath the desk, Georgie's pinkie caught Mary's own, a tiny point of connection that linked them together. It felt exactly like a circuit completing.

Cris Alborja

NIGHTTIME

This artist has chosen not to share the inspiration behind her work.

TAGS
alternate history, aromantic, attraction at first sight, break-up (past), emotional abuse (past), f/f (mentions of), f/nb, flirting, friends with benefits, infidelity (past), meet cute, modern, non-binary, pining, post-canon, soulmates (pseudo), text message fic, third person limited (multiple) point of view

INSPIRATION
Milla Darcy is the seven-times great-granddaughter of Lizzy and Fitzwilliam Darcy. There's a long history of love matches and adoration in her family line, and Milla loves her family history. She also doesn't mind that she herself is aromantic. She still enjoys watching her family fall in love! Enter two dogs, a caring human, and an abrupt upheaval of things Milla thought she knew about herself, and Milla learns that not only is she more flexible than she realized, but maybe she's not as different from her family as she thought.

Sage Mooreland

IT'S JUST YOU

MAY

"ANCHOVY! NO!"

That cry was the only warning Milla had. She looked in time to see a large silvery-gray blur, and then there were entirely too many limbs, heads, and tails for anything to make sense. She was aware enough that "Anchovy" must be the blur and that said blur must be a dog. Said conclusion was reached by the weight landing solidly on her chest and a large tongue bathing her face in enthusiastic greeting.

"Ackglrppfffft!" Milla spluttered, laughing helplessly under the affectionate onslaught. She tried to protect her face enough to focus on what was happening, but between the dog's determination and her laughing, she had absolutely no success.

A second dog appeared, making Milla laugh harder. The second was more interested in licking her arms, but fortunately, a human arrived very quickly after the second dog.

"I'm so sorry—Annie, c'mon. Sam, you're not any better. Let 'em up!" Somehow, the dogs were wrestled off, and Milla, still mildly giggling, sat up wiping her face with the edge of her shirt.

"Are you okay?" The dog owner's voice pulled Milla's attention upward to meet the most beautiful—and worried-looking—light-green eyes she could remember seeing.

Milla nodded, reaching out to pet the silvery-gray bully-mix that had to be Anchovy, straining to get to her. "Hey, hey, you're okay. I'm right here." She smiled at the big bully grin she got in return. "What a cutie you are. Just a big lovey baby." She cooed at the dog a moment longer before turning her attention to the other. This one was an equally large bully-mix, but he was a brindle with a brown-toned coat that almost matched his human's eyes. "So are you, aren't you?"

"You're okay, right?" the person repeated. "You're sure? I'm so sorry. She yanked so hard that she managed to pull the leash off my wrist. She made a beeline for you and basically dive-bombed you. She just doesn't do that, so I don't…" A pause. "Uh. Hi, I'm Liv, and this is Anchovy and Sammich. My pronouns are they/them."

Milla tried hard not to stare, but it was hard to look away from the light-green eyes contrasting against the golden skin, the swoop of thick black hair that dipped into their eyes and made the green that much more striking. "I'm Milla, she/her, and those might be the best names I've ever heard for dogs. I really am okay. I'm used to animals and kids tackling me like that, and I know how to take the hit."

Anchovy managed to wriggle free of Liv's grip and dove for Milla again, rolling to land belly-up and wagging hard enough to swing her butt back and forth slightly.

"Do you need belly rubs? What a pretty girl, of course I will." Milla used both hands to rub the dog's belly, pouring nonsense and baby talk all over her in the process. "Friendly little girl, aren't you?"

Liv snorted. "She isn't, actually. Not at first. She's usually extremely shy and takes time to warm up to people. I've never seen her react to a stranger like this, and I have *never* had her take off toward someone."

Anchovy twisted to slurp Milla's wrist and flopped back to enjoy her rubbies. Milla shook her head with a snort and nodded to the rest of her blanket. "Please, sit. Anchovy's gonna be here for a while, and Sam needs love, too!" When Sam responded to his name and tried to stretch toward her, she reached to scratch his head.

What Milla didn't say was that she wanted Liv to sit down almost more than she wanted to pet the dogs, which was an unfamiliar and unsettling urge. Like Anchovy, she took a while to warm up to people, and that she was responding so quickly to Liv was something she didn't know how to navigate.

Fortunately, the dogs didn't give anyone a chance to argue. Sam immediately sprawled next to his sister for his share. Liv snorted and sat, leaning back on one arm and keeping their shoes off the blanket. "Thanks. And thanks for being okay with my dogs assaulting you while you were trying to relax."

"Honestly, I'm used to a multiple-tiny-human-plus-several-animals form of attack, so just two dogs is new!" She simultaneously rubbed Sam's ears and Anchovy's belly.

Liv laughed, and something swooped in Milla's stomach, startling her almost as much as the flare of warmth when she'd met Liv's eyes. The way she was reacting wasn't anything like her normal aromantic self, and she was a little unsettled by it.

"Well, I don't know how they spotted you or what drew my girl your way, but I'm not mad that she did." They gave Milla a small, crooked smile. "I might have missed out on meeting the prettiest woman in the park. Maybe even Chicago."

Milla felt her cheeks flame up, heat swarming through her body. It sizzled before splitting into a swarm of butterflies in her stomach. "I dunno about prettiest, but I…think I can accept pretty?" She tried not to wince. "Oh, that sounded awful."

"Nah. It sounded like a chance to show you just how beautiful you are." Liv's smile grew a touch. "As long as you're okay with me flirting with you. My dogs claiming you is one thing. I don't want to overstep with assumptions about myself." There was a hopeful look in Liv's eye that unlocked a torrent of words Milla wouldn't normally have shared so quickly.

"Yes, I'm okay with it, but I'm going to be really awkward about it. Like. *Really* awkward? I identify as aromantic, but I like…I like you? I like flirting in general because I think it's fun and it can make people feel really good about themselves, y'know? I just…might react weirdly." *Oh, way to sound like an actual human being…*

"I absolutely can respect a no-flirting boundary," Liv started, but it was a short-lived offer.

"No!" Milla only just managed to not shout. "No, seriously. It's good. It's good *for* me, really. Flirting is good."

"Flirting is good," Liv repeated with a small smile. "So sayeth the pretty lady."

Milla's squeak made Anchovy look up and wag her tail.

July

"The amount of water you're splashing could fill a whole other bowl," Liv informed Sammich as he dove into the fresh water bowl to drink. "There are droughts in Africa. Think of the children."

"Somehow, I don't think that's going to work on him the same way as the famine guilt-trips of our childhoods worked on us," Milla said from the hanging egg chair nearby.

They were lounging in the shade of Liv's apartment building with the dogs under the chairs while the summer night set in. "You're probably right. And honestly, I'd rather the mess than they not drink water."

"I think you're right," Milla said with a grin, and closed her eyes again. One foot dangled to slowly pet Anchovy, and the pair looked deeply satisfied and sleepy.

And good. Liv had to swallow down the urge to tell Milla how beautiful she looked with her soft brown hair tucked into a messy bun with flyaways fluttering idly in the breeze, brown eyes reflecting nothing but contentment before she'd shut them, and how much Liv wanted to kiss her. Not because it wasn't true, but because that was way beyond the level of flirting they'd agreed on. That was happening more and more, enough that Liv was about to give in and accept that they'd caught feelings and reestablish the boundaries. For now, though, they continued to ignore the existence of the feelings at all.

"You still wanna get tacos for dinner?" Liv said instead, using their foot to turn their face into the flow of air from the fan. "The birria truck is two blocks down. Or do you want something cooler?"

Milla hummed. "The truck. They've got amazing agua frescas, and there's that little elotes cart on the corner, too." She paused and then snorted. "Well, now I'm hungry. Rude. How dare you make me aware of my need to consume food?"

"I'm the worst," Liv said, giving Milla a lopsided grin.

"Just awful," Milla agreed, but she was already laughing before she said it.

For a moment, it wasn't Milla that Liv saw, but Jace, and Jace wasn't teasing or being silly or—

"Liv? Hon?" Milla's voice snapped her face back into focus, and Liv blinked a couple of times. "There you are. You okay?"

Liv took a deep breath and rubbed their hand over their face. "Yeah…okay, so that's not the first time I've checked out unexpectedly, and I know you respect it, but I think I should probably explain why I keep doing that. Walk and talk?"

Milla gave them a concerned look but didn't say anything while they got the dogs ready and set off. She just gave Liv the space to decide what they wanted to say and how. They appreciated that consideration, and it made the oncoming conversation easier.

"I told you I'd been cheated on, but Jace did way more than that. He was all about self-expression and following your true self. You know, the kind of person who gets really into tracking behavior patterns to see if there's an aspect of yourself you're hiding."

"I've always thought that sounded more like a recipe for anxiety and self-destruction," Milla mused. "And he probably weaponized it."

"Got it in one. In some ways, he wasn't wrong. It helped me to realize that I'm non-binary, but his gaslighting had me convinced about all kinds of things. He had me hating peanut butter for a while, and I've loved it since I was old enough to have any. I never found out why, other than he thought it was funny."

Milla reached over and gently squeezed Liv's hand, but she didn't speak. Liv turned their palm to hold the offered hand. There wasn't anything but the solid contact of a true friend, and Liv treasured that. It gave them the courage to finish.

"Three years of that, and by the time he cheated and then dumped me, he had me twisted up, convinced I was a failure and the whole problem, terrified to trust anyone ever again. I felt shame for a long time, like I'd betrayed myself and everyone who'd ever loved me by letting him fuck me up so badly."

Milla clearly thought about Liv's words while she watched Anchovy and Sammich circle a smell, snorting when their leashes tangled enough that they bumped together and reversed to untwist themselves. "So that zone out earlier—Jace used to agree that you were awful?" she guessed.

Liv appreciated that Milla kept her eyes on the dogs. It made it easier to finish the story. "In a way. I was far more cruel to myself, and I thought my therapist was going to stroke out; we had a hard talk about that, and I wasn't allowed to use any phrase insulting myself until I could believe it wasn't true and only a 'joke.'" Telling this to someone was pulling out the last of the poison that kept the wound a little painful. Liv wondered if they'd finally be able to put this part of their damage in the closet.

Milla squeezed Liv's hand again as they resumed walking. "So watch myself around comments about self-worth?"

Liv shook their head. "No, don't change your behavior. For one, you're desensitizing me with positive associations to a lot of triggers because you being the kind, wonderful person you are has helped me establish new frames of reference." Liv needed to make sure Milla understood that. "You being you is so good for me, and I can't tell you how grateful I am for your friendship."

They bit down hard on the rest of what wanted to come out, though. Milla was very firmly in the "friends only" box, and Liv would not jeopardize the friendship that they valued so much by mentioning a dream that could never be. Their feelings were their own to manage.

Milla gave Liv her biggest, brightest smile. "You've been good for me, too, Liv. In ways that I'm not quite sure I can explain, but ones that I deeply appreciate."

There was something in her eyes that almost had Liv asking what was wrong, but Sammich saw a squirrel, and the moment was gone. By the time Liv remembered, Milla had left, and all they could do was wonder.

September

Milla was starting to wonder if she'd manifested Liv somehow. The last four months had set her spinning like a top, but she was kind of enjoying the ride. Liv had slotted so well into her life that it felt like they'd known each other forever. They shared similar views on all the important things, from politics to pizza toppings (though there was usually a playful battle over "Please may I have black olives on my half?" and the insistence that two small pizzas were better so that the evil olives wouldn't infect the other half).

The thing she couldn't quite wrap her head around was the conversation about dynamics that had happened a couple of days into their friendship. Liv's reaction, understanding, and insight had been just as difficult to process.

"I'm okay with it. I…" She paused. "So I want to be up front that I'm aromantic. I'm not asexual, but I've been aromantic for most of my life. When I imagine myself in romantic situations, there just isn't anything there, y'know?" She shrugged and rubbed Anchovy's silky ears, the big block head in Milla's lap. "Most people can't understand or feel like I'm using it as an excuse to be a slut."

"I think I get it, though. Your side, not theirs, I mean. It's not that you don't care for the people you partner with. You care, and probably care deeply. You just don't have romantic feelings for them."

Milla blinked at Liv a few times. "Yes. I know you're queer and have more exposure to these things, but most of the community doesn't understand aro people. I…I'm surprised, honestly." What startled her more was the swoop in her stomach, warm and thrilling instead of sick or scared.

Liv hummed thoughtfully while sipping some water. "I can't speak to the rest of the world, but I can say that for me, it makes sense because I understand there are different types of love and care. Also, we're steeped in Puritanical crap, so we're probably lucky that we're not sitting here with people screaming about perversion of the reproductive process."

The conversation had churned in Milla's mind ever since, and she was no closer to understanding what her response to Liv meant. Were those actual crush feelings? Was it something else? It *was* a crush, but not just the physical attraction she was used to. The feelings were distinctly unfamiliar in flavor and felt more like what her siblings and cousins had described in their own relationships.

It didn't help that they had settled into a healthy and very satisfying sexual relationship with almost no hiccups or awkwardness. It was as close to a truly comfortable relationship as she'd ever had, and it felt *weird*.

The four of them were curled up on the couch watching TV, and it felt so good. Anchovy nuzzled a little farther into her lap and looked up with loving eyes that melted Milla's heart. This gentle sweetheart who didn't trust people, who stayed to herself and took time to warm up, had been glued to her from the day she had tackled Milla, choosing to trust that Milla would love Anchovy back. She hadn't questioned her instinct, just thrown herself into loving with all her little pupper heart.

I'm not capable of leaping with such abandon, but…people change. I know that people change. I know that sexuality is fluid, gender is fluid, that basically everything in my life is only defined by how I choose to enforce labels. So…what if I have an exception? What if I'm…demiromantic? Or just Liv-romantic? Interested in something more than just sex and mutual friendship with at least this one specific person. Can I do that? Do I want that? Oh god,

I sound like some gender studies book. Why can't I just…be?

That feeling of "…maybe?" was currently enhanced by the no-fuss way Liv was taking the full explanation of Milla's family. "Remember how we were comparing the lit classes we'd taken in college? And how I sort of…veered off when you tried to talk about how much you like Austen's novels and her sarcasm?" When Liv nodded, Milla continued, "When you said that one of your favorite parts of *Pride & Prejudice* was that it was based on a true story, I kind of had a heart attack because, uh…Lizzy and Fitzwilliam Darcy are my seven-times great-grandparents."

Liv blinked a couple of times as they digested the information. "Before I do anything else, I gotta know. Were Lizzy Bennet and Jane Austen actually friends?"

Milla couldn't help laughing even while she reeled at the matter-of-fact acceptance. "Sorta. Well. I mean, yes, they were friends. But they were also sisters-in-law. Jane and Georgiana fell in love at the same time as our intrepid heroes. It was Aunt Georgie's idea for Aunt Jane to write Grandma Lizzy and Grandpa Fitz's story. According to *family* legend"—and she emphasized the word to make it clear that this was an inside secret—"Fitz all but dared Jane when he said that he didn't think she could do it justice."

"He did not!" Liv stared incredulously. "He hadn't learned anything in however many years he'd been married to Lizzy?"

"Personally?" Milla snickered. "I think he did it on purpose. If the other stories about Aunt Jane are to be believed, she struggled with confidence in her work. She was also as stubborn as Grandma Lizzy, so…"

Liv's mouth popped open in shock before they let out a loud guffaw. "So by saying that she couldn't, he knew he'd goad her into doing it. Tricksy tricksy!"

"Right? And damned near the whole family winds up with the same kind of ridiculous love stories. There's some kind of meeting that creates sparks and a little friction somehow, but everyone finds their true love. There have only been a couple of people throughout the years who didn't."

"You're one of them because you're aromantic. But you're also ridiculously happy being the fun aunt, aren't you?"

Milla was impressed with how quickly Liv put together the pieces they'd been handed. "Endlessly. And there are so many kiddos. Family reunions are ridiculous. Grandma Lizzy and Grandpa Fitz had four kids, and each of them more or less founded their own clans. A couple branches have petered out, a couple were cut off early by wars, stuff like that, but there's enough of us that reunions only happen every 10 years or so, and we wind up with damned near an entire hotel full of people."

They talked…and talked…and talked…about what it was like growing up in that environment, both as part of a famous family and as one of the "odd ducks." Over and over, Liv's equanimity startled Milla and added to those swimming, swirling feelings that she really didn't know how to deal with. By the time she went home that evening, she was no closer to figuring out what the hell was going on in her head, but she had no doubt that she was going to upturn everything about herself in the process of figuring it out.

October 12

> Milla if I don't stop seeing xmas stuff on shelves, i may riot

Liv

> I'm sorry to inform you that you will be rioting imminently as it will be there for several more months. Whats wrong

Milla

> Mom messaged this morning. Asked about holidays.

Liv

> Need a shoulder, a bag holder, or space?

Milla

> Space today, bag holder tomorrow. Gym at 6?

Liv

> See you then

Milla

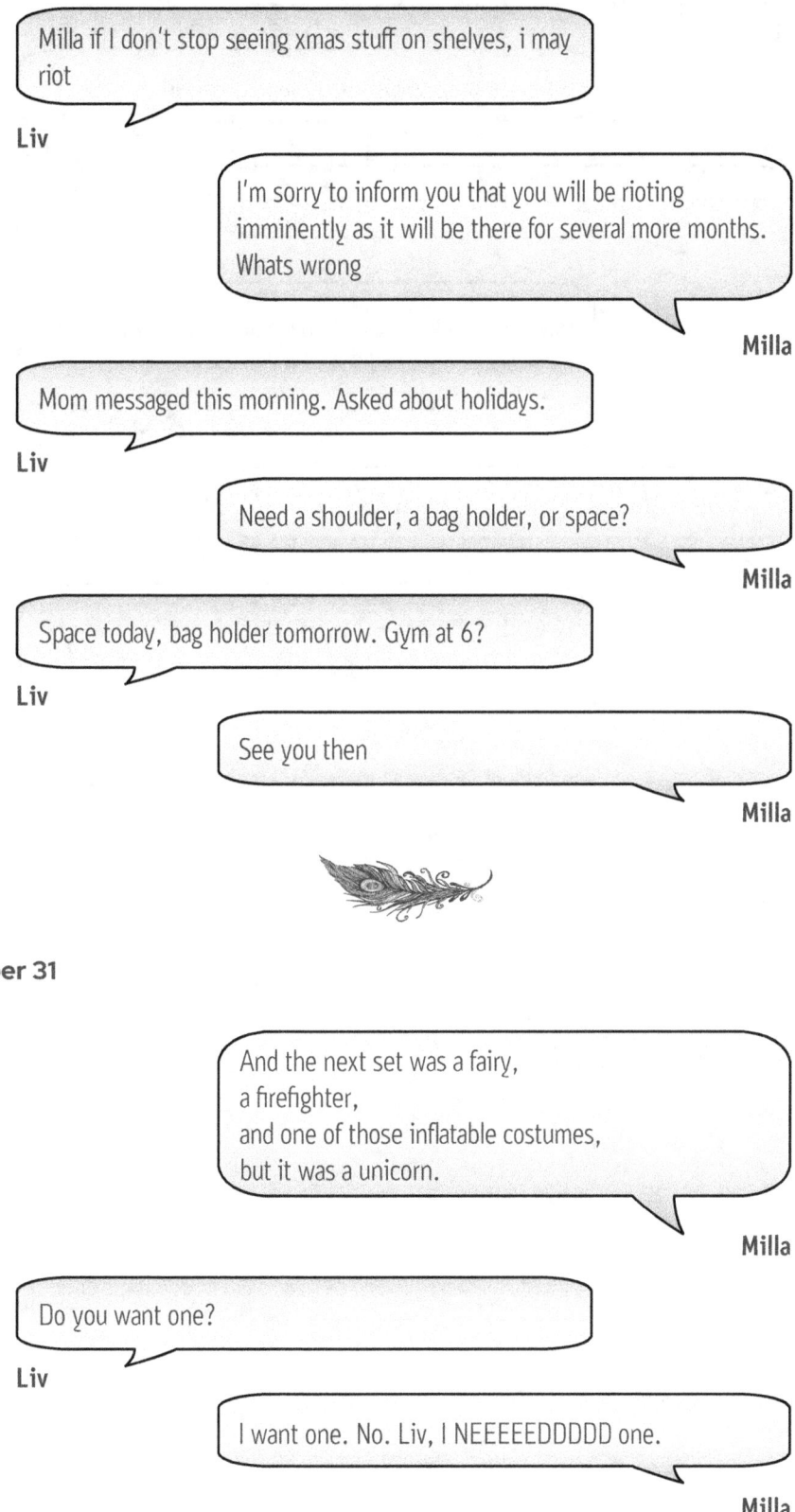

October 31

> And the next set was a fairy,
> a firefighter,
> and one of those inflatable costumes,
> but it was a unicorn.

Milla

> Do you want one?

Liv

> I want one. No. Liv, I NEEEEEDDDDD one.

Milla

You really don't

Liv

But I do. Imagine what my niblings would do.

Milla

You'd be the weirdest Pied Piper of Hamlin ever.

Liv

Have I ever told you that I love your brain and the knowledge contained therein?

Milla

Thank you, madam. It will be here all week.

Liv

HIS ONE'S A GROUP COSTUME!
THEY'RE CHEERLEADERS!!
THEY WROTE A ROUTINE!!!
THEY'RE LIKE SIX HELP I AM DYING

Milla

You're not going to be coherent until after trick or treating ends, are you?

Liv

A deviled. Egg.
a white shirt with a yellow dollop and a pair of devil horns.
A DEVILED EGG.

Milla

Okay, now that's just clever.

Liv

November 28

How go

Milla

Dad's drunk, mom's pouting, grandma's cackling, and everyone else is trying to pretend everything is okay

Liv

Fubn times. Need that rescue call yet?
*fun

Milla

No because Aunt Ella brought her pecan pie and if i leave now i won't get a piece

Liv

Not the pie! Let me know when.

Milla

Aunt Ella baked me a whole one. She also got me, her family, and my brother out of there in one swoop by saying we all needed to go prepare for Black Friday Shopping that night and no one would interfere with that sort of bargain hunting, correct? Have a wonderful evening, Jerry, there's a bottle of water next to your lounge chair and another next to your bed, drink both, Melissa, thank you for dinner it was fantastic, ok bye!

Liv

You hate shopping.

Milla

So does Aunt Ella. She had my pie in the car, and when she handed it to me she told me that she would have to come up with another escape hatch next year or we could just go to her place instead.

Liv

I like your Aunt Ella.

Milla

Me too.

Liv

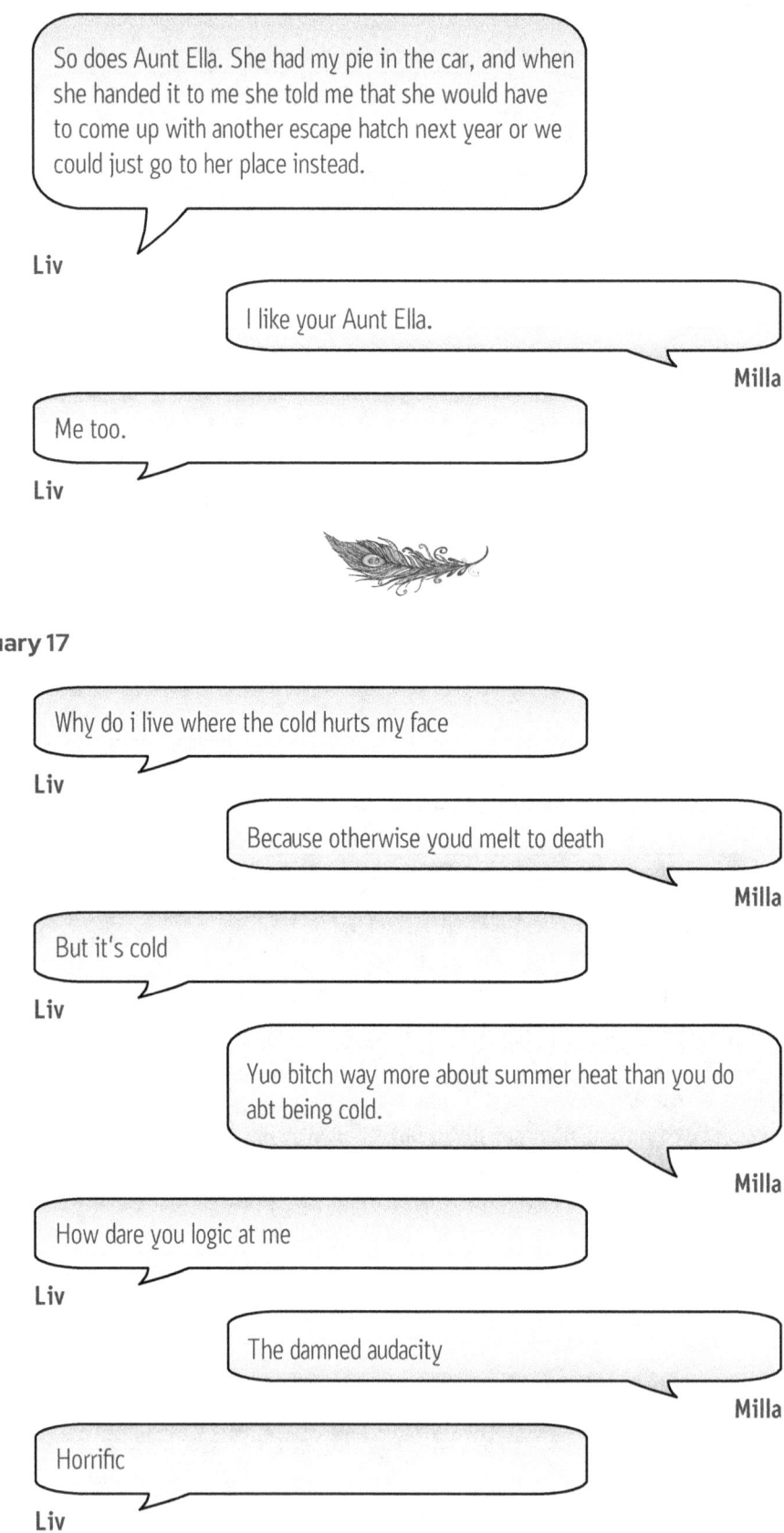

January 17

Why do i live where the cold hurts my face

Liv

Because otherwise youd melt to death

Milla

But it's cold

Liv

Yuo bitch way more about summer heat than you do abt being cold.

Milla

How dare you logic at me

Liv

The damned audacity

Milla

Horrific

Liv

How do you stand me

Milla

I don't. It's a clever ruse.

Liv

To make sure your dogs get walked?

Milla

Of course. Speaking of, we still on for Sunday?

Liv

I don't think I could bear Annie's eyes if I didn't come for our weekly walk.

Milla

You are wrapped around her paw

Liv

So are you

Milla

Touche, Monsieur Pussycat

Liv

March 27

HAPPY BIRTHDAY, MEERKAT!

Milla

You'll eventually stop calling me that, right? And thank you 😄

Liv

Unlikely. Its your own fault for parking on your butt to watch them at the zoo

Milla

So i can call you hippopotamus?

Liv

If you feel it necessary.
You ok?

Milla

Yeah. tired. No one from my family apart from Aunt Ella and my brother sent birthday wishes. Your family sent me more. Uh. Way more. How many of them have my facebook??

Liv

No clue. tbh, Maisie probably found it and sent it to everyone. That seems like her.
Is it bad? I can tell them to stop

Milla

Please don't. I love it. It's mostly just very...new

Liv

They're good at that.
They love you, you know

Milla

I love them. But then, they raised you, and I adore you, so that makes sense.

Liv

You keep up with comments like that and i might swoon

Milla

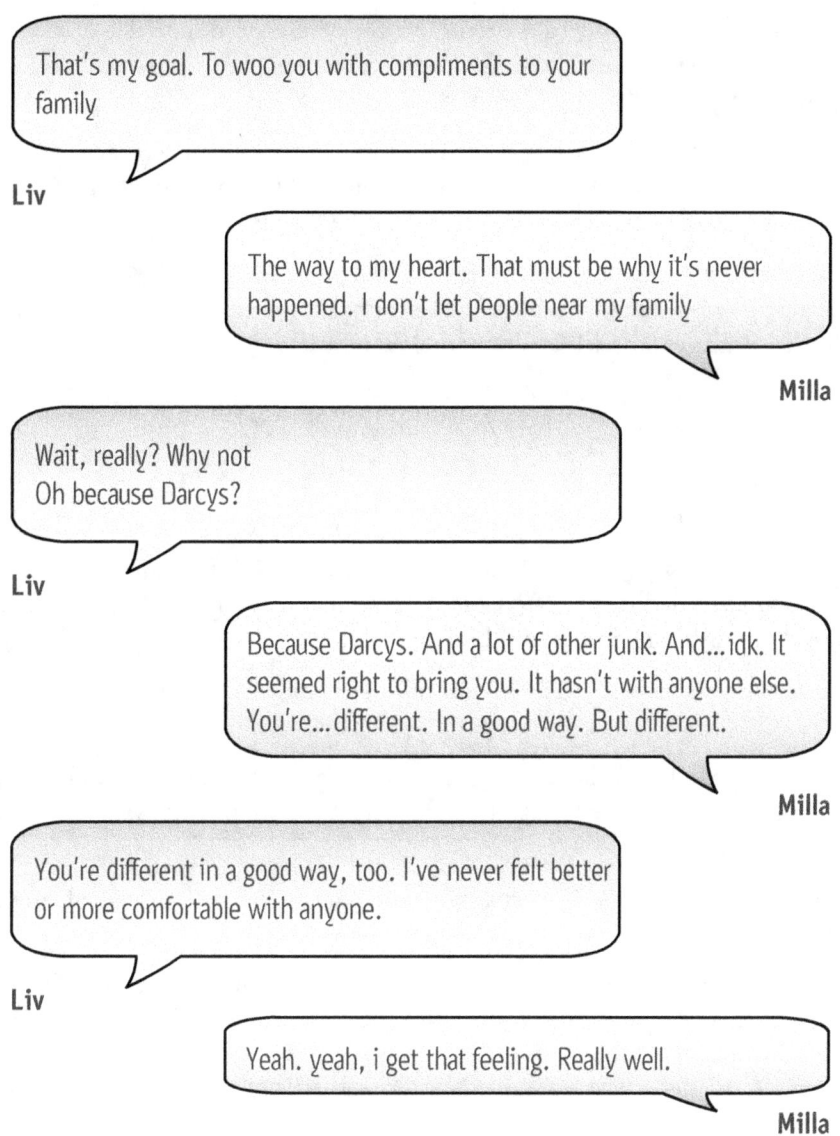

Liv

> That's my goal. To woo you with compliments to your family

Milla

> The way to my heart. That must be why it's never happened. I don't let people near my family

Liv

> Wait, really? Why not
> Oh because Darcys?

Milla

> Because Darcys. And a lot of other junk. And...idk. It seemed right to bring you. It hasn't with anyone else. You're...different. In a good way. But different.

Liv

> You're different in a good way, too. I've never felt better or more comfortable with anyone.

Milla

> Yeah. yeah, i get that feeling. Really well.

Milla stared at the last text she sent and sighed. She did know that feeling, and she had had some long soul searching to figure out what the actual fuck, but it was probably time to be an adult.

She hated being an adult.

April 29

"A little birdie told me that Vera's testing a new menu," Milla said, looking up from where she lay with her head in Liv's lap. "And by a little birdie, I mean we've been implored to come taste test for her. She's trying to figure out what works and what doesn't for the café. I've been told specifically that she needs your less biased palate to make sure I'm not lying to her."

At Vera's name, both dogs lifted their heads and wagged their tails. "You only like her because she feeds you," Liv told them, but they were smirking. "I was just thinking that I wanted to take you out. The Oak Leaf Café sounds like the perfect place. And the weather's nice today, so we'll be able to sit outside with the dogs. Wanna?"

Milla was momentarily breathless at the *something* in Liv's green eyes, and just lay there, looking up at them. The way Liv had said "take you out" had tingled along Milla's nerves. "Do you mean take me out as in on a date?" she asked softly.

Liv's gaze didn't waver when they asked just as softly, "Is that something you'd like me to do? Because if it is, I would absolutely like to make it a date." There was banked hope lurking in their features, and Milla's heart melted a little.

"Yes," she said without even having to think. "Yes, I would like that." She responded automatically to the beaming smile that spread across Liv's face with one of her own. "I'd like that a lot. Shall we go?"

"Lead on, MacDuff!"

"There is no Birnham Wood or Dunsinane, and I have no intention of killing anyone," Milla said with a startled laugh. "Was *MacBeth* your favorite from the Shakespeare class that you took to finish the minor you didn't mean to get?"

Liv grinned. "The Bard got me my minor, a step down from his major place in the world."

Milla cackled. "He'd probably raise a glass and congratulate you," she said, and glanced sideways at them as they walked down the steps and out onto the sidewalk. "I always loved finding the dick jokes."

There were several more snarky barbs about the Bard's plays as they walked, and it didn't take long to get to the café.

When Vera caught sight of the dogs, she clapped her hands excitedly. "Please tell me that you're bringing me these beautiful babies to love on for a while!" she exclaimed, crouching down to offer hands to both Sam and Anchovy, who both pushed close, vying for her pets. "Hi, babies! Oh, I missed you. Did you bring Dad and Mom to dinner to see me?"

Liv choked back a laugh while Milla blushed, but neither corrected her. Liv did give Milla's hand a squeeze, though, and Milla felt her heart and stomach flutter a little.

Bruschetta for the humans and a "plate of tidbits for my babies because they deserve appetizers, too!" started the testing that Vera had requested, and it was difficult to want to do anything but talk about the food for a while.

Effusive praise for the tangy, savory blend of tomatoes, mozzarella, basil, and seasonings, drizzled with balsamic vinegar and sprinkled with flaky sea salt assured Vera that she'd done well, and she kept them well supplied with food and drinks. No plate was overly full, each portioned and paced to encourage them to keep talking. When a chocolate lava cake with caramel drizzle appeared on the table in front of them, Milla looked up at her friend. "Okay, you're ridiculous, and I refuse to believe you just wanted to test a menu on us."

Vera pressed a hand to her chest, giving an exaggerated "who, me?" look before plopping on a nearby chair and resuming loving on the dogs. "Yes, I do. While I really can't figure out if the rest of this menu is worthwhile, this treat is because you two needed to celebrate whatever shifted between you." The smile she gave them was warm and happy before she petted the dogs one last time and disappeared inside again.

Liv studied Milla's face before taking her hand in their own again. As they gently laced their fingers with Milla's, they said, "You don't have to do this if it's not what you want. I know you said this could be a date, but I'm happy with just friendship."

Milla gently squeezed the hand in hers. "I want this. I'm not sure about anything because this is new and weird and I have never done anything like this before. But I feel…different about you. I feel different *around* you. I'd like to figure out what that means beyond what we already have." She hesitated, and then said, "I spent a long time with my therapist talking about how much a person's sexuality or romantic preferences can change over a lifetime if they're willing to stay aware of themselves and work with what they feel instead of what they think they should feel." She brought Liv's knuckles up to her mouth and kissed them gently, an instinctive move that made her cheeks heat and made Liv break into a big smile. "I guess this is me listening to myself and not trying to hide."

"From a family legacy or from yourself?" Liv asked, but their smile was genuine.

Milla thought about that. She wasn't Lizzy, and Liv wasn't Fitz, but maybe there was something to that whole process of interesting paths to solid, loving relationships. She certainly hadn't followed a traditional one. "Both, but really? I think it's just you."

Saro / Legendaerie

"IF ONLY WE HAD BEEN BLESSED WITH A SON!"

There is both a privilege and a curse to being born buxom and beautiful; you are more likely to be desired, yes, and less likely to languish alone on the margins of others company. But to bear the heavy gaze of society's approval is also to be squeezed tight by its expectations.

If only their mother had birthed a son, indeed.

TAGS
character injury (non-graphic descriptions), china, f/m, family, gender non-conforming, historical with cultivation, marriage proposal, masquerading as a person of a different gender, meet awkward, mis-communication, past tense, t4t, third person limited (multiple) point of view, violence (non-graphic descriptions)

INSPIRATION
I was watching a lot of Wuxia dramas when the anthology was recruiting, and while brainstorming my pitch, my mind naturally started putting these two things together. I wanted to explore what would happen if Elizabeth had a choice aside from marriage (as inspired by a *His Majesty's Dragon* x *Pride and Prejudice* crossover fanfiction I've read before in which Elizabeth joins the Aerial Corps.) Thus, in this Wuxia setting, I gave her the goal of joining a cultivation-world rebellion—the Hundred Path Alliance—to avoid her clan's martial arts being "reclaimed" by the nation's military. I ended up focusing more on developing the relationship between these versions of Elizabeth and Darcy, but I hope? the vibes? are there?

Aside from that, I've also incorporated one of my favourite tropes that happens frequently in Wuxia (or at least the costume drama versions): crossdressing! (Or rather...characters present as their birth gender because their "disguise" is needed for them to receive something—education, family's business, etc—or avoid certain threats to their lives.) I liked the trope so much that both characters get to crossdress in different directions! Variety!

Now, the glossary for curious minds:
- Emperor Haojing: 昊景帝 (lit. Vast-View-Emperor)
- Biluoyu Sword Forms: 碧落予剑法 (lit. Aquamarine-Fall-Give-Sword-Rule; Biluo here refers to heaven)
- Er-jie: 二姐 (lit. Second-Sister)
- Feng Ciyan: 丰词妍 (lit. Abundance-Word-Beauty)
- Feng Clan: 丰门 (lit. Abundance-Clan)
- Feng Yingtian: 丰迎天 (lit. Abundance-Welcome-Heavens/Sky)
- Hundred Path Alliance: 百道盟 (lit. Hundred-Path-Alliance)
- Nian Ming: 念冥 (lit. Thought-Dark)
- Xiao Tian: 小天 (lit. Little-Sky)

Xianyu Zhou

IN WANT OF A HORSE-STEALING, TROUBLEMAKING SWORDSMAN

THE FENG CLAN'S Mansion was quiet in the dead of the night. Still, Feng Yingtian kept his movements light while packing his bag: two sets of clothing, a bag of silver pieces, and most importantly, his family's sword-form manual.

The first time he'd seen it was eight years ago, the fifth year of Emperor Haojing's reign. His Majesty had decreed for all cultivation sects without heirs to turn in their cultivation manuals to the Department of Defence and forfeit the lands under their care to the local ministry upon the passing of their current leader. Supposedly, this was to better protect the country's new-found peace and stability by preventing certain sect techniques from falling into unknown hands. The decree had arrived at the mansion in the morning, and that night, Yingtian's father had unlocked the gilded cabinet in the ancestral hall and taken out the manual.

"Such a great thing ruined in the hands of untalented descendants," his father had murmured, leafing through the pages.

Yingtian had stood outside, peering in through the window. The manual was old and yellowed, the paper rasping with the slightest movement.

His father noticed him, yet said nothing. He just quietly, reverently put the manual back and left the room.

Yingtian now rummaged through his room to find a sturdy handkerchief and carefully wrapped the manual before tucking it between his clothes. It wouldn't do if it were damaged in any way.

The last thing he took was his sword, an unexpected gift from his father the morning after the decree had arrived—and along with it had come his first of many lessons on the Feng Clan's sword form. Although it has long gone out of fashion, his father insisted on practising daily. Perhaps it was out of stubbornness or guilt, perhaps out of grief that he would be the last patriarch.

Well, at least he thought he would be the last patriarch. Yingtian had other ideas about that, ideas that required scrabbling up the wall of the mansion and falling less-than-gracefully onto the bushes on the other side.

Leaving the estate was easy but leaving town… The town wasn't big, just spread out enough that he regretted not stealing a horse. As he worried that he'd be discovered, he heard a carriage coming down the path.

He slowed, anticipating some kind soul offering him a ride. He pasted on a grateful smile, yet…the carriage drove past him. The swinging lanterns were just bright enough to illuminate a veil-hat wearing figure who didn't even glance at Yingtian.

Yingtian jogged after the carriage. "W-wait up! Please!"

The carriage slowed, allowing him to catch up.

"I have an emergency in the next town over," he lied. "I'll pay."

The coachman didn't respond.

"I—"

"Get on," the coachman said curtly.

Yingtian hauled himself up before his benefactor could change their mind. "I will remember your kindness for all eternity!"

The coachman remained quiet, focused on steering the horses. It seemed like they—she, Yingtian belatedly noticed her robes—weren't interested in conversing. Yingtian tucked his legs under himself and tried to be as unobstructive as possible. But under the lull of the quiet night, the gentle breeze, and his newfound freedom, Yingtian's eyelids grew heavy. One moment he was watching the bob of the horses' manes, the next…

It was daylight when Yingtian woke.

He carefully stretched his stiff limbs while checking his surroundings. The woman and one of the horses were missing. The one left behind was unhitched, loosely tied to the carriage and curiously nosing around the grass.

Yingtian hopped off the carriage and paced the small clearing. The shiny surface of a river was visible nearby. Logic told him that that must be where the woman had gone.

Seeing that his benefactor was so kind as to entrust her carriage and one of her horses to him, Yingtian figured he should do her a favour. His eyes landed on a bush with brightly coloured berries.

I will feed her horse!

By the time he collected a handful, the woman was making her way back with the second horse. Yingtian jumped into action, stroking the horse's nose and pretending to feed it.

"What are you doing?" the woman demanded, closing the distance between them.

"Feeding your horse?" Yingtian took a step back warily.

"Those are poisonous!" She hurried over to pry open the horse's mouth. "Did it eat any?"

"It didn't want to?"

"Good," she said sternly as she walked off. The woman hitched the horses back onto the carriage and hopped on. "We part ways here."

"Wait. No. Get me to the next town at least!"

The woman stared at him for a moment longer, then spurred the horses on.

Yingtian watched her go in disbelief.

Nian Ming chewed on a piece of roasted meat as she watched the young man stumble into the roadside tavern. His face was red with exertion, hands grasping the door frame for support. Yet he spotted her quickly and he dragged himself across the room to collapse at her table.

"You!" The young man pointed a finger at her. "Terrible!"

Nian Ming continued eating.

"Why did you abandon me in the middle of nowhere?" he asked in a gritted tone.

Nian Ming swallowed. "I don't travel with strangers."

"Fine!" The young man huffed before putting on a fake friendly grin. "Honoured benefactor, could you please give me a lift to the next town in exchange for some money?"

"Not interested." Nian Ming picked up a piece of stir-fried gourd.

"Please. It's urgent," the young man said earnestly. "One of the co-leaders of the Hundred Path Alliance will be in the city soon. I can't miss this chance. Unless I appeal to the Hundred Path Alliance—" The young man sighed, shaking his head. "Why am I telling you this? What would a rich young lady know about martial arts?"

Much more than you do, Nian Ming thought.

"Speaking about the alliance will bring you trouble," Nian Ming said.

The young man blinked. "Wait, you know about the Hundred Path Alliance?"

Nian Ming waved for a tea refill then continued polishing off her food.

"Do you have contacts in the alliance? Could you help me get in touch?" The young man was relentless with his questions. "How did you know about them? Are you also part of…*that*?" He cut off as the waiter approached with a new, steaming teapot. His eyes darted between the waiter and Nian Ming suspiciously.

The young man resumed talking when the waiter left; Nian Ming continued ignoring him, sipping her refilled tea as she planned the next leg of the journey. When she'd arrived earlier, the waiter had complained about bandits in the area. While she was confident she could take down half a dozen men, any more than that would probably mean her carriage could be ruined. If the young man tagged along, however…he was clearly a decent martial artist. He could watch over the carriage.

Nian Ming walked away once she finished her tea. She stifled a laugh as she heard the young man muttering under his breath while scrambling to grab his things. Ignoring him, she mounted the carriage and began to drive away.

The young man came running after her.

"I have said this before but—" The young man huffed as he pursued her. "You are a terrible, terrible person."

Nian Ming was surprised when trouble appeared before sundown. She had thought there was still enough sunlight to deter anyone from trying their luck. That's why she had stopped for a bathroom break. Yet she returned to find one of the carriage windows broken, and the young man—Xiao Tian, he had finally given as his name—worse for wear. His ponytail was askew and there was a large bruise on his cheek.

Nian Ming had arrived just in time to see him untie one of the horses from the carriage.

"What are you doing?" Nian Ming yelled.

Xiao Tian startled, pausing before resolutely mounting. He turned sharply to look at Nian Ming, mouth pressed into a grim line. "The bandits took something very important."

"Wait—" —*for me*. Nian Ming couldn't bring herself to say it.

They had only met yesterday. She shouldn't risk her life for a horse-stealer who was using her as a free ride.

It was nightfall when Nian Ming came across the horse Xiao Tian borrowed tied loosely to a tree on a bluff with a view of the bandit's den.

The place was shabbier than she had expected; she was optimistic about Xiao Tian's chances of survival. Though, one thing confused her: it looked like a fight had broken out and half destroyed the place.

She left her horse and carriage and carefully crept closer.

Even weirder, it was eerily quiet. Were the bandits not home?

When she passed the wide-open gates, she had her answer. There were bodies—hopefully alive—strewn around, and the ground was scorched like a huge shockwave of energy had gone off.

In the flickering light of some flaming debris, there was only one person left standing.

"Xiao Tian?" she called out, barely louder than an exhale, suddenly…wrong-footed. The day had taken a sharp turn, and she was having a hard time adjusting to it. That was all.

Her feet carried her closer, one step after another.

"Xiao Tian?" She braced herself for something terrible. "Xiao Tian, it's me. Are you all right?"

Thankfully, Xiao Tian moved, lifting his head. His face was blank, eyes flat and unfocused. Even in the low light, he looked pallid.

She strode forward just as Xiao Tian coughed, deep, guttural coughs that wracked his entire body. He stumbled backward, barely getting a few steps away before folding over to spit out something dark.

"Don't…look," he mumbled, voice oddly wet.

Nian Ming rolled her eyes, the urge to kick some sense into the young man only tempered by her worry. "You're injured. No need for decorum now."

That got a huff out of Xiao Tian, his body swaying. "Terrible."

Nian Ming caught him before he landed in the dirt, but despite her efforts, they both ended up sprawled on the ground, narrowly avoiding the tiny puddle of blood that Xiao Tian had coughed up.

"I think I'm dying…" Xiao Tian slurred, head pillowed on Nian Ming's lap. He blinked very slowly, fingers wooden as he pulled out a small, old booklet from the chest of his robes. He shoved it into Nian Ming's face. "Keep this safe. Please…"

"What—?" The booklet smacked Nian Ming in the chin as Xiao Tian's arm went limp. She grabbed the book in one hand and righted Xiao Tian's arm with the other, fingers finding the pulse on his wrist. "You're not dying." There was something odd about his internal energy, but his life wasn't in danger. She placed Xiao Tian's arm on his chest, tucked the book under his palm, and looked around. The bandits didn't look like they would wake up anytime soon, but that didn't mean they should linger. "Troublesome."

With a put-upon sigh, she shifted Xiao Tian's head off her lap. There was much to do.

First, she picked up Xiao Tian's fallen sword, sheathed it, and tucked it back into the belt around Xiao Tian's waist.

Then, she took off her hat and used the long straps to tie up her sleeves.

"Right." She stared at her unconscious companion. "You better be very, very grateful when you wake up," she grumbled as she squatted down and gathered Xiao Tian's limbs toward the centre of his body.

With a deep inhale, Nian Ming hefted Xiao Tian's weight into her arms and carried him out of the bandit's den.

Nian Ming shoved Xiao Tian into the carriage. There wasn't enough space for a person to lie down anywhere else.

She even got out her nice blanket for him.

Bone-deep exhaustion came over her as soon as she sat down.

But she couldn't stop yet.

One long drink of water later, Nian Ming settled onto the carriage seat and winced as something angular dug into her bottom. Irritable, she yanked it out with half a mind to throw it as far away as possible before her mind caught up with her eyes.

Biluoyu Sword Forms the title on the cover read.

It must have fallen out of Xiao Tian's grasp when she was getting him into the carriage.

She placed it carefully beside her. A Sect or a Clan's heritage martial arts manual was intensely private. Most disciples never even got to see the original book.

Nian Ming itched to have a peek.

She forced her attention to the young man tucked into her bedroll. Either he was a thief who had stolen the Feng Clan's most treasured possession, or…

In his sleep, Xiao Tian snorted.

The Feng Clan didn't have any men around Xiao Tian's age. There were women, though… Nian Ming had briefly met the Feng Clan's young mistresses, and she couldn't imagine any of them as the young man before her eyes. They were rather nice, ordinary, focused on being perfect brides. None would be involved with their Clan's martial arts. None would wander off alone to seek out the improper adherents of the Hundred Path Alliance… It was unthinkable.

If Xiao Tian were really a thief, then he should be punished by the Feng Clan. If he weren't a thief, this would still be the Feng Clan's internal business. Either way, Nian Ming knew where she should bring him.

Nian Ming shook her head to clear her thoughts and spurred the horses on.

The carriage swayed along the road they had just travelled, heading back to the town they had set out from.

No one would know if she took a little peek within the manual, right?

She dusted off her hands on her skirts and carefully cracked open the book, reading it under the dim carriage lantern. The pages were packed with text, stray notes wedged between the pages. Half of the notes detailed how each sword form could be modified for the note-taking practitioner. The other half were frustrated scrawls about how the practitioner didn't have enough yang energy to perform the more complicated moves.

The tone of these complaints was familiar.

On a hunch, she got up and clambered into the carriage. She tugged Xiao Tian's arm out of the bedroll and felt his wrist, focusing on the flawed thrum of internal energy that she'd noticed earlier.

Xiao Tian had depleted most of his yang energy. He had been practising the Biluoyu Sword Forms, and they were so incompatible with him that they drained him every time he used them, as he had when fighting the bandits.

Nian Ming checked his meridians more thoroughly, and awkwardly confirmed that Xiao Tian had indeed done the unthinkable.

Now Nian Ming understood why Xiao Tian had clung to the idea of meeting the Hundred Path Alliance.

Don't worry, I got it, Nian Ming silently promised the young man. *I'll help you.*

Feng Yingtian woke up in his own bed. His hair was unbound, and he wore only his underclothes under a thick blanket.

For a long, headache-filled moment, he thought he'd never left his room, and the woman and her carriage taking him away in the night had been just a dream.

But the hollow feeling in his bones could only mean he'd used the Biluoyu Sword Forms.

As he sat up, fragments of memories came back.

He had…taken down a bandits' den, hasn't he?

"Er-jie! You're awake!" a familiar voice exclaimed, followed by footsteps and the *thunk* of a tray carelessly thrown onto his—no, *her*—side table. Feng Ciyan, her youngest sister, crowded close. "Do you know who I am?"

Yingtian leaned back because Ciyan was about to poke the bruise on her face. "Yes. I haven't gone stupid yet."

"You could've! You've been unconscious for two days!" Ciyan huffed, plopping down beside Yingtian. "Everyone's worried! Well, Mother is mad, and Father hasn't actually said anything, but everyone else was worried!"

Yingtian opened her mouth, a question on the tip of her tongue, but she hesitated. Stealing the family's manual was a big deal.

Her sister whispered conspiratorially. "Don't worry. I put the manual back."

"How—?"

"The young man—dashingly mysterious, by the way—gave it to me in secret," Ciyan said nonchalantly.

"Young…man?"

"He also left you a letter." Ciyan bounced to her feet, ran across the room, and grabbed a white envelope off Yingtian's study table.

Yingtian ripped it open.

> *Dear troublemaker,*
>
> *Congratulations on not dying. You may think your current situation is worse than dying, but rest well knowing that I have decided to handle your affairs while you recuperate.*
>
> *I told Sect Leader Feng that we were trying to elope, but we ran into some trouble and you blocked a hit for me. I was worried for your well-being so I sent you back and decided that it was only fair that, regardless of our difference in station, I will marry you as my formal wife. This "confession" seemed to be well-received by your mother.*
>
> *Worry not, I am certain that my plan will go well and you'll have what you set out to achieve.*
>
> *I will be back in a month. Please prepare the reimbursement for the gifts I bought your parents according to the second itemised list included in this letter.*
>
> *Stay out of trouble,*
>
> *Nian Ming*

Yingtian blinked and rubbed over the name with her thumb.

Nian Ming?

Wasn't that the leader of one of the most prominent sects?

Yingtian stuffed the papers back into the envelope and crammed it under her mattress. She flopped back in bed, tugging the blanket up to her neck.

Hah! I must still be dreaming!

It was quiet for a few long seconds before Ciyan groaned and pulled her upright again. "No more sleeping, Er-jie! You need to eat, or at least drink something!"

"Wine?" Yingtian asked hopefully.

"Absolutely not," Ciyan said, yanking Yingtian's blanket off. "And no martial arts."

Yingtian sighed.

A month, was it?

She could wait. It wasn't like she could go anywhere in the meantime.

Feng Yingtian had fully recovered when Nian Ming visited again.

Her mother broke the news to her, barging into her room and dragging her toward the vanity. Yingtian played along, knowing things were not as her mother believed them to be.

Then, in a blur, she was making her way to the front hall.

A few steps shy of the wide-open doors, she stopped.

All too suddenly, Yingtian was aware of her heart racing out of anxiety and anticipation. She hadn't tried to contact Nian Ming. She'd tried to forget about her and the short time they'd spent together. But now that she was about to see her—*him*—again, Yingtian didn't know what to think.

Forget it. Whatever happens, happens.

She stepped into the room.

Nian Ming turned toward her. He looked different in men's clothes. His posture was uncomfortably straight.

"I thought you would be speaking with my father, Sect Leader Nian," she said when it was clear that Nian Ming would've been happy to stand there in silence for the rest of the day.

"I spoke to him earlier. I needed to talk to you," Nian Ming replied, holding out a folded invitation.

Yingtian took it, opened it, and read the first line.

The Hundred Path Alliance cordially invites—

She closed it again.

"This is your plan?" Feng Yingtian demanded discourteously.

"You mentioned—" Nian Ming cut himself off and took a deep breath. Then: "Yes. Despite the state of your clan and your personal unsuitability to practise martial arts, you have shown great tenacity and courage. I still cannot agree with your decision to secure a future for your sect by allying with the Hundred Path Alliance, but I concur that it is not a terrible option for an unmarriageable young woman of your station."

Yingtian blinked in disbelief. Was he trying to praise her, or was he insulting her?

"I won't pretend to understand why, but I admire your resolution to help your clan despite not being able to inherit it. Thus, I took the liberty of appealing to the Hundred Path Alliance on your behalf." Nian Ming's words came in quick bursts. "I knew that they wouldn't turn me down."

Yingtian glared at him. Her ears rang, indignity burning hot on her cheeks. "I understand Sect Leader Nian's gesture of goodwill, but I cannot accept this," Yingtian gritted out coldly, putting the invitation down on a side table.

"This is what you wanted," Nian Ming said as if she didn't know that better than he. "Why won't you take it?"

Yingtian had to suck in a deep breath before she felt calm enough to answer. She couldn't afford to offend the leader of such a prominent sect. "Sect Leader Nian, you have my utmost gratitude for your hard work," she managed. "We will prepare an appropriate compensation in return for your very generous favour."

Nian Ming thankfully stayed silent.

Yingtian wished she could look at his face. Maybe then she would know what exactly this ridiculous man was thinking about. But she didn't want to see the silhouette of the woman from the carriage on a guy who she was growing to dislike more by the second.

"Xiao Tian—"

"Farewell, Sect Leader Nian."

Yingtian left the room as fast as her feet could carry her.

Of all the hobbies befitting a fine young lady, Feng Yingtian enjoyed incense-making the most. Smashing away at things in a mortar was a nice way for her to alleviate her bad mood. Though, it usually also worsened her mother's mood at the same time.

So when her father showed up at the courtyard, she figured that it was because her mother had had enough with her poor excuse of a hobby.

"Father," Yingtian greeted, putting down the pestle.

Her father nodded in acknowledgement. "Are you busy?"

Yingtian shook her head, clearing a spot for her father to sit and pouring him a cup of tea.

Sect Leader Feng frowned as he took a sip of the tea, and belatedly, Yingtian realised that it must've gone cold while she'd been imagining Nian Ming as the ginseng root she was chopping up.

"I'll make a fresh pot!" she said.

"No need," Sect Leader Feng said, gesturing for her to sit. "I just wanted to chat. Nothing serious."

Despite his words, Yingtian sat gingerly, afraid of what he was about to say. They didn't talk often, and she could guess what he wished to discuss.

Her father took out the invitation she had turned down and slid it over.

"Father—"

He held up a hand, cutting her off. "Sect Leader Nian is one of the co-leaders of the Hundred Path Alliance." *Wait, what?* "I had only dared to speculate about it in the past, but seeing this, I'm sure my guess is right. The handwriting is familiar. He must've not had time to get a scribe."

Why hide his identity? Why take a month to follow up instead of giving it straight to her?

"You could ask him yourself," her father said, pausing to look ponderously into his empty teacup.

"Father, we're not—"

"You'd make a good Sect Leader," Sect Leader Feng said with a slight smile. "I…have never been courageous or ambitious. I'm glad that you are."

"Father?" Yingtian didn't know how to feel about her father's sudden verbosity. "I'm not following?"

Sect Leader Feng smiled. "Don't play dumb, child. Since you have the heart and the luck to see this through, don't waste it."

Yingtian was unsure what to say. She didn't want to be Sect Leader. She just wanted to keep her family together.

"Does Mother know that Sect Leader Nian has withdrawn the marriage proposal?" Yingtian asked cautiously.

Her father made a noise of surprise. "Has he? He didn't say anything to me."

Unsure of how much of the truth she should reveal, Yingtian chose the quickest way to end the conversation. "That's a relief."

If Nian Ming was put off by what had happened, he didn't show it. He kept up the ruse of their supposed engagement, sending gifts and letters, always in pairs: one addressed to her parents, inviting them to social events, another addressed to Yingtian, telling her about the Alliance members who would be in attendance and how they could help her modify her family's sword form to fit her better. And his gifts for her were always practical: wrist guards, medicine for strained muscles, books on wilderness survival.

He gave her a horse. A well-trained horse.

He never asked her to reply, nor did he get mad when she didn't attend the events. He himself never attended them. It was like he didn't care if Yingtian reciprocated, only sought to help her.

(Ciyan said it meant that he cared about her. Yingtian rolled her eyes at that.)

So it was a great surprise to Yingtian when she spotted Nian Ming at an event—and in disguise, no less. She wouldn't have recognised him if she hadn't met *her* before she met Nian Ming.

Nian Ming had expected to see Feng Yingtian at the gathering—he'd sent the invitation, after all. He hadn't expected her to find him while he was in disguise and hidden behind a rockscape.

"It's been a while," she said.

His plan of pretending to be a stranger flew out the window. It has been months since he heard from her—he'd heard only from her mother. He didn't want to push, seeing how doing so had ended the last time they'd met.

"Mn," was what he eventually settled on.

"You look better like this," she said to the moss tucked into a crevice of the rockscape.

Nian Ming pressed the bridge of his nose lightly, making sure the molding wax there was still in place. A veiled hat would've made him stand out more here, so he'd used a different way to hide his identity. "How did you know it was me?"

"You have a way of standing." Yingtian finally looked at him directly. "But I was talking about your clothes. They're more…flowery."

Nian Ming crossed his arms. "You didn't ride your horse here," he remarked, turning the conversation away from himself.

"Easier for everyone to rent a carriage," Yingtian replied. "Why did you give me a horse, anyway?"

Because you're too poor to buy one that'll be good for travelling long distances, Nian Ming didn't say. He'd had an earful from his sister about how he must, must, must change the way he spoke to people he liked. "Because…it's useful?"

Yingtian hid a snort behind her silk fan, but it couldn't hide her eyeroll.

Nian Ming wanted to ask her to elaborate. He wanted, desperately, to understand her.

"Is that also why you gave me that invitation? Because you thought it'd be useful?"

"They need people like you, people passionate about preserving their craft and making space for those usually excluded."

"Oh" was all Yingtian said, disappointment casting a shadow over her face.

"I—I don't mean it that way! This isn't a recruitment thing! We don't have the budget." Words escaped his mouth in a rush. "They! Don't have the budget. I want to help. Because I can help."

Instead of pressing on the matter, Yingtian took the conversation in a different direction. "You kept up the pretence of us getting married. Why? I can't imagine that you're actually fond of me?"

Silence hung so thickly with awkwardness that Nian Ming barely stopped himself from twitching. "I am. I *am* fond of you."

Yingtian turned her gaze on him, assessing. "Really?"

"I...I read stories about great adventurers. Being on the road together was...classic imagery," he finished lamely.

Yingtian was quiet, and when she finally spoke, it was in a teasing tone. "Were you imagining *A Beauty's Twelve Lovers*? Or *Tryst in the Dark*?"

Nian Ming cleared his throat.

"*Saved From Endless Matchmaking by a Dashing Swordsman*, if you must know," Nian Ming managed. "It's new. Very popular."

Yingtian laughed, soft and sincere. "No one has ever compared me to a dashing swordsman before. I quite like it."

Nian Ming didn't know what to say. He quite liked the way she was pleased to be compared to a man and the way she didn't say anything about Nian Ming comparing himself to a woman. It was the same slight, too-fragile elation that he'd felt when he'd checked Yingtian's pulse and found she wasn't as she appeared to be. Since then, he'd wondered: *Is Xiao Feng...like me?*

"I think I'll quite like saving you from endless matchmaking," Yingtian said suddenly.

"Pardon?"

"Getting married, no?"

Nian Ming stared at her in disbelief. He'd thought he'd lost the chance, that their fake engagement would be broken off any day now.

"It would benefit us both," he said.

"It would," Yingtian agreed, tilting his head in thought. "Would you like your dashing swordsman to ask, or should he just whisk you away?"

"I... Both?"

Yingtian nodded, handed over his fan, then pulled a hairpin from his purse and showed it to her. It was made of dark wood, polished to a shine, inlaid with bits of mother-of-pearl. Beautiful, and neutral enough to be worn regardless of how Nian Ming presented herself.

"Shall I?" Yingtian asked, raising the hairpin suggestively.

Nian Ming lowered her head and allowed him to slide the hairpin into her updo, head filling with a rush as the smooth wood glided across her scalp.

Yingtian looked as giddy as she felt as he whispered conspiratorially, "I never thought I'd get to do that."

"Neither did I," Nian Ming whispered back, carefully feeling the hairpin.

Yingtian took her hand in his. "Shall I whisk you away now?

Nian Ming couldn't help the grin that tugged at her cheeks.

Xiao Feng is *like me.*

He tightened his hold on her hand. "Let's get out of here."

radicalhoodie

(UNTITLED)

Considering what's going on in the world, I really wanted to draw something peaceful about Elizabeth being trans/nonbinary.

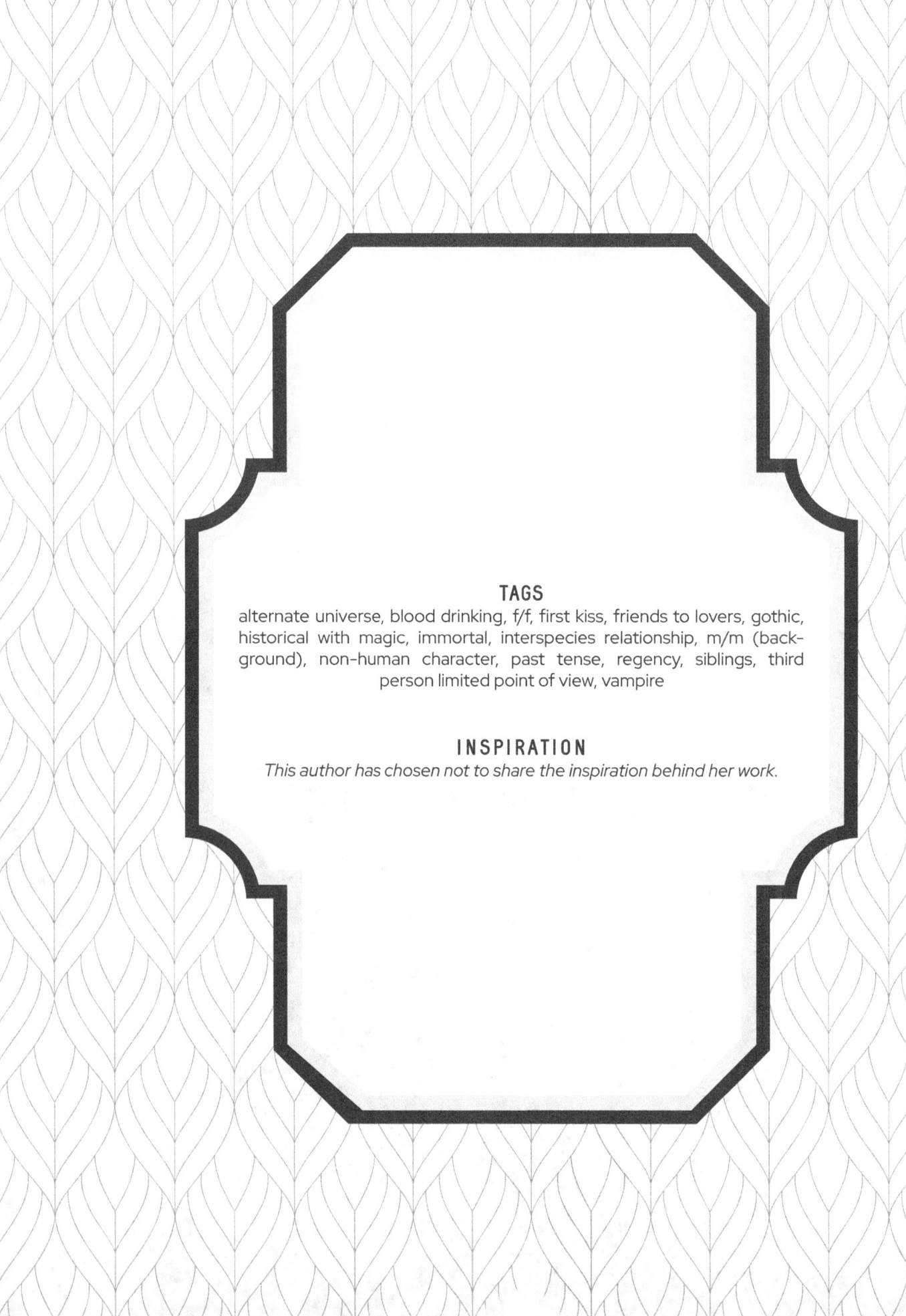

TAGS
alternate universe, blood drinking, f/f, first kiss, friends to lovers, gothic, historical with magic, immortal, interspecies relationship, m/m (background), non-human character, past tense, regency, siblings, third person limited point of view, vampire

INSPIRATION
This author has chosen not to share the inspiration behind her work.

A CONSTANT, FEARFUL LONGING

There are monsters that hunt the night, draining the lifeblood from the living until they weaken and die. Monsters that are pale as ghosts, fast as hounds, tireless, and without mercy.

They burn in the sun, but can only be defeated with oak stakes and fire.

They are called vampires.

Soldiers had brought the tales back from Europe, and spent the winter nights embellishing them for the young ladies of Meryton. The stories, and the reactions they evoked, haunted Lizzy into the first weeks of spring.

She'd longed to flee to Pemberley, but guilt and propriety kept her from it. She wrote instead to her sister, Jane, and begged to be received in London; it was a request quickly granted.

Jane's marriage had made her more pleasant and handsome than ever, and Lizzy could not help but be cheered by her sister's happiness. Jane wore a constant smile which bloomed into joy anytime Mr. Summerfield checked in on them. The weeks passed in such easy, pleasant activity, Lizzy nearly forgot her own distress.

At the end of the visit, Lizzy clasped Jane's hands as Mr. Darcy's carriage waited. "Truly, I cannot tell you how I needed your company."

Jane's gaze held a great gentleness. "Darling Lizzy, you're always welcome. I can see something troubles you, but you have always borne such things in silence. If I can help in any way, please tell me. Surely you have some dream that has not yet been realised?"

Lizzy shifted uncomfortably. She had long known that dreams were meant for more agreeable women. She could hope for comfort, and had achieved it, and now wished only to return to it. "What more could I ask for than your joy, and all our sisters married, and the freedom to visit my friends with a carefree heart? It's you, and your Mr. Summerfield, who have made it possible."

"It's not so much." Jane averted her eyes. "Only what anyone would do."

They both knew it was not. "Don't worry on my account," Lizzy said lightly. "My dream has always been your happiness, and it is granted."

Jane laughed. "Very well. I must take you at your word. Remember me to the Darcys, won't you?"

Lizzy nodded and took her leave, looking back once as the footman handed her into the carriage. Jane's sunlit figure was obscured when the carriage door closed, and Lizzy was embraced by the shadows.

As they left the city, Lizzy discovered that the chill of winter had only briefly been held at bay. The change of seasons and the longer days could not vanquish her memories.

She had thought the stories a harmless diversion at first. But when several townspeople had fallen ill, fear and grief had driven Meryton to the brink of madness. The Darcys, due to their malady, had been the target of the town's ire. It was only distance and a great storm that had kept her friends safe until good sense had returned.

The townsfolk seemed to have lost all memory of their frenzy. But Lizzy was not reassured, even now. She had seen a viciousness in people she'd known her entire life; worse, she had been forced to admit that—while the accusations were clearly false—her friends did have unsettling commonalities with the creatures of the tales. She could no longer be certain of anything.

When at last the footman opened the door onto the bright gardens of Pemberley, Lizzy was relieved to see them before her, as perfect as she remembered. Sunlight spilled shadows and the shine of crystal across the pond. How Lizzy longed for the previous summer, when she had been as calm and clear as that stretch of water.

Inside the manor, she made her way into the darkness beyond the entryway, where the windows were hung with thick curtains and the Darcys were safe from the sun. Georgiana kissed her cheek with a smile as welcoming as Jane's; her voice was so dear it brought tears to Lizzy's eyes. In the face of such pure affection, Lizzy felt weak with relief.

After a more staid reception from Mr. Darcy, Lizzy excused herself to change her clothes. Her memory had not exaggerated how the Darcys' illness othered them. Their skin was yet pale and smooth, their movement yet as easy and quick, the manor just as dark. But their manner was as polite and kind as she remembered, and it was much harder now to imagine that they could be any more monstrous than the people of Meryton who had called for their destruction.

She returned downstairs and joined them in the parlour, and soon she was completely at ease as Georgiana told her the news that hadn't fit in letters. Mr. Darcy spoke indulgently of his sister's talents and encouraged her to show Lizzy paintings and compositions, keeping them busy until dinner. Pemberley kept London hours, so dinner was quite late in the evening, near sunset.

Lizzy's lavish dinner was soup, followed by roast quail and spring carrots. The Darcys had small bowls of nutrient broth, hardly enough to feed a child. The sight brought again the weight of unease, but Lizzy ignored it in favour of Georgiana's quiet conversation.

The Darcys, despite their illness, always had a great restlessness about them and were eager to walk the paths that surrounded the manor as soon as the sun set. Lizzy joined them, and Georgiana took her hand as they walked—an intimacy she had begun the moment the two had met, and which engendered in Lizzy a great comfort.

The bluff where they stopped had a beautiful view overlooking the manor, but the trail to reach it was quite steep, and they stopped while Lizzy recovered her breath.

"I hope no one's been a bother," Lizzy said finally. "The rumours have quieted. I think now that people are out of doors, they have better things to do than spread vicious lies about their neighbours." She gripped Georgiana's hand tightly, and Georgiana turned to give her a soft smile.

"I'm afraid it will only get worse," Mr. Darcy said grimly, his face shining pale in the moonlight. The chill returned to Lizzy's body; she had hoped to be gently ridiculed. "This is our last season at Pemberley, Miss Elizabeth. It is no longer safe for us here."

"What?" Lizzy exclaimed. "Surely, it isn't so dire! You could explain it to them—you're ill, not evil creatures risen from the dead!" Her laugh sounded forced and loud in the hush of night.

"Dearest Lizzy," Georgiana said quietly. "You must know that we cannot." She loosened her grip on Lizzy's hand, but Lizzy renewed her own. Her limbs tingled alarmingly. She felt she must never let go.

"Convince them?" Mr. Darcy said in a sardonic tone. "How can we prove that we, who are pale as marble, who never tire, who never age, who cannot eat as other men do, are not the very creatures they fear?"

Lizzy forced another laugh through the tightness in her throat, and it came out ragged. She glanced at Georgiana, who would not meet her eyes.

Her friend's face was still rounded in the soft lines of youth, as it had been five years ago. Lizzy's younger sisters, whose features had shared that softness, had long outgrown it.

Mr. Darcy sighed. "They are not entirely right about us," he said. "But they are not wrong, and the differences will not be enough to matter."

This had been her fear, Lizzy realised as the world seemed to tilt under her. That they would not refute the accusations. That they would admit what she had, somewhere inside herself, already known.

"So," she asked. "How much of what they say is true?"

Georgiana looked up, and her smile trembled. "We're not dead, I don't think. But we're not certain we're human anymore. We don't know a great deal about it."

"And the rest?" Lizzy swallowed. "How is it you…sustain yourselves?"

"We don't hurt anyone," Georgiana said hastily. "We do— It *is* blood, but we only take a little at a time." She touched her neck self-consciously, and Lizzy remembered the strange collars the women wore at Pemberley.

"You take it from their necks," she said faintly. "How is it done?" In the stories, people were bitten—*savaged*—but then, in the stories, the creatures were monstrous.

"Our teeth grow long when we're hungry," Mr. Darcy said. "We're able to pierce the skin with little damage."

Lizzy laughed weakly. *Our teeth grow long*, as if they were talking about the confirmation of a horse. The timbre of the conversation was mundane, but its content was so outside the rules of society that Lizzy hardly knew what to say. "This is…this is madness. You're *vampires*."

Mr. Darcy tipped his head. "You're taking this well."

"Am I?" Lizzy felt strange, separated from her body. "Well," she mused. "I suppose… When you came ill, Mr. Darcy, one of your servants left you in a great hurry. She scared my maid, Rose, half to death with some vague, horrific stories. She begged me not to come here. I've spent weeks here with you both, and your maladies never progress. The only time Georgiana has seemed weakened was when my aunt and uncle visited. A ruse, I suppose." She smiled fondly at Georgiana. "I'd never known you to beg off a walk until then."

Georgiana laughed softly, her grip once again confident in Lizzy's. "He warned me you'd notice something, but I simply couldn't pretend with you. I cannot be put to bed in the midst of a game or a performance or a walk under the moon. I enjoy myself far too much, and I did not want to hide from you."

"It was reckless," Mr. Darcy said, but there was no reproach in it. "But there is a freedom in being known. I have certainly found it so."

"Have you?" Lizzy asked, leaning forward. "Who else knows? It must be terribly dangerous!"

"Only Mr. Bingley, and the servants who have chosen to stay," Mr. Darcy replied.

The evening's enveloping silence was interrupted only by the clicks and hums of the nightlife, and the occasional fox's scream.

"Are you well rested, Miss Elizabeth?" Mr. Darcy asked. "Would you like to return to the manor?"

She understood him to be offering the comfort of well-lit rooms and the company of servants, but there was no need. "I'm in no rush," she said. "I'd like to enjoy the stars."

Mr. Darcy looked at Lizzy and Georgiana, and a shadow passed over his expression. "I will return, then, and prepare for Mr. Bingley's arrival. The two of you should enjoy the night."

He bowed and then strode away, disappearing silently into the forest.

"You're not afraid of anything, are you?" Georgiana asked with a cautious smile.

"Oh, I'm afraid of all sorts of things," Lizzy said. Her insides churned restlessly. "But I'm not afraid of you." She looked up at the stars and picked out the figures she and Georgiana had amused themselves with in summers past.

The fear that seized her was, instead, that she might one day soon find Pemberley deserted, her truest friend gone forever. She had never felt so strongly with Charlotte, nor even Jane. No other person had provoked in her such a constant, fearful longing.

It was too much to be borne, and grew into a claustrophobic grief. Losing Georgiana seemed inevitable—if not to a riot of terrified townspeople, or to her imminent departure, then merely to the march of time.

"Whatever would I do without you?" Lizzy asked.

Georgiana only shifted closer. They watched the stars hand in hand, and Lizzy felt a chasm crack wide inside herself, in the place where everything that had once comforted her lived.

Lizzy did her best to appear carefree the following day, which began as most of their days did: breakfast at noon with both of the Darcys, then retiring to the parlour with Georgiana.

She was determined to put the revelations and the future out of her mind, to enjoy this summer as she had all the previous. She would fix these moments as firmly in her mind as she had her first meeting with Georgiana—so she could return to them when her friend was gone.

They took turns at the piano-forte. Lizzy had toiled resentfully at it before Georgiana, but her friend's knowledge and excitement had transformed the experience, and Lizzy was determined to show Georgiana the results of that inspiration.

"You've nearly got it," Georgiana praised as Lizzy ran through a new piece. "The arpeggios are much smoother! Only, may I?" She moved behind Lizzy and hovered there, nearly touching. Lizzy nodded, and Georgiana's hands lighted on her shoulders. "Posture changes everything," and she pulled Lizzy against her. The whole of Lizzy's back pressed into the soft folds of Georgiana's dress and the strong frame beneath it. A blush rose mysteriously to her cheeks. "There. You'll play much better if you're sitting properly."

Then, Georgiana sat and held out her hand for Lizzy's. She shaped first her fingers, then her palm and wrist in a soft curve before indicating the keys.

Lizzy resumed playing, her fingers tingling and her body over-warm. She fumbled only once, when Georgiana put a hand at the small of her back to remind her to sit up straight. She'd never felt so flustered by a correction. Perhaps she really had found a passion for playing after so many years.

"That was near perfect! Don't slow here," Georgiana said, and set her fingers to the keys to play in a lower octave, maintaining the tempo and making the piece completely new.

"Oh, I see," Lizzy said, astonished. They played on together, with Georgiana's right hand inside Lizzy's left as the notes moved into a higher register. Their arms brushed, and Lizzy fumbled to a halt.

Embarrassed by her clumsiness, she laughed and stood hastily. "I am not used to such grueling practice. I insist we rest!"

They sat together on the sofa, Lizzy's skin humming, her body restless, and Georgiana rang for tea she would not drink. All the things Lizzy had promised not to think about came rushing back.

"Where will you go?" she asked softly. "Can you tell me?"

A tension rose in the room, and she thought to apologise. Then Georgiana answered, eyes averted. "I think, the coast of France. We've visited before, and there are areas that are quite remote. It would be safest that way, and there are lovely cottages near the sea. There's a wild sort of beauty to it. I think we can be happy there, though there is a great deal we will miss."

France. No distance could be greater. Lizzy would never be allowed to leave the country alone, especially if the Darcys again became the targets of suspicion.

She forced her lips into a smile even as a rushing sound filled her ears. She wanted to grasp Georgiana's hand and refuse to let go. She wanted to cling like a spoilt child and beg not to be left. Her practicality, which had always been a point of pride, had deserted her utterly.

She stood, lest her violent urges take her over, and took the nine painful steps to the piano-forte. "That sounds beautiful," she said, turning her attention to the sheet music and brushing away her unshed tears.

Mr. Bingley arrived just before dinner, and they all ate together. Listening to his news of London left Lizzy free to watch the assembled party as Bingley spoke. He was animated and cheerful as ever, his face flushed and pink as he and Lizzy ate a meal of roast pork and salad. She wondered how he'd taken it when Mr. Darcy had told him the truth of his condition, or if Bingley had guessed and only needed confirmation.

She wondered if he felt as pained as she, to be losing a dear friend.

That night, as she and Georgiana walked the gardens together, she asked how he had taken it.

"You needn't concern yourself that you've reacted badly. You've been more accepting than I had any right to expect. It's all right if you still have questions, or reservations."

"I had a great deal, yesterday," Lizzy admitted. "I still can't reconcile what I've heard with what I know of you. But, I think, I don't need to." She turned toward Georgiana. "I may not understand the intricacies of what you are, but I know *who* you are, and that's what matters. I only wondered how Bingley had come to accept it. His friendship with your brother seems unaffected, and I very much want that for us."

"Lizzy." Georgiana clasped her hands, and Lizzy closed her eyes against a swell of emotion. "You are most extraordinary people, you and Mr. Bingley."

"It is not so extraordinary, is it? I hope you never feared that I would turn so easily against you. We know each other too well for that, don't we?"

"I had hoped, but I understand the terror of it, too. When I was changed, I could hardly accept myself, only, I had no choice. For those who do, to accept us even so…it is a very brave thing, to have a choice and take such an unnatural course."

Lizzy hadn't considered them unnatural, despite reigning opinion in Meryton. There was a divide, now, and she could not cross back, even if she returned there and pretended to be as she had been. She would as soon reject Georgiana as her own sister, or her own limb.

They returned to the garden hand in hand and found Bingley and Darcy playing croquet on the lawn, the wickets just visible as shadows in the moonlight.

"Join us!" Bingley called out. "Darcy is cheating viciously!"

Mr. Darcy laughed. "You can't call it *cheating*—"

They continued bickering pleasantly while Georgiana pulled Lizzy away with a laugh. "Come," she exclaimed. "Let us change our damp clothes while they finish their round."

They raced up the stairs to their rooms, and after she changed, Lizzy went to the window to fix Pemberley in her mind. There was a vast garden, and hills in the distance, but she found herself caught by the interplay of the men on the lawn. She didn't often see Mr. Darcy in such high spirits. He seemed an entirely different man, there, with Mr. Bingley— loose and smiling and unencumbered.

Bingley swung his mallet and knocked Darcy's ball away from the wicket, laughing as it sailed into the long grass. He appeared blissfully unaware as Darcy gestured rudely at his back and stalked toward him. It all seemed in good fun until Darcy grabbed him about the waist, pinning Bingley's arms to his sides and moving his mouth to Bingley's throat. Lizzy gasped, torn between running down the stairs and throwing open the window, ultimately struck voiceless and frozen in horror.

What happened next was more shocking even than the bite she'd feared. Bingley turned in Darcy's arms and they came together—their arms encircled one another, and their hands grasped in each other's shirts as if they could not bear to be parted. Their mouths met and moved provocatively together.

Lizzy had never seen anything like it.

A knock at the door made Lizzy jump; she yanked the curtain over the window. "One minute," she called. Her heart hammered as she opened the door.

Georgiana gave Lizzy a curious once-over. "Ready?" she asked, her brows lowering in a different question.

Lizzy nodded, pasting a bright smile on as if she'd seen nothing at all. Georgiana took her hand, and they descended the stairs together. The moonlit scene that greeted them was perfectly proper.

The memory haunted her through the night.

She'd seen the perfunctory pecks her father gave her mother at breakfast, and the warm kisses Mr. Summerfield pressed to Jane's cheek. Lizzy had known from Charlotte, from Jane, that there were other sorts of embraces to be had by married couples behind closed doors. She'd never imagined anything like what she'd witnessed. Certainly never between two gentlemen. Or two ladies.

It was impossible. But there were many things at Pemberley that were impossible, and she knew them as truth. This, it seemed, was simply one more.

The memory of the scene she'd witnessed grew inside Lizzy like an infection. If she had been able to unsee it, she certainly would have. It was too fundamental a shift to face on the back of the previous days' revelations.

So scattered were her thoughts the next afternoon that she hardly realised that Georgiana also was not herself until her friend had nearly paced a path into the parlour floor.

"Is something wrong?" Lizzy asked at last. She'd believed the night had passed without anyone suspecting the cause of her distraction, but she'd never had Jane's talent, to look unconcerned when she was not.

Georgiana turned to her. "I've been thinking. You've been incredibly generous to us, knowing what we are, but I don't want to hide anything of myself—of how I *live*. I know that our appetites…" She shook her head, and her lips pursed in displeasure. "Perhaps it is best left to imagination, but I'll be dining in my room soon and I— If you'd like, you could come and see how it's done."

Lizzy's mind went blank, filled only with the buzzing of late-night crickets. A shocking vision rose in her mind—Georgiana nuzzling into her neck the way Mr. Darcy had into

Bingley's.

"It's not so awful as you might think," Georgiana said, startling Lizzy out of her reverie.

Lizzy flushed hotly before the true meaning of Georgiana's request sunk in. "Oh!" she stammered. "Oh, yes, let me— I'll just—"

Georgiana took pity on her. "You can meet me there, if you'd like. I won't be offended if you don't come."

Lizzy stared after her, then scrambled to follow. Georgiana needed to know that Lizzy accepted her completely, and Lizzy would not fail her. She hurried up the stairs; her own crisis could wait.

In Georgiana's room, the servant Sarah sat on a wing chair with a strange bench next to it, seemingly a taller version of the kneelers Lizzy used at church.

Lizzy could see that Georgiana was nervous, but she hid it well as she directed Lizzy to another chair at the foot of the bed. "Sarah doesn't mind you watching, but please stay seated there. That will be all right, won't it?" She looked for confirmation from the young maid, and Lizzy felt affection swell in her chest. Whatever Georgiana was, she *cared* for people.

"It's fine, Miss," Sarah murmured. She had already removed her collar and now set a light wrap about her shoulders, tucking it into her frock as if to protect the fabric from a spill. Lizzy shivered.

"You needn't worry, Miss," Sarah told her as Georgiana sat. "It hardly hurts, and there's never any mess, really. Just a few drops, sometimes, so we've learned to use this." She fingered the edge of the cloth briefly and shifted around, tipping her head to expose her neck.

Lizzy knotted her hands as Georgiana knelt on the bench next to the chair and leaned in. She was gentle as she adjusted Sarah's head. "Ready?"

"Yes, Miss." Sarah did not show any concern as Georgiana moved closer and opened her mouth against the girl's skin. Sarah gasped, and then Georgiana's throat was working as she swallowed. The girl's hands gripped the frock over her knees, and her expression was unexpectedly blissful. Her breath came quickly, drawing Lizzy's gaze to the rapid rise and fall of her chest. When Georgiana's hand cupped her neck gently, Lizzy ached all over.

When Georgiana was done, Lizzy saw the pink swipe of her tongue against Sarah's neck, felt it through her entire body. Georgiana turned toward her, and there was one single crimson spot at the corner of her mouth. Lizzy couldn't tear her eyes away. Dabbing delicately with a handkerchief, Georgiana offered Lizzy a shy smile before turning back to Sarah.

"Are you dizzy? I tried to take less this time. Make sure you drink water." She inspected the area where she'd sealed her mouth. "Everything's healed up nicely, just a little bruising."

"You get better each time," Sarah reassured her. "I think the bench helps with the angle. I could have held still quite a bit longer."

Georgiana looked pleased. "Good. Take it easy, now. Do you want help back to your quarters?"

"No, Miss. Truly, I feel fine."

"She fell once, after," Georgiana explained to Lizzy, still holding her hand out as Sarah stood easily. "I think I took too much. It was awful!"

"I'm fine," Sarah reassured her. She walked swiftly around the room twice to demonstrate her strength before Georgiana let her go, and then Georgiana turned back to Lizzy.

"Was it what you imagined?"

"Not at all," Lizzy said. "It was as you said. You didn't hurt her in the least." What Lizzy felt couldn't yet be put into words.

"Lizzy." Georgiana's expression was tight in a way Lizzy had never seen before, distressed in a way she never wanted to see again. "My brother wishes Bingley to accompany us when we go. It feels selfish to ask anyone to come, knowing the danger we put them in. It would be, wouldn't it? Selfish?" Her expression was full of longing.

Whatever emotion gripped Lizzy then could not be named. "There's never harm in asking, is there?"

Georgiana smiled tightly. "Only in the answering, I suppose."

Lizzy did not know what to say. She took Georgiana's hand in hers, and it seemed to be enough.

Lizzy rarely went out during the day at Pemberley—she preferred to spend all the time she could in Georgiana's company. But that afternoon, she found herself urgently needing to walk in the sunlight, to remind herself that doing so was still possible.

Lizzy had come to Pemberley hoping to finally burn away the haunting winter, to find the contentment that had become so elusive since then. Now, with everything she could not unknow or unsee, something had broken open in her that could not be shut away.

Lizzy stood at the edge of the pond for a long time, considering its deceptively calm surface and the currents that must move ceaselessly underneath.

She didn't believe in monsters. Not in the way the people of Meryton did. But she knew that what she wanted, now, would make her a monster in their eyes. She would never again be the person they had known. Georgiana had been asking for her company, she was nearly certain of it. And it felt possible, with Jane's help, or Mr. Bingley's, that her departure would not bring ruin to her family.

Before winter, she had been content with her life. Now, it would only be prudent to be happy with what was offered. But too much had happened since; the current inside her had carved new channels, and the desire that lived there could not be walled away.

Georgiana sat silently at the piano-forte when Lizzy returned to the parlour.

"I had to clear my head," Lizzy said, sitting next to her.

Georgiana nodded. "Of course. I'm glad I didn't frighten you off. I know it must be difficult to see…to really see what I am."

"That wasn't it at all," Lizzy said, turning and taking her hands. "It was only—" She took a deep breath. "I must ask you something, if you'll allow it."

"Of course. Anything."

"I know that your brother and Mr. Bingley are close."

"Yes. They've been friends since they were young."

"But their closeness is more than friendship. Isn't it?"

Georgiana was silent. Then, "It seems you're uncovering all our family secrets this summer."

"Have you ever felt like that for anyone?"

"Have I ever loved someone?"

"Could you love someone that way?" Lizzy opened her mouth, but there was nothing more to say. She could not beg.

"Lizzy." Georgiana breathed her name like a prayer. Her fingers were delicate in Lizzy's grasp, but there was a desperate strength in them as they clung to her.

"I didn't realise what I felt for you, before," Lizzy admitted. "That it is more violent an affection than I had allowed myself to understand. Do you see?"

Georgiana opened her mouth and took a breath, and her chin trembled, and she did not let go. Her smile was the only sunrise Lizzy would ever need. "Sweet Lizzy," she murmured. "I never dared hope. But, yes. I *have* loved someone. I *do*."

The words echoed through Lizzy's body like the ringing of church bells. "Thank God," she whispered, and pressed her lips to Georgiana's cheek. "Take me with you, if you meant it. If you'll have me. Please."

"I shouldn't have said anything, only I couldn't imagine never seeing you again." Georgiana kissed her mouth with intoxicating warmth and then warned, "We'll be cut off completely; I don't know if you can ever come back."

Lizzy had never cared less about anything. She put her arms around Georgiana's waist. "Only say you want me there, and it's done."

"Of *course* I do," Georgiana's slow-blooming smile was radiant. "Oh, I can't wait to show you the sea at night," she said. "I can't wait to show you *everything*."

Such an ecstatic joy flooded Lizzy that she could not imagine anyone had ever felt it before. Was this what Jane had called, so inadequately, *happiness*?

The quiet calm she had longed for all winter now seemed a wretched, useless thing. She felt wild and new and alive. Old doubts and fears could not hope to survive in the restless sea that now surged inside her.

"I will follow you anywhere," Lizzy promised, "and look wherever you direct me. But I cannot imagine any view more precious than this one, right now."

Max Jason Peterson

DUELING DARCY

I love swashbuckling films and books so much that I learned to fence. There's a brief scene in the 1995 BBC production of *Pride and Prejudice* in which Darcy is practicing his swordplay in the salle, and in the book (as well as most screen adaptations), there's a great deal of worry that Mr. Bennet will duel Mr. Wickham. However, other than this, swordplay is strangely absent from Jane Austen! I always thought P&P should have more duels. On this front, the way Bingley wrongs Jane has always bothered me. If I were Elizabeth, I'd want to duel Darcy for inspiring such harm to my sister. And if Elizabeth were me...he'd be Eli. Also, like Elizabeth, I had a close relationship with my dad; and like Eli, I've always felt like my father's son. So I just kept playing with these sorts of correspondences and alternate visions of what P&P could be.

There's honestly a longer backstory to this comic! However, mainly, this art is inspired by my desire to draw the characters of P&P swordfighting. And for Elizabeth to be trans like me. Finally, I really love comics (and illustrating with watercolors) and am just so excited I got to make one.

TAGS

character study, death of a parent (past), death of a spouse (past), didn't know they were queer, enemies to lovers, f/f, m/m (background), period-typical homophobia, post-canon, present tense, regency, third person limited point of view

INSPIRATION

I have always wished that the character of Charlotte Lucas could have had a happier ending; I've often thought that Lizzy might invite her to Pemberley after her wedding, but that Charlotte would struggle to accept the invitation. Particularly in the 1995 adaption, Charlotte comes across to me as someone doing a stellar job at keeping herself completely in check, which makes it really interesting to think about what could happen if, on one fateful night, the boundaries all shifted and she allowed herself to act authentically.

When it comes to Caroline Bingley, I find her to be a delightful minor villain, just a really nasty bully with a sharp wit. I love the idea that all her attacking is done in the name of self-defence—she feels deeply vulnerable as a woman attracted to women, and is lashing out to protect herself.

I wanted to bring the two together in a setting where standards are relaxing and each feels more aware than usual of how hard they are constantly working to keep themselves hidden, and see if perhaps they could help each other to find honesty and genuine enjoyment for the night!

WE CAN ALL BEGIN FREELY

CHARLOTTE LUCAS IS walking stiffly through the woodland, following the familiar track to Rosings Park.

Over her head, the sun sprawls back into a dusky pink sky. The trees soak in the last of its warmth and lean dreamily into a soft breeze. But Charlotte pays them no mind; the muddy folds of the track have petrified into hard ridges in the heat of summer, and she focuses on her steps, on the swish-swish movement of her widow's weeds over her sturdy boots.

It is seven months since the passing of Lady Catherine de Bourgh, and two months since Mr. William Collins followed his benefactor into what lay beyond—devoted as ever.

Charlotte does not look overcome by grief.

She is thinking polite thoughts about her late husband, and thinking polite thoughts about his erstwhile patron, and certainly attempting to think polite thoughts about her own new patron, too. A letter from Anne de Bourgh had come, offering such a very *dear* friend, in the midst of *terrible* loss, the option to stay at the Hunsford parsonage indefinitely. Oddly cloying in parts, strangely formal in others, the letter read as though Anne were trying the hands of different writers as she went. Or perhaps, Charlotte thinks shrewdly as she pauses by the pond on her walk, it is the steering hand of an older and kinder relative that she can sense in places. Colonel Fitzwilliam, or even Mr. Darcy.

As Charlotte's dower money had dwindled, she had snipped flower stems, and read books, and written letters, and taken in the seams of her new black dress as food ran short. She had resigned herself to the looming prospect of a return to her parents' home. Anne's letter is a complicated reprieve.

She glances down at the greenish-grey pond. There are no damselflies to dart over the waters; only Charlotte's own silhouette breaks the perfect reflection of the drowsy sky. Charlotte runs a dispassionate eye over herself at this unflattering angle. Her hands clench, tight skeins, as she seeks but cannot quite find a glimmer of any real feeling in the rigid tilt of her head and neck. A blink, though, and the moment is over. She walks on.

A second letter from Anne had arrived on the heels of the first: a summons dressed up as an invitation, to come to dinner tonight. And now Charlotte steps out of the tree line and onto the grounds of Rosings. The sinking sun offers her plain features, flat body, and unassuming posture some ribbons of gold for artistry and romance; unconsciously, she refuses the gift, holding herself neat and unbeautiful. The weight she has lost leaves her dress hanging off her frame, gapping strangely at the neck and wrists.

She is allowed into Rosings with the usual ceremony, and passes her cloak with stickish awkwardness to a footman with blond hair and golden livery.

"The party is gathered in the Blue Room, Mrs. Collins," he says.

Charlotte's eyes widen slightly at the implication of a gathering rather than an intimate dinner.

"There are many guests?" she asks.

After a moment's hesitation, the footman says, "Not so many as Miss de Bourgh was hoping. But some, Mrs. Collins."

His manner is familiar, almost friendly. Charlotte wonders, briefly, at the reason for his impertinence. His gold coat and the cut of his blond hair is immaculate, so it can't be standards slipping at Rosings Park. Perhaps her circumstances are known to him, or it's the state of her appearance.

"Charlotte?" says a voice as thin and demanding as a horsewhip, and Charlotte turns to see Anne de Bourgh. She cannot help raising her eyebrows, just a fraction.

Anne is approaching, wearing a towering wig and a collar of blue stones around her neck. Her periwinkle gown, sumptuous and shining, looks fit for a royal ball, and the low-cut bodice is practically painted onto her blueish skin. She has rosebud lips and rouged cheeks in the old French style. Somehow, she manages to look too modern and satiny for the musty grandeur of Rosings, and too old-fashioned for anywhere else.

"Miss de Bourgh," Charlotte says, her tone resolutely neutral as she curtseys.

"It's so good that you're here!" Anne says. "I'm sure more people will come. There will be a real party, here at Rosings, at last! I have hired new staff who are much better-looking, and I've prepared a dinner that will make everyone laugh. And then there will be dancing and party games. I have procured libations for the evening."

Charlotte's arm is pinned to Anne's side and she is marched through an antechamber.

"It will be fun," Anne says.

She looks at Charlotte. Her fevered eyes brook no argument.

"It sounds very well-planned," Charlotte manages to say. Anne purses her lips.

"You are always *so* boring," Anne says. Charlotte blinks, left silently aghast by the slight. "Tonight is for having fun, don't you see? It won't work if you don't have fun." Anne almost stumbles over her own dress, and the possibility occurs to Charlotte that Anne may have already partaken of some of her own libations.

They enter the Blue Room arm in arm, and faces turn towards them. The tense, stilted murmuring that had filled the high-ceilinged room falls still, and Charlotte recognises with a sinking dread that Anne de Bourgh must have invited anyone of her acquaintance in the hope of a large gathering. The sea of unknown people is punctuated by a buoy of familiarity: Colonel Fitzwilliam stands from a tufted chaise longue and offers a bow. Charlotte returns a curtsey.

No Lizzy Bennet, Charlotte thinks. No Jane. Neither of the men they'd married. Charlotte herself had received her invitation only yesterday; perhaps they had been sent at too short notice.

"We shall go in to dine," Anne declares, clinging to Charlotte. Her voice was always plaintive, but listening to Anne speak now, Charlotte hears a new, demanding strain. "It will be fun. I have prepared a feast, of sorts. And afterwards, I shall have the trio play for us, and we shall all dance and be merry, and partake of the libations…"

Charlotte happens, at this point, to see another familiar face. At the far corner of the room, her teal gown effortlessly lovely, is Caroline Bingley. Charlotte looks directly into her eyes and finds the expected cool dislike.

Although Charlotte intends to look away, she somehow does not, and the look holds. As Anne continues to talk, Caroline arches an eyebrow in silent judgement, and—in a sudden breach of her long-worn stoicism—Charlotte finds the corner of her mouth crooking into the tiniest of knowing smiles. Something bright and delighted sparks in Caroline's eyes.

Horrified at herself, Charlotte breaks free of Caroline's gaze, her cheeks heating—the polite blood-rush of embarrassment.

"Come, then, everyone," Anne says, strutting through the swathe of people, dragging Charlotte along with her. "Come. We shall dine, now."

Charlotte does not look at Caroline Bingley as she is walked past. She avoids any eye contact; her heart is beating quickly, and the situation seems suddenly a little dangerous.

"Miss de Bourgh," comes the voice of Colonel Fitzwilliam, and Anne stops to swing her voluminous skirts—and peripherally, Charlotte—around to face him. "If you can bear to relinquish the delight of Mrs. Collins's company, I could escort you in to dinner?"

Anne simpers and lets go of Charlotte with a little priggish push. Charlotte offers the colonel her gratitude in a small, tense dip of the head, which is returned.

The colonel and Anne proceed into the dining hall, followed, with uncertain ceremony, by the congregation of guests. Charlotte can hear mutterings, and she picks out scattered words. *Unstable...since her mother...erratic.*

Charlotte swallows, and as she moves to follow the crowd, someone draws level with her.

"I did not expect to see you here, Mrs. Collins." Caroline Bingley's low voice, as always, sounds smeared in dark honey, sweet and sophisticated. Not particularly interested in the reply, either. Charlotte wonders briefly at Caroline bothering to speak to her at all. It puts a fluttering in her stomach. She reminds herself that this is her best friend's enemy.

"Miss Bingley," Charlotte says. She considers leaving it there—but with an unexpected lurch of courage, she finds herself saying, "I thought to hear from Jane Bennet of you at Netherfield Park before seeing you here."

"I do not disturb my brother's peace at Netherfield often," Caroline says, side-stepping the implied rebuke around why she might not be welcome at Netherfield Park by sounding supremely above it all. "You are here alone?"

After a moment, Charlotte answers, "I am."

"I heard of your husband's passing. My condolences." Caroline's response is cursory. They enter the dining room together, and for some reason, Caroline does not drift away to other company. They take seats beside each other. "Where will you go?"

"My plans are undecided. I am being allowed to stay indefinitely at the parsonage."

Caroline says nothing more, which Charlotte does not wonder at; as the penniless widow of a clergyman, she can't provide amusement for long. Charlotte suspects that, sitting side by side, Caroline might feel too close to the kind of dull calamity that usually would not walk its inexpensive weeds through the lavish halls where she belongs.

At the head of the table, Anne stands resplendent as uniformed staff line the wall of the hall, each holding a tureen or a dish. Charlotte represses the thought of craning her neck to see the food about to be served.

The blond footman who greeted her is standing neatly off to one side. Charlotte watches him staring towards the head of the table, and turns her head to follow his gaze; she catches Colonel Fitzwilliam looking back at him.

Colonel Fitzwilliam's face is neutral until, on a breath out, it melts into a little smile at the footman.

Heat creeps up Charlotte's neck and cheeks. She glances left and right, though no one else seems to have noticed what happened. Her heart is beating fast again. She feels, strangely, almost angry at the colonel for having been so terribly obvious.

Obvious about…what, she asks herself, and then backs away from the question as Anne clears her throat.

"We shall dine," Anne says, "on breakfast! Good appetite to you all!"

The dishes and tureens are brought forward and set upon the table. The startled guests watch as piles of eggs, heaps of kidneys and liver, meat chops and sliced bread, and tens if not hundreds of cakes appear. Anne is giggling in a way that opens a pit in Charlotte's stomach.

Charlotte looks to Caroline, whose eyes are narrowed, watching Anne with an expression somewhere between contempt and interest.

"Eat!" Anne demands, and sits. She looks to Colonel Fitzwilliam, who manages a smile and reaches bemusedly for a slice of plum cake.

Following his lead, the rest of the guests serve themselves, whispering to each other and sharing loaded looks.

"Come!" Anne says, her gimlet eyes raking the room. "Is not this fun?"

"Enormous fun!" says a man sitting close by Anne. He has impressive side-whiskers, and an even more impressive impersonation of a man having an enjoyable time. "Breakfast for dinner! However did you think of it?"

"Yes, Miss de Bourgh, how?" asks another gentleman a little farther away. "A stroke of genius. A mark of true wit!"

Caroline lets out a breath in a way that is not quite a laugh, but certainly isn't anything else.

"Mother hen is gone," Caroline says. "Little chick is all alone, and the cockerel meant to protect her has another sweet bird in his henhouse at Pemberley. And so…" Caroline nods towards the gentlemen making Anne flush and laugh. "The scavengers circle."

Charlotte makes no response. She looks to Anne, and permits herself to wonder what it feels like to be sought after.

A servant appears over Charlotte's shoulder, about to pour wine into her glass. Charlotte covers her glass with a stiff hand.

"No," she says. "No, thank you."

Painful hours later, the dining table has finally been left behind, and the guests have been permitted to roam the rooms of Rosings before the threatened dancing, games, and libations begin. Charlotte is doing her best to skulk to a quiet corner in dignity.

"Charlotte, there you are!" Anne says.

Charlotte turns in answer to Anne's call and hitches a polite smile onto her taut face. "Miss de Bourgh," she says.

"Walk with me."

Charlotte does as she is bid, following Anne through a set of glass doors into a porticoed pathway beyond. Anne throws out her arms and takes a deep breath of the outside air, twirling once, and again, and then giggling.

"Tonight is so fun!" she announces, and then looks to Charlotte as though she has performed happiness for the first time, and is looking for applause.

"It is, yes," Charlotte manages.

Anne sits on a stone bench, demanding Charlotte sit too with an insistent little pat of the space beside her. Charlotte complies. Her stomach is aching from the amount of food she ate, mindful of the sparse larder at home.

"You," Anne says, wiggling her finger towards Charlotte, "are my greatest challenge." The rouge on her cheeks is cracking in places, showing the skin beneath.

Charlotte shifts uncomfortably on the bench.

"You have not laughed once, yet," Anne says. "I have paid attention."

"You do me too great an honour to afford me particular notice on a night so special to you, Miss de Bourgh," Charlotte says.

"You are the measure by which I know my success or failure," Anne says. "No matter that I have not yet succeeded. I am sure to win when it comes to dancing. And I have an array of drinks and other things that will liven you up."

Charlotte clenches her fists. Something inside her seems to wobble dangerously.

"I even hid one out here," Anne says, and reaches behind a column to retrieve a bottle and a single glass. "Come, drink."

"Oh…" Charlotte says, wishing to refuse outright but too keenly aware of her position to do so. "I fear the magnificence of the dinner must be allowed to settle."

Anne makes a noise of frustration, but the compliment seems to pacify her. She pours herself a glass of golden-brown liquid and takes a sip.

Charlotte sits awkwardly by her side and wonders whether she can leave. The bottle is on the bench between them, threatening recklessness and wildness and hideous embarrassment, the leave of all good sense and character. Charlotte thinks, incongruously, of Caroline raising an eyebrow at her, and the loveliness of her teal gown. She only barely resists the sudden urge to smash the bottle to the floor.

She wonders at herself. Something is shaking inside her. Or perhaps it is only her hands shaking. Either way, she wants to go home.

"Everyone thinks I'm quite unhinged," Anne says, and takes another deep gulp of the contents of her little cup, leaving it almost empty.

Drawn out of her thoughts, Charlotte's mouth opens in surprise. "Miss de Bourgh…"

"It's true," Anne says. "Before, everyone thought I was sickly and boring. Now, everyone thinks I am sickly and mad. I am not, though. I am set free." Her tone turns soft and dreamy. "No one can see that but me. I am quite free."

She pushes the bottle closer to Charlotte, who pretends not to notice.

"You are not free," Anne says. She drains the last of her glass and then examines Charlotte, her eyes like fish knives, sharp and ready. "You could be. But you choose not to be."

Charlotte looks at Anne's smug face, with its paints and powders worth enough to feed Charlotte for a month, and the shaking feeling becomes in a blink something horrifically huge, hateful, incandescent. Too large and too powerful for such a small moment. Charlotte holds herself rigid and waits for it to pass, but it doesn't. It roars louder. She stands too quickly. Her breath is coming fast.

"I shall go indoors," she announces, and then—because of her parents and her late husband and the sudden weight of shame in her chest—she adds, "by your leave, Miss de Bourgh."

Anne looks up at her, her expression slightly too self-involved to be clever.

"Go, then," she says indifferently.

As Charlotte turns to leave, Anne moves—reaches for Charlotte's shoulder, perhaps to hold her in place, or to push. Charlotte tries, instinctively, to duck away; Anne's hand tightens on the fabric of Charlotte's dress, and there is a sound of tearing.

Charlotte falls. She feels her teeth sink too hard into her lower lip as she lands in an ungainly sprawl.

She looks up at Anne, one sleeve of her dress ripped, and Anne giggles.

"You look silly," Anne says. "That's better than boring, at least."

Charlotte gets to her feet and hurries away without another word, Anne's giggles following her inside. She is quivering, her lips pinched, her hands clenched, every inch of her trembling with the need to remain dignified through such insult—such *vile* insult. Her skin feels tight, her dress feels itchy, and her hair is unravelling. Her lip hurts. Within her, there is the sensation of a single, focused, highly pressured burst in a mighty dam. The rest of the structure shakes and rumbles.

Charlotte marches through the darkened rooms of Rosings, most of them empty—the guests are strewn about the place, each in their own isolated corners of embarrassment. She does not know where she is going, heading blindly down a corridor until she hears a familiar voice.

"Mrs. Collins?"

Charlotte turns to the welcome sight of Colonel Fitzwilliam, his spaniel-esque soft brown eyes concerned.

"Forgive me," he says. "I saw you take a fall. Are you quite well?"

"I…yes, I only need a little…a little time to gather myself." Charlotte thinks that in silence, on her own, she will be able to stop this overwhelming feeling of shifting and shaking.

"Of course—perhaps I can—"

The blond footman who greeted Charlotte at the door steps into the corridor and passes Fitzwilliam a drink. His hand lingers for a moment, and then he leaves, Colonel Fitzwilliam watching him as he goes. Charlotte's eyes flicker between them, refusing to allow herself to draw conclusions.

"I…" She swallows hard. There is a hammering in her head and a tearing in her chest. "I must go."

"Mrs. Collins…"

Charlotte turns quickly and walks away, leaving Fitzwilliam alone in the corridor.

She resumes her frantic pacing of Rosings' dark corners. Her shaking anger at Anne does not ease but only grows. The dam shudders.

Charlotte can feel it twisting her face, seeking release: tears, screams, fury. The feeling is catastrophic and painful, terrible, overwhelming. She digs her fingertips into the palms of her hands and holds it in.

Flashes of anger pound at her as she races through the grand and horrible house. Here, the indignity of cheap widow's weeds, there, the reek of wealth at Rosings. A blond footman and a colonel, and what can pass between two people who could never be wed. The ignored blood-rush and heart-pound when Caroline Bingley held her gaze across a room, and—

Charlotte bursts through a set of grand doors and finds herself in a huge, dark, empty ballroom.

She slams the doors behind her, turns, presses her forehead to the wood, and grits her teeth as she just barely holds on.

"You have found me," says a wry voice, and Charlotte spins, one hand clapping to her mouth. Against the wall, sitting with her knees up and tenting her fashionable dress, is Caroline Bingley.

It is the shock that finally breaks the dam. Unable to stop herself, embarrassingly, Charlotte begins to cry.

"Oh," she hears Caroline say. Her sight is blurred by fat, wet tears, and she turns away, covering her face with both hands.

"I am—I am so sorry—" Charlotte fights to say through the inexorable tide of misery. "I shall—I shall leave—" She tries holding her breath to stem the tears, and it does not work. Charlotte's badly stifled sobs are raw and painful in her throat, too loud, too much. There's a swish of fabric behind her.

"What is this?" Caroline says, and her voice is closer.

"It is nothing," Charlotte says quickly, almost viciously, and then looks around at

Caroline. "Oh—that was rude—"

Caroline waves a hand. "I am always rude," she says. Her honesty makes Charlotte laugh, a hiccough in between sobs. "Come," Caroline says, with a dash of impatience. "You have interrupted my solitude. Am I not owed some explanation?"

Charlotte's knees go weak, and she puts a hand on the door for support.

"No," Caroline says, "come, this is too much—you must tell me what has upset you. Has someone done something?" Her tone is cold with sudden steel.

"Truly, it is nothing," Charlotte gasps. "Well, that is, someone did something. But it—it is not that—" Charlotte breaks off as a sob swallows her voice, and then tries again. "It is only…I do not know, but I think I am tired."

"Tired?" Caroline says, and her voice is just careful enough that Charlotte keeps talking.

"Yes," Charlotte says, and turns to look at Caroline in her expensive and lovely teal gown, anger rippling through her. She can hold back no more; the flood surges. "I am tired! I am tired of being plain, and poor, and sensible, and—and I am tired of carrying the weight of my heart, that insists on asking always for something I cannot have. I try to ignore it—but—but I cannot deny it. I am not all good sense, I am not all sober and solemn, I do not want to follow the wretched strictures and rules any longer. I want something *real*! I want to feel! I want truth and—and to act according to my nature, and—I want—I want—"

"Freedom," Caroline says, unexpectedly. Charlotte is startled by the word, and looks at Caroline more clearly. Caroline's eyes are suddenly bright with a kind of desperate empathy.

Charlotte blinks. "Freedom," she says, as though understanding the word for the first time.

Outside, visible through the wide glass doors on the far side of the room, Anne de Bourgh passes by, her arms out.

"Dancing, soon!" she cries as she goes. "Dancing! Come along! In the Blue Room!"

She is silhouetted—none of the gaudy paint is visible, nor her viperish expression. For a moment she looks, to Charlotte, quite magnificent: unfettered, skirts swirling.

She moves, and the light strikes her differently. The moon's eye falls balefully on the way that her frothy old dress has slipped, revealing even more of her pale, veiny chest.

"She brings a whole new meaning to the phrase 'blue tit,' doesn't she?" Caroline says.

Wiping at her cheeks and nose, trying to steady herself, Charlotte replies, "I don't know what that means."

Caroline snorts. "But you're from the backwaters of Kent, darling."

Charlotte is sure that *darling* is meant to demean her, but it makes her heart beat faster and the colour rise in her cheeks in a way that feels a lot more like pleasure than patronisation.

"It's a bird," Caroline says.

"Oh," Charlotte says, "a titmouse? But what's that to do with…" Charlotte's eyebrows suddenly go up. "*Oh.*"

Caroline smiles, and Charlotte swears that there's a bit of genuine warmth in her eyes when she says, "There, you have it."

"I do."

"Rather cruel of me."

Cruel. Hearing the word fills Charlotte's eyes with tears again. She holds a hand to her mouth as a river of memories floods her. Events and gatherings and meals and soulless nights with her late husband, all greeted with a smile, not permitted the mercy of a bad temper even once across the years.

She thinks about Lizzy Bennet, eyes wide in shock, when Charlotte told her she was to marry Mr. Collins. At the time, she'd thought Lizzy was unworldly and foolish. Now, tonight, Charlotte looks back and sees only a dear friend dismayed at the cruelty she was about to inflict on herself.

"I have been very cruel to myself," Charlotte says. "But if I had my time again, I would have to do all the same things. I cannot change my position." The tears surge again. "And I do not know what happens now. Every day I think that I cannot—I cannot bear to stay at the parsonage any longer. But I have nowhere to go."

"You have friends, do you not?" Caroline asks.

"Yes, but I…"

A moment passes. Charlotte thinks of the feeling of looking at Caroline, and Lizzy's quickness, and can finally name the huge and horrible feeling that has held her back from reaching out for her friend's help: a fear of discovery.

Caroline looks Charlotte over astutely. "Mrs. Hurst, my sister," she says in a low voice, "is very good to me."

Charlotte draws in a breath. She thinks now of Lizzy's kindness, and a little of the weight lifts. Her eyes fill again with tears.

"Perhaps it would not be so very bad to go to Pemberley," Charlotte murmurs, more to herself than Caroline.

Caroline does not answer. Charlotte is quiet, too. Their bodies are close; they are standing as would intimate friends, or lovers. Charlotte wants to stare. She waits for the familiar pricking of shame or sense of propriety to choke the urge, but nothing happens.

The dam is broken.

The tears are flowing.

Charlotte lets herself look at Caroline. She takes in the curve of her neck and the curls of her hair and the length of her eyelashes and the softness of her lips, and the curve of her neck, and the curls of her hair…

Caroline looks back at her.

Something hot and bright grows in Caroline's expression the longer Charlotte does not look away, and Charlotte says, "You look at me queerly."

Caroline only looks some more.

"Yes," Charlotte says, "like that."

"I like looking at you," Caroline says.

"There's another of your jokes," Charlotte says. "See, I understood that one."

"I made no joke," Caroline says lightly. "I like to look at you."

"No," Charlotte says, with a little breath of a laugh that's still wet with tears.

"Do not make me fight to compliment you," Caroline says. "It does not come easily to me in the first place."

"I am plain," Charlotte says, with a novel note of sadness in her tone, as though she truly wished it were not so—perhaps for the first time. "Unusually plain, in fact."

Caroline raises an eyebrow and lifts a hand. She hooks a finger under Charlotte's chin, and gently turns her head to one side.

"Are you sure?" Caroline says.

Charlotte knows she is tearful, flushed, messy.

With a smile that is almost private, Caroline says, "You have a pair of fine eyes, Mrs. Collins."

Charlotte's heart squeezes a little at the sound of the name that always fit her ill. But she doesn't move an inch, finding herself desperate not to dislodge the gentle press of a single finger beneath her chin.

After a moment, Caroline corrects herself. "Charlotte," she says. Charlotte's breath comes a little sharp, and Caroline's gaze flicks across her face as she repeats, "You have a pair of fine eyes, Charlotte."

In the distance, from the Blue Room, there comes the sound of the music starting. Caroline's face shifts into mischief, and she lets go of Charlotte's chin only to take her hand.

"Come," she says, "let's dance."

"I cannot dance," Charlotte says. "I've been crying."

"Perhaps that is the best time for it," Caroline says, and her tone has its usual velvet sarcasm, but her expression is the most earnest Charlotte has ever seen it.

"I do not know if I can," Charlotte admits.

Caroline says nothing, only begins the dance with a smile. Charlotte cannot help but follow, though she tries to move stiffly, tries to maintain propriety; she tries to show that she knows how odd and uncomfortable she must look, so she cannot be caught off-guard and vulnerable by a joke at her expense from Caroline. But her body has cried away its stiffness and its shame for tonight. Her body moves softly, easily. Her body asks for more.

The music grows louder. Caroline is looking at Charlotte as they dance, something in her eyes that looks too mingled with slight hesitation and confusion to be a trap; she is warm, watchful, and the touch of their hands is gentle. It does not change what has gone before. It is not an answer. Charlotte thinks that freedom cannot be claimed in a single moment—unless it can, and it is the first moment when one reaches for what one wants. With shame or without. Crying or not crying. Not dancing, or dancing.

Caroline's fingertips are soft against Charlotte's own. What she wants from this,

Charlotte cannot imagine—but she wants it.

Charlotte takes a deep breath. She almost moves away, as the dance would dictate—and then her body sways back, draws in close.

Four hours later, Charlotte walks home at dawn.

She is wearing a fashionable teal dress that does not fit, under a gold footman's coat to keep her warm. She is pleasantly dishevelled and cannot quite seem to keep the smile from her face.

A soft mist covers the field she passes through. The light is tentative, offering her threads of sparkling gold for her hair, for her eyes.

Charlotte's shoulders are relaxed. She breathes in, and then lets it go.

In a lonely field, for the first time, she walks without stiffness. Without shame. Incidentally, she is completely beautiful.

Zel Howland

A STOLEN MOMENT

The origins of this piece were formed many years ago, when I noted in the 2005 _Pride and Prejudice_ movie that there was a lot of potential of a Lizzy/Charlotte romance in the subtext of their interactions. At the time, I outlined a fanfiction about the two of them running parallel to the canon events of the book, but I never started writing the fic itself. This anthology proved to be the perfect opportunity to revisit the idea, reimagining the tracking shot through the Netherfield Ball in the 2005 movie as ending not on Lizzy standing alone in the dark, but instead finding a stolen moment with her best friend and lover, away from the pressures and rules of polite society.

TAGS

aroace, aromantic, asexual, f/m (platonic), friends, historical, marriage proposal, period-typical understand-ings of gender and sexuality, present tense, regency, relationship of convenience, story diverges from the original work's canon, t4t, third person limited point of view, transphobia (mentions of)

INSPIRATION

On thinking about Darcy and his role in the book, specifically his disdain for the more social behaviors, I began to wonder: what if it was simply that he did not want to be perceived as he was? This, naturally, led me to the concept of Darcy being trans; and, as a heroine that did not fit the general societal mold, I began to think about Elizabeth being trans, as well. Thus came the idea of Darcy and Eli, finding themselves (with an ease not gen-erally allotted to the discovery of one's own identity) in each other's clothes. I think many classics could use a queer lens fitted firmly over the page, and I'm very glad to have done so here.

TROUSERS AND OTHER ODDITIES

THE DEFINITION OF "subtlety" is often lost on those who would polish mirrors until they shone, decorate walls with lavish portraits, hire entire orchestras for an evening's entertainment, and invite countless people into a ballroom until "brushing elbows" is less a turn of phrase and more an unavoidable eventuality. The moves of the contra are not the true dance of these stifling events; the true dance involves more vocal cords and polite smiles, and it is one that Elizabeth, somewhat unfortunately, possesses remarkable skill in navigating.

The issue with this sort of social two-step is that there is no bowing out at the end, no thankful smile as she retreats elsewhere. She has to stand and listen to whatever the topic is, no matter how dreadfully boring, while her thoughts are miles away.

That is where Elizabeth is now: firmly stuck between a Lord, telling her about his favorite hunting dog, and a Lady, giving her a tight-lipped smile that quite clearly conveys "he is off-limits, darling." (If there had been a returning gesture that meant "Thank goodness," Elizabeth would be using it.)

"And he is quite *extraordinary*, you see," the Lord prattles on, "because he understands the English language, being an English dog, but also seems to have some small grasp of French, as well!"

"Amazing," Elizabeth responds with an amused smile. "Is he here somewhere, by chance, that I might dance with him tonight?"

The Lord laughs heartily, while the Lady laughs behind her hand. Someone then calls the Lord's name, and the two are off once more with a polite goodbye. Elizabeth lets out a small sigh of relief and looks around the room for an escape.

There is every manner of person engaged in some form of social chicanery, from her sisters batting eyelashes at charming young men to complete strangers casting eyes at any young lady who dares move. Elizabeth walks swiftly to the edge of the room before any of these eyes land upon her. She finds a small bench to sit upon, away from everything else, and tries to gather her bearings; she's been here for hours already, and there are, undoubtedly, hours to go. Still, the time will pass whether she suffers or celebrates, so she might as well celebrate. Just…in a moment.

She leans her head against the wall, closes her eyes, and, here, she overhears the voices of two men arguing.

"Miss Amy is quite stunning," the brighter of the two offers. "Dark dresses become her."

"Perhaps," begrudgingly agrees the gloomier one, the sole occupant of a nearby bench, "though she knows far too much about flora for a lady of her standing."

"I think she'd beg to differ and do so in a great many words." The brighter one laughs softly. "Truly, Mister Darcy, you are being churlish tonight, and I am half tempted to leave you here and go enjoy the festivities alone."

"Please, do. I did specifically ask *not* to be dragged along."

"And what manner of friend would that make me? Letting you wither away like moss in acidic mud?"

"Well, Mister Bingley, to think you've been ignoring Miss Amy; she very clearly stated moss *thrives* in acidic mud. And here you are, calling *me* churlish."

"Aye, I must remedy this immediately by asking her to dance. And after her, Miss Jane, if she can stand me."

"No one can stand you," Darcy says. It lands as a joke, light and airy, and Bingley laughs. "There seem to be plenty of the Bennet girls for you to pick from. Why her?"

"I do not know yet, and that is what excites me about her." Bingley straightens his own lapels. "Why don't you ask one to dance, then, if there be a surplus? Perhaps Miss Elizabeth?"

Darcy grimaces. "She is rather loud—and not very handsome."

There is a brief silence, then, "Aye, you are *indeed* in one of your moods tonight. I will leave you here after all. Come find me if your mood changes, dear friend. I will speak highly of you to anyone who will listen."

"Please don't," Darcy says, but Bingley is already gone. He sighs and leans back on the bench in some guise of abject misery that has Elizabeth wandering over and sitting beside him, waiting for his notice. "I'm afraid I am not up for friendly company this evening," he says, turning to find the suitably displeased countenance of Elizabeth Bennet looking directly at him. "Oh."

"Just as well," she responds grimly, "for I am rather loud and unhandsome company."

"You were not meant to hear that."

"What does that change? Though, I will take it as a compliment that I am so detestable to someone like you." She looks out at the ball with him as it twists and turns like a living thing. "Unfortunately, I believe you and I are the only ones not fully entranced with the party."

"I thought balls were designed for women," Darcy remarks. "You always seem to get the better end of the deal."

"Better end?" Elizabeth responds, disbelieving. "Men have it better. All you have to do is pick out a suitable partner and dance the night away or discuss whatever you wish, with no regard for if your partner wishes to hear it."

"All women have to do is listen; they do not have to speak more than to maintain the conversation. Surely, you can see how that is easier?"

"Nay, I cannot," she responds with a shake of her head. "In fact, it is altogether boring and dismal to be a woman at a ball. I just listened to nearly an *hour* of a man claiming his dog spoke *French*."

"And did it?"

Despite herself, Elizabeth laughs. "To hear him say it, you'd certainly think so."

"If my dog spoke French," Darcy says, "I would not be wasting my time at a *ball*."

"Would you be selling tickets, then?"

"Of course. Directly outside, as a matter of fact."

"Ah, yes, of course." She laughs. "But *back to the topic at hand*. As a man, you could go on forever about your French show dog, and, as a woman, all I could do is sit there and listen until you got bored or someone stole me away for a dance."

"As a *woman*, there are not the cutting nerves of trying to figure out the right thing to say or of trying to entertain. That falls to someone else. And you get to put ribbons in your hair. Men do not get to do that."

Elizabeth nearly snorts and reaches up, untying a ribbon. "For good luck," she jokes softly, reaching out to tie it around Darcy's wrist. He stares at it in a way that Elizabeth cannot parse. "That is not something a woman should do, either," she admits.

"It isn't," he agrees, running his other thumb along the silken length. "I won't tell anyone."

"Your loyalty is astounding." She turns once more toward the ballroom, where dresses flare out like seafoam tucked too quickly back into the sea. She spies her sisters individually and laughs fondly at them. "I will never understand how they so enjoy this," she offers, looking to Darcy, who is staring not at the ball but at her.

"Miss Elizabeth," he says, and there is something meaningful in the words.

"You're saying my name like it's something holy," she accuses. "Don't."

"I have thought of a way to settle our disagreement."

"Over the dog who speaks French? I thought we were quite in agreement on that."

"On who has the easier lot."

"Ah. Then I am listening intently."

He is still holding the edge of the ribbon—finer by far, Elizabeth notices, than the one currently tying his own hair back—between thumb and forefinger. "What if you and I switched places for the rest of the night?"

"You will have to be more specific."

His face is red, as if he's saying something forbidden. "We switch clothes." Ah. He is.

Elizabeth balks at that, sitting up straighter and looking at the many eyes in the sea. "Even were I to agree to that, I'm not sure we wouldn't be thrown out. Unless that is the point: to see *which* of us gets thrown out first."

"No, no. There are more rooms here than this one. I suggest we find one, switch clothes, and pretend to be each other, or some version of each other. At the end of the night, perhaps we will know who has it easier."

Elizabeth worries her bottom lip. "And if we are caught?"

"I pray we won't be," he says. She hesitates, and he inches nearer. "Just for one night. Aren't you curious? Moreover, aren't you inherently *bored* with this ball?"

"This…would certainly add an element of interest." She eyes his suit. "Very well. Do you know where these other, hidden rooms are?"

"I do." Darcy stands swiftly and walks away, leaving Elizabeth with no choice but to follow.

"I do hope you are not leading me to some grisly demise," Elizabeth tells him as she follows him into dense, candlelit halls. "If you are, might I have a moment to go back and say farewell to my sisters? I'm afraid they'll forget about the horses if I don't remind them."

"You could remind them as a ghost."

"You're not lifting my spirits." She eyes him curiously as shadows dance like the ball disappearing into echoes behind them. "You do seem rather excited about the prospect."

"Murder?"

"Trading places."

Mister Darcy, decidedly, ignores her, testing a door handle and finding it unlocked. "Ah, here. After you."

"Then there are some manners in you," Elizabeth jokes, walking into the room. It's all shadows and mirrors, connected to an adjacent room by an ornate door. "How do we proceed? I have no intentions of providing you a glimpse of even my ankle, Mister Darcy."

"Nor do I wish to see it," he responds, eyes averted. "I shall go to the other room, and when I am ready to switch clothes, I will knock. You do the same, and we will pass them through the gap of the door. Will that suffice?"

"Scandalous," Elizabeth whispers, eyes shining, and Darcy walks hurriedly into the next room. The door that closes between them feels resolute.

Elizabeth undoes the ties at the back of her dress, letting the train of it fall, and shimmies out of it with difficulty. She struggles with her stays, but those come undone as Mister Darcy knocks.

"Almost!" Elizabeth responds, hurriedly pulling off her chemise and standing, horrifically, naked. Her reflection seems to twist and turn as she rolls her stockings off, hopping on one foot then the other.

"Are you all right?" Darcy asks, muffled.

"Yes, quite! It's just— Well, you'll see!" Finally done, she balls up her clothes and knocks. The door opens just enough that they can trade their outfits through the crack. It closes once more, and Elizabeth is faced with trousers and other oddities.

She raises her eyebrows at the array of fine fabrics, laughing to herself as she touches warm silk. "How straightforward," she murmurs, then begins buttoning on the shirt and pulling on the trousers. The waistcoat goes next, she's sure, then the—wait, the socks. She is once again hopping around, though she can hear Darcy doing the same this time.

"Are you quite alright?" she calls back with a laugh, and an ungentlemanly curse leaves Darcy's lips.

"What *are* all these confounding things?"

"*Clothes*," Elizabeth returns, pulling on the coat and attempting to tie the cravat. The shoes are too large, but she laces them tightly to account for it, and…there. That's as close as she can get on her own. She turns to the mirrors to look, still half laughing as Darcy, from the sound of it, falls over.

The suit is too large, for one thing, as it was not tailored to her. The sleeves of the coat are too long, as are the trousers, though she cuffs them somewhat sufficiently. She fastens the waistcoat and watches her hands tug each button through the corresponding hole. She studies herself, then takes her hair and unties it, only to tie it back snug at the base of her skull. Her fingers brush over soft fabric and rounded fasteners.

"Mister Elizabeth," she says to her reflection with a small curtsy and a giggle, then straightens to study herself again. "Mister Eli," Elizabeth says, this time bowing properly. She looks up again from her bow, eyes meeting eyes in the unflinching mirror. "Mister Eli," Eli says once more, quieter, serious, before he hastily straightens and turns stiffly, anxiously, to the door.

"Mister Darcy!" he calls out, wincing at his own voice and suddenly feeling horrible in his own skin. He pulls on the shirt sleeves. "Are you nearly ready?"

"I can't figure it out," comes the downtrodden voice, and Eli laughs to himself and knocks lightly.

"May I help?"

"I am *hardly* decent!"

"Do you have the chemise on?"

"The… Could you describe it to me?"

He giggles. "The white dress."

"Oh. No, I hadn't gotten to that yet."

"Unfortunately for you, I'm afraid that goes on first."

There is a moment of quiet, then another curse and the sound of clothes falling to the floor. Finally, Darcy calls out, "I have the white dress on!"

"Then I am coming in!"

"Maybe you shouldn't—" Darcy begins, but Eli barges in anyway, closing the door behind him. Darcy's face is tinged pink, even in the dim light. The clothes lie in disarray. "It's all very confusing," he murmurs, and Eli gives him a small smile.

"I know," he offers gently, then picks up the stays. "Slip these on, and I'll teach you to fasten them."

And so the stays, the stockings, and the dress itself are put on. Eli takes the ribbon from Darcy's wrist and does up his hair as pretty as any lady dancing a thousand rooms away.

"There," Eli whispers. "Take a look. You're beautiful." He pulls Darcy back into the main room, where the mirrors wait patiently. Eli tries to keep his eyes trained on Darcy, but they keep drifting to himself, instead. He adjusts the poorly tied cravat and feels something…light well up in his chest.

Darcy's fingers are trailing over lace and silk and cotton, barely breathing, and Eli *knows* that look.

"You feel it, too," he says quietly, so quietly the candles on the walls do not hear.

"Feel?" Darcy asks, fingers trembling.

"That you were born wrong."

"Not born wrong," Darcy mumbles, brow furrowed. "But…shaped wrong, perhaps."

Eli takes his hand and kisses it, gentlemanly. "You look beautiful, Mister Darcy."

Darcy dares not turn to him. "Miss."

Eli squeezes her hand. "You look beautiful, Miss Darcy."

The red spreading across gentle cheeks is enough to splay her soul out on full display. "And you," Darcy says with a bit of stammering. "I…I apologize for my earlier remarks."

"Which ones?"

"When I said you were not handsome. I was wrong." She attempts a curtsy. "You're the most handsome man I've ever seen."

Eli hides his smile, shaking his head. "Do be careful with the flattery, madam. Remember your place here."

"My mistake," Darcy whispers, a smile gracing her lips. She reaches out and ties Eli's cravat for him. "Now for our test, I suppose."

"Yes—into the world with us."

Still, both hesitate. Darcy fidgets with her hair.

Finally, Eli takes a deep breath and opens the door to the hall. "After you, Miss Darcy."

"Thank you, Mister…?"

"Eli," Eli responds smoothly, and it feels *correct*.

"Mister Eli. It's a pleasure to meet you."

The hall stretches out around them. "The pleasure is all mine. Shall we?" Eli holds out an elbow, which Darcy easily takes.

"We shall."

Darcy is a vision in swaying skirts and lace, enough so that many faces turn their way as they re-enter the world, the dance floor, and the ball in turn. Eli turns to look at Darcy there, her cheeks stained the most beautiful pink, and can't help but laugh fondly. He takes her hand and leans down, kissing it. "Might I have this first dance, my lady?"

"I am a terrible dancer," Darcy mumbles but lets Eli lead her out onto the dance floor. They fall into rhythm easily, though Darcy was not lying.

"That is simply because you've been dancing the wrong side of it," Eli whispers back, and they keep time as well as they can, even when both falter at steps they've never had to make before.

Darcy is stolen from Eli by a gentleman with high cheekbones and a soft smile, and Eli can't help but laugh as he graciously obliges. Darcy sends Eli wide, panicked eyes, to which Eli just shrugs and grins.

He himself finds the illustrious Miss Amy and asks her to dance, a request that is met with excited acceptance. He tells her about the many plants he's seen wandering the meadows and listens contentedly when she tells him their names. He finds the Lady from before, who does not seem to recognize him, and explains to her the merits of trained dogs performing tricks for money. (He is more amused, however, by the Lady's attempts to imply they have no such dog.)

Many times throughout the night, Eli meets Darcy's eyes across the ball. Each time they see one another, their eyes sparkle. Darcy is surrounded by men wishing to dance with her, and Eli is having a wonderful time speaking as he chooses and seeing the lights in ladies' eyes when he asks them to dance—something he is getting better at.

"Excuse me," a voice asks, and Eli turns to see Mister Bingley with an apologetic look upon his face. "You seem to be making the rounds quite well, so I wished to ask if you had spied my friend, Mister Darcy. He seems to have altogether disappeared."

"Nay, I cannot say that I have," Eli responds in a voice now practiced and deeper. "I think Mister Darcy might be gone for good."

Bingley nods. "It is as I thought, then. Regardless, thank you for the information."

"My pleasure." Eli nods toward Jane Bennet. "That lady over there keeps looking at you, you know."

Bingley turns to look, and Jane quickly averts her eyes, cheeks dusted with pink. His eyes soften. "Does she?"

"Oh, aye. I think you should ask her to dance before I do." Eli means it as a joke, and Bingley must hear it as one, for he laughs as well.

"That is as good a reason as any, I suppose. I cannot avoid it any longer, though I admit I am nervous."

"Ah, nerves are the death of many a fond love story. I'd hate to see them ruin yours."

Bingley turns back to Eli curiously. "I'm afraid we haven't met before. I am Charles Bingley." He holds out a hand.

"I am Eli," he responds, shaking Bingley's hand.

"Eli…?"

"Yes. Eli." He grins and motions again to Jane. "A million love letters are slipping away as we speak, Mister Bingley."

"Right you are," he responds with a courteous nod. "Farewell, Mister Eli." And with that, Bingley is gone toward a hopeful Jane.

Eli finds he prefers bouncing around, speaking to every lady, to spending prolonged periods of time with anyone. No one spares him a second glance as he goes from one to the next, excited to speak and be listened to earnestly. When he glances over at Darcy, she seems content and relaxed to only have to listen and offer responses when desired.

The party dies down slowly, though far too quickly for Eli's tastes, and he feels a hand in his own before long. He glances over to see Darcy, hair in slight disarray from dancing. She pulls him furtively down the hall as the other guests trickle out into the night.

They say nothing until they get back to that room from lifetimes ago, the candles not yet burned out. The moment the door is closed, they both start laughing.

"Truly," Darcy says when she can, "I was correct after all: women have it easier."

A lazy smile still graces Eli's lips. "And yet, I also was correct: men have it easier."

"I suppose it is a question prone to possibility," she responds, there in the mirrored room where silver panes reflect a man and a woman, leaning close, speaking of things they would have dared not even whisper about hours ago.

"I found it freeing to speak as I so chose," Eli continues, "to be heard instead of merely tolerated."

"And I found it similar not having to worry about responding," Darcy replies, "to choose silence and not be hounded about it."

"Then we each have our differing answers."

"I suppose we do."

The candlelight flickers.

"Well," Darcy begins, clearing her throat, "I suppose it is now time to switch back and return to our families and friends before they realize we are missing."

"Aye, it must be." Eli watches as Darcy goes slowly to the other room, as the door closes behind her with hesitation and despair.

Alone, Eli looks at himself once more in the mirror, at the ill-tailored suit and the too-big shoes. He touches gently the round buttons, runs a hand over pulled-back hair. Though his hands rest on the first fastener, they refuse to move.

"Darcy," he calls out at the same time that Darcy calls out, "Eli."

He swallows harshly. "I'm going to open the door now."

"All right," comes the quiet reply.

He opens the door to see Darcy similarly stuck, clothes not the slightest bit undone. They stand in silence.

"I have many rooms at my estate," Darcy finally offers, cheeks stained. "I'd hate to keep our gracious hosts waiting for us to be done in here."

"Yes," Eli agrees unquestioningly. "In addition, I think we'd make quite the spectacle if we came out of here long after everyone else has left."

"Agreed. Then it is settled? You will accompany me to my estate and we shall swap back there?"

"It truly appears to be the most logical course of action."

They sneak out of the room and back to the thinning throng, mingling with guests until they greet the cool outside air and the few remaining carriages.

"How far do you live?" Eli asks gently.

"Not far. Walk me home?"

"It would be my honor."

They set out between tall grasses and rolling lands while the stars watch overhead with bated breath, twinkling just for them.

"Your friend, Mister Bingley, seems quite taken with Jane," Eli says to fill the silence, though his voice does not carry far.

"So I saw. They were staring at one another all night. It's a wonder he managed to speak to her, let alone dance."

"I might have encouraged him." He gives her a small smile. "He was looking for you. Rather, he was looking for a you that no longer exists. I told him you must be gone."

Darcy puts a hand to her chest. "I believe I must be." She shakes her head. "Bingley can get caught up in emotions that do not last. I fear something similar for your sister."

"Perhaps, but I do not think it our duty to decide the extent of their affection."

"Maybe," Darcy responds, unconvinced but at least assuaged. "Did you find any lady there to suit your fancy?"

Eli laughs. "I'm not quite sure I fancy *anyone*, though I did find Miss Amy, and I fear you've been entirely unfair to her."

"I'm unfair to a great many people," Darcy admits. "I found her as well, though our discussion was brief. I think, perhaps, I envied her. To speak without worry, to be charming without trying…she was everything I am not."

"Why do you wish to be charming?"

"Because I've never been. I am…harsh and unyielding and unfriendly. I do not know how to change."

Eli snorts. "Though I agree with your assessment, I do not think these things are the end of you. There is more under the surface. There are worse things to be."

"What would be worse for me to be than *rude*?"

Eli gives her a shrug. "A man."

Darcy turns her head sharply forward, lips sealed, cheeks flushed. The moon rises steadily on.

"Did you find anyone to suit *your* fancy?" Eli asks after the silence finally wears itself ragged.

"Perhaps," Darcy mumbles, then glances at Eli. "I felt more accepted tonight than I ever have before. Or, perhaps, I felt like I *belonged*."

Eli nods. "I know the feeling. It was like things lined up how they were meant to."

"As if it were fate that we meet."

"I don't know that I believe in fate."

"What else would you call this?"

"I don't know," Eli admits, watching his too-large shoes step upon the soft ground. "Fate implies we had nothing to do with it. I'm inclined to believe it was all because of us."

"If we say it was all us, then we have to name it. We have to give it shape."

"What would we even call it?"

"I don't know." Darcy tugs lightly on her hair. "I know I do not wish to go back."

Eli stops walking. Darcy halts as well, turning to look at him. Her dress blows in the wind. "What choice do we have?" Eli asks, voice low and aching.

"You keep asking questions I cannot answer," Darcy says with what could almost be construed as a laugh. "Tonight we both learned things about ourselves—do not deny it, Eli; I can see it in your eyes as plainly as I can see the stars. You are changed."

"Whether or no," Eli responds quietly, hiding his traitorous gaze, "my family is bound to notice if tomorrow they have a son rather than a daughter. I doubt their opinions on the matter."

"As do I mine," Darcy responds, just as quiet. "But I doubt more returning to my past life. I do not fit there. I did not before, and I certainly do not now. I—I think I'd tear myself to pieces were I to waltz back into it as if tonight had no meaning."

"Did it have meaning?"

"I think there has been nothing more meaningful." Darcy takes a step toward him. "Say it. Say that I am not alone. Say it is not merely I who cannot trace my steps anymore."

"It is not only you," Eli says, though he still looks anywhere but at the desperate lady before him. "It feels…agonizing. Overwhelming. I'd run away if I didn't know it would destroy my sisters. But I cannot run away, and neither can you. We are stuck here, whether we wish it or no."

"Forever? Have we tasted the truth of life only to be starved of it hereafter?" Darcy steps into Eli's space, angles her neck to meet his eyes. "Look at me and say this is to be it, and I shall surrender."

Eli finally looks again at the woman before him, there with the wind twisting and blowing her loose hair upon its eddies, sending her dress in waves like clouds threatening thunder. Her eyes are wide and pleading, insistent that Eli himself holds the key to her existence. He opens his mouth, and nothing comes out.

"Look at me," Darcy repeats thickly, a single tear falling down her fair cheek. "Look at me, and say this is it. Tell me to surrender, Eli. If you are going to dash me against these rocks, do it *now*."

"What else am I meant to do?" Eli whispers, voice shakier than he intends it to be. "What other choice do I have?"

"Stay with me," Darcy breathes, then her eyes become harrowed, as if she had not expected the words to leave her lips.

"Stay with you?"

She nods, appearing unsure but forging ahead regardless. "You think no one will understand, but that is not true—*I* understand. I am here, before you, and I *know*. If we wish to exist in this world rather than merely skirt along its edges, you and I…we are bound to one another. We cannot part. Do you see this? Do you understand what I am asking of you?"

"You will have to be plain," Eli whispers back, hands trembling.

"The only way to exist is together, and the only way to be together is to be so by law." Darcy wrings her hands before herself, soul laid bare. "Tell me to surrender."

"I do not love you." Eli swallows harshly. The stars seem to twinkle in time with his erratic heart.

"Nor do I you," Darcy responds the same. "Nor do I ask that you grow to love me—or pretend you even could—in this form of mine that seems to have forsaken me. I—"

"It has not forsaken you," Eli responds softly. "It has finally found you."

Darcy nods, glancing away before looking back. "Tell me to surrender," she pleads once more.

"Marry me," Eli says instead. "We can exist together. The world outside of us will still ask us to be what we are not, but we…we don't have to abandon ourselves entirely. Marry me, Miss Darcy. We can figure it out, together."

"And if we fail?" Darcy asks, barely a breath on the rising wind.

"Then I am glad to not do so alone." Eli bows and holds out his hand, a promise of possibility and change, a promise of ribbons and shoes that fit properly, and Darcy accepts.

There are many things to plan, many people to tell while wearing the guise of past lives, but for now, Eli looks up into the most dazzling smile the night sky has ever witnessed and thinks to himself that he has never seen a woman more beautiful than Miss Darcy, surrounded by the wondrous, endless, twinkling night.

Xanthe P. Russell

DISTRACTED GLANCES

There's a part of the original novel when Darcy smiles down at Lizzy but she doesn't notice, too caught up in her own joy at their engagement. So I wanted to create my own queer version of this moment and play with the idea that there are a myriad of unconscious, smitten glances that they make at and around each other without the other ever realising it.

Darcy and Lizzy are a couple for whom so much of their early relationship is defined by outward contempt and derision such that everyone around them knows that they do not get along. I wished to counter that with a subtle lift of the corner of their mouths, a sparkle of longing in their eyes as they are unable to express the actual love they have for one another because of the reality of the time.

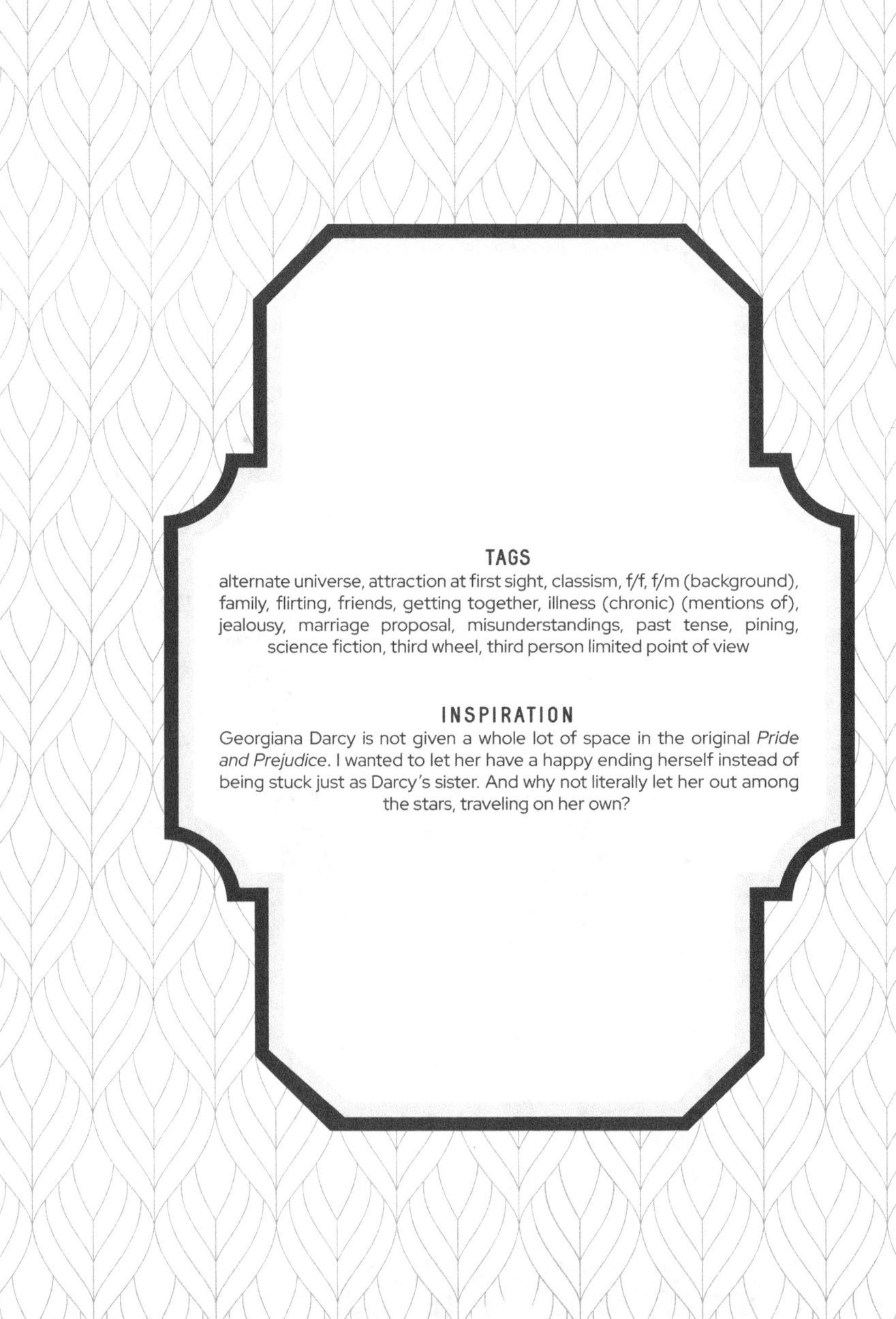

TAGS
alternate universe, attraction at first sight, classism, f/f, f/m (background), family, flirting, friends, getting together, illness (chronic) (mentions of), jealousy, marriage proposal, misunderstandings, past tense, pining, science fiction, third wheel, third person limited point of view

INSPIRATION
Georgiana Darcy is not given a whole lot of space in the original *Pride and Prejudice*. I wanted to let her have a happy ending herself instead of being stuck just as Darcy's sister. And why not literally let her out among the stars, traveling on her own?

Genevieve Maxwell

MUST BE IN WANT OF A WIFE

Panic rose as Georgiana faced the enormity of the bustling gateway. There were so many people, sounds, smells, and bright lights in every color. She was dazzled and more than a little scared, unsure how she'd make her way through it all. Georgiana had been to plenty of dockcities before, and naturally she'd been through gateways, though most of her traveling had been on Pemberley, where she had the option of never setting foot on a planet's soil if she so chose. One didn't need to go through a gateway if one had docked an estate in a proper neighborhood.

Clutching the strap of her bag, Georgiana took several deep breaths and made her way into the throng. Charles had told her to head for the Meryton exit, so she allowed herself to flow along with the crowd headed in that direction.

"Georgie!" a voice called, strong and familiar. Georgiana lit up as she spotted Charles off to the side of the long hallway. She'd never admit she was so relieved to see him, or that Darcy had been right that she might not be ready to jaunt through spaceports and dockcities, out among the stars all on her own.

Charles had been her brother's best friend for as long as she could remember, always kind and able to make her smile. Sure enough, Georgiana spied a small poesy hidden behind his back. She could see Jane hesitate between a hug and a handshake; Georgiana decided that, even though they weren't close, a hug wouldn't hurt. She noted the way Jane's whole body relaxed as they embraced.

Charles hugged her briefly and presented the poesy of glories with a bumbling flourish. Georgiana took it gracefully, inhaling the sweet scent; real flowers were uncommon out among the stars. "It's so good to see you both."

"We're so happy you'll be joining us," said Jane. "As soon as Lizzy mentioned her trip, I suggested you come. It will be so wonderful having you."

Georgiana tried to hide her surprise. She'd assumed this had been Darcy's high-handed idea.

Taking her arm, Charles led them confidently through the gateway. Now that she didn't have to navigate her own way, Georgiana enjoyed taking in the sights and sounds. The three of them chatted easily, and before she knew it, she was whisked away by ground transport to Netherfield.

The first night and day passed quickly. Georgiana needed time to adjust to the stillness of a docked estate, but the novelty of Netherfield was enough to take her mind off her discomfort. There were actual plants growing on the grounds they were docked on. Georgiana hadn't seen so many varieties before—especially the glories—and certainly none that smelled as sweet. She happily anticipated spending much of her visit in the gardens.

The second night, they attended what Jane assured her would be a small dinner party. Small and large were relative terms, and Georgiana was dismayed to realize that for Jane and Charles, a dozen guests was considered small, whereas Georgiana was used to one or two guests at a time. Most of her life, it was only herself and Darcy, and then Lizzy, too.

After the initial introductions, Georgiana was relieved that most guests were no longer focused on her. She knew how to behave at these things, but that knowing never made her feel truly at ease. She was seated in a small group of the younger guests that included Jane's unmarried sisters, Kitty and Mary Bennet, and two from the local Lucas family, Maria and her younger brother John. John was clearly reluctant to enjoy the company of his sister and the Bennets and, shortly, began to ignore them as he concentrated on his handheld viewer. She didn't take any offense at his rudeness: she remembered wishing to do the same.

Kitty was sweet, if somewhat restless. Mary only opened her mouth to instruct them all in how they weren't perfect models of propriety and politeness, though Georgiana found some of what Mary said to be contrary to her own upbringing. She resolved to take her cue from Kitty, who seemed to listen politely without giving any consideration to what her sister said.

Maria was the most interesting of the group. She was shy and hesitant at first, but it wasn't long before she was telling stories about her family. She had a great deal to say about the time she'd traveled in Lizzy's company to visit her newly married sister. It took Georgiana a moment before she realized that Maria wasn't talking about any old Miss Catherine in the huge estate putting on airs but, in fact, *her* Aunt Catherine.

"What did you think of Aunt Catherine?" Georgiana asked after making the connection.

"*Aunt* Catherine? You mean that woman is your aunt?" Maria was practically squeaking by the end of the question. "She was, um"—Maria groped for words—"very proper."

Kitty snorted, and Mary glared at her.

Maria's face turned red as she looked pleadingly at Georgiana.

"It's all right." Georgiana grinned. "Aunt Catherine can be a bit of a pill."

"She's very grand."

Georgiana leaned toward Maria. "Did you know that she wanted Darcy to marry her daughter?"

"Anne? Aren't you cousins?"

"Not real cousins. Our mothers were best friends, so she's always been 'Aunt' Catherine. She thought Darcy shouldn't marry anyone besides Anne."

"So why didn't he?"

Georgiana laughed. "For one thing, he's more than ten years older than her. For another, I can't imagine my brother ever voluntarily signing up for a lifetime with Aunt Catherine as a mother-in-law."

Maria grinned back at her, and Georgiana's stomach swooped.

"Was she angry about him marrying Elizabeth?"

"Furious," answered Georgiana.

Maria looked around at the others. They were engaged in their own conversation and not paying the pair any attention, so she scooted closer on the loveseat they were sharing. "Can I say something?"

"Go ahead," answered Georgiana, with curious anticipation.

"Elizabeth is much more beautiful than Anne." Maria blushed and dropped her eyes.

Georgiana resisted the impulse to take Maria's hand. "I much prefer Lizzy as a new sister."

Maria did meet her gaze then, and the pair smiled at each other in shared judgment of "Cousin" Anne.

Maria's smile stayed with Georgiana for the whole evening. It was the strangest thing, that something as silly as a shared dislike of her cousin could occupy Georgiana's mind long after the conversation moved onto more pleasant topics.

Thoughts of Maria Lucas persisted long after the guests had left for their own dwellings and estates. Surprise suffused Georgiana as she caught a glimpse of her moony expression in the reflective surface of a decorative wall panel. That was an expression she hadn't seen on her face in years—not since she'd almost made the biggest mistake of her life. The initial surprise soon dissipated, and Georgiana couldn't help but realize she was excited—not frightened—by the prospect of her crush. There was nothing artful about Maria Lucas, so she felt safe from repeating the mistakes of her past. In fact, Georgiana was looking forward to spending her weeks in Hartfordship with a lovely, unexpected friend.

As the days passed, Georgiana was in Maria's company as often as possible. While Maria didn't have a formal occupation, she helped out at her family's supply-and-repair station, one of the largest on the planet. Maria had many stories of the clients who came through their doors. Her parents' defunct estate was small and very near their establishment, which afforded the Lucas children an eclectic education in the variety in behavior and people. While grateful her own childhood had allowed her to grow up farther away from such crowds, Georgiana found the stories (and Maria) quite charming. Georgiana felt more and more that there was something important about Maria, something that gave real significance to her shy smiles.

"Georgie," said Charles one morning, startling Georgiana out of her idle thoughts, "something's come up." He was sitting at the head of the table, with Jane and Georgiana on either side. It was a quiet evening after a day of activity under the hot sun, a novelty Georgiana wasn't sure she'd ever adjust to.

"Is everything okay?" she asked. She hoped so, as she cared for Charles and Jane very much.

He smiled reassuringly. "Everything is fine. But the estate will be getting a little addition."

"You're pregnant?!" asked Georgiana, looking to Jane.

Jane sighed in exasperation. "No. I am *not* pregnant. Charles, why would you tease the girl?"

Georgiana turned a scowl onto Charles, who was blushing. "I had no idea how that would sound," he finally stammered. He cleared his throat. "Well, er. I know that your Aunt Catherine wanted to have your company this summer, but you came to us instead."

Georgiana nodded slowly. Even her brother at his most addled would never, ever think that Georgiana would choose Aunt Catherine, especially not for weeks at a time nor when the much more pleasant option of this estate was available.

"Apparently, Lady Catherine has decided that it would be better for her daughter—that is, for Anne—if she had company closer to her own age. She's asked if Anne could stay with us for a few weeks."

Georgiana stared at Charles before glancing at Jane, who merely smiled kindly and shrugged. "She's coming here?" Georgiana asked.

"Yes, exactly," he said, beaming at her. "It will be quite lively having two young ladies staying with us old married folk."

Georgiana's thoughts whirled. Anne was a tedious person who wouldn't know anyone here but Georgiana. Georgiana wouldn't get to keep her time alone with Maria. "What a surprise," Georgiana settled on as a neutral response not tinged by her own dismay.

Charles nodded emphatically. "It *is* a surprise! She'll be here the day after tomorrow."

"O-Okay," answered Georgiana, unsure what else to say. She couldn't very well ask Charles to refuse Aunt Catherine's request.

Jane smiled sympathetically at Georgiana, squeezing her hand. "I'm sure it will be fun."

Georgiana gave a tight smile and let the conversation drift to other topics.

Anne arrived on schedule in a sleek black ground transport clearly not of the common ilk. She stepped daintily out, twitching her skirts into place with a swift flick of her wrist. She didn't look as wan as she had the last time they'd seen each other. Georgiana hoped that meant that Anne's various ailments weren't troubling her as much as usual, though she suspected that was mostly from Anne getting space from Aunt Catherine. Aunt Catherine's exacting standards would drive the most physically fit person to nervous exhaustion.

Georgiana came forward to greet Anne. She noticed how bright Anne's eyes were. They positively sparkled as the two young women embraced lightly. There was a delight in them that Georgiana wasn't familiar with when framed in Anne's face. She couldn't remember a time the two of them had exchanged more than a dozen words when others weren't around.

After pleasantries were exchanged, Georgiana couldn't help but ask the question that had been at the back of her mind since she'd learned Anne was coming. "I was surprised to hear you'd be traveling alone. Why didn't Aunt Catherine escort you here in Rosings?"

Anne tilted her head back in a laugh. "Oh, my dear, you are so *funny*. Mother wouldn't possibly think of uprooting Rosings at a time like this! And it's not like I was by myself. Mother used one of her several shuttles to get me here, and it was fully staffed."

Quite taken aback, Georgiana kept her face neutral. Private shuttles were strongly discouraged due to the disproportionate amount of resources required to run one. The idea of using a shuttle to ferry just Anne across the Black was appalling in its wasteful extravagance. Smiling pleasantly at Anne, Georgiana changed the subject. "We've been invited to a gathering this evening."

"On whose estate?"

"Not on an estate. It's at the Hartfordship Assembly Hall."

"What? We're going to a dockcity hall…for a party…in…*public*?!"

Georgiana bit back a sigh. She had forgotten Aunt Catherine's injunctions against social events not held by a "proper" family on a "true" estate. If it couldn't travel the stars anymore, it no longer qualified. And a building that was never intended to go out into the Black? Georgiana wasn't sure Anne had ever set foot in such a building. "It's a private gathering being held at the hall. It'll be fun. You'll see."

Anne's frown smoothed out at the words. "Of course. You'll just have to take care of me, my dear."

Georgiana's answering smile was a little puzzled at the endearment, but she was happy they had harmony again.

Georgiana was content to sit in silence as they rode to the assembly hall. Anne was equally quiet, though from time to time she squeezed Georgiana's hand. She was palely beautiful in the darkness.

The assembly was full but not overly crowded. Jane and Charles went off with the older couples. Georgiana would have been intimidated at the gathering a few weeks ago, but now, all she needed to feel comfortable was the sight of Maria making her way through the hall. Georgiana lit up in pleasure.

"So good to see you, Maria," breathed Georgiana as they clasped hands and pressed their cheeks together. A faint cough reminded her that she hadn't come alone. "Anne, let me introduce you to Maria Lucas. Maria, this is my cousin of sorts, Anne de Bourgh."

"Pleasure," said Anne coolly, showing hardly any expression at all.

Maria nodded back at Anne's greeting. "I believe we met at your mother's estate."

Anne squinted as she looked Maria up and down. "I believe you are correct."

"It's nice to see you again."

"Hmmm. So what does one *do* at this sort of thing?" asked Anne, waving a hand to take in the entire room.

"Oh, lots of things," said Maria with enthusiasm. "There's cards, of course, and food and drink. Always good conversations to be had. Usually, we end up playing those old-fashioned parlor games like charades or nimble-numbers. Once a month we have a theme night. Last month was 'Reinvention,' so there were all sorts of repurposed gadgets and art. It was marvelous seeing what everyone came up with."

Anne blinked at Maria and then at Georgiana, an indulgent smile on her face. "How charming," she said.

"Sometimes there's dancing, if enough people are interested," added Maria.

"Dancing," replied Anne with an eyebrow raised in question. "How can there be dancing without musicians?"

Georgiana smiled reassuringly at Anne. "Several of those here are excellent musicians and are more than happy for a lively audience at a moment's notice."

"The *guests* perform? How very…quaint."

Georgiana felt her cheeks heat; Maria's enthusiasm had noticeably wilted somewhat under Anne's disdain. "I'm sure we will have a lovely time, Anne. Why don't we introduce you around?"

Anne took Georgiana's arm possessively. "All right, Georgiana. If that's what you want."

Georgiana saw the flicker of disappointment crossing Maria's features and had to take a deep breath to keep her own countenance smooth. She gave Maria a little smile, which seemed to cheer Maria as they made their way farther into the room without her.

The next morning, Georgiana lay in bed wondering if it would be impolite for her to sneak away. Maria had seemed nothing like her usual cheerful self the previous night. Georgiana rolled over restlessly. She knew there wasn't a kind way to ditch Anne when she hadn't even been here an entire sun-cycle. Maria would have to wait. After Anne had been there for a few days, Georgiana would make sure that she reconnected with Maria. Perhaps she would send Maria a quick letter this afternoon, explaining.

With a sigh, she sat up and threw off the covers. The estate was quiet, which meant Jane and Charles were already up and outdoors. They spent most of their time in the impressive flower gardens or visiting with neighbors or doing any of a million other small occupations that Georgiana was happy to marvel at from afar. She herself enjoyed playing the piano in one of the out-of-the-way rooms at least once a day. Traveling on Pemberley wasn't always conducive to practicing, but the stability of the anchored estate made it simple.

She decided to start her day there.

Georgiana hastily threw on some clothes and padded down the series of hallways that led to the piano room. The sunlight streaming in through the windows spoke of a glorious day, and Georgiana made a mental note to show Anne the gardens later.

Fingers flying through her warm-ups, Georgiana's thoughts turned again toward the evening before. Every time Georgiana had tried to have a private word with Maria, Anne had burst upon them in need of a beverage, or an explanation of what those people over there were doing, or an introduction to a young person who had caught her eye. In the end, Georgiana didn't think she and Maria had exchanged more than a handful of words that weren't said in front of everyone. It made her heart ache. But she was sure it would be easier once Anne was more familiar with Hartfordship and its people.

Georgiana moved on to practicing a piece she'd been struggling to master. It was intricate enough that soon she had no room for any thoughts beyond the notes. She was so engrossed that she didn't notice Anne had entered the room until she spoke.

"That's a beautiful piece," she said, beaming to rival the sunlight.

Georgiana was torn between wanting to stop and thank Anne, and resenting that Anne had not waited for her to finish the movement before speaking. She closed out the piece and laid her hands gently on the instrument. It was strange to see this thing of wood and wire in an estate that probably didn't have a single other piece of natural wood in it. Her own instrument at Pemberley was nothing so historically faithful as this.

"Good morning, Anne," said Georgiana placidly.

"I think you said that the gardens here were very fine," started Anne. "Would you like to show them to me? It looks like the weather is agreeable enough to venture out."

Georgiana smiled. "Of course."

The two women left the music room and wandered out to the gardens, Georgiana filching a roll from the dining area as an impromptu breakfast along the way. The day was beautiful, and Georgiana turned her face to the sun instinctively. She loved living aboard Pemberley and exploring new places and being out among the stars, but there was something to be said for real sunlight and real grass beneath her feet, the air filled with the perfume of real flowers.

"Hmm," said Anne.

"What?"

"It's all right, I suppose. But it's rather untamed."

Looking around the garden, with all the flowers in the neat boxes and beds, Georgiana glanced questioningly at Anne. "How so?"

"They've been left to grow every which way! See this bed here? These glories should have been cut back and trained upon a trellis."

"Isn't that a trellis?" said Georgiana, pointing at the stiff frame she could just make out under the greenery.

"Yes, of course," Anne said warmly, "but there's only this one trellis for I cannot tell how many plants. Surely you noticed the glories at Rosings are kept to an individual trellis. That way, each plant is shown off, and it's much easier to find the brown spots and inferior leaves for pruning."

Georgiana looked back at the glories. Truth be told, she avoided Aunt Catherine's gardens as much as possible. Georgiana was convinced that there was no possible way to *not* get in trouble when in those gardens; Aunt Catherine had once scolded her for walking on the path in the wrong direction. Or was it the right direction, but her footsteps were at the wrong angles? Whatever the specifics, Georgiana found it best to be elsewhere, preferably in a quiet room where she could read or sew or sketch without being observed.

"Hello!" came a voice behind them.

Georgiana turned, her face already overcome with a huge grin as she recognized Maria's voice. She quickly went to embrace her. Although they'd seen each other last night, it felt like an age since they'd had time together. "It's so good to see you," she breathed.

"You too. I've missed you… Hello, Anne."

"Maria," returned Anne, the warmth of her voice iced over. "Georgiana was showing me the gardens."

"They are lovely," said Maria.

Anne cocked her head. "I suppose they are if one has never seen the heights that true horticulture may be taken to."

Maria blushed while Georgiana looked confusedly between them. "Come see the pond at the center of the garden," Georgiana said, hoping to restore Maria's spirits; she knew it to be a favorite spot of hers.

"Very well," answered Anne.

The three women walked on, chatting about the weather and the particular blossoms that caught their eyes and the buzzing of insects. Anne was particularly talkative, giving an in-depth explanation of the points of superiority of her mother's gardens. Maria drifted closer to Georgiana during those bits of lecture, and Georgiana loved the feel of the back of Maria's hand brushing her own. How she wished she could be alone in the garden with Maria as they had been so often before Anne's arrival.

They reached the pond, and Georgiana was momentarily lost in its beauty. There was something about the stillness of the water contrasted with the natural bustle of the living things that hypnotized Georgiana. Deep in thought, Georgiana sank on the bench, not noticing the others. She came to herself again, blinking slowly, when someone sat next to her. Looking over, she expected Maria but found Anne instead.

Georgiana looked around. "Where's Maria?"

"She remembered a prior obligation," said Anne lightly. "It's just us."

"Oh. Yes. Just us." Georgiana didn't try very hard to keep the disappointment from her face. She made up her mind to seek Maria out before too much time passed.

Between the weather and a series of unexpected social engagements, Georgiana found another couple of weeks had gone by before she had a chance to even think of heading into town to see Maria. Her letters to Maria had remained unanswered as well. Anne had been pleasant enough company, but her flattery and constant companionship were wearing on Georgiana. Another fine day dawned, and Georgiana was determined to see Maria.

As she was about to leave the estate, Anne called her name. She took a deep breath and turned to speak with her.

"You aren't going out now, are you?" asked Anne.

"Well, yes. I wanted to see Maria."

"Oh pooh. You can speak with Maria any old day. I have a surprise for you."

"A surprise?"

"Yes, and I've just put the finishing touches on it. Please come and see it with me. I've worked so hard."

Georgiana swallowed a sigh and a protest. If Anne had gone out of her way to be nice, the least Georgiana could do was humor her. Afterward, she would head into the dockcity to see Maria.

Anne led her through the house and out into the gardens. The rains from the night before, combined with the strong sun, made everything seem bursting with life. Georgiana wasn't sure what the surprise was supposed to be, as she'd seen the gardens many times.

"Just a little farther," said Anne.

At first, Georgiana thought she was taking her to the pond, but instead, Anne led her into the part of the garden where the glories grew.

"Well, what do you think?"

Georgiana blinked at Anne's expectant look and then back at the flowers. As she inspected them, she realized that the glories had been…organized, for lack of a better word. Each individual glory vine now had a trellis of its own, the intertwined plants rigidly separated. "How…?"

"I mentioned to Charles how much better mother's flowers were kept, and he was so obliging he had this done. I told him it would especially make you happy."

Georgiana frowned. She didn't care about glories in particular. The brutal way that they were now laid out and forced onto the trellises was much less appealing than their earlier natural chaos.

"Georgiana. My dear, dear Georgiana."

Georgiana startled out of her confusion only to be significantly more confused as Anne took one of her hands in both of hers and stared up into her eyes.

"I did this for you, as a representation of my affection. I confess, I came to Hartfordship with an ulterior motive. Please Georgiana, will you do me the honor of being my wife?"

"Wife?" repeated Georgiana, her confusion turned to alarm.

"Yes. I know that our mothers both had planned on me marrying your brother, but really, he didn't suit me half as well as you do. Our families will finally be united as they were intended to be."

"I…I don't know what to say."

"Still the shy one, aren't you? Come my dear, all you have to say is 'yes.'"

"No." Georgiana was surprised at the vehemence behind the word.

"No? Why in all the stars would you not?"

Georgiana tore her hand away from Anne's. "I care for another. And I don't care for you in that way."

"Oh, that little Maria? She is rather pretty. But really, Georgiana, she's hardly suitable for someone of your breeding and quality."

"What?"

"She's only ever left this planet once, when she came to Rosings. She barely visits estates here, either! Her family is in *trade*. Surely you know that she cannot be appropriate for someone of your stature."

Anger broke through the uncertainty of Georgiana's mind. "You will not speak of Maria that way."

"Be reasonable—"

"Let me be clear. I will not marry you and I want you to leave. Today. Nothing you have done here is acceptable."

"Your brother would want this for you."

"My brother didn't want to marry you, and neither do I!"

"Our estates must be united! Think of the power and position we would have. The *order* our union could create."

Georgiana reached into the flower beds and began disassembling the first trellis she could reach. "Go back to your mother."

"Stop that." Anne batted Georgiana's hands away from the flowers.

Georgiana turned on her heel and stalked away.

Anne followed.

"You cannot be this foolhardy. All over a common thing like Maria Lucas. Really, Georgiana."

Her anger got the better of her. She turned and shoved Anne away from her. She told herself later that she hadn't realized that they'd made it as far as the pond, nor that Anne was standing rather closer to the edge than was prudent. The splash she made wasn't nearly as satisfying as her indignant squawk upon hitting the water.

"Go home, Anne," said Georgiana as she strode away purposefully. She had more important places to be.

Though the transport took the usual amount of time to reach the heart of the dockcity, to Georgiana it was an eternity. It was crystal clear now that Anne must have said something to keep Maria away, to make her leave without saying goodbye at the pond two weeks ago. Well, it couldn't be helped now, and Georgiana was prepared to do whatever necessary to get back into Maria's good graces. She only wished she'd pushed Anne into the pond then.

She entered the shop nervously, unsure whether Maria would be pleased to see her. Once inside, she spotted Maria in the back tinkering with some bit of tech. As if someone had tapped her on the shoulder, Maria looked up and saw Georgiana.

"Maria," was all Georgiana could manage. She had so much to say, but the words had dried up in fear.

Maria came out from her workroom. "Georgiana," she said flatly, standing in front of her.

"I'm so sorry," blurted Georgiana.

"Are you marrying that woman?" asked Maria.

"What? Oh. No. Stars, no!" Georgiana suppressed a shudder at the thought.

"Are you sure? Anne seemed confident you would."

"Anne is currently extricating herself from the pond," said Georgiana with relish.

Maria's smile dawned like the sun. "Is she really?"

"It's not very deep, so she's probably out by now."

"And how did Anne end up in the pond?" asked Maria in a teasing tone.

"She tripped?"

"I see." Maria's amusement faded. "And what brings you here? Need something fixed?"

Georgiana took a deep breath. "I need you. I mean, I want. I want you. I want to be with you."

"Me? Hasn't your friend informed you that I am just a low-class, soil-bound gold-digger?"

"She did. But she's in the pond, so…"

"Did you throw her in the pond…for me?" Maria's eyes were wide with astonishment.

"I did it for us."

Maria stepped closer. "'Us'?"

"Yes, us." Georgiana looked at the floor, unsteady. "If you want there to be an 'us,' that is."

Maria lifted Georgiana's chin with a gentle touch. "Of course I do."

"Really?" Georgiana was breathless at the thought.

"Yes. You sure you don't mind"—she waved her hand to take in the store, the workbench, the bit of grease that stained her clothes—"this? I've rarely been out among the stars…"

"I'll give you all the stars you want. And if you don't want any, well, I can learn to live on the ground." Georgiana would give Maria everything she had, if it meant they could be together.

"I think we can find someplace in between," said Maria softly.

"I think we can, too," agreed Georgiana.

Georgiana intertwined her fingers with Maria's, not caring where one of them ended and the other began.

THE MEETING AT PEMBERLEY

In the novel, Lizzy Bennet's view on Mr. Darcy changes with her visit to Pemberley, and I thought about how it would go if her meeting Georgiana was what changed for Lizzy. I wanted to place their encounter in the lush setting of the house. In my painting, Lizzy's aunt and uncle are being shown Mr. Darcy's portrait, but what catches her attention is Miss Darcy.

TAGS

aromantic, bittersweet ending, character injury (graphic description), f/f (background), first person point of view, kidnapping, lesbian, magic use, military, non-fanfiction story inspired by the source material, present tense, science fiction with magic, siblings, vehicular injury, war

INSPIRATION

When I looked for inspiration in *Pride and Prejudice*, the plot of Lydia's elopement with Wickham stood out to me most. I decided to transport it into more modern times with a new set of characters, an ongoing war, and a bit of magic.

ALONG THE WAY

I THOUGHT THE envelope would be thicker. More money than I've ever seen, yet thinner than my thumb. Beige. Unimpressive.

It'll take me forever to pay it off. Hell, the way the prices are going, gouged by war and greed, I'll have to sell my kidney to settle it.

I need that envelope so I can leave his suffocating flat. I had expected Daniel's home to reek with old money and new tech, but was met with a shrine to adventure in places I couldn't afford to even dream of: regional art, foreign instruments, travel photos. The couple eating diamond-shaped fruit straight from a strange tree in the photograph behind Daniel seem to laugh at me.

Daniel puts the envelope down with a *thump* and covers it with his clean, pampered nails. "What do you need it for, Martha?"

I don't like his tone or his question. He agreed to give me the money when I begged for it; now he might take it away if he doesn't like my answer. Like it's even his damn business.

Yet as long as the money is in his hands, I have to play by his rules.

"My sister's missing."

"Wanda?" A deep crease appears on his forehead. Is that concern, or is he trying to remember whether I have other sisters?

I nod to put him out of his misery. "I have to find her."

Any decent person would offer to help with the search, even if I wouldn't accept it. Or at least, they wouldn't obstruct: take their heavy hand off the envelope, let me trace my sister's steps and safely bring her back.

Not Daniel, though. Daniel looks at the envelope, then back at me. "The gas prices aren't that high yet, are they?"

Is he checking if I'm dumb, or does he think I'm greedy? If going to the gas station himself weren't beneath him, I bet he'd fill the tank for me and keep the receipt.

"This isn't gas money," I say. Then quieter, but clear so he doesn't miss my meaning: "She's not in the district."

He gets it.

"Are you sure? The Buffer's a big place."

I hate that name. The Buffer. The zone between vicious slaughter and heavenly peace. A belt of poverty and misery that the enemy will have to plow through once they burn down the outer rim and go for the Bullseye—the capital city, their goal.

Just last winter I lived in Santel. Same crappy building, but the plumbing still worked, the power was on 24/7, and the laughter of children carried outside. The only war they knew was with snowballs. Now, everything is part of the Buffer, and no one can leave without paying the price.

"She left a note saying she was leaving the Buffer. Only one way a sane person can go."

"She get a call?"

"Does she look like a 23–67-year-old male to you?"

"She's a Healer, though."

I don't miss a beat. "She's a nurse in Dr. Alman's clinic, if that's what you mean."

He smirks. "Why run, then?"

I shrug. "Love made her stupid." Wouldn't be the first time. I don't get what it is about love that makes people do senseless things.

"So there are *two* people in the Buffer reckless enough to leave?"

"I don't know where she hails from, but a soldier could talk her way through a turnpike, couldn't she?"

"If Wanda's with an active-duty soldier, they'll have to come back. I doubt she can get more than a few days' leave."

"Or she's defecting."

Daniel snorts. "And do what? They'll drag her back unless she flees the country."

"And leave Wanda to fend for herself with no money or way back."

"She'd need a lot of money and connections."

"Look, I don't know Kantar's entire life story. She—"

"What did you say?" Daniel's eyes grow wide.

"Private Kantar. That's the soldier's name."

"Isabel Kantar?"

I pause. "I think so. I never met her. Wanda was taking care of her at the clinic. Friend of yours?"

"An old friend," Daniel says as if he doesn't have time for the mundane details. "She was here? In Santel? How long?" He leans forward like he's about to shake the information out of me.

"About two weeks." There isn't much I can offer—all I know is what Wanda told me. "They brought in a bunch of soldiers from an accident, even though there aren't any more Healers here."

Daniel takes it in, nervously biting his lip. "Did Wanda heal her?"

Not this again. "Wanda doesn't—"

"Wanda healed my broken arm two months ago. She's not as committed to keeping her Gift a secret as you are."

I stare in shock. I knew Wanda was reckless, but *this*? Could he still be bluffing? The alert in his eyes suggests otherwise.

I capitulate. "Are you gonna report her?"

He shakes his head. "She might be in danger."

"I know. That's why I need—"

"No, I mean she didn't go to the Bullseye," he says. "Isabel would never defect. If you want to find your sister, you have to go west, not east."

He's not making sense. If Isabel took Wanda to the west, that would mean they went— "To the front line?" She couldn't have taken a civilian there. "If Kantar reported Wanda, there are procedures."

"And you'd have a gendarmerie knocking on your door, yes. That's why I don't think she reported her. I think what she needs is an unreported Healer."

"What for?"

Daniel pushes a hand through his hair. "I don't know, but I think I know where to find her."

"Let me guess: in Arlon?" I don't hide my sarcasm. The main battleground of the last months. A town torn in half by missiles. The last stop before the Buffer. Sounds just right.

As he nods, I can't hold back a snort. "Listen, if you want to, take the money and try your luck in the Bullseye. You don't even have to pay me back." He pushes over the envelope. "Or you can meet me tomorrow at dawn, and we'll find her together. I'm going either way."

My fingers itch to grab the envelope. I have no reason to trust him, let alone risk my life on his word. Wanda is reckless and follows her heart too easily, but would she follow it into the war?

But his reaction feels genuine: the way his entire demeanor changed when he heard Kantar's name, his confidence in his own words. Besides, no one would offer that much money unless he was sure he was right.

The vision of my little sister, scared and alone among the flying bullets and exploding buildings, used and ditched by Kantar, stands vivid before my eyes.

"Let's say I believe you," I say cautiously. I don't like this, I really don't. But if I make the wrong choice, the Bullseye can't compare to leaving Wanda at the frontlines. "What's the plan?"

"Did they see Wanda?" I ask as Daniel slips back into the driver's seat. In front of us, a soldier opens the gate.

"Isabel crossed yesterday with another female soldier they didn't ID," Daniel says. "She must have given Wanda a uniform."

I try to imagine my gentle, scrawny sister drowning in folds of camo.

The car starts rolling toward our demise. My muscles tense as if bombs are waiting right behind the fence.

But beyond there's only quiet, clear sky.

The road dives into the tree line, their crowns bright green in the pale sunlight. The forest embraces us with its shade. Even at the high speed, I don't miss the puckered, ripe raspberries adorning the bushes, same as every year.

This time, there's no one to pluck them, take them home, turn them into the sweetest jam.

The forest ends abruptly, right at the bank of the wide band of the Tanne River. This is where Santel really ends—not the arbitrary border. This river is where Dad taught me to swim the year he got sick. Three years later, I taught Wanda to swim in the very same spot.

As we pass over the bridge, it dawns on me that, when the defense of Arlon fails, blowing up this very bridge will be the last-ditch effort to slow down the enemy before they come for my home.

Will the Bullseye open for the hundreds of thousands of people from the Buffer, or will they let us burn to save the elites who hide there?

I cast my eyes down and notice something next to my foot. I pick it up: a picture of Daniel, a few years younger, and a girl with stormy hair, bright eyes, and freckles. They're posing in front of a tree, grinning from ear to ear. Their teeth and lips are bright blue.

"Isabel?" I ask.

Daniel glances at the picture and hums a confirmation.

"What's with the blue teeth?"

"Sapphrines," he says, like I'm supposed to know what that is. "My great-grandpa brought saplings from his travels. Only one grew. It's the only one in the Peninsula."

"Wow," I say sarcastically. Rich folks even have their own unique trees. "Did you make your fortune on the fruit? I've never heard about it."

"No, the fruit rots so fast you can only eat it straight from the tree."

"Isabel lived with you, but you never…?" I change the topic. I couldn't care less about Daniel's love life. I just want to make sure that once we find Wanda and Isabel, I won't end up with love-triangle drama on top of the war drama.

"No, nothing like that."

"Why not? She's pretty. You're not terribly ugly."

Daniel snorts. "Just don't fall in love with me."

Even though he's objectively good-looking, and even if he weren't a rich douche, I'd be completely safe. I'm not the falling-in-love kind of person. Wanda says it's like her not being into guys, just that I'm not into anyone.

"Yuck!" I say like a child who caught their parents kissing.

He bursts out laughing.

I join him.

We drive through abandoned fields and villages where only the most stubborn residents remain.

When I was a kid, trips to the hospital in Arlon felt like they took forever. Now, the hours pass in the blink of an eye; once the car climbs the hill, familiar blocks rise before us. Several have turned black from smoke and fire.

I force my eyes away and look for distraction in conversation. "Why aren't you in the Bullseye with all your rich pals from Villa-land?"

In the south, Arlon sprawls out almost all the way to the silver-edged cliffs washed up by the ocean—a gorgeous view, claimed by the old-money families and their obnoxiously sprawling mansions. And among those mansions is Daniel's old home.

"It's not called that," he says, rolling his eyes. "By the time they got Arlon, the Bullseye had shut the gates."

As if he couldn't buy his way in.

"Don't tell me you believed our boys would stop our good ol' neighbors from coming for your mansion."

Daniel gives me a stern look. In the first days of the war, our army's pushback was so strong, we all had hope of victory. But the truth is, we were done the moment the bombers speared over the mountains. The only thing the resistance succeeded in was making the process painfully slow.

"I wasn't brave enough to volunteer," Daniel admits. "But I stuck around, waiting for the call."

"How noble." I don't hide my mockery. "How old are you, again?"

He might've avoided the twenty-eight-up call fair and square, but he's not younger than the boys who left last month.

"Situation's changed."

"Your feet got cold?"

I can't blame him. If it wasn't for good old sexism, I'd have already marched to my death. In Daniel's place, I'd have used every beige envelope at hand to spare myself.

In a way, I have.

His throat bobs up and down.

I wait.

"I needed more time."

He sounds so solemn, I almost feel bad for him. I could drop it, but curiosity takes the better of me. I match his tone. "What happened?"

Daniel curses and stops the car. I follow his gaze.

Ahead of us, the bridge that leads to Villa-land, bypassing the main Arlon area, no longer exists. What's left leads straight down the canyon to the raging river.

I swear, too, with much less finesse.

"You can wait here. I'll find Wanda and Isabel, and come back for you," Daniel offers.

Stay in the middle of nowhere alone? I'll pass. "You won't manage to drag Wanda away without me."

Daniel gives me a moment to change my mind before turning the engine back on. "East Arlon is supposed to be safe. It's not far."

We pull back to the main road. Right past a roundabout, urban buildings line both sides of the road. As a warm welcome, a distant *bang* makes me jump in my seat.

"It was Isabel," Daniel says. When I give him a questioning look, he explains. "You asked what happened. It was Isabel."

I'm grateful for a distraction. "What did she do?"

"We were friends our whole lives." There's a heaviness in his voice that I haven't heard before. "Then she robbed and betrayed me. It hit me hard."

The betrayal part I get, but what could she possibly have stolen to hurt him so much? Surely not money.

"What was it, a family heirloom?"

He stares at the road ahead, silent, as if he didn't hear me. Maybe it was too personal: we aren't friends, after all. I look away.

"It'll sound unbelievable," he starts, slowly, as if picking his words carefully. "I didn't believe it myself, at first. But she—"

The windshield shatters. The blast knocks the air out of my lungs, the sound from my ears. The world erupts. Metal curves around us. Agony explodes across my forehead, spreads through my skull, spills to my eyes, searing hot. I blink through blood and smoke, gasping for air and choking on it. The car stands still in a dust-made twilight.

"Daniel!" My voice is raspy, drowned out by the ringing in my ears.

I reach for him, sense movement.

He's alive.

I keep searching until I can make out his silhouette.

His chest—it's wrong. A flat piece of metal the size of my forearm sticks out of it. Bubbles lather the blood on his shirt.

His hand circles over his chest, fingers flicking. I force it down—if he hits the shrapnel, he'll die.

I look around, mapping our surroundings through the settling dust. Ahead, there's a fiery crater in the asphalt. Behind us, the buildings might provide protection.

I unbuckle my seatbelt and shift to undo his. My head pounds. I hover my palm where it hurts; I move my fingers. Daniel's wandering eyes lock on mine, and I freeze, then grit my teeth and push through the pain. I open the door and set my feet on the ground, then get a good hold on him. I pull, and slowly, so slowly, slide him out. The ringing in my ears begins to subside, replaced by the sound of Daniel's futile gasps.

I manage to get him out of the car and set him on the ground. He's too heavy to carry, so I drag him, walking backward toward the alley. I force myself to stop glancing at the sky.

Once we reach safety, I lay him down and drop from overexertion. Daniel's eyes are closed, but his chest still heaves. For now.

I glance around the empty alley as I kneel next to him. "Daniel, can you hear me?"

His head moves slightly and his eyes flutter, but he can't keep them open.

"I'm sorry," I say, wrapping my fingers around the shrapnel, the other hand steadying his chest.

I yank out the piece of metal. From lack of air, Daniel can't even scream in pain. A stream of blood pours from his chest. My hands hover above the wound. I draw from the adrenaline that rushes through my veins, from the panicked energy, and I focus on Daniel's lung.

I bend and stretch my fingers to call upon my Gift.

For a moment, when it's not coming, I'm scared it atrophied from years of disuse. Then a dim green light blooms beneath my palm, seeping into the wound like a thick foam.

I conjure an anatomical image of lungs from the old biology textbook. It's foggy; I can only hope I'm close enough. I should've studied harder, should've read the books Wanda borrowed from Dr. Alman. I should've known she was healing people. She didn't care what she jeopardized, if they forced us to conscript—she'd run right into it. Did she do it for the high of holding someone's life in her hands? For this rush, keeping them alive with your whole being?

Focus on Daniel, I remind myself as my Gift flickers. I stem the bleeding, but his left lung is in shambles. I must piece each vesicle and vein together before his body shuts down from lack of oxygen.

As the process goes on—so much slower than I'd like, so much more complicated than healing Wanda's scraped knees before Mom convinced me not to flaunt my Gift—my strength dwindles.

I strain until the organ is whole.

Daniel takes in a sharp, deep breath, as if trying to suck in all the air from the alley.

"Welcome back," I mutter, my own breathing shallow like I've run a marathon.

As I'm mending his skin, footsteps resound in the alley. I douse out the Gift's light. Too tired to panic, I cast my eyes at the approaching soldier. How much did he see? Is he one of ours or here to kill us?

"Martha?" Though distorted in my ears, I recognize his voice right away, before his face emerges from the shadow. Sal, a good friend who volunteered long before his time. "You can't be here."

"Our car was struck." I turn my eyes to the mangled wreck. We have no way home.

"You were damn unlucky to get hit with a stray," he explains, crouching next to Daniel. "How is he?"

"Could use stitches, but he'll live." I got him here from the brink of death, and I can't help a small tickle of pride.

Sal pulls out a first-aid kit, hands me a pack of gauze for my head wound, then starts tending to Daniel.

"Did you heal him?"

He knows the wound's been tampered with. All those years I managed to conceal it, yet the one time I play hero, I'm caught. I open my mouth but no sound comes out.

Daniel's glance meets mine, then he rolls his eyes. "I did," he says.

I blink, surprised. Why is he taking the fall for me? What will he do when the call comes and he doesn't have the Gift?

Unless—his hand in the car, the familiar flicking of his fingers…is he a Healer too?

"You healed yourself?" Sal's as surprised as me, though for a different reason. Self-healing is possible—were I alone, I'd have long healed my pounding head—but in the state Daniel was in, it would've been impossible. Luckily, Sal doesn't know that. "You're one tough cookie."

I hide my relief; Sal would never understand how I can refuse to fight.

Sal helps him sit up and asks, "Where's your uniform, soldier?"

"Shipping off in two weeks." Daniel doesn't hesitate. "Got delayed for health reasons."

"We'll be happy to have you." Sal grins at him, as if Daniel were about to join a party. "And don't worry. As a Healer, you'll be well cared for. You guys are precious. Especially now."

Daniel frowns. "Especially now?"

Sal looks to me for whether he can trust Daniel. I nod.

"They haven't sent us new Healers or soldiers in a while. I'd say they're running out, but—" He hesitates. "Rumor has it, the capital is keeping them for the main defense. Fighting along the border has spread us too thin."

The implications are clear. "They're sacrificing the Buffer to protect themselves?"

Sal looks uncomfortable accusing the country he pledged allegiance to. "We gotta save the heart at all costs, right?"

I couldn't disagree more. The heart of our country isn't in Bullseye. It's in the people. But the politicians and the elites don't care.

I say nothing.

"Are you going to say something?"

We walk toward Villa-land like a couple of zombies, leaning on one another. Daniel's weak from blood loss and near-asphyxiation, I from healing him and my head's incessant pounding.

Once we reach Daniel's home and find Wanda, we can rest there. I'm trying not to worry about our way home; hopefully Daniel has another car in his garage.

"Thank you for saving my life," Daniel says sincerely.

"Sure." I'm caught off guard. That wasn't what I meant. "Aren't you surprised?"

"That you've been hiding your Gift to avoid conscription?" Daniel sighs and stops leaning on my shoulder. "I get it. You don't care that they'll take our home as long as you don't risk anything."

"No!" I protest too aggressively, and my head forces me to slow down. "I care, but we don't stand a chance. How is sending our people to die helping?"

"What's the alternative?"

I don't have a good answer. The only way to stop this war is by surrendering, learning their language, and hoping they treat us as equals. It's shitty, but if it curbs the death toll, isn't it better?

"Are you really leaving?"

Daniel nods. "Got my date. I'm ready."

A strange wave of melancholy comes over me. We're not friends. Before yesterday, we'd barely exchanged a few pleasantries. And yet. "Aren't you scared?"

"I'm scared as fuck," he says with a nervous chuckle. "But maybe with one more soldier, our chances get a tiny bit higher."

I offer a sad smile. "Maybe."

We arrive at a mangled, gold-plated gate.

Daniel pushes its wing. "Welcome to my neighborhood."

Admiring the glamorous, overblown villas when my tiny flat might soon cease to exist makes me even more nauseous, so I glue my eyes to the pavement. I follow Daniel at the pace my head allows. The last length of road until I find Wanda stretches endlessly until Daniel stops abruptly.

"No!" he screams, panicked.

He dashes toward a strange, tall house sculpted from metal and mostly-shattered glass—the offspring of a lighthouse and a greenhouse. I expected his home to be an elegant, old-money mansion, not something so bizarre.

Daniel kneels among the cinders, before the burned tree at the dead center of the house. It must have been tall and magnificent, but now it's just a three-story-high, used-up matchstick.

"Daniel?"

His palms dig into the thick layer of ash. I lay my hand on his shoulder and drop down beside him. Before my eyes, his expression turns from shock to bottomless grief.

My heartbeat races. Is he grieving the tree or is there, in this ruin, something I have yet to discover? Isn't it just the heirlooms, sofas, and clothes that have turned to dust?

My head spins; I'd have fallen if I weren't already on my knees.

Was Wanda here when a stray missile hit the building and set it ablaze? The smoke filling her lungs, choking the life out of her, flames consuming her flesh, and ash burying her bones.

I can't look, can't risk finding her charred remains. The ash clogs my throat as I gasp; charcoal obscures my vision until everything goes black.

The last thing I hear is Daniel calling my name.

I'm floating. Waves bob my body up and down. The river carries me across our wounded homeland. Above me the sky is black and gray, like dust.

No, not the sky. It's debris: the shattered road, scattered chunks of concrete torn from buildings.

It's not water that carries me but Daniel. My head's too heavy to lift. My mouth is cottony; I can't form words, but my grunts get Daniel's attention.

He gently puts me down. He looks concerned as he helps me sip from a water bottle. The water is uncomfortably warm, but it's wet, which makes it perfect.

"Where's Wanda?" I ask, once I can speak.

"I was wrong," he admits. "Isabel didn't take her to the tree."

"Why the tree?"

"Why didn't you tell me your head hurt so much?" he asks instead. "We should've gone to the hospital right away."

"I'm fine." I just need to replenish the energy I used on healing. "Was that your grand-pa's tree?"

He nods. "I used to joke that Isabel was only friends with me because of the tree, she was so obsessed with it. Now I'm not sure it was a joke."

"The fruit can't be *that* good."

"It's extraordinary, but it's not about the taste. She believed it's connected to the Gift. She got deep into its history and all sorts of conspiracies."

"I've never even seen that tree. It couldn't have given me my Gift."

"You're right, you're born with the Gift…but it can be taken away."

Things click into place: Daniel's fingers over his wound, his depression after Isabel's betrayal. After she stole something from him.

"It worked." It's not a question.

He hums in confirmation. "The night they announced obligatory conscription for the Gifted, we were together, eating sapphrines and talking about my murky future. I don't know what she did, but I woke up three days later without my Gift or my best friend."

"And you thought she wanted to do the same to Wanda?"

"She'd have picked the wrong sister, right?" he says with a sad half-smile.

The implication that I'd happily give my Gift away feels like a punch in the gut. Without it, I'd be safe from combat, but violence shouldn't be a condition for keeping a part of me intact.

I lean on Daniel the rest of the way to the hospital.

The nurse that takes me in insists on calling a Healer despite my protests. I'm not a soldier: if I refuse to fight, the least I can do is not waste their resources.

I'm prepared to swat the Healer's hands away until I recognize the girl approaching my bed.

Wanda.

"What are you doing here?" she asks me with wide eyes.

I should be the one asking, but the pink Healer scrubs match her rosy cheeks, her fingers poised to call on her Gift.

She's right where she's supposed to be.

"Mom and I were so worried about you." I expected anger; I have none. "What were you thinking?"

She doesn't answer. Instead, she places her hands over my head. "Concussion?"

The pounding from the accident is gone with a blink of an eye. Has she always been this good, or is it a matter of practice?

"It was my only chance to help Santel," she says quietly, cleaning the dried blood off my healed forehead. "If I conscripted, they'd keep me for the Bullseye defense. When Isabel told me—"

"Is she here?" Daniel interrupts.

"She's usually healing in the field, but I saw her a moment ago." Wanda looks at him with pleading eyes. "Don't report her. I begged her to take me."

"It's okay, Wanda. I can handle this," interjects a stern voice.

Isabel is standing right behind Daniel, an echo from the picture. Neither of them carries that lightness anymore: she's all military hardness, and he's broken.

Daniel turns, jaw tense, yet he's so much calmer than I would be. He's staring her straight in the eye, wordlessly saying, "*Go ahead. Handle it.*"

Under his glare, Isabel softens, hanging her head. "I'm sorry," she says. "I hoped with time you'd understand."

"Understand?" His voice is harsh. "That you'd always envied it? That you were so obsessed—"

"No!" Isabel cuts him off, brow knit in surprise. "I never—I tried to save your life."

"Never thought to ask me first?"

"I wanted to protect you. You aren't made for war." There's a tenderness in her voice, her eyes. Perhaps a glimmer of the girl who'd been his best friend, who cared about him so much she'd sacrificed their friendship and chose to go to war—though being a non-Gifted woman, she'd never have to—to spare him from this hell.

And for nothing: in two weeks, he'll be putting on camo and a brave face, risking his life anyway.

Daniel laughs humorlessly. "And you were?"

She doesn't answer.

Truth is, no one's made for war. It's not fair that any of us—soldiers, Healers, civilians, cowards—has to go through it.

"I've always planned to give it back," she says, quietly.

Before Daniel can answer, tell her that she can't, that the tree is gone, a commotion switches the atmosphere in a heartbeat. A crowd of wounded gets rushed in, stirring a mix of chaos and structure. Shouted orders and screams of pain. Every doctor, nurse, and Healer knows what to do. Wanda and Isabel hurry away to their new patients.

They put a groaning, bloodied soldier on my bed as soon as I jump off. It's his arms: both barely hang on. A nurse sedates him, calling for a Healer but getting no response. Everyone, including my sister, is busy with the soldiers on the brink of death.

This one, with regular medical care, won't die…but he will lose his arms. I look at his convulsing face—young, but not the youngest; he managed to make it through months.

Does he have a son at home whom he'll never be able to hug again? A daughter he'll never teach to swim?

I should leave and let the doctors work. If Daniel and I can figure out a way home, I could be back in my room tonight, safe for a little longer.

I step around the nurse and stand behind the patient's bed.

"I'm a Healer," I say.

I hover my hands over the soldier's arms.

I curve and stretch my fingers.

I call on my Gift and begin to heal.

GIRLS' NIGHT IN

In a modern version of *Pride and Prejudice*, soon after her wedding with Mr. Darcy, Elizabeth is still getting to know his family, notably his younger sister Georgiana and his cousin Anne, who are both close to her age. After Anne, who is chronically ill, has to cancel a night out with the Darcys, the girls decide to stay in and chat instead. When the conversation turns to gender and sexuality, Elizabeth discovers many things about her new friends, and perhaps even a thing or two about herself.

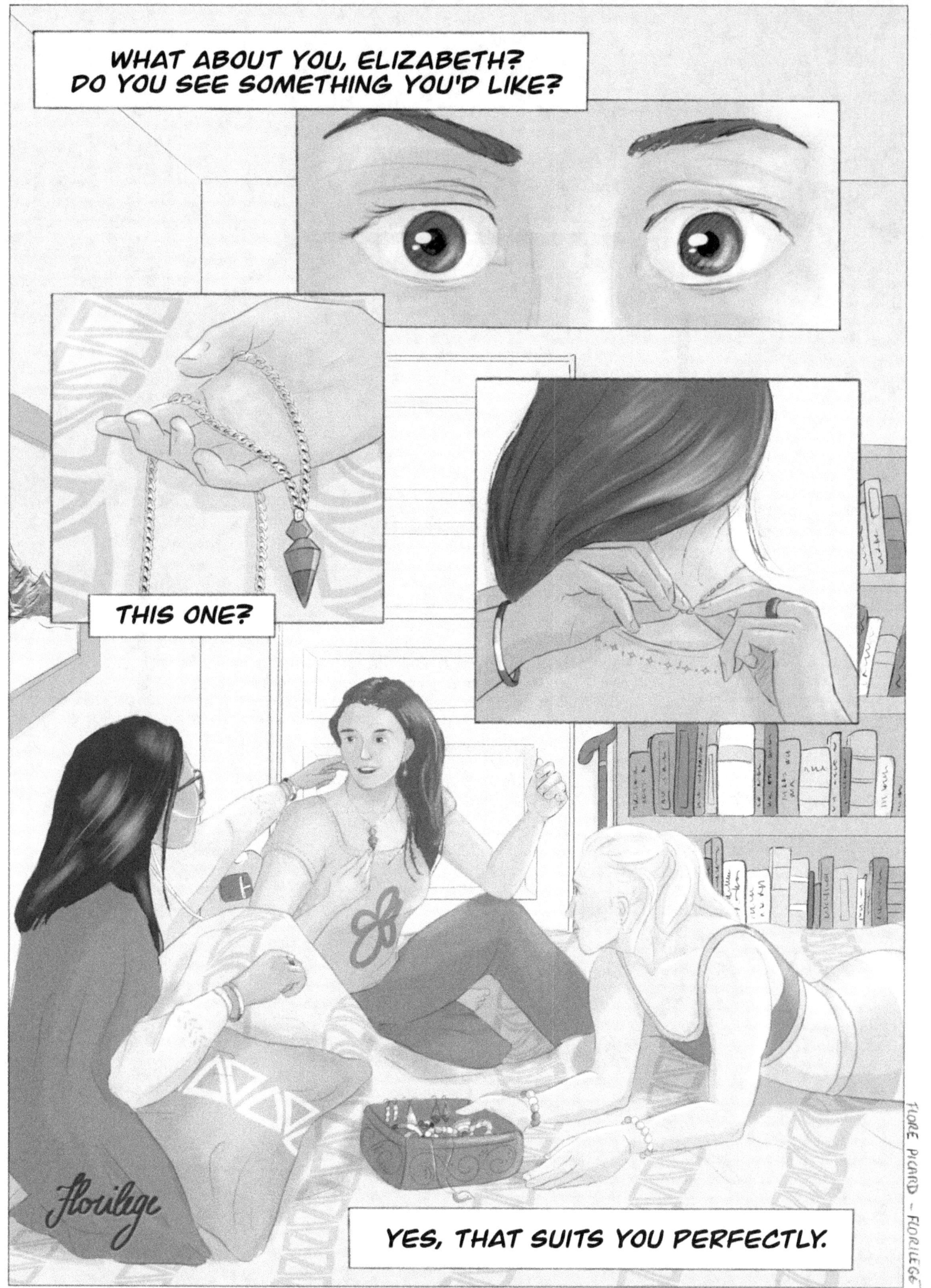

TAGS
anxiety, coming out, epistolary, f/f, historical, lesbian,
post-canon, present tense, regency, second chances, siblings,
third person limited (alternating) point of view

INSPIRATION
Kitty feels to me like the most overlooked Bennet sister. For most of
the original *Pride and Prejudice*, she is only Lydia's tag-along, helping to
conceal her elopement but otherwise not taking much agency in the story
herself. I wanted to explore what that girl coming into her own life might
look like, and felt a lot of queer kinship with the way it probably left her
feeling out of step with her peers, like her life was on a different schedule
than everyone expected of her. I wondered what would happen if Kitty's
flirtations with men were all blatant mimicry of Lydia and only an attempt
to fit in, and what she might do if she met an attentive, pretty
girl who woke up all sorts of feelings that she'd started
to think were only exaggeration.

KISS AND TELL

When a white-faced maid shakes Elizabeth awake, her first thought is that there must be a fire. She doesn't know what other reason a servant still in a dressing gown would have for waking her in the middle of the night. She sits bolt upright, alert for screams or the smell of smoke, but the night seems quiet. The maid is holding a candle, casting flickering shadows about the room.

"My deepest apologies for waking you at this hour, Missus," the maid says. "Only, there's a bit of an emergency and I do think you'd want to know."

Elizabeth scrubs a hand over her eyes, willing her brain into action. "What sort of emergency?"

"It's one of your sisters, Miss."

Elizabeth's heart surges into her throat. Without meaning to, she grabs hold of the maid's arm. "Who?" she asks. "What's happened?"

The maid squeaks.

Elizabeth forces her fingers to release. "My apologies. Please, tell me what's happened."

"It's Miss Katherine. She's not hurt, far as we can tell, but she's just—shown up here. In the middle of the night." The maid bites her lip. "She's asking for you, Missus, and she won't say anything about what's happened, and I am very sorry to wake you, but—"

Elizabeth is already getting out of bed. "Thank you for coming to fetch me, Anna," she says. "Please, pass me my dressing gown."

Within moments, Elizabeth is downstairs, wrapped in a dressing gown and slippers. The servants have brought Kitty to one of the more intimate sitting rooms, where Elizabeth and William like to spend their evenings together. There are still a few coals in the grate, so it is not quite so chilly as the parlor would be at this hour. Elizabeth spares a moment of thanks that the Darcy servants care more for compassion than propriety.

Kitty springs to her feet the moment Elizabeth enters the room. Elizabeth has time to register the tear tracks and blotchy redness of her sister's face, and then Kitty is flinging herself across the room and into Elizabeth's arms. Elizabeth catches her in as tight a hug as she can manage. The poor girl is trembling.

"Kitty, darling, what's happened? Are you hurt?"

Kitty shakes her head into Elizabeth's shoulder and lets out a muffled sob.

"All right, you're all right. I've got you."

Elizabeth lets Kitty cry herself out afresh on her shoulder, trying to suppress her imagination as it runs wild with reasons that Kitty might have shown up with no warning in the middle of the night. Last Elizabeth heard, she was spending a few weeks at the country home of a new friend, a Miss Linscott. Their mother has been writing to Elizabeth all summer about *the wonderfully handsome and charming Mr. Linscott, £3,000 a year, not quite as well as you or Jane have done for yourselves of course, but quite acceptable, don't you think, Lizzy dear?*

Dear God, Elizabeth hopes Kitty has not repeated Lydia's mistakes.

And if that Mr. Linscott has done something even worse than seduce her under false pretenses, Elizabeth will—

Best not to finish that thought until she's gotten answers out of Kitty.

When the sobs finally slow into shivery, hiccuping breaths, Elizabeth guides her back to the settee. She pulls a spare handkerchief out of a drawer and hands it to Kitty, who makes a valiant effort to wipe her eyes, though they are still leaking.

Elizabeth tucks a strand of hair behind her sister's ear. "Can you tell me what happened?"

Kitty sniffs, loud and inelegant. "Can I stay here tonight?" Her voice is so small.

"Sweetheart, of course you can. I'm hardly going to send you back out in the middle of the night. How did you even get here?"

Kitty's bottom lip trembles. "There was a coach," she says. "Into Bollington. And then I walked."

"You *walked* from Bollington?" Elizabeth is aghast. That's almost six miles away. No wonder she'd shown up at such an hour. Her sister walked all the way here in the dark? *Alone?* Elizabeth realizes her grip on Kitty's hand is turning white-knuckled and forces herself to relax. Kitty's lip is trembling more forcefully.

"I couldn't go home," Kitty says. "Mama wouldn't understand, and—and I couldn't—" The tears boil over again.

Elizabeth gathers Kitty into her arms once more, stroking her hair. "All right. It's all right." When Kitty's tears slow once more, Elizabeth sits her back upright. "You're sure you're not hurt?"

Kitty shakes her head. "It's not—it's nothing like that," she says.

"Then anything else can wait until you've had some sleep," Elizabeth says firmly. "Anna told me they've prepared a room for you. Did they take your bag up already?"

Kitty bites her lip. "I didn't bring one."

The jolt of imagined fears sears through Elizabeth again. She schools her features to stillness. It wouldn't do to have Kitty see *her* upset right now.

"We'll find something of mine we can pin to fit you. I'm sure Anna has already found you a spare nightgown." She takes Kitty's unresisting hand in her own and interlaces their fingers tightly. "Come on."

For a glorious instant when Kitty wakes, she doesn't remember where she is. Then she moves her legs, and her whole body groans in aching protest, and the entire awful mess of yesterday comes rushing back.

God, she's ruined *everything*.

Her eyes grow hot as the tears threaten to well up again. She squeezes them shut. She can't start crying again the moment she wakes up. She made quite enough fool of herself blubbering all over Lizzy last night.

She gets out of bed slowly, stiff and sore, hissing as every blister on her feet makes itself known when she stands. She rings for a maid, and one is at the door so fast she must have positively flown up the stairs.

"What time is it?" Kitty asks her. The sun is streaming in through the curtains, already well up into the sky.

"Nearly half past ten, Miss. Mrs. Darcy instructed you were to be let to sleep as long as you needed, but I can bring up a breakfast tray right away if you like."

Kitty presses a hand to her face. "Please," she says. "Um. Can you let Lizzy—Mrs. Darcy—know I'm awake now?" What on Earth Kitty is going to *say* to her sister, she has no idea, but she probably can't hide in the guest room forever.

The maid bobs a curtsy. "I've got some dresses pinned that should fit you well enough, Miss, if you'd like to get dressed before you speak to her."

"Oh. Right. Yes, please." Kitty must be exceptionally stupid this morning. Or maybe she's always been exceptionally stupid. Yesterday would certainly seem to bear that out.

The next hour passes in a haze, but Kitty does feel marginally more like a person by the time she has eaten and gotten into fresh clothes. She makes her wincing way down to the sitting room, where Lizzy is waiting for her. Kitty sees the concern etched on Lizzy's brow, and her stomach instantly plummets. For a moment, she's worried she's about to lose the entire breakfast she just ate. She can't tell Lizzy what happened, but she has to offer some explanation for her presence. She has no idea what she should say.

"How are you feeling, Kitty?" Lizzy asks.

Kitty parts her lips, but no sound comes out. The crease in Lizzy's brow deepens.

"Can you come sit with me?"

Kitty moves gingerly to the sofa. She sits with her hands folded in her lap, unable to meet Lizzy's gaze. For a moment, they're both quiet.

"Kitty," Lizzy says softly. "If you don't want to talk about whatever happened, I'm not going to make you. But I need to be sure you're all right."

"I'm fine," Kitty says. The words come out stiff and unnatural.

Lizzy tilts her head to the side. "Have you killed someone?"

Kitty jolts and turns to stare at her sister. Lizzy's mouth quirks up slightly. "Well, then, whatever's happened, it's not as bad as murder."

"*Lizzy.*" Kitty glares at her, but something loosens in her chest, just a little.

Lizzy's expression grows serious again. "You don't have to tell me everything, but can you tell me *something*, at least?"

Kitty takes a deep breath. "I had an…argument with a friend. And I—oh, Lizzy, I'm sure I overreacted but I just—panicked."

"Mama wrote that you were spending a few weeks at the country home of your new friend—Miss Linscott, wasn't it?"

Kitty feels all the blood drain from her face. Lizzy's eyes widen in alarm. She puts a hand on Kitty's arm. "Kitty, if they hurt you—"

"*No.*" Kitty pulls away from her touch. "No, no, they didn't hurt me, it's not—it's not like that."

Lizzy visibly hesitates. "Mama also mentioned there was a Mr. Linscott," she says carefully, cautiously.

"He was a perfect gentleman the entire time I was there. It's nothing to do with him, truly." Kitty watches a mix of relief and confusion wash over Lizzy's face. She feels perversely irritated. "I'm not Lydia." Her voice comes out in jagged edges, angrier than she'd realized she was.

"I know you're not," Lizzy says, "but—"

Kitty hurtles to her feet and barely manages to avoid doing a humiliating somersault over the coffee table. "No man has touched me. I am not pregnant, and I am only so ruined as taking a stagecoach unaccompanied to get here has made me. The Linscotts were—nothing but kind. I promise."

"I believe you," Lizzy says. "I just—don't know what else it could be, which means I don't know how to help."

Kitty turns her face away. "I don't need help." She hesitates. "Just—I can't face Mama right now. I need a place to stay for a few days until I can. That's all."

After a moment, she sees Lizzy nod in the periphery of her vision. "You can stay as long as you like." She hesitates another moment. "Shall we write to the Linscotts to send your luggage?"

Kitty's heart surges into her throat, and for a moment she's terrified she might be sick. "T-tomorrow," she says. "I can do it tomorrow."

Lizzy hesitates, then says, "All right. I'll let Anna know to pin another dress. We can go to Lambton to see about getting you a couple new things, if you like."

Nausea slowly receding, Kitty gives her a weak smile. "Perhaps in a day or two, when my legs are no longer so sore?"

Lizzy reaches up and tugs her back to sit on the couch. She brushes a ringlet of hair out of Kitty's face. "Get some rest. I have some letters of my own to write, but the servants will fetch me in an instant if you need me, all right?"

Kitty closes her eyes. "All right."

By the evening, she feels almost normal again. She's able to sit at supper with Lizzy and Mr. Darcy, who seems remarkably unperturbed by her unannounced and unceremonious arrival. He asks her so kindly about her summer, about whether she'd like to go into town, about anything and everything except the Linscotts. Kitty feels a strange and bitter ache at the careful avoidance of the topic. It's meant as a kindness, she knows, and yet it only makes her awareness of the absence beside her expand. She worries it like the hollow of a lost tooth, silently, compulsively.

She doesn't cry again, and still when she falls into bed that night, she feels as empty as if she'd sobbed herself dry.

Kitty has been sitting in front of the blank letter for almost an hour when Lizzy comes in. She glances between Kitty and the empty paper and says nothing. Kitty wishes she would—scream, or demand answers, or something. Maybe if she *has* to talk about it, she'll find the words. Instead, Lizzy retrieves a couple bits of embroidery from the drawer and hands one of them to Kitty.

"I always admired your birds," she says. "You had a far more deft hand for their anatomy than I did."

Kitty accepts the thread and bends her head over the pattern, trying to find where Lizzy had left off. The soft *pitter-patter* of a light summer rain is rhythmic and soothing against the window. They are silent for almost half an hour before Lizzy speaks again.

"I get lonely in this big house sometimes. After the chaos and close quarters we had growing up, sometimes I worry that William and I might get lost and wander for days before we can find each other again."

"It's not the same with just me and Mary at home," Kitty says, frowning over an odd angle of the bird's wing. "I've really heard my share of awful piano."

"You must miss Lydia. You two were always attached at the hip."

Kitty's fingers still. She feels Lizzy look up at her when she doesn't answer. "I suppose I do. Or, I suppose I do sometimes. But—" She sets the embroidery down and looks up at Lizzy. "I don't think I miss being her—accessory." She bites her lip. "That's too mean. I meant—"

A different version of this conversation rushes her memory. Adelaide's sharp brown eyes softened with understanding. An ungloved hand laid across her own. *It's perfectly normal to be scared of being your own person.*

"Kitty?"

Lizzy's concerned voice drags her back to the present. She blinks and presses the needle into the skin of her thumb—not enough to bleed, just enough to ground herself.

"Sorry. I only mean that Lydia has always been so—certain of herself." She glances up at Lizzy. "You know, even when she ran off with Wickham—I know it was stupid but—at least she didn't do things halfway. I envied her confidence."

"Lydia is a…force of nature," Lizzy says. "I don't think I can necessarily praise her for it, but—" She considers, untangling a piece of thread that's snagged against the fabric. "Then again, if she weren't such a whirlwind, she wouldn't be Lydia."

"I don't know if I've known who I am ever since Lydia eloped."

The words tumble out of Kitty before she lets herself think about them. They land in the silence, cushioned by the sound of rain. Lizzy sets her sewing down. She opens her mouth, but Kitty feels more words spilling out before she can stop them.

"All anyone ever says to me is to ask me if I miss Lydia or if I've met a husband. I haven't met a husband, and no one seems to know what to talk to *me* about. I can't even blame them! I don't know what I would ask myself about, either! I'm not well-read like you, and I don't go to parties without Lydia, and I don't even have a terrible hobby to inflict on others like Mary. You and Jane and Lydia were all gone, and I realized that I wasn't—that there wasn't anyone for me to talk to or anything for me to *do*. Except get married to whatever man Mama could find, and I don't—I don't know if—"

"Kitty—"

"I don't think I want a husband." She blurts it out, the words stark and far too loud.

Lizzy looks startled. "You still aren't even twenty; you have plenty of time to think about what kind of man you want to marry."

"But I don't want one. At all. I kept following Lydia around because I thought if I did, I would—eventually I would understand! I watched what she did, and I tried to copy her, and it never *worked*, Lizzy." Kitty feels heat rising in her face. She's crushing her embroidery, she realizes, and tosses it down. The needle skitters across the table, prevented from falling into the carpet only by its attached thread.

"I thought maybe she was just making it up, how excited all those men made her, that she was putting on a show, because I never felt any of the things she talked about." Not until two days ago. Butterflies rise in Kitty's stomach. As quickly as the words have come, they desert her in a wave of nausea.

Kitty staggers to her feet, wincing as her still-tender blisters protest the sudden weight.

"Kitty, wait," Lizzy says, standing as well, trying to catch her hand. "Please, stay. Talk to me."

Kitty is already shaking her head. "I couldn't go home to Mama because I can't—I don't want to explain this. Please."

Lizzy takes a long, slow breath and lets it out. Kitty shudders with the effort to wait for a response and not simply bend over and be sick.

"Very well," Lizzy says. "I'll be here if you change your mind."

Kitty turns from the room and flees.

The next afternoon, Kitty finds her sister in an isolated reading nook near the back of the house. Lizzy starts to stand when she sees her, but Kitty gestures for her to stay.

"I want to talk."

"All right," Lizzy says slowly. "Do you want to go somewhere you can sit down?"

Kitty shakes her head and sits on the edge of the ottoman, twisting her hands together.

She doesn't want to talk, not really. She still doesn't know if she can put any of this into words. However, the longer this goes on, the more tangled and ugly the secret gets inside her chest. She can't breathe for the fear that someone will look at her lips and somehow see the deed painted there. She needs it untangled, and for that, she needs help.

Once, she might have gone to Lydia with these concerns—if it were a man, she would have gone to Lydia—but thinking back, Kitty can't find a moment when Lydia actually helped Kitty talk through a problem. Lydia wanted to move, to flit from person to person and place to place and leave problems behind like bad dreams. When Kitty asked her to listen, Lydia's solution was always distraction: something shiny and new to take her mind off her troubles.

Kitty isn't sure, but she feels somewhere deep in her gut that the only thing more heart-breaking than laying out this whole messy explanation would be leaving it to fester as a secret forever.

"You know I met the Linscotts when I was in London this summer."

"Mama said you were sitting next to one another at a play."

Kitty nods. A corner of her lip twitches up, the ghost of a smile. "Ade— I mean, Miss Linscott and I laughed at all the same moments. We talked a little during the intermission, about how long we'd be in London and what our plans were, and then after the show, we walked out together and we just wanted to keep talking. So we planned to meet at the park for a walk the next morning, and we walked for hours. I've never enjoyed the park so much.

"After that, we simply kept making plans, almost every single day. And I realized she was the first friend I had who was…all mine." Kitty swallows. "She wasn't someone you or Jane or Mama had introduced me to, she wasn't one of the girls Lydia got flirting tips from, she was just…someone who liked me. *Me*, all by myself."

Lizzy nods. "I was happy, to hear you were making friends in London."

"We became friends so quickly, it almost frightens me. Only, I felt like I could talk to her about truly anything." Kitty hesitates, elects to probe slightly. "Is that—what it's like with you and Mr. Darcy? You can say anything to one another and you'll enjoy the conversation because you just…like one another so much?"

Lizzy laughs, a tinkling sound. "A little different," she says. "*We* argue, William and I. We both need something to argue over every now and again." Her eyes soften. "I can tell him anything, though. If I have something I want to talk about, I know he'll listen."

Kitty nods. "Yes, that—it's—it's been so nice to have someone who I felt like was really listening to *me*." She waggles a hand in the air, trying to mitigate her next words. "You know I love Mary and Mama, but… Well, sometimes…"

"I know. Oh, I know," Lizzy says. She gives Kitty a tentative tap on the elbow. "So she listened to you?"

Kitty tilts her head back. Even the ceilings are fancy in this house, done up with murals and exquisite stonework. The frothy blue lines of a stormy sea fill her vision. "I discovered I had so many things to say. So many of my own thoughts and opinions. Somehow, I hadn't realized, but when she asked…" Kitty shrugs. "I don't imagine they are especially smart or important opinions. I am not as well-read as you. But still, I had them, and they were all mine."

She takes a breath. Lizzy is quiet. "Miss Linscott felt…similarly fond," Kitty continues. "We were spending most of our time together. So when she was planning to leave town, she invited me to come back to their house. Perhaps I was…a little too afraid that if I did not follow her, I would lose her friendship."

Kitty bites her lip. She'd felt a sort of terror at the idea of losing Adelaide, as if she were a dream who might disappear entirely the moment Kitty let her out of her sight. Adelaide's offer to bring Kitty to the country with her had felt like a lifeboat in a storm.

"And it was wonderful to be spending time with her, and her family were all lovely, and I thought I was having the best summer I could possibly have hoped for, but then…but we were sitting in the drawing room one day, right next to each other because she was showing me her sketchbook, and she—" Kitty covers her mouth with her hand, remembering warmth and softness. She looks at Lizzy. "I really don't know if I should tell you this," she says, worrying the inside of her cheek. "I don't…know if I know how."

Lizzy reaches over and takes Kitty's hand, pulling it away from her mouth. "You promised you didn't kill anyone," Lizzy reminds her, with a half-smile. "I promise, whatever it is, it will be all right."

"She kissed me!" Kitty blurts it out before she can think about it any longer. All the blood in her body tries to make its way into her cheeks. "She just—kissed me. Not a friendly kiss on the cheek, but a *real* kiss, on the lips, and she said that she felt about me the way we're supposed to feel about men, and I didn't know what to think so I just—left."

Lizzy stares for a moment.

Kitty curls in on herself.

"But, Lizzy, I think I—I might—I wasn't ready to kiss her, but when she did, it didn't—it didn't feel bad."

It had felt confusing, and then it had felt terrifying, but for one blink of a moment in between those, it had felt like she was soaring.

Lizzy is squeezing her hand.

Slowly, Kitty manages to look up.

Lizzy's smile is awkward and uncertain, but it is a smile nonetheless.

"Well, this has the benefit of being much less frightening than anything I've imagined over the past three days," Lizzy says.

Kitty wants to melt into the cushions. "Don't you think it's—wrong?"

Lizzy ponders for a moment. "We have something of a habit of inadvisable matches in this family," she says eventually. "If you wish to hear about practicality and morality in marriage, I must send you to spend the weekend with Charlotte and Mr. Collins."

Kitty can't help the face she makes, and Lizzy snorts, the awkwardness bleeding from her expression. She reaches to grasp Kitty's hand in both of hers. "Really, Kitty, you cannot think I would disapprove of your happiness." Kitty's lip quivers. Lizzy's brow creases. "She *does* make you happy?"

"She makes me so happy I almost can't endure it."

"Well then," Lizzy says, "we can figure out everything else."

Kitty lets her breath out slowly. Her heart is still hammering far too fast in her chest, but some of the panic is seeping out of her. "Thank you," she says, her voice small.

Lizzy squeezes her hand. "What I think," she says, "is that I am very lucky to have a sister who trusts me so."

Kitty can't help it then: a tear slips out of her eye. Lizzy has a handkerchief out in a moment. Kitty pulls her hands free to dab at her face.

"I don't know what to do next," she admits. "She must think I'm awful."

Lizzy flicks her on the nose. "Well, you won't know if you don't ask."

Dear Adelaide,

First, let me apologize for the manner in which I left your estate. It was the most dire insult to your hospitality and kindness, and I regret it more deeply than you can imagine. If you throw this letter straight into the fire without reading it and cut me out entirely if we ever meet in London again, I shall not blame you. If, however, you <u>are</u> reading it, then allow me to express the hope that you will find it in your heart to forgive me.

Regarding our conversation the day of my abrupt departure, I can only say that I was very foolish and unprepared to acknowledge certain of my own thoughts. If you wish to broach the topic again, I think you will find me far less prone to panic.

If you can even find yourself so far moved as to wish to endure my company once more, then I should like to visit you again. We never did complete our count of all the naked cupids in your family's art gallery.

I must conclude this letter with an entirely uncharming, practical request: please send my luggage to my sister Elizabeth Darcy's address at Pemberley. My sister has been most reassuring in my confusion, and it is truly only under her eye that I am able to compose this letter without perishing of mortification for how I have repaid your kindness. Still, she insists that if you are as good a friend as I purport you to be—and you are certainly far better than my limited vocabulary can contain—you will be pleased to know I am well and that I would prefer your forgiveness to your silence.

Yours in contrition,

Kitty Bennet

Dear Kitty,

Thank God you finally wrote. I have been in an absolute state for the past few days wondering where on earth you could've gone. Your sister is a wiser woman than both of us: I am far too much relieved to be angry, except possibly at myself. I have felt sick with guilt for days that I drove you off into some horrendous situation. Rob is always telling me I need to be more patient.

If you would like to resume our discussion from before you left, I shall. However, I feel it necessary to be clear that I shall love you always as a friend, and no other decision you might make would negate that.

At any rate, I believe I acted rather too hastily. If I may suggest, let us continue our friendship somewhat more slowly from this point on, to be sure we both truly know each other.

This letter ought to be arriving with your trunk. Do let me know if we have left anything out.

Yours always,

Adelaide Linscott

"Well?"

Kitty looks up from the letter. Lizzy's expression is curious but otherwise carefully neutral. Only the grip she has on her skirts gives away her anxiety. It eases Kitty's heart further to know her sister was so worried for her. She manages a tentative smile.

"You were right. She still wants to…" Kitty rolls a few different phrases around before landing awkwardly on, "…talk. At least. We'll see."

A smile flashes wide and bright across Lizzy's face. She reaches over the coffee table to catch Kitty's hand and squeezes it hard.

"That's wonderful, Kitty."

Kitty takes a breath so deep it hurts and slowly lets it back out. She looks down at the letter again, lets her eyes catch on the "*Yours always,*" and lets the warmth of that phrase spread out through her chest.

"Yes." She feels her careful, nervous smile relax and spread across her face. She squeezes Lizzy's hand back. "Yes, it is."

Dearest Adelaide,

I regret tremendously letting you worry and feel guilty on my behalf. Rest assured, I am positively drowning in embroidered birds and good company. My sister and her husband, Mr. Darcy, insist I extend you their greetings and heartfelt wish to invite you for dinner at the first opportunity.

You have been a dearer friend than I ever hoped to have since my sisters began finding husbands. I find every few moments, there is some observation or little joke I wish to turn in your direction, only to find you are not there.

I would like very much to get to know you better and more slowly. Perhaps we may begin with letters, and I may write down all the funny little things I would say over the course of the day and collect them for your amusement. Meanwhile, please write and tell me how your newest painting is going. Your sketch of the arborway looked positively magical. I hope I shall see the completed version soon.

Love always,

Kitty Bennet

INDEX

About the Creators

ACERIEE

Hi! I'm Aceriee and I draw sometimes. I've been drawing all my life, but after falling into the *Supernatural* fandom in 2014 I've mostly focused on fanart.

CRIS ALBORJA

I'm an illustration and comic artist from Spain. I've got a nursing degree, but I decided to pursue my passion. I have studied Illustration at EASD Pablo Picasso in A Coruña and comics at O Garaxe Hermético in Pontevedra. I have done cover art for an anthology called *Infiniteca* by Retranca Editorial and comics for *Altar Mutante*, *Nai dos Desterrados*, and *Abraxas en Cuarentena* fanzines, as well as in *Gaspariño 21* by Retranca Editorial.

MAY BARROS

I'm a Brazilian writer, artist, and game designers located in Rio de Janeiro, with short stories published in anthologies like *Keep Faith* and *Momentum*, as well as a self-published short story, *Journey Home*. My art is focused mainly on women and fantasy themes, but I've reconnected with my first fandom recently, *Inu Yasha*, and have been making a lot of fanart and fanfics!

TÉA BELOG

Téa is a hypothetical writer and artist, a professional procrastinator, and a merch hoarder. When they aren't working on personal projects, they moderate zines and bake the same loaf of bread over and over again. From their pile of WIPs, they've managed to self-publish one book and are currently working on other manuscripts to eventually release into the world. Until then, they remain the worst gamer on Twitch and like to spend their free time ranting about books and thinking about fictional lawyer video games.

E. V. DEAN

E. V. Dean is a writer with a decade of fanfiction writing under her belt. She's embarking on her original fiction adventure with the angst tag kept within arm's reach. Her favorite excuse not to write is watching Jeopardy.

J. D. HARLOCK

J. D. Harlock is an American writer, editor, researcher, and academic pursuing a doctoral degree at the University of St. Andrews. In addition to their work at *Solarpunk Magazine* as a poetry editor, and at Android Press as an editor, Harlock's writing has been featured in *Strange Horizons*, *Nightmare Magazine*, and the Science Fiction & Fantasy Writer's Association Blog. You can find them on LinkedIn, Twitter, Threads, and Instagram.

RASCAL HARTLEY

Rascal Hartley is from the southern United States, and when they aren't busy hiking or collecting various bones, you can find them curled up in their favorite chair, writing. Their favorite author is a tie between Jack Kerouac and J. R. R. Tolkien, but the book they re-read every year is *The Last Unicorn*.

A. L HEARD

A. L. Heard is an aspiring writer from Pittsburgh. She's been writing fanworks for over a decade and self-published her first novel, *Hockey Bois*, in 2021. Some of her short stories have been published through the indie press Duck Prints Press, where she also contributes as an editor. Ultimately, though, she spends her free time writing about characters she adores in worlds she'd like to explore: contemporary romance, historical fiction, science fiction, and fantasy. In between writing projects, she works as a language teacher, plays hockey, tours breweries with her boyfriend, and spends her evenings playing dinosaurs with her two sons.

ZEL HOWLAND

Zel (they/she) is a writer and artist currently living in Los Angeles with their partner. When not writing, they spend their time painting, embroidering, analyzing literature and TV shows, and playing *Dungeons & Dragons*. They are the author of many a fan-fiction, as well as the novel *The Shadow of Ophelia Walker*.

ILGAKSU

Full-time fandom cryptid, Furby enthusiast, and the human embodiment of that one gif of Elmo on fire, ilgaksu was born and raised in an undisclosed location, has lived in several others, and now currently resides in [REDACTED]. Their interests include collecting haunted toys, using their artistic practice as an excuse to forget to do their laundry, and playing with fictional men like Bratz dolls. They have not unclenched their jaw yet today, but they did remember to drink lots of water.

LUCY K. R.

What is there to be said for a person such as Lucy K. R.? Her mother remembers her requesting a cookie, and when she was denied, amending "What about *two* cookies?" Her friends once observed her, when startled in a haunted house, to scream, run face-first into a wall, and then yell "Sorry!" Her wife, she claims to have met "soul-first," having collaborated in art and writing before ever meeting as individuals. Among the line-cooks of her restaurant, it is said she performed Ylvis's "What Does the Fox Say" at a Christmas karaoke party without ever glancing at the screen. In her dojang, she was heard to pronounce a fondness for sea salt, as it "May have touched a shark once." When she briefly majored in bass performance, while alone in the practice rooms, she would write musical themes for her characters rather than drilling études, until she could not escape her love of stories any longer. They say all these things and more, but to meet her "soul-first," you need look no further than "I Am For You" from *And Seek (Not) to Alter Me*, "The Hollow Mass" from *She Wears the Midnight Crown*, or "The Three Mic'O'Tears" from *Aim for the Heart*, all available from Duck Prints Press.

LYONEL LOY

Lifelong maladaptive daydreamer, finally working up the courage to write those daydreams down. Spends time cosplaying as a Responsible Adult With A Job.

MCDAD ARTS

mcdad is a Latine illustrator from the American Southwest. He currently has an MLIS for Librarianship and Data Science, as well as a med for secondary education in English and Art. His BFA was in Illustration and his BA in English Literature. He loves school and is working on programming and systems' analysis whenever he has free time to study. He's currently freelance illustrating but has been an art director, project manager, teacher, and local barista. When he's not busy with illustrating or school, he can be found as the forever

DM of his friend's *Dungeons & Dragons* group or reading yet another book. His one minor career goal is to make shirts for hardcore bands—one day.

MIKKI MADISON

Mikki Madison has been writing stories since she was seven years old. Her favorite genres to read are romance, adventure, fantasy, and cozy mysteries. (Coincidentally, these are also her favorite genres to write.) This is her fourth anthology with Duck Prints Press. Her stories appeared previously in *And Seek (Not) to Alter Me*, *He Bears the Cape of Stars*, and *Aether Beyond the Binary*.

When she isn't reading, writing, or searching for new anime, she can be found baking, doing puzzles, walking her foster dog, playing Pokemon Go, or consuming a truly unhealthy amount of tea. She has also written under the name M. K. Mads.

GENEVIEVE MAXWELL

Genevieve Maxwell is the pen name of a queer writer living in Michigan with a husband, their teenage kid, and a couple of cats. She has always been a storyteller, it just took a while for her to start writing the stories down. Genevieve writes fantasy and short-story romance and whatever else seems like a good idea at the time.

SAGE MOORELAND

Sage Mooreland (they/them) is a city-dwelling gremlin from Chicago. They are embarking on the adventure that is their 40s equipped with three amazing partners, one very ridiculous eighteen-year-old biological offspring, and a fleet of teenagers and twentysomethings who've adopted them through work over the last several years. Sage put themselves through the torture of grad school and now holds a Bachelor's in English and a Master's in English and Creative Writing—Fiction, to which they say, "Now I have expensive pieces of paper that make it seem like I know what I'm talking about."

Sage has been writing since they were wee small, entering their first writing contest in fifth grade/at ten years old. In high school and college, they made small offerings to school literary magazines, and they have done eighteen years of National Novel Writing Month. As their writing career grows, they hope to provide stories that are entertaining, caring, inclusive of all, and full of the stuff of which dreams are made.

NOTTESILHOUETTE

Notte has been writing for over a decade and has published short stories, interviews, articles, poetry, and more. Her fiction tends toward introspective, character-driven short stories, often laden with metaphor and double meanings—she loves flowery imagery and poetic prose, and making characters suffer in the name of growth. More than that, they love using fiction as a way to connect with others: both through the text and through the process of writing.

When they're not writing, they're probably reading or on a VC with friends.

TALIESIN OWENS

Taliesin is a queer author who grew up bouncing around Europe and the US and currently calls Chicago home. They've been writing stories since they had to pester their mom to help them transcribe their words on the family desktop computer. They work as a stage manager, dog walker, bartender, and hold a Master's degree in Humanities, with a focus in literature. No amount of school or chaotic array of part-time jobs has yet managed to stop them from reading and writing voraciously. They can also occasionally be found doing calligraphy, baking, or getting really excited about Shakespeare.

LINNEA PETERSON

Linnea Peterson (they/them) is an autistic writer and marketer from Minnesota. Their creative writing has appeared in *Five Minutes*, the *Oneota Review*, *Verbal Promiscuity*, and *Teen Ink*. They have also published articles in the *Minneapolis Star Tribune*, *Living Lutheran* magazine, *Twin Cities Geek*, and the *Twin Cities Daily Planet*. They have two complete-but-unpublished YA novel manuscripts and many more ideas that they are hoping to publish someday. Fanfiction has been their primary hobby and special interest for the majority of their life, but they also enjoy songwriting, volunteering, attending local live theater, and going on long walks.

MAX JASON PETERSON

Max Jason Peterson (he/they, maxjasonpeterson.wordpress.com; EliotQueliot on AO3, Instagram, and Tumblr) loves creating Queliot fanart and fanfiction for *The Magicians* (Lev Grossman, SyFy). As a writer and artist under various bylines, Max has a number of art, poems, stories, and articles published. Favorite artistic media include watercolors, colored pencils, and black-and-white photography, with seventeen pieces shown in exhibitions, including the statewide Virginia Artists Juried Exhibition.

FLORE PICARD

I'm a French artist and writer who loves drawing both fanart and original art, and I have a passion for patterns and systems, for the beauty at the edge of chaos and the complexity of being human. I tend to draw and write queer and disabled characters finding themselves and each other and learning to take up space in the world.

KENDALL PLETCHER

Lifelong doodler, painter, and impressive mess-maker. Took the high-school *Pride & Prejudice* curriculum far too seriously and has never looked back. Currently living in Somerville, Massachusetts with her patient fiancé, perfect cat, and far too many art supplies.

RADICALHOODIE

Hi! I'm an Italian artist whose passions reside in *Ace Attorney*, *Star Trek*, and all things silly. Lately, I've really been into making visual novel with friends!

J. RADIN

J. Radin has had a lifelong interest in history and a love of fantasy media, both of which are major components of her art. She loves to make narrative pieces that focus on their subjects, often in quiet, introspective moments. She also sews historical costumes and cosplays whenever she can find an event. This is her first published piece of art, and she is very excited to see it in print.

ELIZABETH ROSE

Elizabeth Rose, freelance artist and graphic designer living in Michigan. Has been drawing for many years and is currently going back to school to get an art-based degree.

EM ROWNTREE

Em Rowntree's first foray into the world of writing was with a story called *The Magic Land* that featured a unicorn and a flying carpet the size of a country, and they've been chasing that high ever since. They've been sharing their writing online for almost seven years, and have had poems and short stories published in anthologies. They live in the UK.

XANTHE P. RUSSELL

I'm Xanthe, she/they, a queer freelance portrait artist based in the United Kingdom! I love using art to express my love for a variety of things, including TV shows, films, music, and many other things! I mainly work digitally, although I love to dabble in traditional art from time to time and am heavily inspired by art history! I'd describe my style as realistic but slightly zany, and I especially love being able to play around and experiment as much as possible! My work has been featured in several fan zines and other independent publications over the years, and I genuinely love having the opportunity to work with other incredibly talented and lovely people!

SARO / LEGENDAERIE

Saro is a multimedia artist with over fifteen years of writing and art experience under her belt. From early comic publications in the *Neopian Times* (a user-submitted newspaper for the long-running pet website), to several fandom zines over the years and an Honorable Mention award in the final round of the 2022 NYC Midnight Rhyming Story challenge, Saro has long enjoyed combining her visual and literary skills with her love of collaboration and community. She brings to this collection a love of Jane Austen and a hope to add further depth to a comfort media she has long shared with her adoring mother and two older sisters.

VEE SLOANE

Vee Sloane has authored a novel, several short stories, some poetry, and twenty-two-years' worth of fanfic. She lives with one lovely spouse, one rambunctious clever child, and one sleepy cat.

SHEA SULLIVAN

Shea Sullivan is a life-long writer living in upstate New York. As a late-blooming queer person, she enjoys writing about complex characters coming into themselves and finding comfort in being exactly who they are.

Shea's day jobs in computer programming and middle management have molded her into the patient, sarcastic, big-hearted, frustrated human she is today, but it's what she does outside the 9–5 that really excites her. When she's not writing, she can be found painting, napping, making quilts, watching documentaries, and trying not to adopt more animals, usually with a cup of tea in hand.

TOMOWOWO

I'm an artist located in Mexico, drawing since I was little. I've been in few fanzines with my fan art. I love video games and watching others paint. I recently married my fiancé from the US. She's a wonderful person and an amazing author who has many publications! When I'm not drawing, I'm either playing with my cat or taking care of my plants.

DEI WALKER

Dei Walker (she/her) is a queer New Englander abroad, having spent almost half her life overseas. She currently lives with her family in Beijing, China. When she isn't writing, she can be found knitting, scuba diving, or playing games (video or tabletop).

TERRA P. WATERS

Terra is a scientist by day who lives in the Pacific Northwest with her family. She has been writing fiction as long as she can remember, and has always told her partner of 17 years that if she weren't a scientist, she would be an author. During grad school, she discovered fanfiction and immediately began writing her own. After many years and several fandoms (including *Teen Wolf*, *Hawaii Five-0*, and *Stranger Things*), she returned to writing original fiction. To date, she has self-published two novellas in a '90s-nostalgia polyamory comedy series, and has drafted two YA/NA sci-fi novels. When not doing science or writing, you can find Terra indulging her yarn addiction and knitting.

A. A. WESTON

Alex, AKA foxymoley, (she/her) is best described as a jack of all trades, but she practices digital art more than anything else. She just wants to make things and change the world for the better.

A. D. WILLIAMS

A. D. Williams is a storyteller first, and a human being third. Or fourth. Honestly, the jury is still out on the human thing. She holds a deep affection toward grotesque creatures, is an avid admirer of characters who appear twice before dying offscreen, and thinks that any novel can be improved by the addition of a snake. When she isn't bent into pretzel-like configurations in front of her computer, Williams can be found watching clouds and trying to entice the local lizards to scamper into the palm of her hand. The lizards have yet to pity her. But she's also a dreamer, so she hasn't lost hope yet!

AMALIA ZEICHNERIN

Amalia Zeichnerin (she/her) lives in Hamburg, Germany. She is a disabled queer woman with a chronic illness and lives in a polyam polycule. Amalia mostly writes original fiction (SFF, cosy Victorian mysteries, queer romance) in German and has also one English *Star Wars* fanfiction on AO3, with one of her favorite shippings, StormPilot. Amalia likes to draw and paint, especially fantasy world maps, character portraits, and sometimes also fanart. Amalia's hobbies include pen-and-paper RPGs and LARPing; these also have inspired some of her writing and artworks.

XIANYU ZHOU

Xianyu Zhou is a translator and aspiring garment and plushie cloning specialist hailing from a coastal city in the tropics. Despite staying a 20-minute drive away from the nearest beach, they have yet to visit one, preferring to dwell in their darkened room luminated by a table lamp and the ever-shifting RGB of a CPU fan. They have the tendency to accidentally wander into new and exciting forays such as joining Duck Prints Press (and enjoying it!), learning to sew (stitching and unstitching the same part of a "coaster" for the nth time) and working on their language skills (watching shows to scrutinize and take notes about how their subtitles are written).

JAGODA ZIREBIEC

Hiya! I'm Jagoda or MizuShiba. I am a game dev artist currently working on a few unannounced titles. In my spare time I love to join collaborative projects like this or charity zines. I'm located in Poland and currently live here with my family. Aside from art, I'm interested in collecting dice and playing TTRPGs with friends.